and the
STARS
began to
FALL

by

Madeleine de Jean

TELEMACHUS PRESS

Cover design by: Telemachus Press and Madeleine de Jean

Cover images:
© Copyright iStock/173572510/Bartosz Hadyniak
© Copyright iStock/178149253/kevron2001
© Copyright iStock/522871533/carton/king
© Copyright iStock/539337150/Photoslash
© Copyright iStock/1007532674/Davel5957
© Copyright iStock/1068309286/simonkr
© Copyright iStock/1331559863/zhongguo
© Copyright iStock/1190295119/ktsimage
© Copyright iStock/465266885/Nerthu

Interior images used with permission as credited beneath each photo.

Publishing Services by Telemachus Press, LLC
7652 Sawmill Road
Suite 304
Dublin, Ohio 43016
http://www.telemachuspress.com

Contact the author:
http://www.madeleinedeJean.com

Library of Congress Control Number: 2021922083

WGAW Registration Number: 2141714

ISBN: 978-1-951744-96-0 (eBook)
ISBN: 978-1-951744-97-7 (Paperback)

FICTION / Historical / Ancient
FICTION / Alternative History

Version 2022.01.03

and the
STARS
began to
FALL

TABLE OF CONTENTS

Part II – The Rest of the Story … Keeping our Bargain

DEDICATION

OPEN ON: *Inspiration*

I would like to dedicate *AND THE STARS BEGAN TO FALL* to my friend, Dr. Elizabeth Wace French, archaeologist. It was a question I had for her about a short story her father, archaeologist Alan Bayard Wace, had written that first connected us. And since that letter in 1986 Lisa has been not only a friend but a great guide, taking me and sending me on adventures into the past with archaeology.

To you, Lisa, I dedicate this story in gratitude.

And to my granddaughters, Chiara Mathilde Adams, and her sister, Valerie Wehring, I also dedicate this story in hope that they too will lead lives of adventure and joy as did Elizabeth Wace French.

In honor of Elizabeth Wace French, twenty percent from the profit of each book will be contributed to the Institute of Mediterranean Studies (www.griffinwarrior.org), in support of preservation of finds from the grave of the Griffin Warrior at the Palace of Nestor, in Pylos in Greece.

AUTHOR'S LOVE LETTER TO THE PAST

FADE IN: *Imagine*

SETTING:
    Place: The Desert
    Date: September, <u>2021 A.D.</u>

DEAR READER, LONG have I been amazed by our assumption that every society that preceded ours was in every way less civilized, less advanced than ours; the farther back in time, the less civilized.

Lack of evidence, lack of tangible proof, is the usual rationale for branding all of the past as less advanced.

Suppose tomorrow the perfect storm of destruction arrived here. Imagine collisions from the sky meeting those from the earth, joined with intentional use of tremendous forces from sentient beings from inside as well as outside this planet, all occurring simultaneously. What of our great, advanced, civilized society would remain for anyone to discover some thirty-two hundred plus years later, in 5277 A.D.? All those satellites that keep our incredible technological inventions functioning? Gone. Fallen from the sky. Mobile phones? Computers of all varieties? World Wide Web? Lost in the Cloud? Or bits of trash to be found, perhaps underneath tons of rubble. All our fast, humongous modes of transportation? Trucks? SUVs? Bits of colored metal. Likewise fabulous ships and supersonic planes. All our advanced brains, filled with so much knowledge. The answer is the same: gone without a trace. No assembly books attached. Likely, future archaeologists will determine ours to have been a very primitive though widespread society. Perhaps they will be able to find enough to determine that we were 'barbaric' also in terms of our humanity.

After years of study, of reading, research, and visiting, I have come to the conclusion that for the special moment in time between 1500 B.C. and 1185 B.C., in that special space, the Peloponnesos in Greece, there existed a most-advanced society, a civilization capable of things that today are still beyond our ability politically, scientifically and socially.

When at the convergence of a perfect storm, that whole society collapsed in 1185 B.C., any humans who survived either had fled far away prior or were reduced to the subsistence of cavemen. No more writing, no more communicating through technology. All gone. These few survivors were reduced from the pinnacles down to hunting and gathering to survive, - like the cavemen we study in grammar school — and to storytelling around fires at night to pass to the next generations any information about their past. Humans are born storytellers, especially in turbulent destructive times. And so were they after the catastrophe of 1185 B.C. Until finally, after almost five hundred years, writing returned, and those stories that had survived were written down. We give the name Homer to that writer. Over those hundreds of intervening years, because knowledge of details, objects and technologies described in those old, first, stories had long been lost along with all points of reference, new names and terms that could then be understood were given by the man we call Homer to describe what he could fathom of what those original stories had detailed. Like the sound of Zeus tossing lightning bolts heard coming from a clear sky during the day, when he describes Odysseus' final trip home. Today we would understand this to mean the breaking of the sound barrier.

Other instances of the far-advanced society can be found hidden in archaeological discoveries. As in 'advanced Optics'; *optics*, that necessary invention to assist weak-eyed humanity to reach outside our planet's boundaries; optics to search under our oceans; optics to search our solar system; optics such as take us outside our star's system and into the vastness of the far universes: advanced optics such as we are just rediscovering. For example, in 2015 A.D., at the site of Nestor's Palace in Pylos, Archaeologists from the University of Cincinnati, Sharon Stocker and her husband-partner, Jack Davis, with their teams, uncovered the Tomb of the Griffin warrior. Among the extraordinary finds they excavated are some that call out *optics*. In the tomb, from a lost bracelet, was found a 1.4 inches wide agate with most intricate carvings. The carvings depict a battle scene with figures in perfect detail, some only 1/100th of an inch in diameter. In precise detail, on the arm of one small but intricately detailed figure is an identical bracelet with a stone exactly like the one found. Astonishingly it was discovered, by using advanced optics, that on that tiny, tiny stone was an identical battle scene perfectly carved in infinitesimally small detail. None of this could have been carved (nor appreciated) with the naked human eye, or without finely ground specialized and mechanized tools. The optical advances in precision magnification and in light refraction this small stone's carver needed would signify a society that had developed such which would allow it to scope out not only the very tiny but the very far away as well; to explore not only all the reaches of this small planet and underneath into the world of our oceans, but to view and reach into universes far in outer space as well. Such optics as we are only rediscovering in this 21st century A.D.

Not only in tombs are astonishing remains to be found. In 1901 divers in the Aegean off the coast of the Peloponnesos uncovered a mechanism that was so puzzling, so foreign to any scientific knowledge we possessed at the time, it was put away into the back archives of the National Archaeological Museum in Athens. In the 1950s curiosity brought it out for study. Again its use was still foreign to any who inspected it. But by the 1960s when yet again it was inspected it began to garner interest as a form of something we were just beginning to explore, a form of something we called 'Computer'. This mechanism, now called the Anti-Kithera Mechanism, continues to be studied to this day, and is on display in a special room in Athens' National Archaeological Museum. It is still being studied as a form of computer still not understood. And divers are searching the Aegean near the island of Anti-Kithera for more parts of this computer mechanism.

Lest we overlook something we today consider very basic, let's talk about plumbing. That invention of the 20th century A.D. which keeps society clean and reduces the horrors of plague, among many other advantages. Not until just prior to and just after World War I did homes in Europe and this continent begin to have flush toilets, baths and kitchens with hot and cold running water with plumbing to carry away the wastes by septic or sewerage: engineered plumbing. Even the great Roman Empire had only public baths and toilets fed and cleaned by gravity flow from aqueducts. However, at Knossos and Mallia on Krete and in the city of Thera on Santorini since the 1600s B.C., and later on the Peloponnesos in the 1400s and 1300s B.C, in King Nestor's Palace and in Mycenae's Palace complex, there was universal plumbing with flush toilets, shower baths and kitchens with running water based on a huge engineered system of pipes. All of which was forgotten for millennia after the fall of that society in 1185 B.C. How many other traces of that society's advances, still foreign to our current-day knowledge, exist, still hidden away until we might comprehend?

Therefore, I believe it is reasonable to postulate a society far more advanced than ours: a society not only capable of time-travel but one that was also socially capable of living in peace among themselves and among their confederation neighbors as well.

It took that perfect storm of geology, astronomy, physics and human intelligence, coupled with fear, to converge and destroy it all.

Every time I walk up to Nestor's palace today, I see, I visualize and I step into a much different scene from the one that remains thirty-two hundred years after the destruction. I open my eyes, and there before me I see the pixels reforming, shimmering into focus. And I enter a magnificent, shining, vibrant-with-technology City on a hill. I feel a population buzzing around me in this state of amazing inventions. Most of all I feel a humanity: a community joined for society's interests.

Dear reader, I have been asked what this my story is: Is it Historical Fiction? Is it Sci-Fi? What? Both, maybe. And more. This story is the unfolding of my dream of Pylos. And the medium that is best suited to unravel and depict my dreams as they unfold like flowers, the medium devised by visual dreamers at the turn of the 20th century such as Georges Melies and the Lumiere brothers, is the motion picture medium. So here I will unravel this story, pixel by pixel, scene by scene, moving between times in the same places and dates, like a screen-writer preparing scene by scene the movie so it unfolds vibrant and alive to you, the viewer.

Please take my hand and enter this story as we FADE IN to that world...

PART I

In the Beginning…

PROLOGUE

FADE IN: *Sky-Full of Falling and Exploding Star*s

SETTING:
> Place: High balcony, Palace of King Nestor
> Where: Pylos, Greece
> Date: 30 to 31 May, 1190 B.C.
> Time: 11 p.m. to 6:15 a.m.

(N.B.: Dates and times are stated as registered today in 2021 A.D.)

AGAIN. THERE. THERE they were. He took his binoculars and was almost blinded by the array, by their brilliance.

There. And there. And far over there.

He shivered in the warm night air.

Again tonight the stars were falling. Like last night. And the night before.

Again, Nestor stood on the palace's highest balcony, watching them drop into the sea far to the north. These falling stars were of far greater concern than the comet that was doing its best to conceal the falling messengers. Heavenly messengers were converging. Beautiful. Terrifying.

It was the anniversary of the 1214 Mycenae disaster, and the old King had a bad feeling. Twenty-four years. Twenty-four. Unconsciously his fingers drummed out the number. "One off from the ominous twenty-five," he mused.

Almost directly above him, the huge comet streaked lower and lower in the evening sky, its coma reaching and arcing behind like a thing of brilliant glory or a predicator of doom.

"Everyone likes to ascribe intelligent powers to comets. So which is it this time?" The King's thoughts were racing. "Glory? Or Doom?" At least what he was seeing behind the coma of this comet was not the rain of fire that had happened over Mycenae in 1214. With the anniversary of that catastrophe so near, were They, whoever *They* were, using the date as a reminder that They existed? Or of Their power? Perhaps. Though, of course, he had no idea who They might be. Or indeed that They existed. Imagination? He could be quite imaginative, especially when it came to matters of state. "Not quite imagination, Nestor," his thoughts recalled him to those unexpected and unwanted visitors from other worlds at Troy: His Negotiations for Confederation had turned into all-out war.

"Glory? Or doom?" he called to the falling stars, breaking the stillness of the night.

In the brightly lit city of Pylos below his palace, Nestor knew that minds as brilliant as that heavenly interloper were hard at work on this question. And in the observatory high in the hills above, in the outskirts of Khora and also below in laboratories on the great promontory of Iklaina, stretched out toward the triple harbors in the sea below, astrophysicists and nuclear physicists, cosmologists and engineers and oceanographers were, even and especially at this hour, studying not just these natural phenomena but those strange sounds and lights that had begun as a sort of extra accompaniment three nights prior in the skies over the Sea of Io, the night the stars began to fall.

"Could it possibly be," he thought, "that those celestial representations are out there reminding us of the long-ago fable of Daedalos? Behind that metaphor where the Old Ones hid the reality of the magnificent technologies they had discovered about the uses of nature for the advancement of civilization?"

His drumming fingers and intense stare belied his quiet stance. "But," he spoke softly into the still night air, "if this is a dramatic replay of the Fall of Icaros, meaning the Fall of Krete in 1450 B.C., and then of that other-world Trojan 'experiment' on display as a warning out there ..." Well the old King knew, then their civilized Union of Kingdoms should be afraid. "Or is this display simply another natural phenomenon which my scientists could potentially harness and learn from?"

While his eyes watched the falling stars and arcing comet and his brain sorted possibilities according to what he knew to be, another part of The King's mind turned to the new possibilities of things totally unknown. Maybe his physicists or cosmologists or astronomers knew about things he did not. Then there were the other possibilities he had intimated. Maybe those he feared most.

"So much of what I've seen has been from this balcony," he reflected. He had first stood here with his grandfather and great-great-uncle. "How many years now? Ninety-three? Ninety? Well, no matter. Time passes differently according to what is needed."

So while his palace slept, out here Nestor stood and continued to ponder and watch this natural or contrived phenomenon. He released a held breath, forced his fingers to loosen their grip on the balustrade and paused his racing thoughts by looking over at his harbors and remembering times past.

"Which is what old people do." He laughed. He did so, perhaps more than he should. "No, no. From such introspection over memories, like my memories of the day construction began on the warehouse complex down there," he stopped pacing and pointed into the distance, "by recalling such moments, by mulling over what I learned about the workings of society, about ... well, I actually learn more."

And at those blurted words, he looked up and another memory was released. "I myself was born one-hundred years ago under the sign of a comet," he murmured, and that thought made him smile. At that time, his father had announced that the comet signified that his son would be as great a warrior as his great-great-uncle, who had come across the Middle Sea from Knossos and Kidonia in Krete, himself born in a time of another comet, "now some one-hundred and forty years ago," Nestor tapped his fingers and calculated aloud ... "in another such a time when stars fell from the skies." He picked up his binoculars. But in that time, they had not been prepared for the seas rising up to meet the stars, bringing catastrophe and collapse to the whole island and its satellites, putting into deep freeze much of that extraordinary civilization of invaluable, Daedalic-like knowledge, some of which they were still recovering and piecing together. Whole colleges, enormous worlds of thought, were still being recreated. "The loss of people was the greatest of that devastation: the human brain, the most-powerful computer and library." And that thought summed it up.

On the other hand, also at Nestor's birth, his mother, she had often told him, had looked into her baby son's blue eyes and predicted that his comet signaled that her son would become a great leader, bringing the light of peace and the brilliance of learning to all his people.

Oh, gosh. Just thinking of Mama, he became young. And as clear as the comet above came the returned aroma of her rose-scented perfume to suddenly envelope him. "The amazing sense of smell makes time travelers of us all," his great-great-uncle, the Griffin Warrior, had once told him, recounting how the "collective sense of smell, the aroma of home, the aroma of safety," led them here to begin anew. Nestor could hear his voice. He looked out across the City and over the sea. Too many memories were taking him away from where he had to be now in thought.

"Well, yes. Oh darling Mama," his voice broke strangely. He had made her proud. He had been and still was a peacemaker with all the kingdoms of the Peloponnesos. And he would return to this memory. But now, there were more immediate and pressing needs for his computer up there to ponder.

Throughout his reign, he had worked hard to diplomatically join all the societies around the Great Sea in an Economic Common Union. Together they grew it into a technology-wise paradise in which humanity ruled. Extensive and continuous trade throughout that now-Federated Union assured the joined peoples of a better life with education and abundance. That accomplishment had not been easy and often fell short and sometimes apart. But once again, schools around the Great Sea were open to all within the confederation and were staffed with searching minds, offering a better life to all who availed themselves of the riches that recovered and uncovered knowledge offered. It had taken decades, but once again, particle physics and quantum mechanics, combined with theories of universal gravitation, were being used by teams of scientists to open paths in space-time, using, as well, the amazing sense of smell to create further avenues of many forms of travel and protection. "That sense of smell!" With the emphasis on protection. Not destruction. Protection by a brotherhood of man.

Several seemingly great inventions had been ruled out by him and the United Council, such as the internal combustion engine horseless chariot, which would have caused huge air pollution. Egypt led in that debate. They had ruled it out a generation before. Most of all, they had again universally voted down that atom bomb. The split atom did many wonderful things for his society, especially in medical research and inventions numerous, but would never be used in war against others. The planet and humanity could not recover from such horrors as would be unleashed in the air, on the planet and deep in the oceans. "All life would be in a deep freeze," his chief physicists had advised. It had happened before, in the Time of Giants, when this planet, with simultaneously converging outer forces, had erupted in combinations to unleash unprecedented destruction.

So, using their knowledge and under his oversight, instead the peaceful sciences — astronomy and geology, engineering and oceanography, physics and psychology — were studied and explored by inventive and seeking minds with an eye to solving the physical problems known to humanity, delving always into the past to correct and protect the future. Medical science laboratories combined peaceful results of the split atom with those from quantum mechanics and created instruments to cure and heal illnesses of all sorts, leading to happier and more-productive citizens. Their hospitals accepted not only anyone from the City-States of the Peloponnesos, but patients from all the Common Union's members as well. Every day he could see ships unloading litters into waiting vans to take new patients to treatment centers, centers named for the god of healing, Asclepius, signified by the image of the healing snake twining his dreaming cup and staff. At 100, Nestor himself was an example of Aesclepian bio-regeneration sciences. And down in the town below him,

in buildings well-made with movable substructures for stabilizing and
materials to withstand most dramatic, earth-shaking events, lawmakers
met and were in constant communication with their counterparts
throughout the Commonwealth Unions, assuring stability for enjoyment
of the better life the support systems promised each and every citizen.

Many called all these wonders Magic. Indeed, there was an element
of magic, if by that one meant calling on universes that were too small
and too swift and therefore invisible to the human eye. And using
theories based on intangible numbers. The results could appear magical,
of course, even to him, the so-called Wizard of Peace. Like the stories he
had heard from his friend, The Great Ramesses, of those long-ago, those
traveling Magi, who convinced his people of the power in music and of
how to sing the old high notes with which they lifted enormous boulders
into place. Or tore them down. But there were no rabbits pulled from his
hat. Such feats were based on solid theories of physics, his scientists
assured him. Yes, harnessing those powers of nature using
interferometry, like lightning and the sun's rays to give light and heat and
communication, as well as space-time travel, harnessing ourselves to the
sun, such seemed magic indeed.

But then again, many were those so-called wonders that he had
refused for his world. Those refusals had taken a lot of talk, a lot of
convincing. Like that internal combustion engine his sons had really
wanted so they could drive up and down and all around like crazed
people, causing pollution and danger. They had argued. But he had
managed to convince them that though it was slower, the solar-powered
engine would move those chariots where they needed to be without the
need for pollution or horsepower. Until an emergency occurred. Such as
happened one night when his son Thrasymedes's first son was about to
be born. The horse was reliable even at night.

But still there was an unmistakable element of magic about things
one could not touch, feel and see, like the powers generated by the sun,
of which Egypt had long known and used. There the sun was called Sun
God. Yes. Magic, perhaps like the life led by his great-great-uncle,
symbolized by the griffin lying in peace with the lion. Magic from the
human heart. Or such like his with Agamemnon of Mycenae and

Menelaos, his brother of Sparta. Well, he did not always convince them of peace. He, too, had spent millions and ten-plus years of his life in Troy trying to increase the Confederation for Peace. Instead he had lost his first son there.

Magic. He had done his best during his long life to fulfill his parents' dreams for him, to become a great warrior and a great peacemaker. Magic, indeed. With the return from Troy for many, finally even for the Playboy of the Great Seas, Odysseus — days of war, he thought, were over and done. But as he looked again at the sky, behind and beneath the coma of the great comet, stars were still falling. Had too much peace caused restlessness among the citizens? Had too much peace caused restlessness and or enmity at so much plenty from nations unknown, peoples not within the Union; in people perhaps in need? Were all things conspiring against their Confederation to end such perfection? Perhaps those even more knowledgeable but fanatically crazed with anger, as Clytemnestra had definitely been? Was she a key? Possessed by negative energy called evil? Well, she had caused such destruction, one could say she was a living atomic bomb, such as he had rejected. It had taken her fourteen years, but even after her demise, her evil persisted. And how she had succeeded! Mycenae was teetering on the brink, about to collapse from her catastrophic years. Tisamenos, Orestes's son, was doing his best to overcome. But there was no more infrastructure there.

"Will I send aid? Or will Tisamenos join us and his father here?" the King wondered aloud. "Were there unknown enemies of such anger against peace out there conspiring with the universe?" his thoughts were grim. "Perhaps I've encountered them before, those interfering strangers, the Great Ones from the sky who arrived at Troy"? Interior alarm bells made his pulse sing.

The stars falling again arrested his attention. Each time he thought he had solved one giant problem, another arrived. Like those stars. He would have to discuss this with his sons, Thrasymedes and Peisistratos. Even with the son of his old friend Ramesses, Seti II. Seti had problems of his own, but the kingdom of Egypt was flourishing. He would send an emissary, perhaps pulling the strings in Krete for the space-time unit, not used often. Nestor stretched and turned to go back inside. He himself was now too old for war. But as a peacemaker, he still had to do his duty. Thrasymedes was king now. And Peisistratos his second in command. He would call for them in the morning. Now he had to think.

The old King walked into his office, which was directly off his special portion of the balcony. In here were all the memories of his eighty years of mostly peaceful rule. There the frescoes by Aliana, great-grandmother of his darling daughter-in-law Nepthaulia — herself the great niece of famous Merope of Mycenae — frescoes of the giant argonaut creatures that stood for the powerful-yet-peaceful use of the sea's waters, shone at him in all their still-brilliant coloration gleaned from Egypt, which excelled in gradations of sea shades from ground lapis. And then his favorite. He turned and walked over. Every time he encountered it, he was held spellbound. As if enchanted, he reached out a hand to this copy of the much-older fresco, the original still decorating his throne room two stories below, with the griffin, symbol of their ancestor. Depicted were griffins lying in harmony with lions, painted from stories told to Nestor's great-aunt by the Griffin Warrior of the magic in the land, of the forces in clouds and in trees and in song, forces from winds and the sun, with which the Old Ones had imbued this society: "Peace is Strength." That was the motto of the Griffin Warrior, the last words issued from his dying lips, Nestor's great-aunt had told him. The Griffin Warrior had come from Knossos and Kidonia to renew here what had been lost there.

"I came guided," the warrior had told Nestor's great-aunt, "guided by our collective sense of smell to this precious, rich land, here to carry on and expand the learnings of our lost, once-great sea-nation."

The warrior had died too young. But not before establishing the first cities and universities and economic enterprises right here, starting from the two natural harbors below, and then building arsenals, first for creating the means of spreading peaceful enterprise between the societies of his ancestors and Pylos, and then to expand and stretch between all the neighboring nations who wished to coexist in peace for prosperity.

So it was, still today, only far, far expanded. Nestor crossed to another area of the room and looked at the map of the cooperating countries and societies of kingdoms with some pride. But that rumbling coming from over the sea outside brought him back to here and now, and he turned away from peace with a troubled mind. Were these signals from the skies signaling that it was time for another catastrophe? Another reversal of what is expected? Magicians use that all the time to lead the eye in a certain direction. But catastrophe also means winding up of the plot. Magicians use that all the time, too, to unexpectedly reveal yet another collapse. He made a prayer to his guiding spirits to ward off such destruction of all they had accomplished since the last.

"Never again!" the Confederation's members repeated at the beginning of each joint meeting. He had made certain that any scientist in the employ of Pylos really understood and welcomed that motto. But had he and the confederation made certain they were prepared for a destructive rogue force?

He reached across his desk and touched, then clasped and kissed, his little statue of his dear daughter-in-law, Nepthaulia. And as though Nepthaulia whispered to him, he looked again toward the door to the terrace.

"Could it be that the times have become right for this wrong to occur? That we ourselves, he and all the citizens of this confederation, in our enthusiasm for promoting our great and good and peaceful societies, had, in fact, spread the word to the envious, to those whom the Federation did not reach in its peaceful embrace? Or," — a face popped into his mind — "maybe it was the over-talkative Odysseus? He was not that foolish, was he? Or was this a simple display of the great, natural cosmology his scientists were studying now at this moment in their observatories and laboratories? Would they give him another answer tomorrow at their meeting? Or perhaps were they simply all, all of them, too naïve and unprepared?"

He kissed the little figure of Nepthaulia and put it back in its place. He rubbed his eyes and reached out to the miniature, framed painting of Eurydice.

"I think it is time. I must ask you, darling Eurydice, to call out The Girls. Yes, the time is right."

Sitting in his large chair at his immense desk — (that he almost dwarfed), he took the portrait in his hands and kissed her lips. How he loved this woman. How much he and all their people owed this extraordinary woman. His bride to this day, often in his absence his very self, she becoming king when necessary when he was gone, like that last, great almost-catastrophe over at Troy. Eurydice had taken care of every fear while he was off at Troy. And in his absence had done far better than he would have had he been here. As with those economic successes she had encouraged Agamemnon and Menelaos into with their vineyards, she had also urged cooperative expansion with all their economies. While those brothers were creating a huge consolidation effort with Troy, they were paying zero attention to many of their industries and were leaving behind no backup plans, especially for, as Eurydice saw it, their vineyards. But by incorporating all the vineyards of the Peloponnesos into a Co-operation, she had created their huge Integrated Peloponnesos Wine Industry, joining together, with their own, those vineyards of Mycenae and of Sparta, where the missing leaders had left behind no such replacement as a Eurydice. Throughout their world, that wine industry, which emanated from Pylos Harbor, was now known as "The Wine-Dark Sea Industry." Then she had overseen that of their olives, creating specialty markets, both the gastronomic markets and, for that of the perfumes, capturing within the oil the essence of rose from the special rose cultivated by his mother on their floral farms from the western interior down toward the sea.

Most of all, there was Eurydice's phenomenal idea, truly an idea which saved them more than the others put together: her leadership in and expansion of The Societies of the Khorus Girls of Pylos and the Khorus Girls of the Peloponnesos, societies called Khorus Korai. These societies of young girls and women had, by their magic intervention with the natural elements, saved the harvests over and over, thereby saving all these economies and, indeed, the city-states. What a woman! Oh, Eurydice! He kissed her image again. When replacing her portrait, his fingers brushed the little statue that proudly stood as the symbol of that special group of Eurydice's 'Singing Savers' of whom and in whom he took great personal pride. He was their patron here and throughout the Peloponnesos. As was Eurydice here their foundress and head votaress. But of this one, this special Khorus Girl, this Nepthaulia, and of her little sister, Khloris ... of these he was most proud. Nepthaulia was his angel and that of this city-state of Pylos. She was their savior. Oh, that had been quite a night when she had saved this kingdom by harnessing the powers of clouds and winds and song with the whole khorus of Pylos. And because of her actions that incredible night, in 1205 the tradition began: that of creating these little figurines. Nepthaulia and her sister, Khloris, and the khorus had saved the city, he was positive, from one of those great moments of certain catastrophe, which would definitely have led to total collapse here. Will they be able to do so again?

"Ah, darling Nepthaulia." He again picked up her little statue and gave it a kiss. Now she was, in actuality, right next door in her home, his and Eurydice's daughter-in-law.

Tomorrow would be a long day. He would likely be awakened by that group of astronomers coming to give their reports. He had better get to bed. He pushed back his chair and stood. Only then did he notice a sheaf of pages he had not seen. A report from those very cosmologists. He sat back down. Oh. What he read gave him such a jolting thought, he later could not remember having risen from his desk. When his wits returned, he was standing again at the balcony, looking into the night sky where the comet's tail continued sweeping, now in a greater concealing arc. With his binoculars, Nestor looked more carefully behind that brilliant, silver arc, where he could see those stars continuing to fall in even greater numbers and brilliance.

"Oh, no!" thought Nestor. "Everyone, including Pharaoh, I myself, every one of us has been too focused on the seas, preparing as our people are, down there right now, below in my arsenals, creating bigger and better ships to combat the People from the Sea, as Seti II calls them. 'Our new and biggest enemy,' as Seti's missive said. But," he felt himself shouting to himself, "it is the Sky People, people from the stars! The STAR People!" Uncharacteristically, his fists pounded the balcony while his thoughts raced. "We must prepare for designing innovative sky-ships with which to meet the necessity of confronting the people from the stars before they wreak havoc again."

Though these thoughts raced, he stood still, still watching.

"The Confederation," he shouted to himself. "In our conservative, peace-loving wisdom, we had decided of all possibilities our scientists have as formulae in their hands, the ones to focus on developing were those for medical cures and on those creating solar power. And some others ... those were for emergencies only. Like the space-time travel contrivance. It was housed far enough away, in the back hills of Krete, and overseen by a committee which made sure its use was most infrequent and only for true emergencies.

"Like for The Playboy of the Great Seas, when he was still out there, shocked by war or not, Odysseus had been making a mess of things. That had been tolerated for some eight long years. But each day while he was away from his kingdom, at home in Ithaka, things had accelerated to the point of inter-confederation alarm. Then, ten years after the end of Troy, Odysseus's son, Telemachus, was spotted secretly leaving home. And naturally, the Confederation feared Telemachus' absence would lead to an all-out war, including the use of weapons of mass destruction thought to be held by some of those rabid contenders for the Ithaka throne and lands (from where they could exert, in secret, an unlimited force). Quickly Nestor, in order to avoid the catastrophe of war again, had pulled rank and sent a *fait accompli* to all confederation members, declaring he was going to use the space-time travel device to get Odysseus home. Odysseus, unaware, enticed by the daughter of King Alcinous of the Scherians, was soon captured and returned to Ithaka in time to avoid war. Was it now again the time to declare another *fait accompli*?"

Unfortunately, no one had spotted in time a countermeasure to Clytemnestra's machinations. "Is this now another such time? A time of greater, again unexpected, need?"

Would Nestor's sons be in time this time right here in his Pylos? Would his administrators?

What Nestor was seeing this night might mean, and almost certainly did, that someone in the inner circles had leaked the secrets of the Confederation and they were being warned that they were on some doomsday list set for destruction. Could this, too, be attributed to Clytemnestra's lingering curse? Possibly. Power and attention.

Clytemnestra. Oh, gods! The psychoanalyst had described Clytemnestra's character vividly, detailing a strange form of what they called schizophrenia. Not multiple personalities but, essentially, no personality. She was constantly seeking to know who she was. And unfortunately, in the vacuum of a personality, she had become an animal, unconcerned with the results of her actions, simply needing, craving action, resorting often to violence and overweening rage to immediately destroy whatever bothered her, crushing it like a fly. Guilt never crosses such a soul. Anger had become this queen's very self.

But her son, the hero Orestes, was made of different stuff. His goodness and decency and leadership had been nurtured and encouraged by the family of Theseus in Athens, where Orestes had been raised as a son, to where he had fled when his father was away in Troy and his mother had taken up with the vicious Aegisthos. But his very goodness weighed on his soul, so he could not forgive himself for murdering his murdering mother. Acquitted of any wrong, acquitted of avenging his father's murder by Wisdom herself and a group of his kingly peers, among them he, Nestor. Though Orestes had taken up the mantle and served as king at Mycenae, finally his guilt and Clytemnestra's evil spirit had destroyed him, daily seeping like water on porous stone. He was porous, poor lad. Well today Orestes's son, Tisamenos, was doing his best in that haunted and doomed city-state, Mycenae. While here in Pylos, just down the hill, Orestes hid. The only place Nestor thought Orestes could find himself truly forgiven was there in the home of Nestor's darling son Peisistratos and the remarkable Nepthaulia. There Nepthaulia did softly sing to him of the murder by Clytemnestra of Cynthia, Nepthaulia's grandmother, and of her great-aunt Merope, when Mycenae's Khorus Girls had become Clytemnestra's Fire Girls. There, in Nepthaulia's home, Orestes had found salvation in hearing the stories of tragedies caused by his mother, working them like beads through his fingers to soothe his soul. And in that home, there could Orestes forgive himself and learn to love himself again. Poor lad. Poor, heroic lad.

But maybe murdering Clytemnestra was not enough. Her evil was so deep, it penetrated into the very hills, soil and soul of Mycenae.

Mycenae had become a dark place. Those evils of Clytemnestra had been passed on to others, as perhaps these Sky People were demonstrating. Perhaps those Sky People, who disrupted peace at Troy, were responsible for Clytemnestra?

Or … or could this possible onslaught out there have been the ignorant result of talkative Odysseus showing off to the very ones who possessed some half-knowledge of the evils of the split atom? Or was he still in touch with those aliens who appeared at Troy?

Nestor felt the uselessness of knowledge. Perhaps scientists themselves had unwittingly disclosed crucial information needed to be kept secret. Most likely it was a combination that gave power and information to these, the possible Sky People. He needed to know what was happening out there. How else could he possibly save his people? Maybe this hunch he was chewing on would pay off if he spoke in time, as when, fifteen years ago, in 1205, another hunch had paid off.

Meanwhile, in a cove off to the side of the King's desk, the King's secretary, tired of pretending he was scrutinizing and replying to the latest letters sent to King Nestor, like this one from the king of Media, was now too exhausted by the struggle to sit upright and simulate focus. His head was slowly sinking toward the desk. But suddenly, instead of fighting to keep his eyes open and his back upright in his chair and his finger on the words, suddenly he heard through the fog in his brain, "Stelios, Stelios! Come! Let's go!" Stelios's eyes fought to focus on the tall figure of the old king striding toward him.

Despite the fear and the urgency, the king smiled. Stelios was struggling to pretend he was awake. But Morpheos was winning. Stelios was not only highly intelligent but totally loyal, and Nestor valued his judgement highly. So instead of allowing this young man his deserved rest, Nestor was going to take him along. He reached into his pocket for a handkerchief to wipe the drool from Stelios's mouth. But his fingers closed on something different from linen. What? He felt it and pulled it out. "Oh, little Nepthaulia." Unconsciously, when jumping up from his desk an hour ago, he had returned the statue not back on his desk but to his pocket. "Unconsciously?" What would his professors of human behavior and psychoanalysis say? Likely they would smile and explain that Nestor unconsciously knew he needed special protection and advice from this symbol of survival. In his other pocket he found a handkerchief and wiped Stelios's dribble. Then he touched his secretary's shoulder and shook it gently.

"Put on your coat. It's chilly out."

The king grabbed his own warm coat, and Stelios staggered to his feet to help him.

"Hurry," said the old man. "We must get up to the observatory."

"Sir?"

"Come, lad. Let's off!"

Stelios, still trying to stay upright, got into his coat and started running in back of his master down darkened corridors. As they raced past the corridor leading to the private rooms, Stelios yawned inadvertently as he wished for his comfortable, warm bed and darling wife. But a large hand kindly urged him forward.

"She'll be there when you return, lad."

Word had spread from the guards on duty in the corridors, and when the King and Stelios got downstairs to the palace's entrance, the king's chariot and driver were waiting.

"Sir, where to?"

"The observatory. And quick."

An advance chariot and driver were already starting swiftly in front, going uphill to prepare the scientists for the king.

Stelios followed the king's stare, so his too was held on the comet and the stars falling over the Sea.

Though Nestor was looking up, he was not thinking of falling stars. Not now. Now he was thinking of who could save them this time. His fingers touched Nepthaulia. His mind wandered back to the days when he was far away at Troy. It was in large measure thanks to the society of Khorus Girls that his cities had been saved. Eurydice had continued to make sure each city-state had such an organization, whose head votaresses were trained by her. As the mother of Nepthaulia and Khloris then had been, and now their daughters. With their numerous sisters in the khorus, they had since indeed saved Pylos many times from disasters caused by the forces of nature. Could they do so again, by some universal magic? His fingers caressed again the little figurine in his pocket. She and her sister were his touchstones, his lodestones.

"Little Nepthaulia," he whispered, "help me now." In fact, he would not rely on prayer. He would ask the real sisters and Eurydice to call a special meeting of the Khorus Korai of Pylos. Tomorrow. Today.

The king had been greeted formally but warmly by the chief of staff of the observatory. He had just arrived after being called from his bed with the information that the king was on his way.

And now Nestor, after an hour with the chief cosmologists, an hour focusing and studying through the great telescopes, said it: "Do you think it is possible?" He wiped his eyes. He was tired. Dawn was about to arrive.

"Yes, yes. Well, of course, sir, if we have this knowledge, others could have come by it, too."

"Possibly by theft," spoke the physicist.

"This is what we were alerting you to in that report. The sky." From his colleague.

"So, tell me what you really think this is about." The old king looked at his scholarly administrators. "Are you saying these others certainly have the technology and decided to use it? That unforgiving technology? That which we refused?"

"First, we know," the astronomer pointed outside, "that there is a large, natural, astronomical exhibition happening. Comets and asteroids, joining some likely exploding dying stars in this extraordinary display."

"However, and in addition." His geologist stepped forward, went to the telescope and looked again. "Yes. There it is." She gestured. "Look, please." Each stepped up and spent moments gazing at the explosions in the sky. "Look lower and you will see multiple eruptions that do not come from the sky but are soaring into the sky from, it seems, many mountains spewing into the heavens. Tons equal to that technology we chose to ignore. I await images from our satellites.

"That thrilling burst you see invading and accelerating the volcanic exhibit out there could be the reinforcement created by aggressive and learned societies of which and whom we are ignorant. This planetary body is larger than we have yet fully explored, sir." She bowed to the king.

"But, though we are learned about our universe, we know not all people will choose the path of enlightened development ours has. If these sights really are their warnings, signaling they have the technology, then, yes. We do not believe these sorts of signs are saying they will use the technology as we have. Certainly not for peace, as we do."

The gerontic king murmured as he again looked into the telescope. "As our images will show you. Or? Or could there be another determination?"

"Of course, these could be truly natural geological and astronomical phenomenon. But," his astrophysicist picked up the thread, "so far, some causes play fickle and elude us. And it is possible that there is a confusing confluence of geology, astronomy and distant peoples colliding with physics. This could be coming from us, that we have fostered a traitor who has stolen our well-guarded secrets of the cosmos and of the atom. It's no longer a secret, may I remind you, sir, that we have space-time travel, though most have no idea what the words mean. But Odysseus, in his ignorance, spread those words all about fifteen years ago. Again, let me state, in his ignorance. And again, let me state that most have no idea what the words mean. But for some special rogue ones, fifteen years is plenty of time to … to learn and to harness."

"Well, space-time is not necessarily a technology that would signal destruction, is it? What do you advise we do?" The King looked again. Then he stepped back and waved a hand. "You, sir," he said, indicating his secretary.

But instead, the director of nuclear sciences stepped forward.

"Sir, one moment. Clearly, there really is another element involved." He nodded to the geologist.

"Yes?" Nestor's famous eyebrows raised as his hand waved that scientist forward.

"I should explain more, sire. The Earth herself definitely is entering into these displays." She again pointed to the differences between the exploding sky and explosions into the sky. "Here and there and there." Taking the King by the hand, she stepped onto the balcony and pointed. "Some of those are marks of Earth's protests. But those. See. Look," she said, gesturing to the astrophysicists. "Those displays there have 'human-caused' written all over them. But they also come from the sky. Many things are converging from Earth's own forces with those from other heavenly earths. Together, earthlings and sky people, I believe, are joining. As they have in the past. Our distant past."

The king kept her hand and looked her in the eye. "And not so distant," he murmured.

The secretary coughed. "Yes. And, sir, there are societies, not learned ... fearing and fearful ... out there making their way here, I have heard, coming here over the seas, seeking destruction for extinction, not for gain. Simply to destroy. They are of little love, not touched by the great understanding and love of the powers of women, as you have guided us to be. Fearful and destructing men who will destroy us if they can."

"Sir!"

The old king looked around and watched the youngest of the scientists step forward, to the obvious surprise of the elders. The director advanced forward with a hand raised in protest.

"I want to hear what he has to say," the king indicated the Director to step back.

"Sir," the youngest continued, "this man," he indicated the king's Secretary, "is correct. There is a coincidence ... no, a convergence happening. This convergence is not a coincidence. This time, there will be a perfect storm, as our geologist is saying, more perfect than just the people from the sea. The earth, the heavens, as you all clearly see, with those sea marauders. They are all converging. And perhaps also with sky people. Yes. Their personal and collective sense of smell is leading these foreigners, all these marauders, here. From all directions. And they converge with geology and astronomy by design. The sky people and the sea people are both using the warring earth and heavens not to hide themselves and their intent, but to sow terror and fear. And to destroy. I fear some powerful ones have not forgotten Troy."

The other scientists, except for this youngest who had joined the secretary and geologist, looked at him strangely.

"I do believe it," the secretary said.

"And I," the king said. "I know our collective sense of smell led us here on our peaceful quest for a new home. Our unknown ancestors arrived here and left that sense of how they believed this was the place for us to come to, to advance civilization. They had gone as far as they could across the sea. And look. We did find it. We have created. And maybe now ..." The old king looked again at the explosions in the sky. "Maybe now it is time for others to discover their destiny. And for ours to disappear from the scene."

All the faces in front of him showed shock.

"Sir."

"But sir!"

The king smiled kindly and waved them silent.

"Sir, you are correct," he said, indicating the director. "And you, madam, and you. All of you. The use of space-time travel is only one application of the great knowledge. And," he added, turning to another physicist at his side, "what we are looking at here does not demonstrate that they have yet quite mastered all that technology needed. But the storms converging do indicate man and many earths, including this one, are joining forces for one huge bang."

The head physicist had not been pleased with the junior colleagues speaking out. "Sir," he said, replying to the king, "against such unknown adversaries, whether from this earth or from others, who perhaps by these actions show they plan to use such as we have decided never to, we can do nothing. Except wait and send ambassadors of civilization with invitations to join our nations of peace. Unless ..."

"Yes?"

"Unless you wish us to rush to production. We have all the materials ready. Sir, if people out there already have these weapons of mass destruction, it is highly unlikely a peaceful offer will do much to change minds set on destruction. They do not want incorporation nor conquest. If so, they would not be showing off these weapons such as we think we are seeing demonstrated in the skies."

"Then we had better start preparing for the worst in many ways," the king said, "and pray not to need. Though against invasions from advanced societies, I cannot see how our most-destructive forces could do more than destroy us for them."

The old king of peace was a realist. As they neared the door, the king turned. "Their personal and collective sense of smell is leading the foreigners our way. Maybe foreigners from the stars, maybe foreigners from the unexplored reaches of this, our star. Yes, maybe it is our time to disappear from the scene. At the same time develop further our space-time travel, please. Maybe we should be on the move. To new homes."

At tomorrow's meeting with his sons, he would spell it out. He would advise what they must do and when. Then he would call the Council. Sadly, some would be missing and much missed. Ramesses. Agamemnon. And he would call the khorus. There was much to organize and prepare. And it would take time to prepare.

"It's past my bedtime," he said. "Do not let the musings of an old man concern you. Come." He smiled sweetly and grabbed the shoulder of his secretary. "Home."

At the formal entrance to the palace, the king was put into a solar sedan chair and zipped off to his quarters.

Stelios went to the offices to tidy up. Finally, the very sleepy secretary waved the lights off. He stretched. Yes, tomorrow would be another early and late day, he was sure. He toddled off to his quarters, down many dimly lit corridors and down staircases, past offices where writers, their fingers flying, were hard at work transcribing the latest activities and economic enterprises. Stelios reached his own not-bad quarters. He was kept in great comfort by the very kind king. The very kind queen, he should add. After a good, warm shower, into his comfortable, warm bed he jumped, already dreaming of where he would most like to be: in Pylos Bay sailing under blue skies with his friend, new-King Thrasymedes. Suddenly, as sleep was sealing his eyes, he was awake, thinking of what the old-king was thinking about at this same time; catastrophe and collapse.

In his great chambers, while his darling wife slept, Nestor, still watching the stars falling and, holding again the figurines of Nepthaulia and her sister, Khloris, remembered the night in 1205 when their actions had saved this Pylos kingdom. The old king held the tiny, clay images close and prayed. And heard again the words of the younger scientist. Then he remembered another event in that fateful year of 1205. Not long after the Khorus saved the kingdom, all of the people of Pylos's eight vineyards and their cities were joined in celebrating the harvest festival honoring the sea god. Unexpectedly into this celebration Prince Telemachus had arrived seeking help for his besieged Ithaka, from which Odysseus was still absent. At that moment, Nestor had known that the lesson Telemachus needed to learn had to be impressed upon him at lightning speed. How to accomplish this while Prince Telemachus was cavorting and celebrating with Nestor's own princely sons? Then wisdom and wine guided him … "that special eleven-year-old wine."

"Our collective sense of smell!" he almost shouted.

He well knew how the personal and collective sense of smell was a magic carpet to space-time travel, from which to instantly learn and return; a carpet that appeared where memories were so vibrant. And such did happen then, when, at the end of that festival day, all the princes, including Telemachus, attended the formal wine tasting Nestor had quickly organized. He knew this wine tasting would instinctively bring all those attending to a moment in 1216, when all the men of the realms had been negotiating at Troy. The moment, encapsulated in the aroma of the wine of that vintage, Nestor knew, would instantly bring forth the message that Prince Telemachus needed to attend to with great haste. This message, the king's inspiration had told him, could only be learned through a shock delivered instantly through the sense of smell. Indeed, as soon as the princes inhaled the initial aromas of that eleven-year-old wine, they were transported at warp speed back to those autumn days when, standing at the sides of their mothers and grandmothers and aunts, they had helped harvest that wine. All the men were at Troy. The year 1216 had become The Vintage of The Ladies. And, instantly, in 1205, through the memory delivered in that aroma, Telemachus had understood how much his mother needed him. And returned to Ithaka just in time to rescue their throne with his conveniently returned father, Odysseus. All thanks to the sense of smell. Today, Telemachus was king in an again peaceful, prosperous land.

"Well, maybe not so peaceful tonight," the king mused, looking again at the stars falling into the sea. Likely Telemachus was on his way here again. He would have seen the stars falling before Nestor had. Telemachus, now his own son-in-law, along with Nestor's daughter, Polycaste, and their people would come with Nestor when the moment came. That was not magic but a collective bond. And for that, the Khorus Girls and his wife would be their salvation.

"What will we do?" he thought. "Will another Griffin warrior come along to lead them with kingly fervor, strength and background knowledge? Could Thrasymedes be the one? Will he be the leader as they start a brave, new world all on their own?" He reached for and clasped Khloris's image to his breast and kissed it before getting up and gently placing her safely on his bedside table alongside Nepthaulia. He turned again to the display outside. "Will there be Khorus Girls to save the kingdom, to put all to right? The gods will it!"

His last thoughts before closing his eyes were of the sight of Nepthaulia flying through the rain and of the singing of the Girls who caught her, of tossed Khloris soaring into the clouds, carried by her birds, and of the raindrops blurring his vision. He could hear them singing.

"Tomorrow," he murmured. Tomorrow, Tomorrow" He slept.

CHAPTER 1

FADE IN: *Magical Mystery Tour at Bronze Age Archaeological Site*

SETTING:
   Place: Archaeologist's Office and Museum, Mycenae
      Archeological Site, Greece
   Date: 30 to 31 May, <u>2021 A.D.</u>
   Time: 11 p.m. to 8:45 a.m.
(coincidings of dates and times of day, and of <u>B.C.</u> and <u>A.D.</u> are <u>not</u> <u>coincidental</u>)

MARGARET BENSON'S BIGGEST find, the one that had elevated her to this exalted position, was the discovery right out there on the citadel of the Bronze Age city of Mycenae: the grave of the last great king of Mycenae. On that day, when she had pried from his bony fingers a small figurine of a girl that the king had clasped to his breast as he died, Maggie had no idea she would spend the rest of her life seeking to know why this figurine was so important to King Tisamenos, son of King Orestes, grandson of the great Agamemnon.

  Margaret was the current lead archaeologist at the excavation site of the Bronze Age city and palace citadel of the world-famous Mycenae. And was naturally proud of this appointment, following in the bootsteps of a long line of famous archaeologists. She had this position because she was a problem solver, excellent at sniffing out and getting to the facts underneath all the rubble.

Maggie had been born loving a good mystery. She admired and sought to emulate great magicians. Years ago she had read that in 2,700 B.C., a magician in Egypt had produced balls out of thin air. That image stuck with her. So when in 1980 A.D., Maggie saw on T.V. David Copperfield levitating over the Grand Canyon, she was hooked; and in 1983, when she was an impressionable fourteen-year-old, while watching him make the Lady of Liberty disappear, she decided to join the ranks of magicians.

Margaret was in her groove when solving Sherlock Holmes's mysteries and challenging her wits before reading the denouements of Agatha Christie stories, as she still did with the mysteries posed by Clive Cussler and James Lee Burke. Harry Potter's tricks fascinated her. When J.K. Rowling came to Mycenae, Maggie had taken her around to show her the magic they were unveiling from millennia past, and over dinner that night they talked magic.

Her mother had always called her Imaginative, "too Imaginative for a practical job," she often warned. Maybe Mother was right.

One fateful day during a summer holiday in Manhattan, while her mother and aunt went to get their hair done at Bergdorf's, Maggie, enjoying the freedom to discover the great city, had wandered up the steps into the amazing New York Public Library, past those guardian lions who had, as she passed, (she was sure) roared softly to her. Inside, having stated her mission, she had been directed to the rare archives. While waiting for the librarian, who had gone in search of a special volume of Harry Houdini conjurations, she had inspected the quiet, dramatically lit room with beautiful cabinets. Attracted by a pin-spot shining down on a green, baize-covered, double-folio-sized volume with a brilliant, gold impression, she had gone over and found her life's work: "ILIOS, Heinrich Schliemann," she had pronounced shakily, her hands in the air, like a conjurer pulling forth life and breath from this object, this great wizard's tome.

"Would you like to see this book also?" the librarian asked.

Maggie nodded. "Yes, please," she whispered, and she followed the archivist, who was walking toward a table where she deposited the Houdini book. She turned and smiled at Maggie. "I'll get you some gloves, too."

Three hours later Margaret met her mother and aunt in front of the 21 Club. So as not to be late for lunch, she had to run.

"I'm." She jumped up and down to get their attention. "I'm going to be ..." She waved her arms and shouted across the street at them, both touching their hair, looking at their watches. She crossed Fifty-Second Street, dodging between taxis and running to hug her astonished mother. "I'm going to be an ... an archaeologist!" She got it out between hugs and kisses and praise for the hairdos and while going down the steps into the restaurant.

"Take that by me again," her mother said, smiling as the waiter placed the napkin on her lap.

So Maggie told them how archaeologists were like magicians, uncovering and revealing amazing things, like the Bronze Age city of Troy.

"You were always too imaginative," her mother said, laughing, and she told the waiter she would like the crab cakes.

That day everything around Maggie felt bathed in a golden light. That was in 1986. Margaret Benson had become that archaeologist. And things in her life often still felt bathed in gold.

Now, at well past midnight on May 31, in 2021 A.D., Margaret Benson, archaeologist, stood in the middle of the office of the lead archaeologist in Mycenae, Greece. Her office. For two more golden days.

She looked around and knew she would have to fight to concentrate on the real work of the next few days. She was finding that hard, looking at all these loose ends surrounding her, each filled with things left undone, and memories, each and all of which she had to let go of, tie up and pack away. Two days. This meaningful clutter right here and all around in her office, that normally comforted her, had awakened her and so worried her brain fibers she could no longer sleep. She had dressed and driven up the hill from her residence at the Hotel Belle Helene in the middle of the night, hardly concentrating in her anxiety on what she was doing. Two days. Well, she did reflect on her way up that her headlights shining into the guard's house had wakened the tired night guard. Yes, there he was. His head peeked out, and she had waved and tooted. Then she had driven into fog higher up, making her concentrate. The headlights shone eerily on the Lions over their Gate.

"For lions who are thirty-two hundred and seventy-one years old, you are definitely looking good," she congratulated them. And she heard them roar silently into the mists. She parked close to the back entrance of the museum, where there was really no parking. But going down that walkway on foot at night was spooky, as her predecessor, Lisa French, had warned. Now she stood in her office and the memories flooded over her, talking to her from all the articles and photos, and she was somewhat undone by it all. Well, well. How had they passed so fast, the years that had made these memories? Twenty-five. All the clutter told her that, as in excavation, each strata of stuff demonstrated a timeline. This was her strata, The Margaret Benson Strata, about to end here, 1 June, 2021 A.D. It was marking her last days here, at this desk, in this small office in the museum of the great, magical, monolithic, once-city and palace of Mycenae from the 1300s B.C. And her twenty-five years of accomplishments deciphering that magical time were on paper and staring at her. All this stuff was hard evidence of her magical time. She looked around and, picking up a photograph from her desk to put into a box at her feet, sighed, ran a hand through her long, blond hair, grabbed a stray rubber band and pulled her tresses through it then pulled back her chair to put the box on the seat.

"Well, here's to you Girls and all that goes with you," she said aloud, indicating the evidence of her research on those figurines she called "The Girls," tapping the photograph of the three types of tiny, clay figurines, named by Dr. Lisa French, "Tau," "Psi" and "Phi," ascribing to them these letters because their characteristic stances made them resemble those Greek letters. Two thirds of them, the Tau with their arms stretched out like the letter T, and the Psi with their arms in the air, seemed the most animated. But she also loved the Phi, who looked, indeed, as some called them, "fashionistas," with their enigmatic, mannequin-like, fashion-show runway appearance. They were, no matter what initial was ascribed to them, elegant and charming, "full of personality," she announced as she stopped and stared closer at the photo and kissed the images.

"My girls. Maggie's Girls. We've been on quite an adventure together these last twenty-five years. And in two, well, no ..." she looked at her watch, "in one day, your big reveal will take place. If only it could be with a fashion show with live mannequins dressed like each of the three types. But, sob, it will be more subdued. And, oh gods, my book all about you will be presented to my professional colleagues at this secret farewell party." She sighed. "Many opinionated archaeologists will be here, armed with a copy of the book. What will they say about my conclusions? Well," she said as she tucked the photo into the box, "too late now to worry." But she knew she was talking to the wind. She was worried. Had she solved the mystery of who and why these little statues were created, and were so loved?

Startled by a huge rumble from the mountains outside, she turned swiftly, only to survey more of what was left to accomplish. And in that moment she felt many emotions.

Like excitement. Yes. Maggie was excited.

She was excited because she was about to move up to an even bigger position in the world of archaeology. Only recently she had been chosen as the archaeologist to lead a team in uncovering the Mycenaean remains under the Acropolis in Athens. Because five years ago she had discovered a special link between Bronze Age Athens and Mycenae and the Kingdom of Pylos in the west, she was now given the dream job of directing-conjoining all Peloponnesos excavations from the triple harbors in the southern Ionian Sea overlooked by the palace of Nestor, to Agamemnon's Mycenae, and all the way east to Athens. A dream assignment she had coveted since those first discoveries at Athens's Acropolis five years ago.

That dream had been fostered by the most-particular find here in Mycenae: the clay figurine clasped to the breast of King Tisamenos. Since her first golden days here, these little figurines had become a focal point in her life's work and in the lives of many other archaeologists, all of whom were trying to discover why these girl figurines were significant to their culture. Conferences had been held, bringing to Athens, Stockholm and Cambridge archaeologists from around the globe with theories and discoveries, all trying to discern what these little girl figurines were all about. Each figurine was so filled with a vibrancy, a life that they almost demanded all the attention and focus lavished on them. But so far, no one theory had proved satisfactory.

Margaret was somewhat surprised to find that in her reminiscing, she had walked from her office and up the dark corridor to the museum room where many Girls were displayed. And there *she* was, this one, her particular figurine. The one that changed her life: her cover girl. She tapped on the glass at her "Merope," the one who fifteen years ago, in 2006, had been discovered in the shaft grave of Mycenae's last king, Tisamenos, buried with him in the last days of Mycenae. But, to Maggie's amazement, when she had recently studied the clay with which Merope had been formed in order to pinpoint the date she had been made, she had discovered that Merope's clay was not from Mycenae. Except for three other figurines in the cases, plus the one standing next to Merope, all the other Girl figurines grouped around these had been made from the pure, local clay of Berbati, just over that rumbling mountain above her office. However, these five were made not of local Berbati clay, but of clay from Pylos, quite a distance away west on the Ionian side of the Peloponnesos, in the area of King Nestor's palace.

Maggie knocked on the glass at her Girl. "That must have been quite a distance to cover back in those days." Sometime in 1205 B.C. was the date ascribed to when these five had likely been made. "Yet here you are." The shaft gravesite where Merope had been found was just a stone's throw from where Maggie now stood, right out there near the citadel of Mycenae's palace. The sight, that day, of the king clasping his tiny treasure was so touching that Margaret had with particular tenderness removed her from his bony clutch.

"Well, Merope, this is kind of a goodbye. My last day here with you is tomorrow. So, please, after all this time together, could you answer the question I've asked every day since I learned that you came from Pylos? How did you get here? Why did you, Merope, come here, to be quite obviously cherished by the last king, the Son of Orestes? That must have been around 1185 B.C. And by then you were already a twenty-year-old creation when, having been removed from home in Pylos, you were buried here in Mycenae. Who had loved you before your trip here? And why were you brought here to be dearly loved by this last, great king?" A mystery voyage with an element of Magic.

Maggie turned her attention to Merope's neighbor. Not long after this magical mystery discovery of the Merope traveling figurine, Margaret had discovered ... "You," she said as she tapped on the glass at Merope's neighbor. Another mystery traveler. "And you have become the mysterious '*link*' which is sending me on my next voyage." She too was made from the exact clay as Merope, by the same potter from Pylos, also around 1205 B.C. She, too, had been uncovered by another chance. And she, too, had been discovered not where she was made, nor found here in Mycenae. Instead, Maggie had found her in 2016 A.D. at the Athens Acropolis. And when investigating her clay to discover her age and origin, Maggie had been once more amazed to find that this little one was also made of that same clay from Pylos. And for some reason, she had taken to the road, this time not stopping until she had arrived all the way in Athens, where Margaret had found her after more than thirty-two hundred years, unbroken, still smiling and waving her Psi-shaped arms. Why had these two, related, clay figurines, along with their three neighbors, gone travelling so far from their home? For what reason would someone long ago bring each to a new home, arriving, according to the strata each was found in, near the end of all this, at new homes just before the collapse of this great Bronze Age civilization? This was a unique phenomenon, because of which Margaret had now received a grant to study this double mystery. Her new headquarters would be in Athens. There Margaret would have multiple resources to learn more about the mysterious journeys these figurines had taken. So Margaret was excited to begin solving this mystery, excited about this new beginning.

In only two days, this mystery would send her on a new voyage. Thus and therefore, Maggie was sad.

She had been in this office in Mycenae for twenty-five years. Here was home. She lived just down the hill at the Hotel Belle Helene.

There, too, was home. The Dassis family had become her family. Margaret walked back to her office reflecting on how much like family she felt here. From her desk, she picked up and closed the journal she had been reminiscing over the afternoon before, the journal in which she had documented these finds. "Merope," she had heard one day, not long after she had found the little figurine buried with the son of Orestes. While cleaning her off, Maggie was sure she heard a small voice say, "Merope. My name is Merope." But though, apparently, Merope could be talkative, Maggie had yet to hear from her why or when she had come to Mycenae from Pylos. Nor why she had been obviously cherished by the last king of Mycenae. Then, when Maggie brought the figurine found in Athens back to Mycenae, and placed her in the glass case next to Merope, Maggie was sure she then heard Merope say, "Welcome, Nepthaulia! Welcome, my darling." So Maggie had ascribed the name Nepthaulia to this other Pylos-made figurine. Colleagues smiled when thinking about her naming the figurines.

"I do know you can talk." Margaret leaned into the hall and called into the dark corridor. "And I presume you knew each other in Pylos, where you were made. When will you tell me the rest of this story of your relationship and of your travels? Better hurry things up, both of you! All of you!"

She turned back to her work and was tucking the journal into the box with the others when another sudden rumble from the mountain in back of the building made her drop it and look up through the clerestory windows. All these years and she still was spooked by the rumbling from those double mountains standing sentinel up there.

Her watch announced the hour: 4 a.m. The rumbling increased, giving her an unpleasant feeling, unnerving. Two more journals went in, and she sealed the box. She knew she would have a good home in Athens. And very exciting work. And that work would return her frequently to Mycenae. But still. With less than joy, she picked up the box and carried it over to top a pile of others. The piles marked an ending with sadness.

She stretched and reached up to a high shelf to get down other books and papers.

"Well, let's be frank about it," she stopped with this stack of books in her hands. "I am not just sad. Frankly, I am also quite worried." Worry was definitely contributing to her unsettled feelings. About? She boxed those books and grabbed more things for the box. Oh, well, yes: *That Book*. That book was worrying her. Her book on these Girl figurines, from which prototype cover little Merope looked out and now waved as Margaret turned away. Her book, which so many colleagues were interested in reading, was due here today. She checked the date on her phone: May 31. Tomorrow all those interested scholars, gifted with a copy, would be scrutinizing it. Were her conclusions correct? She plopped down into her chair.

"Yes, be honest, Maggie," she said. "You always sought out a mystery waiting to be solved. So let's see if you solved it. Time to put it out there and soon you'll know, dear girl. Too late now to worry."

She stood, grabbed another box and began filling it. From the mountains in back came another huge rumble and the lights flickered. She put three more books into the box, and when she stood, what she saw told her she had better get on with it. 4:30 a.m. She still had a lot of packing to do. How she wished she could abracadabra all this into self-sealing boxes, snap her fingers, and shazam! But rabbits really did not easily come from hats.

"Let's abracadabra, Merope!" she called back up the hallway toward the museum where the figurines were. "Come on, girls, cha-cha-cha!" She turned around three times and clicked her heels for good luck. "Gosh, Maggie, you're getting silly-giddy tired." And on that note, she got a new wind and began on more boxes.

8:00 a.m. She stretched and surveyed all the boxes and empty shelves and knew she had accomplished a lot in the last three-plus hours. Yet still, as she looked around at more books, papers and notebooks spilling from shelves and drawers, she wished again for some J.K. Rowling magic. A little Houdini. Today, already May 31, and tomorrow, the 1st of June, 2021. Oh, she would need to call on all her conjuring skills. She waved her hands at the remains of days of research and excavation, but none of what remained to be packed disappeared. She felt her tummy rumble. She had left the Belle Helene last night because all this was weighing on her, and she could not sleep another moment. Now she looked through the high windows to see the clear morning light. Her watch band agreed with her tummy. It told her it was definitely past time for breakfast in the dining room. She stretched and went to find something to drink, but that worry about her book's conclusions started nagging at her again.

"How wrong have I been?"

She opened a bottle of water from the cooler.

CHAPTER 2

FADE IN: *Interior: Hotel Belle Helene, Mycenae Village, Greece*:
"Something is missing."

SETTING:
   Place: Hotel Dining Room and Back-of-House Area
   Date: 31 May, 2021 A.D.
   Time: 8:30 a.m. to 9:30 a.m.

AGAMEMNON GEORGE DASSIS put down his hot cup of sweet coffee. Something was bothering him. What? He had slept well. *Check sleep.* Today, very early, his wife had begun working on their taxes. She predicted she would be at this for three days. She loved working on taxes, "making everything come out right," she said. *Check his wife.* The housekeeping staff had arrived on time and was humming along, cleaning and making the rooms lovely for the long-term guests and the new arrivals. *Check the staff.* Their long-term guests and that couple from Athens were all in the dining room by 7:45, enjoying their breakfasts. The Athens couple had extended their stay and were off to visit Epidauros. They left fifteen minutes ago. Everything was on schedule. *Check the guests.* All was in order. Oh! Flowers! No. Fresh flowers would be brought in by his nephew in about thirty minutes. So? What was bothering him? Gingerly he took another sip. How he loved this sweet coffee.

"Oh!" He snapped his fingers. "Ah-ha! Dr. Margaret!" That was it. No check for Dr. Margaret. She was what was bothering him. Dr. Margaret would be leaving them in three days. Dr. Margaret he had known almost all his life. So? Agamemnon paused and gave it some thought. He and Kati-Selene should invite her to dinner tonight or tomorrow and make something special. Some of her favorites. Oh, and a gift. There certainly should be a gift. A special, personal gift. What would be fitting for someone who was like family? Dr. Margaret Benson had moved into La Belle Helene when he was only four years old. Twenty? No, twenty-five years she had lived here in his hotel. Back then, of course, it was his father's hotel. When she arrived looking so tall, blond and American, he had fallen in love. His first love. She had been to his first family Pascha communion and to his high school graduation. And had come to Athens with his parents when he graduated from hotel school. Bringing a gift. She had been at his wedding last year. She was a like a member of the Dassis family, and now (was it three days only?), she was leaving her home. He had to do something special. He would ask Kati-S's advice. He turned to the sideboard.

"Well, maybe," he poured another small cup for himself, "maybe a few cases of the Dassis family wines she so enjoyed? Sent to her new apartment in Athens? She had some favorites and, well, why not? Why not send a case every month?" He shrugged and sipped. "She is family." He would get his uncle's agent in Athens to arrange the deliveries. "But, hello, where?" He turned and peeked into the dark dining room and looked around. "Oh! That's it!" He smacked his brow. "Dr. Margaret was not here for breakfast with the long-term guests today." She was usually here by seven, at her table. Seven-fifteen at the latest. Maybe with the move, she was packing and had not yet had any breakfast. He would ask the housekeeper on her wing to bring coffee over. And those rolls she so loved. He put down his cup, wrote a note and put it on top of the housekeeper's list. She would find it when she finished the rooms on this end of the inn. He went back to the sideboard on the buffet in the dining room to refresh his cup and, glancing into the glass-fronted panes, stooped to flatten the cowlick on the back of his dark head.

At six feet, two inches, Agamemnon was evidently a Dassis. All his ancestors were tall. His father, six feet one inches tall, had described how his great-great-grandfather, also an Agamemnon, at six feet four inches, had towered over the great, but diminutive archaeologist, Heinrich Schliemann, when he had first come to ask about renting a room. The Dassis family could trace its lineage in Mycenae for ten generations, to there, just northwest in the hills, up in their hilly vineyards that overlooked the Bronze Age citadel of Mycenae. His great-great-grandfather always said their stature proved they were evidently descended from "those Mycenaeans." He firmly believed their ancestors had survived the cataclysm and collapse of 1200 B.C., as the family called the great demise of the Bronze Age. Agamemnon straightened and picked up his cup, adding more hot coffee. "Was that the same catastrophe and collapse Dr. Margaret often discusses with her assistant, Allison, over dinner?"

The housekeeper from Dr. Margaret's area raced over, shaking her fingers at him. "*Oxi, oxi,*" she whispered. "No. No. Doctor is gone. Gone when I arrived." She ran past, moving her cart to another wing of the hotel.

Agamemnon slowly sipped his hot coffee and gave it thought. "Gone?" He stood in contemplation for a moment. "Oh. She has gone already to her office. So much for her to do up there. And we should be helping." He turned and sipped. "I know," he thought. He would have his nephew Menelaos-Stavros bring a thermos of hot coffee and some of the fresh-baked sweet rolls she loved to her office in the museum. Usually, his wife would be the one to bring coffee and rolls when the doctor left too early. But today was the first of the 'three-day tax marathon,' as his wife had called it when she had closed the door to her office that morning.

Kati-Selene loved to do taxes. This she announced one day not long after they were married. And that was just fine with Agamemnon.

Agamemnon paused a moment to return to the buffet and take a roll for himself. Yes, his grandmother's recipe was quite exceptional.

Perhaps he should write a 'Belle Helen Cookbook.' He was told Americans were crazy for cookbooks, especially cookbooks from famous places. "And this place," he thought as he looked at the walls covered with memorabilia, "is certainly famous. Look at all this." He gestured and walked back toward the collection and gazed at the names and the dates. "Well first, over here is the writing of the great Heinrich Schliemann from 1876. And here and here in so many letters requesting his rooms again and here requesting more rooms for his wife, Sophia." Indeed, in 1876, when Schliemann first came, this was his great-great-grandparents' home. And they rented him a room. Then, when more and more people came requesting a room or two, like the king of Brazil, when he wanted to see Schliemann's excavations, the family decided to move next door and enlarge the place and put in more plumbing and create a hotel. Look at all those names! Agatha Christie! Faulkner! Eisenhower! President de Gaulle! Ernest Hemingway! The list was famous and long. "Yes, yes, a cookbook will be a surefire success."

"I wonder what General de Gaulle had for breakfast?" he thought, putting down his empty cup. "Or Agatha Christie? That would sell lots of copies." He was envisioning all those books as he went back to work. He stopped by the hall table and wrote a note to his nephew to come find him as soon as he arrived with the flowers.

CHAPTER 3

FADE IN: <u>B.C./A.D.</u> Simulcast:
   Winding Up the Plot Leading to Catastrophe and Collapse

SETTING:
   Place: Int.: Archaeologist Office and Museum, Mycenae, Greece
   When: 31 May, <u>2021 A.D.</u>
   Time: 8:45 a.m. to 9:45 a.m.
(you know the B.C/A.D. simulcast of events by now: just check the B.C./A.D. listings.)

"8:45 a.m.," SHE ANNOUNCED. "YEP!" Maggie stretched out of the bent-over packing position and happily plopped down into her desk chair. "Yep! 8:45," she repeated out loud as she flexed her long legs. The piles of boxes lining the walls and stacked all over showed she had accomplished most of what she had needed to in the last nine hours. She swiveled the chair and surveyed the small office, once-filled but now almost empty of her twenty-five years of accumulation. Twenty-five years trying to solve Bronze Age archaeological mysteries here at the awesome Mycenae itself! Right here, where she had been lead archaeologist for the last twenty of those. For the first five years she had worked as assistant to one of the best mystery solvers of all archaeology, Lisa Wace French. She turned in her chair and got up from her desk to take down a stray volume whose pages were interspersed with notes on the DNA of the Atreidai ... She closed it, packed it and marked the box. She did some stretching exercises, then stood tall, looked around, and felt proud.

She, Maggie Benson was, after these adventures, *en route* to uncover not one but two of the greatest as-yet unsolved Mycenaean mysteries in modern-day archaeology: one totally hidden, covered over by the Classical Age, a mystery from the Athens Acropolis, from 1300 B.C., when kings had lived up there, and when mysterious religious and civic ceremonies had taken place at night, deep underground. Today, all those Bronze Age foundations and sub-surface staircases were hidden beneath the Classical Age surface, the surface seen and climbed over by millions of unsuspecting tourists each year. She would be excavating those long-hidden mysteries. Secondly, capping that off, was the much-coveted assignment of consolidating and expanding the ongoing Bronze Age excavations in the western Peloponnesos area, which had been under the sway of Nestor's Pylos. This would mean working closely in conjunction with the prescient wife-husband team from the University of Cincinnati, Shari Stocker and Jack Davis. Their work, Shari and Jack were discovering, could end up being greater in scope and discovery, perhaps, than even those discoveries found here at Mycenae. She, Margaret Benson, was the conjurer appointed by the chairman of the New Acropolis Museum in Athens to join the three sites into one great project, working with these teams of archaeologists. What a dream! She was excited and proud, naturally.

Maggie looked about. "All done. Almost." This packing was almost done, yes, but there was still all the rest. More in her rooms at Belle Helene Hotel. Oh, Allison would help her with that tonight after dinner.

So she hummed as she began filling another box. Then she moved over to her desk and rearranged the last pages she had placed into a folder, marked it and put it into the box before turning to leave the room. Walking around stacks of boxes, she continued up the ramp and down the corridor toward the museum's front room, where The Girls were exhibited inside glass cases. Lisa's Girls and her's were on display here. Her contribution, she could see and count, was slim compared to those figurines discovered by Lisa and before by her father, the splendid conjurer, Alan B. Wace. And these others, like this precious one here, found by the magician, Heinrich Schliemann.

Light from the clerestory windows provided dramatic effects of dazzle and shadow as Margaret turned back to her Girl, little Merope. Merope was different from most of The Girls, and at last Maggie had discovered why. Not only was her dress in an innovative style, but her clay was different, as was her firing. Those differences were what had started Maggie's voyage to find Merope's origins. Margaret had chosen Merope for the cover of her new book, perhaps because of her mysterious travels ... one of the mysteries Margaret was now *en route* to solve. But had she solved the most-obvious mystery? The basic mystery: Why had the Girl figurines been created; what was their purpose and what had they done that made them so loved?

Margaret took a deep breath and sighed. She had a very large hole in her psyche and in her stomach, too. Accompanied by that larger feeling ... Feeling? No. More like a positive. Positive she had still not gotten it right; not solved this conjuring trick of who, what and why they were. Not gotten right the very thesis of her book. She was still tossing balls in the air and hoping they would turn into birds. Is that why she thought she kept hearing ominous rumblings from somewhere outside? Most likely, the rumble came from within. And then there was the fact that her assistant, Allison, had secretly invited all — well, many — of her critical colleagues to a celebratory reception right here, where each would receive a copy. Tomorrow. Tomorrow? Yes. Tomorrow, the day before she was to drive away.

"Be honest, Margaret," she chided herself. She had wrongly stated the central premise of the book and had thereby come to wrong conclusions. "You're an overimaginative worrier!"

She turned around to The Girls. She tapped on the glass. "Were you figurines made to represent khorus girls of imaginary khoruses for little girls to play with? Or were you goddesses to be prayed to?" Oh, gosh. Now Maggie knew it was not just her ears but her eyes playing tricks. Merope was waving; really, actually waving. Margaret closed her eyes and counted to three. But when she opened them, Merope's waves were now accompanied by that ominous rumble outside. Then other girls began levitating off their pedestals and shelves, jumping up and down and shouting. This was truly bizarre. Something was wrong with her eyes. Margaret turned and closed them, then turned back and opened them. But instead of clearing things up, now she saw Merope vaulting high, shouting, flipping and jumping with all the rest. This was no *Night at The Museum* film. This was happening. She again closed her eyes.

"NO! You did NOT GET IT, Maggie! All wrong. Look at me! After all this time. Believe me, there is no more time to get it right! We are NOT figurines. We are real girls! REAL girls, Maggie. And YOU are out of TIME." Merope shut up but kept waving.

"Well, that's crazy," Maggie said, "an exaggeration at the least." She took a turn about the room, seeing the girls in other cases also jumping and waving. "Real?" she said. "What the dickens do you mean by real? Of course you are real, you darling, real figurines." She tapped on the glass. But that was obviously the wrong thing to say. Maggie stood back in shock and true amazement.

"WRONG, MARGARET. WE ARE REAL GIRLS!"

Margaret watched, stunned at how loud the little figures could shout and by their acrobatics. She really needed to get some sleep. Was this like Scrooge's bit of undigested beef? Certainly, part of what Merope had said was true. Inside each, they did have personalities and spirits like real individuals. Their makers must have been true magicians, in tune with Earth's essences. "But." She stood and stared at the commotion. "But when I hold one of you, my eyes and hands tell me what I am holding is clay. And when you shout, like now, and jump up and down, I have to figure this is some magical trick your makers imbued you with. What else? Some lifelike spark that defies the ages, like the works of the great Mesmer, able to return to the past." Margaret continued, thinking to herself, "These figurines of clay do have that inimitable spark, that unduplicatable *je ne sais quoi*, that bit of humanity that created objects normally do not. What else has made them so well loved? So loved not just by children and affectionate women but by the greatest and fiercest of warriors in their times. What?" Her own Girl, little Merope, had been clutched in his dying moments by King Tisamenos.

Margaret stopped her train of thought for a moment and watched the show get wilder. DNA made her almost one-hundred percent certain that the king to whose breast little Merope had been found clutched was the son of Orestes, the grandson, therefore, of Clytemnestra and Agamemnon; the son of Orestes, who was not only accused of murdering his mother for murdering his father, but was later acquitted and freed by Justice. As Maggie stood quite still and watched the commotion in the cases, another connection arrived as if on a bolt. After a time here as king of Mycenae, Orestes was known to have given the Mycenae kingship to his son before returning to live in Pylos with his friend, Peisistratos, youngest son of King Nestor. Then, Maggie pictured the moment when she discovered this other figurine, Nepthaulia, in Athens. Athens! Another connection! Definitely there are texts in the New Museum in Athens stating Orestes had returned to Athens from Pylos with Peisistratos, then King of Pylos, at the end. The End. So there it was, at the right time, 1185 B.C., and another Pylos connection. She peered into the glass and spoke back to her Girl.

"Is that what you have been trying to tell me, Merope?" she tapped the glass. "Did your little figurine come to Mycenae from Pylos with Orestes?"

Maggie tapped again the window, behind which all the figurines were still shouting and jumping.

Merope stopped her aerobics and stared back at Maggie while the rest continued their antics. Maggie was now freaked out. Maybe, finally, she was on the right track about one mystery? She took her keys and shook her finger at the jumping and shouting figurines.

"Please stop," she said. "I will do what I can to rectify my mistakes. Please. STOP!" And they did all stop the commotion. So she opened the case and removed her Merope, staring fixedly at the rest lest they begin again.

What could it all mean? To what did it point?

Margaret carried Merope with care back to her office. Suddenly she stood still, listening, then turned back quickly toward the dark corridor. Footsteps? No. Only another basso rumble from those mountains above the citadel. Only? The continuing rumbling was unnerving, but just then it had sounded like footsteps shuffling in back of her.

"Too much unnerving is going on!" she called out. And took a deep breath.

Calmly, front and center she lovingly and carefully placed Merope on her desk. To her surprise, Merope surveyed the office then turned with all the dignity of a nine-year old and walked over and sat down on the edge of a book. — Magic?

"Why am I surprised?" Margaret asked aloud. "I know I'm imaginative. But this is not my imagination, is it?"

Merope stared back at her.

"Did King Orestes bring you here to his son, Tisamenos? And why would the figurine of Nepthaulia be brought to Athens? By whom?"

"Please, Margaret, sit and listen and learn." Merope pointed to Margaret's chair. "If you are prepared."

Open-mouthed, Margaret nodded and pulled out her chair. "I knew you could talk."

"First of all, and once again, Margaret, I am not just a figurine. What you are seeing is a clay representation," she said, gesturing at herself, "a representation of a real girl named Merope. I, Merope, was born right out there, in Mycenae, in the time of King Agamemnon. Then, some nine years later, in 1214 B.C., as you term it, a catastrophe occurred. And this catastrophe, which is about to be repeated, is what you are going to rescue us real girls from. And at the same time, save yourself."

Margaret loved magic, especially when it felt and acted so real. She entered the moment totally. "Merope, we are back in the land of sleight of hand. Your clay proves you were made in Pylos. Why do you say you were born here in Mycenae?"

"Because though you *think* you are, you really are *not* understanding what you hear. Because you are looking at a clay figurine, you are continuing to assume wrong things. I know it is hard to look at and hold the clay me and understand a different reality, Margaret. But listen and learn. This is not really magic. But it is Different." She pointed at herself. "What you are seeing now is just a stand-in, a clay representation of the very real girl who is named Merope. Can that be impossible to understand? Remember, everyone in your 1870 A.D. thought Schliemann was a phony when he announced he was uncovering the real city of Troy because it did not look the way they had dreamed Troy would. But, in fact, he had done so. So here you are, assuming you are speaking to what cannot speak, hearing words you really could not hear, if, indeed, they were coming from clay. Look beyond what you are seeing and hearing and understand that the world is not just what your eyes can see, that there are amazing, real universes and creatures that are invisible to your eyes until you actually find them. And that by some physical use of space-time, the real girl from Mycenae in 1214 B.C. is really here talking to you through the medium of clay in real time. What you see and hold is like a map to the real me. Can you believe that what I am telling you is true? You do it every day. You believe in worlds you have not yet made visible, so please believe me. Most of us real people who lived up here in 1214 B.C., including King Agamemnon, were destroyed by a catastrophic event: a curse-caused catastrophe. You think you know about the catastrophe of 1214 B.C. here? Oh, there is more. Much more."

"No, no!" Margaret was conflicted. As a magician she believed what she heard. But as her mother's daughter she could not stop herself. "Your clay proves you were made in 1205 B.C. Not 1214."

"Please stop referring to me as clay. Please hear my story; the girl named Merope's story. There is not much real time left. I was a real girl born in Mycenae in 1223 B.C. Born in a house not far from where we are right now. For this brief moment, we real girls are offered this small portal into your time so Clytemnestra's curse can be reversed. Before it is too late, let me tell you more about that catastrophic curse of 1214 B.C."

Margaret shivered when she heard the words "Clytemnestra's curse." Though she was an archaeologist, she had a childish terror of Clytemnestra. — Merope was still talking, she realized.

"Queen Eurydice put that curse on hold until the time would be right," Merope said. "And now is that right time. And you are the chosen one. Chosen to reverse what Clytemnestra did to us. It occurred here, and it destroyed all of us; all the king's khorus was destroyed by that curse." She stood and faced Margaret. "And that is what you need to know of the power of evil so you can save your own life and mine. Tomorrow, Margaret. Tomorrow, through that small window in space-time, you will snatch us from that long-ago catastrophe as it converges with the next catastrophe set for tomorrow. When that window between converging times opens, if you act swiftly, you will rescue us after all these millennia. And you will save yourself as well. There will be only one small window when our times converge. And I plead with you, listen to my story, then do as I instruct. Please. When I tell you. If you act, you will save your own life and mine and of all my team of Khorus Korai. And, Margaret, please sit down. You are towering over me."

"So you *were* made as part of an imaginary khorus?" Margaret asked.

Merope frowned and pointed to the chair.

And Margaret sat. And spoke solemnly to the small figurine. "Of course, Merope. I would love to know exactly who it was who made you. Made you in the exact image, as you insist, of the real girl named Merope. And then tell me about your travels from Pylos here to Mycenae." Suddenly she looked back through the open door into the dark corridor. Footsteps? Again? She was sure she heard them. Again she heard a great basso rumble out above the citadel. Unnerving. She was hungry and tired. But maybe she was finally getting somewhere in her search for why these figurines ...

Merope was frowning and agitated. She stood up.

"Margaret! You've got to move past the figurine part. That is a story you will be told later. I promise. If we both survive what is coming tomorrow. But now, hear my real story. Whatever else is bothering you just now, like whether you got it all wrong in your book, is not the point anymore. Save that for after you save yourself. But, if you do not listen to my directions about fleeing, you will cease to exist. You will never get to Athens." She stomped one foot. "You will never solve any of the so-called mysteries or problems about us and about so much more that you wish to. Why? Because you will be destroyed in the collapse that is going to happen tomorrow right here. Can you understand that? But if you pay attention NOW and listen, and RUN when I say RUN, you will not only save yourself but all of us real girls. And in so doing, you will uncover what is still a true mystery. So, on the first of June 2021 A.D., tomorrow, when I say RUN, you RUN. Whatever else is bothering you, forget it. It is no longer of any importance. There is going to be a huge catastrophe on the first of June in your time, and you and I and many others are in grave danger. Put any other problems about your book on the back burner and pay attention to what I am saying to you, Margaret Benson. YOUR life is in danger. And so is mine. Does that grab your attention?"

"Okay, Merope, I'm listening. I will do as you say," Margaret began to enter the magic. Merope nodded and returned to her seat on the book. Then Margaret remembered all those people coming tomorrow and what she would say to them. "But please, Merope, you have this one last chance to help me correct my mistakes in my new book. Then I promise I'll put it on the back burner. I've been wrong publicly before. I'm a big girl and can tell the world of archaeology I am wrong. So, Merope, what were all of you? A make-believe khorus or not?"

"FORGET THE BOOK!" The little figurine jumped up, marched over to Margaret, picked up a pencil and tapped Margaret on the forehead. "You're a brilliant woman. This is like magic, but is no magic trick. Your imagination is not playing tricks on you. This is no sleight of hand rabbit hat trick. Yet I am a real girl using this clay medium to reach you. It really is showtime, so get with it. I'm going to give you a timeline, as you like to say, Margaret. A timeline of past catastrophes and collapses from so far back, neither you nor your colleagues have gotten that far. And then I will finish with this timeline of tomorrow's catastrophe that will destroy you, Margaret, if you do not heed my words. This is no longer about any mistakes in a book. This is about life and death on the first of June in 2021 your time: Your life or your death. Tomorrow. And mine." She stood straight and stared at Margaret. "Mistakes in books will be taken care of, if you live."

Margaret solemnly looked back at the little statue and thought how brave this tiny creature must be to somehow, magically, speak to her of things that must be quite serious. At least to her. "Catastrophe and collapse!" Was her imagination playing tricks? She had long wondered about that past collapse here at Mycenae. Much recently recovered evidence from the collapse of 1214 B.C. was being investigated by her field geologists. Many were the suspected, substantial, geological events from the 1200s still-hidden underneath this surface. This happened to be a favorite topic of Maggie's with her assistant, Allison. In fact, into her Box #1, destined for her desk in Athens, she had just packed a geological report she had received two days ago. She looked into the eyes of the little figurine. Was this tiny statue going to reveal all? Answer all those questions? Margaret watched the large, encircled eyes of her figurine. Maggie was excited. Her fingers tingled: She licked her lips.

"Please go on, Merope," she said.

Merope stood all of her four inches tall and began. "Margaret, I am no figment of your imagination. And I am giving you this chance because you are the chosen one to end the curse on us." She took center stage on the desk and gestured up to the windows. "Thunder in our mountains, such as you hear now, once presaged rain and then foretold ruin and death. Then all who worked for a better life here feared for themselves at its unsettling sounds. As I see you still do."

She turned and faced Margaret again. "First is the story of our Khorus Korai. When I was born, I was told that story. I will relate that history, and then Nepthaulia will tell you more.

"To introduce Nepthaulia's stories, I'll begin with the line of catastrophes followed by collapses." Little Merope took the stance of a great orator and began. "Here in the Western Peloponnesos and in the islands of the Great Inland Sea were once amazing societies that experienced several periods of catastrophe followed by total collapse. A geological reality often converging with human greed. Sometimes a comet predicted the doom and stars fell, giving warnings before all that made human society magnificent, before all learning of arts and sciences, all governing in harmony offering humanity a share in these achievements, before all were destroyed and before times of true darkness came in like the tides, returning to primitive existence, hand-to-mouth subsistence, those who survived the impacts and the severe, lingering aftermaths.

"Collapses of great civilizations and the ensuing catastrophes are as creative as they are devastating if we can wait long enough. And if enough survive.

"Margaret, as you know, this whole land of the Peloponnesos has been formed by thousands and thousands of years of catastrophe and collapse. Here, these mountains and valleys of Mycenae and Berbati and Midea on the other side of those mountains above us were formed and reformed over millennia and will be reformed again. Soon enough you, too, will witness it. And your long-held assumptions will be revealed if you believe in my image and listen to this story.

"Comets have long, long blazed through our night skies, so confusing the great creatures that shook the earth while hunting food that they stopped in their tracks to gaze in shock and awe. Early man cowered, awed by such sights. Then showers of meteors lit the skies, and again awe gave way to terror as one or another collided and entered earth's atmosphere to crash in fire, meeting fire from volcanoes spewing and disrupting all life once more, shrouding the planet in darkness, causing seas to flood coastal villages while all vegetation in the hills and valleys was incinerated by firestorms before being blanketed under snow. And that was the prehistoric pyrotechnic prelude to the total darkness which finished off ninety-percent of all life here.

"Yet life crept out of the ashes. And while most of those humans who managed to survive were too busy surviving to think twice about what they had witnessed, there were those few of inquiring minds who contemplated and counted and began noting and repeating the stories of histories of civilization between the sequences of catastrophes followed by collapse.

"Long after, the first recorded catastrophe and collapse was in 3500 B.C., as you note our time today. This one was caused by the planet and by men who knew how to use the earth and harness its physical gifts. Many truly learned people died, and most who survived did so by savagery and plunder of all they encountered. They spread destruction until they destroyed themselves, and all past knowledge of physical and cosmological sciences was lost.

"Fortunately, man's mind is swifter than the return visit of a comet. Gradually, out of these ashes of despair, some few learned humans began again, and centuries later, many such survivors banded together for civilization on the great islands of the Middle Sea. Thus before there were more catastrophes, formidable universities in magnificent cities with universal plumbing and sustained agriculture, with economies connected harmoniously to a global network to create prosperity, existed where only collapse had been. Like in Thera. You think New York City and Paris and Athens are great cities? Well, you should have seen the amazing cities of Akrotiri and Knossos and Kidonia and Pylos. Metropolises. Like right here in Mycenae. Krete and Santorini formed the hub.

"By 2500 B.C., as you note it, banks of knowledge of heavens and Earth were again established by peace-loving people. Universities of learned and seeking minds were established, and laws to promote peaceful use of such knowledge for the good of all like-minded citizens became commonplace. Life had become once again not subsistence but of comforts that had long disappeared with the past collapse. Again, the island of Santorini became known as the Island of knowledge, a gem shining in the sparkling sea, filled from shore to shore with storage houses and banks of knowledge which were funneled to their neighbors. All the great learned secrets of the good life, using and harnessing the powers of our planet, were there stored. Branches flourished and made more branches on the sister island of Krete, where the spirit of the earth was revered. But Santorini was the mother of all knowledge.

"Goodness and plenty seem to breed greed and viciousness, even from beyond the barren stars. Again, in 1600 B.C., after four hundred years of increased knowledge of how to use the bounties of the planet and its cosmos, another confluence of man-made events met up with earth-made catastrophes to converge. And the whole of the Island of Knowledge collapsed into the Middle Sea. Waves reached to the stars and all was washed away. Neighboring Krete was prepared. On that island, where the knowledge of the earth's sciences had been brought like seedlings on the chariot of the goddess, mother of Dionysos, there flourished learned princes like the great-great-grandfathers of the Griffin Warrior; like the little queen, the Potnia Theron, who was in communication with the Pulse for Connectivity of all the planet and all creatures. And as soon as the stars had begun falling from the skies, notifying those knowledgeable of what was coming, they set out in their well-made ships, sailing across seas and skies in time and space for safe harbors. And thus from their prepared vessels, the survivors of the Catastrophe of the Islands in 1600 B.C. began anew in new outposts on the western Peloponnesos in revolving contact with the mother's offshoots.

"Santorini had been utterly destroyed. Because the colleges and universities and centers of knowledge of all kinds had spread to Krete, where more could be accommodated, humanity was not utterly destroyed this time when the stars began to fall. Krete, though crippled, had retained, through judicious planning, much of its storehouses of learning and centers of civilization. And by 1500 B.C., from their observatories and laboratories and medical centers and universities both in Knossos and in Kidonia, wise men and women continued and expanded the work which uplifted civilization. They harnessed the waves of the sea and the waves of the sky, producing light-filled cities, cities of great comfort to the inhabitants, finding as well, cures for illnesses and expanding possibilities on all fronts. The work of the ancient, wise magicians went on. Some great ones sailed often across the sea to the western shore of the Peloponnesos, spreading their knowledge inland-up from that nature-formed perfect bay, the bay where several harbors were soon developed. Among these wise settlers was the great-great-grandfather of Nestor. He was a physician and an economist as well. He planned those first harbors in two bays and a complex of settlements on the hillsides overlooking. Iklaina it was called. There in the high hills of Iklaina, astronomers built observatories. Then above, in his newly designed Kingdom of Pylos, the larger and more-adventurous centers of learning were established, first by his own son, the father of the Griffin Warrior, and then by the Griffin Warrior himself, the great peace and knowledge-loving prince. They remained in close contact with their brothers on Krete. Life in the dual centers was pleasing and prosperous and exciting for the citizens, many of whom ventured back and forth for learning as well as for holidays. Many scientific and medical innovations began in the Peloponnesos and were sent back to Knossos and Kidonia and Mallia.

"Then an astronomer discovered that the same asteroid, from which particles had broken off and plummeted into the sea some hundred and

fifty years before, was waking up in the heavens and particles were likely
to come within our atmosphere again. There were also flurries of war
arriving from the seas. But all such convergences were dismissed like the
bothering of flies by the great sea and air power that was established
between Krete and Egypt.

"Pylos was the lone dissenter.

"Then all together, as if the gods had planned collapse and
catastrophe in 1350 B.C., everything converged. The heavens fell,
causing a tsunami and climate disruptions, and the hungry and angry
arrived with the force of surprise and desperation. Precautions had been
taken in Pylos and Iklaina and, finally, with much persuasive talk, in
Egypt as well. But on Krete, which certainly knew better, any such
precautions were delayed until it was too late. No tunnels or caves had
been constructed for living underground, as had been in Pylos. Peoples
from the other sides of the world who had been displaced by the lack of
harvests began voyaging west and east toward our Inland Sea. Container
ships carrying wine and grain and oil and unguents and perfumes
brought the word while unloading and refilling. Into our well-made
harbors, they brought the word of the catastrophe arriving from the 'Sea
Peoples.'

"Here in the Peloponnesos, our people were prepared. Even as the
kings' seafaring warriors defeated the usurpers, our astronomers were
hailed and saluted and honored as the saviors which they were.
Catastrophe, however, on Krete meant a large collapse needing
assistance. Our young Griffin Warrior in Pylos sent aid and scientists and
people to reinvigorate the economy and society. Athens sent aid as well,
as did rich Mycenae. All the people in this land worked in harmony and
defeated a catastrophic collapse. An integral part of that harmony was
the formation of the Khoruses of Korai, harmonizing with the elements.
In the wake, Iklaina joined closer to Pylos, together becoming an even-
larger economy with inventions your world today still cannot
comprehend. Today visitors to the ruins of Nestor's fire-stormed palace
gaze at baths and toilets. But would they believe the glories of cities with
universities and economies that your great cities and people today do not
yet fully enjoy?

"In 1290 B.C., into this renewed prosperity was born the greatest and best of leaders. Nestor. At the birth of the son of King Nelius, the announcing comet was heralded by learned ones as a messenger bringing the word that this birth was a predictor of peace. And indeed, for his long reign in Pylos and truly in the whole of this Peloponnesos land and far beyond, Nestor proved the truth of the prediction. Nestor married a consort worthy, Eurydice. Together they changed and made their land even better, even more-prosperous for those who stayed within the Confederation of Peace.

"But in 1214 B.C., beyond and outside Nestor's control, over here in Mycenae, lively elements of evil converged again, and there was another devastating catastrophe. Mycenae's catastrophe of 1214 B.C. was intensified and double-sealed with an evil curse. Which curse was broken into two phases. In the first phase, we, the Khorus Korai of Mycenae, were captured in mortal peril. Where we are captive still. The second phase of this curse, what might be called a Cyclops of Stone, a boulder of immense proportions, waits all this time because of the blocking forces of good generated by Queen Eurydice against what our evil queen did to us. Right here, since then, since 1214 B.C., this phase has been waiting; precariously waiting with that boulder for the magician who can break the spell of evil. And rescue us in time. Tomorrow is the day; that time has arrived. The curse lingers, teetering on the edge, more visible than ever to those with sight. The second phase of Clytemnestra's curse is about to roll. And you, Maggie, are that magician to rescue us.

"It is that catastrophe, that catastrophe from 1214 B.C. that never finished rolling to collapse, against which we need to take action, together, right now, Maggie. The second phase of that catastrophe is due tomorrow, the first of June, 2021 A.D. If you act when I tell you, Margaret Benson, you will be hailed among the greatest of archaeologists because of what you will accomplish with what will be unveiled to you. You are that magician we have waited for all these millennia who can break the evil and save us.

"But if you do not accept your role, if you do not save us, you, too, will be buried under that collapse for future archaeologists to find.

"This concludes the timeline history of many of our catastrophes and of this most-imminent collapse, Margaret. Now the rest is up to you."

Inappropriately to the seriousness of the moment, Margaret's tummy rumbled. The mountain replied with a huge, hungry rumble of its own. Beyond hunger, she was tired. Oh, yes, she was. But after hearing the incredible and, from what she knew, most plausible story from this little clay representation in front of her, she shivered with excitement. She jumped in.

"Merope, I know time is of the essence. I am no longer worried about my book … much. But, well, in all honesty …" Thoughts swirled in Margaret's brain. So much she wanted to know. But she was getting the picture. And time was short. She sat up straight and started again. "Please tell me more about who you are, Merope. What made you so famous and well-loved?"

Merope listened intently to the mountain's still-lingering rumble. Then she turned her large, black-circled eyes back onto her questioner.

"I believe you will help us tomorrow," Merope said. "Therefore, I have a small moment longer to explain more to you. Obviously, I was not universally loved. Else I would not be here, begging you to save me. So listen well. Here is another Time-Line of us Korai. Long, long ago, we began, khoruses of Korai, singing, dancing khoruses of girls." Merope began.

"Ah. Back to the Khorus Girls. My favorite girls." Margaret picked up little Merope, give her a kiss and put her back on the desk.

Merope returned to sit on the book.

CHAPTER 4

FADE IN: *Day at the Museum*

SETTING:

    Place: Int.: Archaeologist Office and Museum, Mycenae, Greece

    When: 31 May, <u>2021 A.D.</u>

    Time: 9:45 a.m. to 1:00 p.m.

"ALL WE GIRLS were real girls who later became your girls, Margaret," Merope said.

"Is this some sort of riddle?" Margaret asked.

"I'm trying to be clear because there is little time for you to decipher. Listen! Before we were figurines, we were all, in successive generations, members of a real, loved and then much-respected organization. From the beginning we were called Khorus Korai: the singing Girls."

Margaret pushed back her chair and opened her mouth.

Swiftly Merope jumped up. And with a finger to her lips, ran toward Margaret. "Again, let me remind you to listen well. I have no time for repeating. Time will catch us unready if you ask more. That would prove fatal. So, first: khoruses of real girls. We were an alliance. An alliance begun in Krete and developed and fostered in the mainland of the Peloponnesos.

"We started as a way of celebrating. Celebrating life. We were living girls and we loved to be together, like all young girls; loved to sing together. We sang the unique songs of our towns and families, preserving and continuing for generations our heritages. We started for friendship. Now you know all from me you need to know to save us. And to save yourself before the cataclysm." Merope looked solemnly at Margaret. "And the rest of this story I leave to Nepthaulia to tell."

"I'm beginning to picture it: You were the first Khorus Girls," Margaret said.

If clay could smile, Merope was doing so now. "We were. Long before The Rockettes, we were. Actually, there were radio waves when we began. Though what you call radio was unimaginably different, then. We were the Khorus Girls, and what we did made us sort of immortal." She stared at Margaret, whose eyes were drooping. "Are you hearing me? Because the most-important part is yet to come. Lucky you, we started this conversation before the very end. Then there will be no explanations. So perk up if you want more. Nepthaulia is about to take the stage."

Margaret blinked twice and rubbed her eyes. "I am listening. Tell me." She yawned; She was quite sleepy. But what she was hearing was incredible. She also had a fleeting thought that she might be on the verge of insanity. But often she felt that way just when she was about to make an important connection. So she got up, walked about, took another long drink of her water and sat back for more.

"Ready?" Merope asked. "The time is ready for Nepthaulia to tell you the rest. Nepthaulia?"

Suddenly, even louder rumbling from the mountain distracted and unnerved Margaret. The room grew dark. She leapt up, pushing back her chair. Through the clerestory window, she saw the ominous sky. But Merope had walked across the desk, following her, and reached out for Maggie's hand. Led by Merope, she returned and sat.

"Nepthaulia really is her name?" Margaret said. "Nepthaulia: another enigma, also from Pylos, yet found by me in Athens." She was intently watching the little figurine. But any reply was interrupted by loud knocking in back of her. Startled, Margaret swiftly turned from her desk, pushing back her chair, and stood in front of little Merope in a defensive, protective position.

And there Menelaos-Stavros was, knocking at her door, bearing a basket exuding enticing aromas. Aromas that overcame fear and surprise. Maggie, with alacrity, bounded over and gave him a swift hug then, without further thought, grabbed his arm, pulling him along while reaching for another chair. But it was covered with books. "Oh, you're in good time, Menelaos- Stavros. Come in. Let's get you a front-row seat." She waved him to sit next to her. "You're an imaginative and thoughtful young man. Come, take a seat. And learn."

"Don't worry, Dr. Margaret," he said, indicating a corner of the desk. "I'll just sit right here …" But his sentence was cut off and he stepped back, staring at the little figurine sitting on a book.

"Gosh, Menelaos, what marvels have you brought in that basket? Whatever is in there smells truly delicious. I am starved," Margaret said. She stood up from peering into the covered basket to see him staring at the figurine. "Pardon my lack of manners. Meet Merope. She's my Khorus Girl. Merope, say hello to Menelaos-Stavros. Yes, indeed, let's all have some of what Menelaos brought. And you, Merope, please continue your history."

Margaret took out a Thermos and two cups. When she turned to hand a cup to Menelaos, she saw that he was dumbstruck, still staring at Merope.

Menelaos-Stavros was trying to talk. His lips were moving. And he tried to reach out for the cup Margaret was offering him. But no words came. And he did not quite grasp the cup.

"Have one, please." Margaret reached in and took a warm roll for herself and bit into it before she addressed Menelaos's trance. "Oh, you'll get used to it. She's normally quite talkative. Merope, don't let the cat get your tongue now. Menelaos-Stavros is a good friend. And I know he will help us at the moment of catastrophe. Won't you, Menelaos?"

Speechless, he nodded his head and whispered, "Yes, of course, Dr. Margaret. Whatever you need." He could not drag his eyes from the little figurine.

Margaret poured herself coffee and turned to see Menelaos nodding at Merope, trying but again unable to talk. She pushed a cup over to him and again offered the napkin filled with beautiful, brown rolls. "Oh. Sorry." She put down her cup and jumped up from the chair she had taken. "Help me move these books so you can sit and enjoy with me."

"She was talking, Dr. Margaret. I heard … These are, are … are really very, very heavy, Dr. Margaret," Menelaos stammered and then dropped a pile with a bang. "Oh, sorry."

"Sit and enjoy! Yum." She took the Thermos from his shaking hand and filled his cup. "I was starved. Thank you so much for this wonderful breakfast. I shall miss breakfasts at Belle Helene." Maggie's voice wavered. She snuffled again, took a large swallow of coffee and, after another bite and sip, put her cup down, relieved to see Menelaos sit and take his cup. "I hope you do not think I talk to every statue in the museum, Menelaos. Merope here is quite special. Aren't you, Merope? Please stop your silliness and say hello to Menelaos." Margaret poured another cup for Menelaos.

But Merope did not say a word. In fact, she was now standing stock still, just as she normally did, looking exactly like a figurine again.

"Oh, Dr. Margaret." Menelaos shook himself out of the spell and turned somewhat reluctantly to Margaret. He began again quite shakily and had to put down his cup, "Oh, Dr. Margaret, you are so wonderful. Even statues talk to you. I will miss you so much. Please, please don't go." He put down the roll he had reached for and instead took her hand. "I want to be an archaeologist like you, want to work with you. Please don't leave us." His gaze drifted over to Merope. "You agree, don't you? She should not leave us?"

"Well, that's great news, Menelaos, that you want to be an archaeologist," Margaret said. "And think, when you are an archaeologist here, Merope will be here, too. She will get used to you and then she will tell you marvelous stories, too, especially once you are sitting here at this desk, which if you apply yourself, you will one day. And after all, I'm only going to Athens, where the wonderful university is with many archaeological resources. Why can you not come to Athens and study with me there? In fact, Thanassis, your cousin, is planning to do so. You could drive in together or take the train. And get a place at the university and work with me. Then," she turned to gesture at Merope, "you will have stories to tell Merope." She turned and picked up a brochure from a box. "Here, take this brochure from the archaeology department at the university."

"Do you really think I could get in?"

"Of course. Apply yourself and work hard as a guard here, like Thanassis, and listen to and learn from all the archaeologists and you will definitely get in. Now Menelaos," she looked up and saw the clock on her desk and the look on Merope's face. "I've got to hurry. Only one more day, you know." She saw his face cloud. "Finish your coffee and roll while I continue with these boxes." She finished her cup, stood and went on filling the box in front of her. "Oh," she said, turning back to Menelaos, "you are invited, I forgot to tell you. Please tell your Uncle Agamemnon and Aunt Kati-Selene. You are all invited at one tomorrow afternoon for a lunch up here. Oh, thank you so very much." She poured the last drop in her cup, finished it, took the last morsel of roll and brushed crumbs off her lips, packed the basket with the Thermos, cups and napkin and closed the lid. "Thank you so very much. Yes, I shall miss you all very much." And she reached and gave him a big hug. "I'll miss you, Menelaos-Stavros. So promise you will come to visit and check out the department."

Menelaos tore his eyes from Merope, took the basket, turned quickly and almost ran out but then suddenly zipped back in. "What is it you want me to help you with, Dr. Margaret? A catastrophe?" But he wasn't looking at her. He was staring again at Merope.

"After the lunch tomorrow, I will need your help. Remember, tomorrow afternoon after the lunch, come back here. Oh, and," she called at his retreating back, "tell your Uncle Agamemnon I'll be back in a few hours for a late lunch today." She wondered if he had heard her, his departure was so swift.

~~~~

"Almost one-hundred-percent done." Maggie looked up and saw that it had suddenly become half past noon, and she was again extremely hungry. "I had better get back to the Belle Helene to that lunch." But before she put action to the thought, she found other things that needed filing and packing. Again, she became too involved to remember what she really wanted. When her watch chimed one p.m., she stood and looked about at all of the clear space and piles of taped boxes. "I think you have done it, Maggie. Almost." Then she looked over at Merope, quietly waiting, just like a statue.

"You frightened Menelaos-Stavros," Margaret said, picking up Merope. "Come along. For today I have to put you back where you belong. There is lots I have to think about from all you have told me. And we will have our time again with Nepthaulia as soon as I have finished the packing at Belle Helene." She kissed the little figurine as she walked up the corridor to the room where Merope lived. "Most of all, I promise I will do as you say. I will be prepared to follow your instructions tomorrow."

As Margaret locked the case, Merope turned to her neighbor and gave her a little nudge. When Margaret walked down the corridor, she heard Merope's voice: "It's your turn, Nepthaulia. You tell her."

Margaret turned back to the room of glass cases filled with girls all looking at Nepthaulia. All the other lights seemed to dim as Nepthaulia's spotlight brightened and she took center stage.

CHAPTER 5

FADE IN TO: *Time in Space Where and When Dates and Times B.C./A.D. Co-exist*

SETTINGS:

    Place: Athens High Citadel, Athens, Greece

    Date: 31 May, <u>1185 B.C.</u>

    Time: 1:30 p.m. to 2:15 p.m.

Simulcast with:

    Place: Archaeologist Office, Mycenae, Greece

    Date: 31 May, <u>2021 A.D.</u>

    Time: 1:30 p.m. to 2:15 p.m.

Nepthaulia Speaks:

"LAST NIGHT, I dreamed I was home again in Pylos.

"Was it the sound of the rain that brought me home? Or the beat of my heart?

"Or the variable elasticity of space in dreaming time?

"Or my loneliness for home? Yes, all that. I want to go home. But home is no longer.

"Home as it was. With all the eyes. I see.

"Many are the eyes I see shining in the rain, staring at me.

"Eyes. Waiting. For rain. Calling clouds. Begging, 'Rain.' Then eyes in the rain.

"Eyes calling me to jump and soar. More and more. No more.

"I was not home. And from here, at the land's end, here, high on Wisdom's promontory, answers from home cannot be heard.

"Please listen to my dream, to the story of home.

"Maybe it was my mother's voice. Selene's voice always carried me home.

"She and her mother, Cynthia, want me to remember and tell of the Khorus Korai.

"To tell our story. To you.

"So we are not forgotten. So you can save Merope. And save yourself, Margaret.

"Tomorrow. Before it is too late. Before elasticity constricts.

"The Girls' story stretches ever so far back. I begin now, at the end.

"And I assure you, it is the end.

"Today, it is again almost the important month of June. And this year is 1185 B.C.

"The end here approaches. And the end, one as devastating, approaches you.

"Your eyes look at me. So, looking back into yours, I sing words passed to me.

"I begin with who we were, with what we did.

"All we girls who became your girls, Margaret."

Nepthaulia's voice reached Margaret's ears in song.

"We were an alliance, an alliance begun by the great-great-great-grandmothers in Krete and developed and fostered in the mainland of this Peloponnesos.

"We started as a way of celebrating. Celebrating life in song. We sang the unique songs of our towns and families, preserving and continuing for generations our unique heritages. For friendship we started; for salvation we continued.

"Together, our voices rising and blending, soar, as we did, soaring all together amongst flowers,

"With lions and turtles we sang and soared to the music of the hills.

"In once-upon-a-time land, we danced in hills, in many hills of many great kingdoms.

"Once upon a time we twirled as we sang, vaulting high in the hills.

"Vaulting, as the Great Goddess taught, sailing into the clouds we called.

"Vaulting with birds we called, vaulting and clapping and soaring, catching our sounds in echoes, calling for universal harmony. We called the clouds, we called the birds, we sailed in harmony. We were Dream Catchers. For our kings, for our people, for Society.

"In tuneful harmony. Together happy. On surrounding, reverberating hills.

"In the hills of Knossos of old; in the hills of Nestor's Pylos; in the hills of Mycenae the once-great.

"In the hills of Elis the new, the hills of Girted Tiryns, in hills surrounding our seaside kingdom of Ikliana, we sang. Oh, Margaret, how we sang. Can you hear? Listen as I sing from the hill of the Acropolis, where I am today with my husband as the last day nears. Hear how we sang.

"Sang for our kings. And their kingdoms. To the gods. And for ourselves.

"Some say, the old ones, that we sang our kingdoms of advanced learning into being.

"Certainly, we now know our songs kept our kingdoms alive.

"You see ...

"We called the birds.

"We sailed the clouds.

"We danced the rain.

"And we caught the dreams.

"And the dreams came true.

"We were the Khorus Girls; we were Khorus of Korai.

"We sang of our amazing differences and of our common heritages.

"Despite all the technology, ours were harvest societies, and we sang good clouds: harvest-creating clouds. An alliance with technology and a celebration of the earth we were.

"Then one day, in 1214 B.C., as in all Once Upon a Times, their calling became Kingdom-destroying. And they became Girls of Fire.

"They were forced to sing. Forced songs confused birds; called wrong clouds.

The birds would not come in that time of evil. That time of Curse.

"Cursed by that evil queen.

"After, there, in Mycenae, they no longer danced nor sang nor vaulted nor called upon the bounties of the earth. There was no leaping into harvest-saving clouds for the Khorus of Fire.

"Now, no Khorus Girls will sing there again.

"Now we no longer sing.

"Not there. Nor here. Nevermore. All is finished. What began with the evil Queen spread and we are finished. Now, in 1185 B.C., our once-great society is finished.

"Nevermore will khoruses sing in our kingdoms by the sea. Finished.

"Kings are no more. Finished.

"Dreams have fled. Clouds will not come. Finished.

"Song is gone.

"The beginning of this end arrived with the evil Queen in Mycenae.

"Nevermore do Khorus Korai call clouds in Mycenae.

"Nor even in Elis.

"Nevermore in Sparta or Iklaina.

"Finally, sadly, nevermore back home in Pylos. No voice is there to call us to sing.

"With our songs went the clouds, went the harvests, went The Girls. Then went the kingdoms of universal knowledge. Now all is finished.

"Songs, clouds, birds, girls, kingdoms, dreams: all gone because of one evil queen.

"Margaret, hear me now. Hear our true story.

"The Once Upon a Time story of our beginnings.

"And now of our endings. The story of who we were. And what became of once-real girls.

"The Khorus Girls of the sea lands. And how we became your figurines.

"It was the sound of her voice.

"In dreams, it is Mother's voice.

"Mixing with her sister Merope's voice and Grandmother Cynthia's.

"They called me back, me, Nepthaulia, back from the high citadel of Athens to call to you for rescue in 2021 A.D. You, Margaret, who found me, who found Aunt Merope. Please rescue those real Khorus Girls tomorrow."

Later, Margaret could not remember walking back to her office, but she knew she was listening to the voices of Nepthaulia and Merope telling her all she had to remember to save them tomorrow. She sat and completed more work at her desk and then …

"… I look out and see your eyes staring into mine, asking for answers," Merope said. "Please, Margaret, remember all you hear this time. The story you were listening to of who we were at the beginning all the way to the end in 1185 B.C. came to you from my niece, Nepthaulia; speaking to you from 1185 B.C. to where she fled carrying her own figurine. Just before the end of it all. Before the final catastrophes. Nepthaulia was the last in our long line. Nepthaulia was the last queen of Pylos. And the last Khorus Girl. And I, your special Psychic Girl, Merope, I take you again into our history in case you need assurance that I am not a figment talking to you in your dreams. The second and final part of the catastrophe is set for tomorrow.

"You want the stuff of fairy tales? Yes? Among the good, here in Mycenae was an evil Queen. And our last chance, ours and yours, is offered by good Queen Eurydice's counter-curse against evil."

CHAPTER 6

FADE IN: *Nike*

SETTING:
> Place: Interior: Archaeologist Office, Mycenae, Greece
> Date: 31 May, <u>2021 A.D.</u>
> Time: 2:15 p.m.

THE HILLS SURROUNDING the museum building rumbled, and the rumbling resounded throughout the rooms. The little statue stood front-and-center on Margaret's desk. Hadn't she returned Merope to her case in the display rooms? Margaret looked as solemnly at Merope as Merope looked at Margaret, making Margaret realize how brave she must be to somehow, magically, speak to her of things that must be quite serious and now involved her as well.

"Merope." Margaret tried not to slur her words. She was so sleep-deprived she felt slightly tipsy. Things tilted in and out of focus. She grabbed the edge of the desk and things righted. She blinked and focused. "Merope, how did you get back here on my desk?" Margaret watched the solemn eyes of the figurine.

She looked so brave there on the desk. "Not as brave as worried, Margaret," the figurine spoke. "This is a last warning, so I appear here for emphasis. Please listen. Time is about out on this one. Understand, you are not hearing this from a clay figurine. I am a real girl and my representation is here to give you notice of your one last chance. And one last chance for myself and all my sisters."

Before her eyes closed, Margaret knew she had to go soon. Lunch at the Belle Helene would be a very late lunch, indeed. But she was overwhelmingly tired. And then her pen fell from her fingers, and before she knew it, her head sank onto the desk. In her dream, she heard the familiar voice again. She tried to push out of the dream to hear clearer.

"Queen Eurydice gives you this one chance to reverse the evil queen's curse. But you must RUN when I tell you. Take nothing but me, your 'Psychic Psi' girl, and RUN. Tomorrow. My cloud-calling songs will end the rumbling and open the door ... open the door ... open the door."

The rumbling in the hills almost drowned out the sound of the elevator door.

Margaret tried harder to push up and out of the dream. "I will open it. I will open the door. I will save you. Speak more precisely. What actually, exactly? Tomorrow?" Then her cell phone buzzed. She had a long way to come back mentally to understand and put this call on hold. When she did, she was startled. She thought she had heard singing about clouds. "What? 'RUN? Open the door?' Where?"

Indeed, over the phone's second line came that familiar voice: "Margaret, save us and yourself from the evil queen's still-living curse! On June first you will run when I say. Take me. I will guide you and you will find the door to the real me. To us all."

Rumbling from the hills actually shook her office and shook her wide awake. There was no figurine on her desk. Instead, there was her phone. Had she been asleep? Margaret turned the volume up.

"Oh, little one, keep telling me: the evil queen? First of June. That's tomorrow." She cradled the phone then looked at it and saw there was a strange lot of numbers that dialed nothing. She shook the phone and frowned. "From what exactly will I, can I, save you? What door?" she said. "How," she wondered, "can I be hearing this figurine from 1214 B.C. speak and sing on this phone?" But she then realized the contradiction in what she had just thought.

"No," she said aloud, "she is not a figurine, yet she is. But on the other hand, she really is a real girl. Or was."

Margaret kept the device on speaker, sat it on the desk and gestured at the rumbling universe, talking into the speaker. "Merope, repeat those instructions because I'm missing something. Lots. I put all I thought I had learned about you and your friends into that book. And tomorrow, before I rescue you and save myself, I've got to defend, or contradict publicly, what I wrote. Contradict it, I now know. I have been wrong. But I also know I must forget the book and all my errors, that I must RUN when you say RUN. There are two things happening, and I'm on a limb here. A shaky limb. Tomorrow ... you warn me about tomorrow. You are right. Tomorrow I have to tell them all, the small-but-important group of colleagues coming to surprise me, that the book I have published is wrong. Hello? Are you still there? So I am frightened of tomor ..." She wiped a hand over her eyes. Oh, gosh. What was she doing back at this spot? She had promised to forget about that book and concentrate on what mattered: the catastrophe that would strike tomorrow.

Again, she heard scraping from the corridor, but she was too involved to pay much attention and there was so much background noise from those darn mountains.

She shook herself and stood up. The sounds, the notes, the words of khoruses and clouds and harmonies and catastrophes and elasticity of time all were clear and swirling around her, brilliant like notes from a silver flute. She reached into the air as though to gather them.

"After all these years? Yep! It's about to be ... Indeed, Margaret, it is almost showtime. And you've got a bad case of nerves," she said to herself. She turned around. And sat back down. "Maybe the books will not arrive. Let's hope. Please, Merope, let those books be delayed. Oh, if only you could delay the surprise day of which I am supposed to know nothing. But that is definitely not your message."

"No! No! What I am telling you to do has nothing to do with your surprise day," the voice continued through the speaker. "You will get through that just fine. The people coming are your friends. True, you now know you were wrong in what you wrote. But while you have finally understood that part, you also know that is not my urgent message. Okay. Once again. Before it is really too late, Margaret. Tomorrow after that surprise meeting, you will have one small window in time to take this clay copy of me and run when I say. There will be zero time to hesitate. I will tell you the rest of what you must do when we are running. And do take that guard, Menelaos-Stavros. With him, and me, by running without hesitating for anything and by following my directions, you will save us from the curse. Save us all. But if you hesitate and get second thoughts of your own making, then ..."

"Oh, I know," Margaret said. "That terrible curse will get me, too. Okay, I get all that. But tell me. Then what? If I act, what? If I fail to act swiftly, what?"

"If you act, you will be amazed by what will happen. If you do not, you know the answer: We will all be lost and so will you. Lost forever with us. You will, with us, be cursed."

"Who're you talking to about a curse, Dr. Margaret? While I brought these cartloads of these boxes off the elevator, I've been hearing bits of this odd conversation. I'm really curious now. It sounded ominous. Lost? Curse on her; a curse on you. A curse, Dr. Margaret?" The voice of Thanassis, the new head guard, joined the noise of his gurney and jolted Margaret. "And such a beautiful voice saying all that. Take Menelaos-Stavros, too, huh?"

Letting go of the sounds, letting the notes sail away into background rumbling, Margaret turned and jumped at the delightful sight of Thanassis's smiling face. She gestured at him to come in.

"To my special girl, Thanassis. My 'Psychic Psi' Girl. Merope. Well, all of them, really. They are all my special girls by now, Thanassis. And probably all psychic, too. I hope you will not find me too bizarre. But it is she, especially, with whom I've been talking, listening to, most," she chuckled, "for the last fifteen years, ever since I found her. And now there is some message of great urgency. Tomorrow after my final presentation here, after that I, with Menelaos, must run to save them. Oh, Thanassis, I do not know really what it is I must save them from. Or how. And I must save myself, too. Maybe it's all a little beyond me. I guess I should wonder about my sanity."

"Well, I heard her. Obviously, she answers you when you ask. I heard her telling you about those ominous things."

"Your cousin Menelaos-Stavros also visited earlier. He heard her. So, maybe we let it stay in the family? Oh, yes. And, well, it is ominous sounding. And in that vein, it seems I have misrepresented, misunderstood her full meaning, and now she's frighteningly concerned that I am not understanding the grave urgency to save them. 'From what,' I ask? She clearly says tomorrow I will have one chance against the ominous and that when she says run, I must take her and drive or run to the hills up there and open a door. Your cousin Menelaos will come to help. For which I am most grateful. But, and so, like most things here, they kind of answer and kind of don't." She gestured. "Like most things here, at the citadel of Mycenae, they are sort of not … they are sort of, kind of yes, and kind of are not …

"Real. But not. How about they hang in the air?"

"That's it! You've said it! They, my Merope Girl especially, her histories, the voices of the others, even the citizens of the past whom sometimes I feel brush past, they all kind of hang in the air over the cherry trees out there, waiting to be plucked, pulled into focus from shifting time. I guess I'm not the right plucker. They mostly drift past my reality into another …"

"Oh, Doctor, may I disagree? You are the best plucker, I hear. The best. There is nothing that's beyond you. Yes, the best. 'Since Dr. French,' they say. And they say that Mycenae is now again famous around the world because of you. You two. I think it's because of you."

"Thanassis, that is a compliment indeed. Dr. Elizabeth French is a great archaeologist with whom I studied and worked. And emulate. She has been here since she was quite little, raised here. Did you also hear that her father was the equally great A. B. Wace? With him, Dr. French is responsible for most of what you see here today. And how you see it. But now, Thanassis, my special girl figurine is interrupting me, saying something urgent will happen tomorrow. A door will open through which I can save her and her friends, wherever they are, the real girls all these figurines represent." She gestured back toward the rooms where they were displayed. "And that I, too, am threatened by the curse of that evil queen. This curse only I can break by taking her, her representative figurine, that is, with me and then running to the hills up there when she says 'run' tomorrow. Doing that, I will break the curse, open that door and save them. Is that clear to you?" She stood and looked through the clerestory window. "Save the real girls these figurines merely represent. Then to make me really want to do this thing called running up into those hills, she added that while doing that, I might be destroyed, too." Her laugh came out more like a cough.

"Keep telling me all these stories, Doctor. I, too, sometimes think I see and hear things and people and then they just — *poof!* — disappear." He pushed a box aside and sat on the very edge of the desk. "I reach out and what I feel is nothing but air."

"You, Thanassis, are about to sit only on air. So, push those boxes more. Recently, the figurines, those down the hall there in the cases, have been talking about …" Instinctively she lowered her voice. "About the queen, Clytemnestra. Today, Clytemnestra was more than intimated as Evil Clytemnestra and menacingly so. Clytemnestra put some curse on them, these girls. And somehow, now, on me, too, if I act. But if I do not, then the girls, the real ones, are lost forever. And I will be doomed by her evil, too."

"You know, that's not so strange, Dr. Margaret. I sense, sometimes feel, her presence right there," he said, pointing toward the outside. "Yes, a very menacing, angry, striding presence, Doctor, down there, down below the cherry trees." He shivered.

"What I heard just now was that the evil queen cursed all the real girls who these figurines represent," Margaret said. "Because of which curse something dreadful happened to them. Now, suddenly, I will have one small window, tomorrow, through which I can jump, no, drive, to save those long-ago real girls from this long-ago dreadful curse." Margaret's whole body seemed to shiver. "Actually, Thanassis, you're not the first guard to say you sense such. Does she really haunt the place? I've never allowed myself to believe it. Well, not exactly. Until today."

A sudden and greater rumble came from the mountains and, unconsciously, Margaret grabbed Thanassis's arm.

"Like that, Doctor?" They laughed. "Oh, don't worry, Dr. Margaret, that's nothing. Certainly not a phantom." He stood and turned around as though making sure, then turned back. "Actually, more than hers, I often feel *his* energy, positive forces, especially when I am walking through and near his Lion Gate, like last night while I patrolled into the fog, the lion-like energy of the great Agamemnon. I know that sounds foolish. But I really do, Dr. Margaret. His energy seems to counteract, contradict the oppressiveness I feel from her. Agamemnon was the Great High King, was he not?"

"Indeed. Oh, Thanassis, I'm relieved that you are here for this chat. I truly need someone like you to talk with at, this … now. 'Tomorrow,' my Merope actually said, 'First of June 2021, your era,' is when I must save all of them. Ah! I'm back to it again, her big point: Her figurine and all the figurines all my colleagues are so wanting to talk about at conferences and in papers were really actual representations of real girls. And tomorrow, 'first of June, 2021, in my era', is also the big day for me with those colleagues, during which, thanks to this part of the news from Merope, I will now have to admit I have been wrong in what I wrote — published — about those figurines." She looked about her crowded surroundings. "But I'm not to worry about that. That does not matter because if I do not run when she tells me, I will be dead." The boxes were covering every inch of space in the room. "Let's do find a place for you among all these." And, searching for a place to move the boxes, she noticed the gurney he had tugged into the office. It, too, was filled with boxes. She stared at them and cleared her throat. "What are those?"

"Oh, there are more in the corridor. Well, let's see, shall we?" But there was simply zero space. "Where do you suggest, Dr. Margaret?" Boxes coming and boxes going were absolutely everywhere.

She waved her hands. "Could you please, just for tonight, stack and store these big ones down in your office? And that little one? In the morning, the museum in Athens is sending the van to collect them. That way, they will already be safely there when I get to my new office in three days. If you can bring them to your office, that will save the driver and guards a lot of time tomorrow morning. All except this one, box number 1.

That one's for Allison." She grabbed a marker and wrote Allison's name front and center.

Thanassis loaded the large boxes and replaced them with the smaller new ones, putting all but one on the floor. The last one he put front and center on her desk. "Well, Dr. Margaret. Shall we?"

"If we have to, please let it be you to do the so-called honors. I am loathe to face what I fear is in them."

"You don't want to see?"

"I was hoping to delay showtime. But seeing as I am almost grown up, I had better."

Taking his cutter from its sheath on his belt, he did the honors with one slice. And with a gesture, stepped back.

Margaret's hand actually was shaking as she parted the top and peered in.

"What do you see?"

"Wonderful things!" She laughed and held up the top copy. "And not so wonderful. Yep. It is showtime. Nothing I can do to avoid all my mistakes being made public now. Look, Thanassis. Here she is! Tatatara! Psychic Girl figurine. No! Figurine representation of the real Psychic Girl, Merope, who talks to me. Who sings to me. Who tells me that they were real girls who sang for the great King Agamemnon. Little Merope, when she was a real girl, was a member of the Khorus Girls of Mycenae. The Dream Catchers." She looked at the book closely and then gave the cover image a little kiss. "I've been asking of and listening to you for all these years. And now ... well, whatever." She turned to Thanassis. "All I've interpreted and perceived of what I found is in here now for others to judge." She thumped the book down. "Judge. Tomorrow. Then, the day after tomorrow, I'll have to change and correct it. If I'm still alive."

She put the book back in its box. "There it is. Far beyond my being foolish in the eyes of my colleagues is this truly life-or-death reason why I must be prepared to act fast tomorrow, saving her and them all, and myself; the curse. The same curse as doomed these once real girls. At last I will save them and save myself. Question: How can I save girls who lived in 1214 B.C. from the evil Queen Clytemnestra's curse? And if I cannot do that, then I am doomed, too! And if I do succeed, what then?"

Thanassis took the book. "Oh, Dr. Margaret, she's so cute, her eyes
so alive." He handed back the book. "I'll happily help you save her.
You're right: Let's ask her to get more specific about this finding and
saving from that long-ago curse. Curses, Dr. Margaret, do sound
ominous. And long-lasting. Definitely not good." He flipped through the
book. "Dr. Margaret, why is this figurine, your Psychic Girl's figurine,
the one you chose to be on this cover? What is so important about them
all that you write this whole book about these little statues?" He
examined pages of pictures.

"Well, who were all these figurines? Is that your question? And to
answer that, I have been aided by, I thought, since I found her and first
began to hear her, Merope, telling me who they were. But I have not
listened well nor well understood her. Now, with her clearer explanation,
I've also gotten a new picture of her era, of 1214 B.C. As you say, as do
many archaeologists, many of my colleagues, these figurines are most
enchanting. In the last few years alone, there have been three
conferences attended by archaeologists about what these figurine girls
were all about. Here at Mycenae, people come up and ask — ask you,
perhaps, ask the guards in the rooms back there, certainly, ask us when
they see us — what they were. Ask what these cute, darling, chic figurines
were doing all those millennia ago. Some eminent archaeologists say,
'Look, their dresses obviously were designed by the best couturiers.' You
see," she said as she paged through the book, "there were different
fashions, in fact, several differing dress fashions and makeup styles used
over the years. Look here at the dark eye patches, so Parisian, so current!
Indeed, my chief opponent, Andrew Stark, says these were models,
fashion mannequins, used from 1400 to 1200 B.C, models used to sell the
then-current fashion, showing its annual changes. Like photos shown in
magazines like *Vogue* and *Harper's Bazaar* today in New York and Paris
and Milan do. Well, who can say he is wrong? Also, some very bright
people believe they were goddesses. Found in cult rooms. Who is to say
they are wrong? But why, then, did some sculptors keep making copies of
them year after year for years? Why were these little figurines" — she
tapped the cover girl's picture — "made, and not just here but in many
places? What did they represent that was so very important? It had to be

more than dress fashions for great warriors to wish to be buried with, clasping them to their hearts. Late Bronze Age sculptors in two Kretan centers made some; sculptors in Pylos made very special ones; sculptors in Elis made plenty; near Bronze Age Delphi they were made. In Tiryns and Argos. Later, thousands were made to ship around the Mediterranean to their thousands of fans. So even way back then, between 1230 and 1200 B.C., these little girl figurines were famous, kind of like Barbie Dolls of 1200 B.C. or famous sports figures. But more. Far more important than dolls. These figurines made their owners feel better about themselves. More secure in difficult times? Perhaps. So, why? According to Merope, these figurines represented real girls who saved their kingdoms, which was obviously very important. I guess, their fans wanted to have these representational figurines as a reminder, to hold like comfort blankets as though they could pass along, transfer even, in times of need some great good the real girls once did. If, indeed, the real girls saved their owners in life, maybe these representations would escort the possessors safely into the next kingdom. Is that it? People back then had to have known for all these to exist. So I have tried to make it my job to try to find out what it was they did, what exactly endeared them to so many. But now Merope tells me that I have not understood that precise moment in time. You know, an archaeologist's interpretations in these rarified realms of archaeology often cause conflict in the ranks. And now, on top of that, today, as clear as the parts you heard over that phone speaker, Merope announced lots more of that ominous message about tomorrow. A curse on me. Tomorrow, if I do not go or run fast to where she tells me, the evil queen will take vengeance on me, as she did on them. These real Khorus Girls of Mycenae will be forever doomed, and so will I be. Would any sane person wish Clytemnestra would take revenge on them? Instead, I wish to delay tomorrow's show time."

She took a pen and wrote "3235."

"How, Thanassis, can they be alive and therefore savable after thirty-two-hundred and thirty-five years?" She held out her hands. "And can you believe that beyond all these fears, I also have to pretend I do not know the first part of tomorrow is happening? That book presentation event is supposed to be a big surprise for me. Ha-ha! Oh, dear, I am shaking, Thanassis."

"Oh, Dr. Margaret." He took her shaking hands in his and held them steady. "What she said was no dream. I heard her. I heard her voice speaking to you on that phone. So I say do not worry! I will be here with you, ready to help you. I'm a great runner, Dr. Margaret. You just have to let me know when to get here. I'll be ready to run with you. And Menelaos-Stavros is a great runner, too." Her hands were no longer shaking. "Dr. Margaret, as for this surprise part of tomorrow, I cannot believe anything you write can cause enmity." He took the book and carefully looked at it again. "Is she that one?" He pointed down the dark corridor.

She gave his shoulder a pat. "Well, come along. Let's take a look. Maybe she will tell you the specifics more clearly."

Together, they walked toward the exhibition rooms. All the figurines were softly illuminated by the lights in the glass cases.

"Many of the first figurines in here were unearthed by Heinrich Schliemann," Margaret said, "others by Professor Wace, and more by his daughter, Elizabeth French. Some, this and those, by me."

"And there she is. This is the one!" Thanassis pointed to the central girl in the first case. "There she is! Cover girl." He tapped the glass and put his face very close. "You have a very sweet but determined voice," he said, waving. And kept staring. "She's so young, Doctor. Too young to cause controversy or generate a curse. But I can believe she is a representation of a real girl. I have heard what the visitors say. Everyone who sees her must feel her vibrant personality, her life force, feel her passion for whatever she did. It almost jumps at you out of the clay. Dr. Margaret, what can she, the real girl who lived here in Mycenae long ago, have done to that evil queen to have a curse put on her?" He turned to Margaret and took her arm. "Yes, I will help you save her. I would love to save her. I want to meet her. To hear her voice again and see her smile. And help you, too, Dr. Margaret. Do not worry. I will be here. Whatever more you know, tell me so I can really help you."

"You can feel through the clay, as you say, that though young she may be, she can also be quite forceful once she has something that she needs to get done. The real girl Merope was, must be, enchantingly formidable." Margaret then turned to look hard at Thanassis. She smiled. He, too, looked enchantingly formidable, though he did not look much older than fourteen. But she knew he was going to college in September to study classics. And he did look as though, when in need, it would be good to have him around.

"Why are you not in school, Thanassis? I thought during this semester you worked here as head guard only on weekends. I fear it was you I woke last night as I came up the hill, tooting."

He still had his head against the glass, staring at little Merope. "I can feel Merope's life force, feel that she is alive," he said. He tapped on the glass, "Hello, enchantingly formidable Merope." He turned away, looked back at Margaret and took a breath. "Oh. No problem about last night. I was dozing instead of making my rounds. And you see, Doctor, this is the beginning of the Rogation holidays, so school is on holiday. I had the opportunity to replace the other head guard, Phaestos. He wanted to assist his family in their vineyards outside of town in the hills up there." He turned back, again pointing to the little statues in the case. "And why, Doctor, are some of them waving while these are folding their arms? What I think …"

In the light of the case, something on his hand glittered almost blindingly. Margaret blinked and reached out to touch the bezel on his ring. "That's very old."

"Yes. My grandfather's grandfather found it in his vineyards before Dr. Schliemann's arrival. The doctor told him the same: that it was very old and that he should take good care of it."

"Where were his vineyards?"

"Where they are still, up above in the hills to the west of here. Not far from those of Phaestos's family."

"And your mother's cousin is Agamemnon, who today is in charge of the Belle Helene."

"You've known us all a long time, Doctor."

"Well, Thanassis, all of this famous place," she gestured to the whole of the site, "made famous in this era first by Heinrich Schliemann, is your place.

You've, through your family, lived here thousands of years. And we are interlopers."

He hung his head with pride. She could feel his pride. She touched his arm.

"I want to learn all I can, Dr. Margaret. I'm sorry you are ... that you are, you know, leaving."

"That other cousin of yours, Menelaos-Stavros, said the same thing a couple of hours ago. Well, though I will no longer be at this desk every day, or down there in the trenches, I will now have my office in Athens in the New Museum, where all these records are going tomorrow. Besides, as I told Menelaos, I know that you will apply yourself and I'll see you walk into my classroom, and with him, too. Before that, I expect to see you whenever you can in Athens. And I will introduce you at the university. And my assistant, Allison, whom I've asked to replace me, will be here. You will enjoy getting to know her very much."

She turned to walk back to the office.

"Wait, please, Doctor."

She turned back.

"I'm really interested in this," he said. "Why are some, like these here, waving and others folding their arms?"

She looked carefully. "Do you see them waving?" — Were they showing off for Thanassis?

He looked at her. "Many of them do seem to be waving," he said, turning back to the lighted case.

"Well," she said, pointing, "what do their positions look like to you? Have you asked them? Obviously, you heard me talking to Merope. So perhaps they will speak to you, too."

They stood side by side and looked at the various girls in the cases. Margaret sighed, tapped the window and spoke softly into it.

"I, with Thanassis, will save you tomorrow." She waved back at her special girl. "Cover girl." She looked at Thanassis. "They are worried, Thanassis. Usually their gestures are friendly and welcoming. But, Thanassis, today I see and feel that they are warning us and begging us to do as Merope tells me as soon as she tells me tomorrow afternoon. Oh, what else to do when one hears voices from figurines thirty-two hundred years old?" She started back toward the office and then stopped. "Your question's answer may be complicated and long. And very adventurous. Are you feeling adventurous?"

He nodded vigorously.

"So please, yes, after all the famous and great have gone tomorrow, come back and begin your archaeological studies by helping me get out of here and achieving what Merope and her team want, and maybe then, together, we will find the answer." She turned again. "And wear good running shoes." She continued back toward her office, "As you can tell, Thanassis, they now have me more than a little frightened." She stopped and took his arm. "I am sort of rocked back to realize how frightened I am by what I heard Merope say. Rocked to know I hear a figurine who is not a figurine but a very real girl. Crazy? Then I remember what she is saying. An ancient, still-living curse is on me, too, whether or not I act. But of overwhelming importance to all these real girls the figurines represent, there is something I must do that will save them and that will also save me. And therefore also save you if you agree to come along. And Menelaos, too. Over the course of all these years, they have become like my own girls. Of course I must do what I can to save them. But from what? And where are they, these real girls? Real girls that were born when Agamemnon was Great King here? That becomes a frightening mystery. There is no way. Yet she says there is."

"I am excited about this," Thanassis said. "Whatever happens I will be here to protect and help you. I love a good mystery. Add me in as your teammate in saving them and you. And I've got great running shoes to save myself as well. Do you?"

"Got my Nikes. And Thanassis, we will find her. The real her. Her, with all the rest. Somewhere up there." She waved her arm to indicate the whole site. "It might be fun. Until now, I had thought them found." She turned back to the girls. "Where are you, my real girls, where will Thanassis and I find you?" She tapped the glass of several of the cases filled with the little figurines then turned back to him. "You tell Menelaos-Stavros about running shoes and ..." She patted his hand. "Thank you. I, too, am beginning to feel a good excitement, a positive vibe, now that you will be along."

Her words were drowned out by thunderous claps and loud rumbling from the mountains just above them with blinding flashes zipping past the clerestory windows. This time she grabbed his arm. She could see his mouth moving, but the noise prevented Thanassis's reply from being heard.

"Wait," he signaled. He was about to repeat what he said, when all the lights went out.

"Don't worry. It's nothing, Doctor. Nothing. It happens here all the time." Thanassis turned on his phone's flashlight. And suddenly, as they turned to them, hundreds of shining eyes shone out, eyes of the girls.

Margaret turned to walk back to the office.

"It's almost showtime, Margaret!"

She zipped back around.

"Did you hear that, Doctor?"

"Did you?"

"You know I did. Having heard it once, I would recognize her voice anywhere." He took Margaret's arm. "Come on." He stopped. "Doctor, that was not a dream. Let's get your things. I'll bring the boxes. You get the elevator. And after we get this organized, I'll be back tomorrow to get you out of here. Together we'll solve this. With Menelaos-Stavros. He's a good guy to have in an emergency. We'll find her; find them. I, too, am frightened. I will not let you down. I will not let anything happen to you. That I promise you, Doctor Margaret. Like you, I'm not sure where the real girls can be or how we are to save them. But I know together we will solve this mystery. If at any time before then you discover you know more about where we are to look, you contact me at this number." He gave her his number and could see her agitation. "Don't worry. Tomorrow we will find her. I want to meet Merope."

"Merope's voice was so serious," Margaret said. "'Urgent,' she kept saying."

"I'll be here to help and to protect you. Urgent is now my motto, too."

And the mountain gave another ominous rumble.

Thanassis took her hand. "I am going with you to meet her. So! Nikes! Do not forget. Menelaos will be prepared, too."

CHAPTER 7

FADE IN: *Selene in Triple Time*

SETTING:

     Place: Interior: Margaret's Bedroom, Hotel Belle Helene,
          Mycenae Village
     Date: 1 June, <u>1214 B.C.</u>
     and
     Date: 1 June <u>1205 B.C.</u>
And simulcast with:
     Date: 1 June, <u>2021 A.D.</u>
     Time: 3 a.m.

THE LITTLE FIGURINE came unexpectedly into Margaret's dream. Margaret sighed when she saw tears running down its little face.

"My name is Selene, Merope's older sister, daughter of Cynthia of Mycenae," she said. "And now, in 1205 B.C. as you say it, I am mother of Nepthaulia and Khloris of Pylos. I break into your dream, Margaret, to tell you needed specifics about the real Khorus Girls of Mycenae. Some history. And I urge you to do exactly as my little sister asks. I join her and Nepthaulia in begging because of my terrible guilt. The Khorus Girls are in this situation because of me. I speak to you of both the horrors of an event of 1214 and of an event of 1205 because I was there at both. If you wish to live to complete your work on both events, do as Merope says."

"What event of 1205?" Margaret said, trying hard to grasp what Selene was saying. "Yes, tell me, tell me." She moved her mouth and hoped she was heard.

"After an event in this year of 1205 that saved our kingdom, the figurine representations of many of us were devised so the Khorus Girls would be remembered for what we did. By then, 1205 B.C. as you reckon, some nine years after what happened at Mycenae, few suspected that the evil queen's curse could continue. They were wrong. But now, at last, in 2021 in your era, the one moment when that curse can be broken has arrived, and my sister, Merope, can truly be saved. By you, Margaret. Where the Khorus Girls are, from where you will rescue them, there is no time as you experience it. That curse keeps them suspended in zero time. You are their only chance. You will surprise that curse by swiftly emerging through a back door and rescuing the Mycenae Khorus Korai of 1214 B.C. Margaret, step swiftly, silently, through that back door. Merope will direct you to them. Trust her."

Delicately she wiped her tears on her striped sleeve and continued.

"Merope has told you how we, real girls, first formed into and then became famous as Khorus Girls long before we became memorialized in all those figurines you found. Naturally, long have I known that story, our story. Since I was very little, my mother, the lovely Cynthia, the khoreographer of our khorus in Mycenae and the votaress of the goddess, told how our khorus of girls began here in Mycenae. And stories of our long evolution in many kingdoms. Some Merope has told you. And today, the first of June, hear and heed what I will further convey to you, both to save yourself and to save them. The situation is grave. And its deadline is dead serious. Grave and dead. You must and you can save them. From eternal obliteration. Today the one chance and the last chance is going to arrive. You alone possess the key.

"Our history both grandmothers told us as they rocked us to sleep, as they fed and trained us. How the khoruses developed. Our aunts told us as they too trained us for the khorus. My little sister, Merope.

My cousin Althea. And I. And I, much after, also told the story while training my own daughters in Pylos.

"But even as I begin to relate this, there is that dry, rumbling thunder in Mycenae's mountains. Once such thunder presaged rain. But today, the first of June, 1214 B.C. and the first of June, 2021 in your era, Merope says this rumbling foretells ruin and death, which includes you because you will work today to break the curse of Clytemnestra. As all of us who then sang for life feared for ourselves, now we fear for you, too. So listen, learn and act fast. Act as soon as that chance opens, as soon as Merope gives the signal.

"If you want to know our club's whole history, it is also the story of four good queens, the originators, the creators of the khoruses. Long ago, Queen Aerope, upon her marriage to King Atreus, brought the harmonies here to Mycenae. And Queen Khloris, when she married King Nelius, brought them to the kingdom of Pylos. And their cousin, Queen of Elis, Evarete, did the same there. Call upon them and the fourth good queen, younger Eurydice who married Nestor, and went beyond all the others with incorporating our healing singing. So, call upon the good queens and break the curse of the evil queen. Four good queens against one evil.

"Once upon a time, long, long ago,

"in kingdoms by the sea,

"lived princesses and goddesses

"and a wicked queen, of course.

"And we? We, long before I, we were the girls of what you today call fairy tales.

"But there were no fairies then. Long, long ago.

"In a kingdom, or two, by the sparkling great sea, it did all begin.

"We, the Khoruses of Korai, all began a long time ago.

"Okay, I hear you want more. You want a goddess. There was definitely a goddess. The great mother of Dionysos, Kybele, came down from the east in her lion-drawn chariot, spreading great dreams, she taught my great-great-grandmothers and their sisters, in that kingdom across the sea, how to call the clouds to give harvests, to give joy, to give more and better lives to our technologically advanced kingdoms.

"You want more. Those princesses you want. Two princesses brought us to these shores.

"There was the beautiful Aerope and her sister-in-law, Khloris. Together, they brought us to sing for their kingdoms, and the good kings of these kingdoms united us all to sing.

"But you want the stuff of fairy tales. Of course. Naturally, among the good, there had to be an evil queen.

"Then, about the time of my grandmothers, The Girls began to develop more amusing, delightful and more-effective ways of acting in harmony with and in harmonizing with the elements. Because of these developments, more girls came to sing. And here on the mainland in our palace kingdoms, we learned how to swing with birds and how to leap with them into the clouds that our singing enticed. Then another broadening development began when the leapers started leaping and clapping while they sang, vaulting into those clouds. Then vaulting higher with birds to tickle the clouds. Soon their dress had to change to accommodating fashions, as you have noted, but for a special reason. Our fashion changes were practical. One was a style of dress that they could use to send leapers soaring into the heavens by those Tossers. They used a large, closely woven garment into which the Vaulters jumped and jumped higher and higher. The waves of the cloth, as wielded by a circle of girls, sent the leapers higher into the now-low clouds we called, soaring into the realms of the birds. For our wonderful, evocative dress, which arose from a need and which also depicted colorfully our specialties, some did call us 'fashionistas.' Like The Lightning Girls with stripes to shake while calling the lightning. And then came a life-altering development: The Rain Girls with the shimmering gowns like rain with their protective and practical polos rain hats. Our black eye patch makeup against the shimmer of the rain, or moon glare, or the sparkles of the rain or of the sun, soon followed, making quite a stir. All of this fashion was created for real girls for these real reasons: to draw forth the elements and protect the girls from harm.

"Such as when we acquired birds, which first joined for their love of song with the leapers; then the birds learned to soar alongside and around and over the girls and the clouds; and then they learned to assist in our leaping higher with amazing results. For this our designers created cloth of tight weave that fitted closely. These the swingers would remove from over their shoulders and, welding the two ends like a swing, swing themselves higher into the birds' realms. And soon the birds, joining this swinging game, would help the girls by taking the ends of the cloths and bringing the girls swinging into the clouds with them.

"The clouds loved the singing and the leaping as much as the birds, and so girls and birds created a harmony with clouds. And the clouds would sail and puff to our harmonies. And thus the famous Cloud Khorus Korai began because the clouds came to their songs. And clouds do special, life-saving things. Like birds do with The Bird Korai. And then the wind joined the fun soaring beneath our wings of clouds and birds and songs.

"Margaret, remember: 'Good queens, clouds, birds, with wind,' an important mantra.

"Suddenly, as I speak to you today, coming to you from over the eons, I am coming to you from a specific moment early on that morning on the first of June, 1214 B.C. The Khorus Korai of Mycenae have suddenly stopped harmonizing and a terrible silence hangs in the air, anticipating more of the dreadful rumbling. Which has brought me abruptly back to this place in this moment and to what we Khorus Girls are doing. Now, in Mycenae in 1214, I am fourteen years old and am, back in time, frozen, standing on the hills above the palace citadel of Mycenae, not singing but silent. Listening with all the khorus to the rumbling of those fearsome hills. As you in your era are doing right now.

"I look over and see our Leapers have suspended their leaping and also stand silent, listening as the mountain reverberates with that sound. Their posture projects that they have some knowledge of what it means for them personally: this reverberating, the basso rumbling. This peculiar rumbling that comes without further results but to bring the musty, putrid smell of death, that they have experienced. Today, long ago, back in time on this most fateful of days to which this rumbling returns them, I am suddenly aware that they are all also watching me, waiting for me to do something. Their songs are suspended in the air, their last note hangs there, hangs on that moment as, with worried eyes, they wait for me to continue my leap. But it does not happen. Something else does instead: Brought upon us by that evil queen's jealousy of my mother, Cynthia; for jealousy and with a murderous curse, did the queen end us on the first of June, 1214 B.C.

"And that is why, though frozen in time in that moment, we are also here now today with you. To warn you and beg you. These girls had vibrant and vital lives suspended on that day by this evil queen. So I too ask you: Be brave and bravely break the curse and free the girls at last. Rescue my little sister, your special girl, little Merope, and her friends. And our mother. Without you, we are condemned, cursed to eternal oblivion. If you listen carefully to Merope, she will sing the cloud-calling songs that can end the rumbling in the mountains and open the door to her and all our Khorus Girls."

"Margaret." Now it was the voice of Merope speaking. "You have heard from Selene. And I, Merope, say, we all have confidence in you. You will GO, you will RUN! Today you will rescue us."

After no sleep the night before and a good, winey lunch-dinner with Kati-Selene and Agamemnon, and Allison, Margaret had fallen into a dreamless sleep last evening. Now she tossed and turned. She whispered, "I will do as you say. I will save ..." Just as she was falling into another deep sleep, her alarm woke her.

"Oh, God." She looked at her cellular and switched off the alarm. The day of reckoning had arrived. A great rumble from the mountains outside her room made her push the covers off with a certain defiance and swing her legs over the side, feet into slippers. She looked about her room. "All packed and ready to go, Mags," she thought. After the festive meal, she and Allison had gone over the details of the paperwork from Box #1, things needing Allison's attention. And now here it was: her last official morning in this room that had been home.

"Well," Maggie thought. "I had better get going. It's going to be a long and exciting day." Her phone read 5 a.m., June 1, 2021. "A.D." she added.

That ominous sound rumbled down those mountains. Maggie shook her fist in its direction.

CHAPTER 8

FADE IN: *Remembrance of Things Past*

SETTING:

    Place: Int./Ext.: Hotel Belle Helene, Mycenae Village, Greece

    Date: 1 June, 2021 A.D.

    Time: 8:30 a.m.

AGAMEMNON HEARD THAT rumbling, that *nothing*. He refused to hear it. It was absolutely nothing, so he pushed it away and reached for the guest list.

Towels for tonight's guests were his first task of the day: twelve large, twenty-four smaller and twelve fluffy bathmats. Oh, and there was that one room occupied by the Americans. So he reached up to the top shelf, the washcloths area, and retrieved two. He wrote out room numbers; the younger housekeeping women often mixed things up without the room number attached. Next he turned to sheets. All had been well-laundered and pressed; his wife's doing. How pleased his grandmother would be to see such. He pulled out what his list called for and numbered them, then adjusted his running inventory to match. Kati-Selene would be cross if he forgot. And when he turned to walk to the kitchen, thinking of his grandmother and the sweet-smelling sheets and then of another sweet, hot coffee, he heard that nothing again. Nonchalantly ambling toward the pantry, he stopped to add sugar to his cup, checked his hair and then, going on through the darkened dining rooms, opened the sliding glass doors. And stepped into warm sunshine.

Sipping, leaning over the front balustrade overlooking the main street, Agamemnon saw that there was still that slow procession of cars, now with no end in sight. They had been passing since before the shutters had been raised across at Elektra's Greek Pizza Palace. To his right, Agamemnon could see that down the road Nikos, cap in hand, was now standing in front of his just-washed windows, scratching his bald head, a curious look across his face. Judging from all the clean tables with neatly arranged chairs up and down the road at all the cafes, restaurants and shops, it seemed not one of these cars had stopped, certainly none to consider Elektra's pizza or coffee over there at Nikos's. Definitely no one cared about the history over here at Belle Helene. Agamemnon finished his small cup. Maybe they would stop for lunch later? He would get out the flags. And some flowers from the garden. Yes. And a fresh bouquet in Dr. Margaret's room for her very last night. He thought all this as he tried to get that one, last, sweet sip. Yesterday evening they had really enjoyed laughing over a lovely late-lunch, early-dinner prepared by the tax-preparer. Kati-S, too, liked Dr. Margaret a lot. They would both miss her.

He leaned over the balcony. It definitely was not that nothing sound that had turned Agamemnon's feet back out here to the balcony. That was nothing. But while Agamemnon had also not thought much of the few cars he had seen while savoring his first hot coffee two hours ago, he now joined Nikos in curiosity. When those cars had first begun passing through the dusty main street of Mycenae, not even the perpetually prone dog, whose territory was the middle of the road between Elektra Pizza and the Belle Helene restaurants, had raised an eyebrow. Still, the cars continued passing silently. The villagers, his neighbors up and down the street, who constantly sat on their deep terraces fanning themselves, feigning nonchalance, kept fanning and whispering in early morning lazy conversations.

Agamemnon leaned back and breathed deeply the intoxicating perfume of the first flowering wafting across from the vineyards. The sweet aroma of violets coming from the hilly vineyards of red grapes mingled with the enticing — what was it? He knew; he just couldn't quite ... He breathed deeply again, and immediately he was transported in time back there: a beautiful pear just picked from his great-grandfather's tree. And taking a bite, he breathed in its fragrance. He was only four years old. And just as suddenly as he grasped and breathed in that aroma of pear, he was twenty-nine once more and standing on his terrace here and now, breathing it in, that pear-like aroma given off from their white grape vineyards.

"Pear!" he almost shouted. And breathed deeply again the springtime vines-in-flower scent of pear. Annual scents that marked the beginning of the wine season. Aromas blown over from the white varieties of Kidonitsa grapes in his uncle's vineyards in the northwest, the aromas coming from up there behind where he stood, from vineyards some ten generations in the family, made it lovely to be alive here, today. He wiped his finger inside the cup to get that very last sugary drop from the bottom of his cup and breathed deeply again. The scents marked that soon enough there would be lots of guests coming in from the surrounding vineyard hamlets for the annual Rogation and blessing of the vines-in-flower. But not today. He took his cup from the balustrade and was halfway back to his sheets when ... mid-step through the pantry where he deposited the cup ... it happened again: that non-sound, that nothing. At the deepening rumble, he turned and ran back through the front dining room and out.

"'Rain ends flowering!" He heard his grandfather's urgent tone in his head. "God! No rain! Please!" Agamemnon almost shouted as he prayed aloud for the newly flowering vines' safety. But he sniffed again and stopped. He found no scent of impending rain. He breathed in again. No ozone. No. The aroma of ozone was clean and brisk and elevating: It smelled "green." It meant "rain on the way." But not this. This new-added scent that blew down from the mountains with that 'nothing' non-sound was not elevating. No. It was a dry, sort of dangerous, musty, putrid smell not signaling rain. As he stopped, no longer seeing the passing cars in the street, he thought, "What is this new, dangerous smell telling me?" And again that nothing rumbled in the hills. He went inside to get the shears to cut some flowers for Dr. Margaret's room.

CHAPTER 9

FADE IN: *Curst Forever*

SETTING:
>Place: High Citadel and High Hills above, Mycenae, Greece,
>Date: 1 June, <u>1214 B.C.</u>
>Time: 9 a.m.

Simulcast with:
>Place: Archaeologist Office and Museum, Mycenae, Greece
>Date: 1 June, <u>2021 A.D.</u>
>Time: 9 a.m.

"HIGH ON THE hills above Mycenae, all the Khorus Korai had stopped harmonizing, stopped leaping, stopped all song and stood silent, listening to the rumbling reverberating, knowing what it meant for them," Selene said to Margaret. "This reverberating, this basso rumbling. This new, peculiar rumbling that came without further results other than that smell of death.

"My reminiscing with you, Margaret, in your era today, now stopped as abruptly as their song.

"Where I was on that hillside, I felt all their eyes looking at me.

"The girls were watching, The girls were waiting for me to do something. The songs were suspended in the air as they waited for me to continue my leap. They waited for me to somehow save them. — But there were tremendous forces I knew nothing about. Listen and learn our fear ..."

~~~~

... As she cleared out all the last-minute details, like finding and attending to memos long stuck on shelves in her office, Margaret was experiencing, through the voices that came over her cell phone, a sort of front-row seat to that same day in 1214 B.C. She put one more book away and tossed stray items into her purse. And she knew they, those Khorus Girls in 1214 B.C., were waiting for her to do something. Their eyes, she could feel, were all upon her. And she was ready.

~~~~

Selene continued the story:

"'Why have they stopped singing?' Clytemnestra, at the citadel palace, in her counting house, was counting her jewels and dreaming she was in her great-goddess magic car, being pulled through the air by her lions. She hated being interrupted from these important, early morning dreams. 'Why have they stopped singing?' in rising crescendo she shouted, throwing down the necklace of rubies. And the dream car, no longer pulled by those lions in her mind, came to a screeching halt. Though more jewels glistened in her hands, she could no longer pretend to be the great goddess. But still she acted as though she was. 'WHY have they stopped singing?'

"Her twelve assistants came running. She stepped through them like through mist. Shoo! She waved. They shooed into corners and cupboards lest she lash out.

"'Why are they NOT singing?' She raced into the new king's chambers and found him looking in the great bronze mirror, drinking the morning wine from the great cup. 'WHY? Did you not give orders?

We need … I WANT RAIN. NOW!' She shimmered as she stomped. 'NOW!'

"'But dearest!'

"'Now! Do not dearest me. I said RAIN NOW.' She ran and threw open the window and took a deep breath. 'Do you smell violets? Do you?' She dragged him over. 'Do you? Do you smell pears? DO YOU?!'

"'But, darling —'

"'Of course you do NOT. Well, you should. It smells more like poo out there. SO I WANT RAIN NOW!'

"'Dearest. It's too early. The farmers. The vintners. They all say it is too early. Rain now will not help. In fact …'

"'I do not care what they say. Peasants. But listen to me! That war is over, over there.' She gestured far away. 'And I want green grass and vines in flower when he comes marching home! I TOLD YOU YESTERDAY!! GET THEM TO SING RAIN NOW! Or else. Sing CLOUDS. Or else!' She stomped her foot and lowered her voice to that menacing tone that terrified the skin off him. 'HE will want to smell those flowers for some damned reason or other.'

"So once again, he, the once-again-new-king, called out all the various khoruses of girls. He issued an edict that they 'all immediately attend and perform.' There was a 'new order of greatness predicted,' he dictated, 'for Mycenae.'

"'Only the Khorus Korai,' he said, standing, perfumed and dressed for the occasion and proclaiming from the bastions. 'Only they can and will end this killing drought and usher in the New Age of Gold. As they had once opened The Lion Gate to the world with their songs, they must now sing clouds, sing rain from the clouds: Sing the flowering. The Khorus Girls must reopen the gates to the gods!'…This death in the vines was 'all their fault,' the once-again new king proclaimed from the high bastions.

"And though it was too early for her humor, the queen actually took to her actual car and whipped the horses, which she perceived to be lions, fast and faster. She thought she was flying.

"And fast and faster we saw her car coming up the road to the hills, the dust rising behind," Selene continued.

"And we, the Khorus Korai, heard her screaming and saw the dust. Our notes still hung suspended in the air as we waited. And the mountain gave a huge rumble. With it came that smell of death.

"Our mother, mine and Merope's, the lovely Cynthia, was the votaress of our order of Khorus Girls. High-Priestess of the moon and Chief Cloud Caller. She inherited these titles and roles because her mother-in-law, my Pylian grandmother, Aliana, had held, had stood and acted in these roles before Mother and had passed along the role. But heritage was only a small portion. Of all those in my mother's group, it was universally acknowledged she actually deserved most to take the place of head Votaress. In the group, she was universally acknowledged as the goddess's chosen. Except for one dissenter. That one, the queen, Queen Clytemnestra, felt she herself was the only qualified one.

"'Why have you stopped singing?' The dust was blowing in the queen's mouth, and she spat the words. The queen was in her magic car, still dreaming herself great goddess, though it was no longer being pulled by lions.

"'Where is she?' She shook her reins at me, Selene. 'Well, answer me, girl. Where is that pretender, Cynthia? Get her.' She hated being interrupted, but she hated not being answered more. With a flying leap, she bounded from the chariot at us. 'Until she gets here, I'll lead all of you,' she practically screamed, 'and YOU.' She shook with rage. 'You go get that fat cow, that Cynthia.'

"Mother was not a fat cow. She was a beautiful, young woman. And she was at home in town below, nursing her new baby, our brother. Though no one dared say so. And at the too-close crack of the queen's whip, my aunt, Thalia, ran to her cart to get my mother.

"'Meanwhile, I will lead you in the singing for rain.' And the queen started singing the first stanza.

"Oh, gods! 'Restrain yourselves,' my eyes implored the girls. 'No laughing. No hands over your ears.'

"Not to worry. The queen would not notice our talking eyes. She was screeching and yowling to the skies. And I was relieved knowing they all understood my eyes signaling.

"After half an hour enduring this, as the queen took another deep breath and stepped forward, lifting her arms, screeching the opening bars of the third stanza of the Hymn to the Clouds in a flat, high-C minor, veering dangerously to other non-notes, suddenly giggles erupted, uncontrollable giggles of a nine-year-old.

"She stopped on an electrifying warble and whipped around, eyes flashing and rolling like those of a mad horse, her arm pointing like a saber directly at the still-giggling uncontrollably and now red-faced child.

"'YOU!' she screamed. And on feet far fleeter than I could have imagined and in a demonic rage, she fairly lifted and flew at the offender, that arm now reared to strike. I saw the picture of terror on the offender, her hands protecting her face while she cowered before such fury.

"Oh, Merope! My darling Merope. I ran like a deer and jumped to stand in her place to take the blow.

"But before any such could fall, an arm grabbed that of the queen.

"She reared, roaring at such effrontery. And turned to face my mother. In back, the mountain roared louder.

"The dust was still settling behind the wheels of Mother's chariot, the horses snorting and stomping from their haste.

"'Please, Madame, strike me.'

"Clytemnestra was not used to nor was understanding of competition. Ever. And now, thwarted in her rage, she turned to confront whoever it was who had dared to say that and found herself staring at the face of her most-despised competitor. Her blow fell hard on our votaress. The mountain behind roared louder and shook us all. And from the blue sky, lightning steaked past and hit the hills opposite, setting the dry stubble on fire.

"Merope and I stood riveted, watching with all the others. Soon Mother recovered, though her face was scarlet, water pouring from her eyes, her nose streaked with blood.

"Mother was the votaress and High Priestess of our Order of the Moon. Unfortunately, at this moment, her position was not only opposed by the queen; she had stood between the queen and what the queen wanted. And that no one had ever done and survived.

"'You dare! I am Head Votaress, you cow!' she screeched at my mother. 'You wish to take my place. Then do. But for that I want rain. You will call the rain to put that out!' She pointed to the flames. 'You will call until you drop unless you succeed, you, you, you fraud! I will get rain from you if you have to make yourself into rain! Today! Get rain today or else!' And with that, she spat in my mother's face. And with that, she ran, jumping through the air into her car. Certainly, those imaginary lions pulled her in the car. But we could clearly see that the real horses did not wish to. Slowly, her magnificent vehicle turned to leave.

"And our votaress, scarlet of face, nose and eyes dripping, stood, arms uplifted to the skies, and began the hymn again, the hymn to the clouds, to the birds, to the winds and to the universe. At that second, the midday sun was dimmed and a full moon suddenly appeared and shone its beams directly on her votaress.

"She turned and stared, the evil one did. Then she reared in her car and raised that arm again and pointed.

"'I put a curse on you all. Damn you each and every to eternal silence. And oblivion!' And the sky again, this time above her, parted and a bolt of sizzling green seemed to make a crack in the very sky and then came into her hand, and she pointed at Mother and then at us all. And the bolt sizzled over her and cracked like a whip in her hand. And for an instant, we did see her in her chariot drawn by lions lift into the air, and she, the evil queen, shrieked and flew away.

"Only a second later, after Mother had blessed us with a healing-of-evil blessing, when we looked back, did we see her down the hill, the chariot normal, lifting dust as the poor, confused horses tried to avoid their mistress's sharp harassment. But they could only do as the gods had fashioned them and continued downhill, lifting dust behind. We did hear her calling and screeching. 'CURST YOU ARE! ALL OF YOU! FOREVER DAMNED TO SILENT OBLIVION! And any who try to revive you so-called Khorus Girls! RAIN! Or eternal, SILENT OBLIVION! CURST!'

"Clytemnestra was smart enough to realize that Mother's opposition had freed her from herself having to produce. The opposition had gained her freedom to make that cow, Cynthia, publicly responsible. As her imaginary lions pulled the queen's car to the palace, again she was singing.

"The guards, wishing for earplugs, pretended they were deaf.

"'Bitch!' the queen screeched as she descended. 'She's in for it now!' And she shrieked, flinging lashes at all and sundry as she entered the palace, striking the head doorman for sheer pleasure. 'Forever damned to silent oblivion. SILENT! Do you wish to be?' The doorman fainted.

"And then the mountains shook town and palace and rumbled. We in the hills felt and heard it, shaken to the cores."

"And thus Mother had arrived. She had left the babe at home with the nurse. She knew this queen better than to bring the baby. But she had no time to bring food or drink, either. She did not plan to be with us long. Well, she was mistaken. She thought she knew this queen. But she had never encountered such before. Poor Mother. Poor us all. Curst by the evil queen.

"Behind us the mountains rumbled and shook. And in-streaming clouds turned violently red and redder."

~~~~

"Maggie, this is Merope again. You heard Selene, my sister? That wicked, evil queen cursed us, Maggie. As she flew away in her lion-pulled carriage, she cursed us. She promised us 'silent oblivion. No one will know any of you ever existed, you so-called Khorus Girls. I curse you to SILENCE. And any who try to revive you. Cursed to eternal damnation of silent oblivion!' she screamed as she flew away. 'Rain. Or silence. Eternal oblivion!' That is what you will rescue us from today. Selene will tell you all you need to know to save us and yourself."

Margaret still had three last-minute things to take care of, like the phone calls she had to return, before clearing out and leaving everything as it needed to be for her successors. Though the little statue of her Merope was front and center on her desk, all the conversation was coming through her cellular. At the sound of a second voice, she turned to the screen. And another figurine took center stage.

"Please listen well, Margaret. Again it is I, Selene, sister of Merope, trying to get through to you."

"I'm listening, believe me," she gestured to the device as she touched little Merope. "I think I know what you want, what Merope needs me to do. I will do my best, believe me. But first I have so much to …"

"No, no, no. Forget what you have yet to do. What will any of that matter if you are destroyed because you did not do exactly as Merope will direct? That evil queen has never forgotten. Her curse worked then. And still does. Until you. Believe me, there is no time as you know it where we are. The evil queen wishes eternal, total oblivion of us all. Oblivion of who we really were. You are our only hope to tell everyone how we were not clay figurines. After all this time, there is this one chance today of surprise through a 'back door'. Now is that day, Maggie. You must, please, step in quietly via that back door, step between the evil queen and her curse. Save us. Please beware the consequences of not being careful enough. Today we are using all our strength to help you. But you must do as Merope tells you. Then will we be freed and known again. Merope will lead you on."

CHAPTER 10

FADE IN: *Here Comes the Bride*

SETTING:
> Place: Int./Ext.: Mycenae High Citadel and Hills Above
> Date: 1 June, <u>1214 B.C.</u>
> Dual timeline interacting with:
> Place: Archaeologist Office and Museum, Mycenae, Greece
> Date: 1 June, <u>2021 A.D.</u>
> Time: mid-morning

MAGGIE PUT THE very last personal file of various site photographs into her briefcase and, turning to survey her almost-former office one last time, gave a sigh. With all this urgency to save her girls and herself, and the urgency to get her belongings out of here before everyone arrived for her big surprise, and the stage fright of knowing she had to somehow confess or ignore her errors in the book these surprise guests would be receiving from her, she had been hard-pressed to get these final things organized. She knew the guests had begun arriving a few hours ago, and several were having discussions in the large meeting room across the courtyard, about her book. "Paranoia," she self-diagnosed. Others, she could see through the windows, were up on the citadel site, talking and likely remembering their student excavation days. And now, satisfied it was done, she could give total attention to the magical, crazy, frightening day.

Front and center on her desk, little Merope was waving her arms. "Still doing the impossible?" Margaret said.

"DID you hear, MARGARET? Hear everything Selene told you? Well, here we are. Today. And I, this little Merope figurine who is waving her arms and moving her mouth, will lead you to discover the real us; real girls for you to save from eternal oblivion." She turned, then turned back again to stare at Margaret, who had suddenly discovered under her desk another box, another one marked "Allison." Margaret started stuffing things into that box while attending to Merope's words.

"Margaret. Are you with me?" Merope said. Margaret nodded at Merope while she taped the Allison box shut. Merope put her hands on her hips and did a good imitation of stomping one foot.

Margaret ran and put that Allison box on the gurney which was being wheeled out. And turned to little Merope, putting her hands on her hips. "Merope," Margaret said, stomping her foot, too. "I have been listening to you for two days and nights. And I will do exactly as you say. I promise."

"Remember that I am well-hidden and well-cursed with all the rest. And so now are you. Cursed. Even hearing and acting as and when I tell you to, even then you may be destroyed like us. To avoid that, as soon as you can, as soon as your guests leave, YOU LEAVE, TOO! RUN with me, this figurine."

With a determined look at the little Psychic Psi figurine, Margaret took from a bag a pair of Nikes, showed them to Merope, put them on the floor near her chair and nodded at little Merope.

Merope continued. "Good! And remember these magical words: good queens, clouds, birds and WINDS. I with you will sing them like a saving mantra. Depend only on me and on yourself. And those cute guards."

"Good queens, clouds, birds. And WIND!" Margaret tried it out and smiled at Merope

Her cover girl pointed to Margaret's cellular screen. And center stage in stepped again her sister, Selene. She was still on a high hillside and was pointing to the south. And as Selene began to speak, the little figurine morphed into a real girl, standing on a hillside.

~~~~

"As if her Clytemnestra curses and enforced labor of us was not enough," Selene said, "khoruses from Tiryns and Argos and Berbati and Midea were dragged out by that horrid woman, and from their hills, their sounds carried so we could hear that they, too, were commanded to sing the rain from the clouds. And we were forced to begin again. With renewed vigor, we had to sing for what was counter-indicated by the farmers. Day and night, we were to sing until …rain. So we sang. We sang under this duress, this curse. The hills were dry; the vineyards were about to flower, definitely not now needing rain. But no matter. The queen and her again-new king, knowing nothing but results, demanded rain. So, on the dry, stubbly hills, high and lower, all day with little staggered rest, we khoruses petitioned at each of Earth's and at heaven's gates, the clouds, the sea, the sun and the moon and all of creation, to end this drought and usher in the new age of rain, the new-king's new age of gold, such as had been for more than three-hundred years back to when the khoruses began. Now two of Mycenae's older Tambourine Khorus Girls collapsed. One died. And one Soarer Khorus Girl failed to jump high enough, her song not high enough to reach her birds, and she plummeted to earth with commensurate tragic results. The gods had shut their gates. And were keeping them shut. Heaven's gates seemed as fortified as Mycenae now was. This is what happened …"

Using a small mirror, Margaret combed her hair and put on some lipstick.

"Margaret, pay attention," little Merope said, reaching for the lipstick to take it away. Margaret put it in her purse. "Listen to the rest of this dreadful unfolding."

So Margaret sat once again in her chair while Merope sat on the edge of the desk, and they listened as Selene recounted the history …

~~~~

"'... They are thwarting us on purpose,' the queen, back at the palace, sat and combed her hair, continuing her tirade. 'TEACH them!: That the new granary needs filling ...' Her hair was falling out, and this annoyed her. 'That the wine casks are empty, waiting; That the spring and the cisterns are running dry. And better yet, if they fail, I shall cast a further spell on that mountain and they will be utterly destroyed. Either way, they will be. If you like any of them — your sister, your mother, your aunt — you will make sure they do not fail. They will sing the rains. Or no one will ever know they ever existed.'

"So the once-again-new-king persisted. Now ordering his favorite game, he ordered the town leaders to whip any girl who faltered.

"Though they paraded into the hills bearing whips, the under-palace guards, none used one whip. 'They' were their wives, mothers, grandmothers some, girlfriends, aunts, sisters, babies. Not one whip was used. Until the palace guard was forced to whip the mayor. Still no whip was used against us, the now-sacred Khorus Girls. And thus, the beginning hour of the afternoon began to our continued chanting and jumping and rhythmic crying to the unhearing and cloudless skies.

"Suddenly, thunder and its rumbling grew more ominous and built as it leapt from peak to peak, spreading whispery rivers of high clouds, soaring down through the valleys between with anticipated torrents of sounds which reverberated sending high, increased, streaky rivers of moisture coalescing into and spreading strands of streaming clouds. These whispery rivers of high clouds began gyrating which caused rumbling and more rumbling in the hills, high and lower. Building into torrential sound. It was too early for summer storms by some thirty days. Not until after the flowering of the vines had finished were they to come. "What to do?" the people whispered, huddling behind doors, afraid to look at the ominously red, cumulonimbus-mammatus sky.

"And the roaring. Such roaring sound once presaged rain. Until it foretold death. And all who had worked for life feared this new order of desperation. Everything was upside-down since the usurper had arrived to seduce the silly queen. The aborted flowers rained down into the dust, falling from the vines' stems. All the harvests were in jeopardy. Even the roses had refused to bloom.

"Under duress, we continued despite jeopardy and failure."

~~~~

"'They met me in the moment of success.' Once more the Queen, in her counting house, counting the rumbling, now also began counting the approaching military rhythms. She could picture in each rumble, in each resounding step of the army, the return of her lord, her husband, the Once Great King. Soon, soon, she would command for the candles to be lit throughout the palace and bonfires on all the hills. Soon, soon, she would put on her finest. Soon, soon, the banquet servers would stand in anticipation in the immense doorway, twisting their napkins. The wine stewards had opened the oldest and best wines to let him remember when ... when he had been beautiful, when he had been potent, when he had been The Great King. She returned to her crème pommades, and to her counting. And now she petitioned her advisors: 'Oh, all you forces down in there, come to my aid.' She stood in the great, open window facing the hills, her face white with crème, her arms open. The hills high and lower were now ablaze in sentry-set alerting flames. 'Come to my aid.'"

"Ravens swooped and cawed high in the hills. And the Rumbling answered her. 'We come. We come, great queen. We are on the way. This is the night. Get you ready.'

"The khoruses, suddenly silent, stood sniffing the musty aroma of death on the hills higher and lower, and with that death smell we knew they had forsaken us: good queens, clouds, birds, winds. We stood and listened. From that vantage, we saw the newly kindled flames announcing the coming of the king leap up and spread from peak to peak.

"And too soon, it was near. He was arriving.

"The queen, heart fluttering like a girl's, looked down into the town below, bright as day in welcoming torches and lanterns. Behind the marching troops, his beautiful new car floated up the long highway, curving into and through town and, with ceremony, to the beating of drums and non-exuberance of the populous, to the tossing of spring's dried, dead flowers.

"'Where are his damned Khorus Girls when needed?' the queen said. 'Where is the rain? Curst they will be! That fat cow? I'll get her. I'll show them.' But now she had to turn toward the non-cheers and silent roars from those peasants as his car passed them and made its way closer. Now it was coming elegantly and silently under The Lions, 'his Lions,' he would say. She smiled. She could see better as it halted a moment, him questioning the guards at the new granary, him pointing at the reinforced and extended walls before continuing up the processional way, the people amassed on either side, amazed at the splendor of his car, welcoming home their old king, silently waving long branches from dead palms to fan his way. And now his procession was quite close, so close she could see his new girl was shaking. And beautiful. As she once had been. Oh, yes, he did love red hair.

"Before the car was totally stopped, he stepped down, showing his authority over it all.

"She walked forward, arms uplifted, her gorgeous, silk gown shimmering with gold in the torchlight. 'Come, my lord. Welcome, my king. All is prepared.' He returned her uplifted gesture to the cheers of the troops. She sniffed. 'Your bath awaits, my dear.'

"Taking a deep breath, he stepped into her embrace. 'The vines should be in flower,' he said as he kissed her forehead. 'I smell no violets. No pears. Where is my khorus? Why are my people less than enthusiastic? Why that granary?'

"'Thank the gods you are back!' she said, signaling a guard. 'Cheers,' she hissed between her teeth to the guard. Then, with a large smile, she turned back to her lord. 'Follow me. Come.'

"'Don't!' came as a sort of broken cry from the shaking girl still in the car. 'DO NOT!'

"'Follow me.' The queen held tight the king's arm. 'Please.' And he walked at her side and into his palace. In back of them, the rumbling from the hills competed brilliantly with the now-enthusiastic cheers from the townspeople.

"She smiled, noting that the girl was now following, too. 'Here comes the bride,' she hummed. And the guards, her guards, surrounded the girl with red hair and escorted her so nicely.

"As he accepted his golden cup, the hinges screeched and the great, copper doors of the palace clanged shut for the night. And the hills gave up an enormous rumble. And the townspeople slowly, silently went home to whisper behind closed and locked doors.

"And in the sunburnt, rumbling hills, high and lower, the torch flames lighting his return as dark fell, also very slowly, one flame less at a time, like our songs, one note at a time, died.

"'We met in the moment of greatest success! Remember?' The Queen whispered to her advisors.

"The hills reverberated, 'Remembered!'

"'Remember well my devotion to you. Remember to grant my revenge. They must not ever be found to tell this tale. Destroy them all. FOREVER! SILENT!'

"'Remembered!' the hills sang back.

"She moved from the window. She had other more-important things to avenge just now.

"And the singing in the hills changed to rumbling and rumbling …"

CHAPTER 11

FADE IN: *Nothing? Nothing!*

SETTING:
>   Place: Int./Ext.: Hotel Belle Helene, Mycenae Village, Greece
>   Date: 1 June, <u>2021 A.D.</u>
>   Time: 11 a.m. to noon

KATI-SELENE LOOKED up, wondering what had disquietingly disturbed her counting. Deep into counting and adding up their taxes, something abruptly interrupted her. Frowning, she put down her pencils and listened. It happened again. Quickly, she stood; her chair, abruptly shoved, falling to the ground, her heart beating faster.

"Oh, that rumbling!"

That rumbling echoing between the hills above the citadel had always disquieted her since her first visit to meet her husband's family. Now, when it happened at night, she snuggled closer to her husband. That awesome, dry sound reverberating off the double mountains, rushing down the valley, was like an avalanche arriving. All the villagers feared it, she knew. Not that any ever spoke of it. But she could see eyes seeking other eyes, looking for reassurance, but there was never any. Kati-Selene was not sure what caused their fear and the reason for their silence. What could be so terrifying no one could give words to it?

Not even her husband. When she had asked, he just looked at her, shrugged and said, "It's nothing."

Before she knew it, she had crossed through the Belle Helene's double parlors and adjacent museum. At the open glass front door, she stopped to stare across the terrace to the street and the passing stream of cars. And suddenly new curiosity moved her with a strange new urgency, and nine fast, long paces took her across the terrace to the balustrade. Old Street Dog was awake and, with one eye, was looking while he wondered too at the procession continuing around him. But she could tell it was not the cars that had awakened him. His eyes found hers and stayed. For a long moment they looked at each other, and taking a deep breath, she calmed. Then, shading her eyes, she turned her head and leaned over the balustrade to stare down the long, eucalyptus-lined road toward the National. Instantly, her mind changed questions back to wonder about all these cars. Cars going up to the citadel, a few, maybe even six a day, unless it was high summer, was the normal order. But this line, today, almost bumper-to-bumper, was not. And that not one person in one car seemed interested in stopping for anything along this street definitely was not normal.

As she walked down the terrace steps, she woke the cat, who curled its tail, twining Kati-Selene's ankles, curious, too. She stooped to pick cat up and walked to the edge of their parking where it met the road. Cars and more cars, all the …

"All the way from the National Road, it looks."

Kati-Selene had not noticed her husband standing in the shadow till he spoke. She reached out and took his hand. "Is it the blessing of the vine flowers today?"

"No. Not for maybe another two weeks. Smell those first, those intoxicating red aromas?"

"Violets." She pointed. "Aga, not one car stopped. Look. Not at Elektra." Old Dog had finally decided to move from his spot in the middle of the road. When a car paused, he lumbered sleepily across, stopping to pee on the car's tires, then over to the couple. The cat jumped and hid between Kati-Selene's legs, hissing. But she then twined around Old Dog as he lay at the foot of the cool, marble steps.

They were partners. "Not one has stopped anywhere. Not even for a café at Nikos's. He looks worried. Oh." Kati-S. took a deep in-and-out breath, "— And 'pears'. Pears, Aga. The white vines have begun flowering too. Just today, I think."

Agamemnon walked into the street and looked. "Yes. Well Nikos definitely has something to worry about." The Kafenieon's tables were still empty. Not one car in their parking. Nikos waved his handkerchief in the direction of his mother-in-law and turned back inside. Eva, Nikos' mother-in-law, was dusting the tables and chairs and sort of leering into the passing cars and was now the only other person Agamemnon could see. "An eccentric. Wonder what it's like to live with her? Oh, sweetheart," he turned back to kiss her hand, "you're so right: pear, from our white grapes. The fleeting, flirtatious aroma of pear. No wonder grandfather took so to you. Such temptation."

"What's all this about?" Kati-Selene retrieved the cat. "Don't you think one car would stop for a drink and at least contemplate lunch?" She stood again at the terrace balustrade and watched Spiros across the road watching, too, little Anthula in his arms waving at the cars. Kati-Selene waved, too. Then she twirled in the sunlight. And cat waved its tail. "It really smells like a world of violets and an orchard of ripening pears. Imagine grapes smelling of violets and pears." She patted Agamemnon's arm and again looked at the procession. "They should stop and smell, at least." She inhaled again. "It's like a paradise. Don't you think so, you little flirt?" She shook the cat gently who purred and reached to caress her. Suddenly, "little flirt" jumped and pounced on sleeping Old Dog.

Down at the curve in the road on this side, she now saw Orestes's wife, Korintia, seated at their table closest to the street, fanning herself, sipping a glass of wine. She had on, Kati noted, her nicest blouse. Korintia called out, "Waiter!" and with a grand gesture, pointed at her glass. "Another!"

"Good advertising," Kati-Selene smiled. "Aga, it's early, but maybe you should bring out a few glasses and a bottle of wine so we can sip and laugh and advertise Belle Helene." She arranged a couple of tables and chairs and moved over the vase he had set out. "Menelaos-Stavros brought the flowers early. Where are the rest?"

"I did that," Agamemnon replied. "He's late today. I put some in Doctor Margaret's room, too."

Kati-S put out her arms and hugged her husband. And they stood at the balustrade watching the slow parade of cars. "Well, I cannot imagine they love sitting in those cars and not having something. — Aga?" She paused and took another breath of young spring. But just then "it" happened again. "Aga, did you hear that? That rumbling? — Aga?" She turned but he was gone. She could hear him talking and saw him inside the dining room, hunched over his cellular. At the shrill sound of Eva's voice from the Kafenieon, Kati-Selene turned back. And burst into a laugh. Eva was now actively talking, proselytizing into the passing cars, leaning in, touching shoulders when possible. Across the road, Korintia was also staring at Eva.

"Here! Stop! Here. Café! Cakes!" Eva shouted. "Better lunch than there." Eva was now pointing at Korintia. "Much better than there." Her arm wavered as she saw Kati-Selene watching her, smiling at her, and it wandered back across the road to point at Pizza Elektra and Spiros. "Much!"

Spiros turned and took Anthula inside. Eva was getting deaf and her raised voice carried up the quiet road.

As amusing as her neighbor's dissing, Kati-Selene was far more puzzled by the cars, now going even slower as more came, bumper-to-bumper. "Aga?!" This time she called; then turned, walking back toward the open door. She could see her husband was inside and still talking into his cellular. "Agamemnon!", she called, "there must be something happening up at the citadel. All the cars are going up there."

He punched off and walked toward her. "Yes. Doctor Margaret is being celebrated today. They have invited us to come up for lunch."

"Well, why not? Okay!"

He had to turn fast. He caught up with her, already in their bedroom, opening drawers.

"Aga? Aga, did you hear that rumbling?"

He stood in the doorway and watched his pretty wife put her lovely Athens frock over her head. She slipped into her pink pumps.

"Well? Did you?"

"It's nothing. I keep telling you. Nothing."

He could see how happy she was to be going. So happy, Aga felt a combination of guilt and some sadness. He would make a reservation at the Saint George in Athens and take her to a nobby wine bar and a fancy restaurant. Her birthday was in twelve days. He had totally forgotten how beautiful she was. Like now. He reached out to help with her necklace. She froze. And he heard it. And again. And she was in his arms, crying.

"Oh, Aga, what is it?"

He reached down for the fallen necklace. "What? It's NOTHING!"

"You hear it. Why pretend? Nothing?"

"It's nothing, sweetheart. Nothing."

As Agamemnon opened the door of the car for Kati-S to enter, Menelaos-Stavros raced past on his bicycle.

But suddenly, he wheeled around and made a circle in the road, calling out.

"Uncle Aga, I forgot. You and Aunt Kati-Selene are invited to lunch for Doctor Margaret up at the citadel." He waved and stood up, his legs pumping him up the hill.

"You also forgot the flowers," his uncle said to himself as he started the car.

CHAPTER 12

FADE IN: *Confrontation and Murder, She Wrote, on …*

SETTING:
  Place: Int./Ext.: Mycenae High Citadel and Hills Beyond
  Date: 1 June, <u>1214 B.C.</u>
  Time: almost evening
In syncopated simulcast with:
  Place: Archaeologist Office and Museum Buildings, Mycenae
    High Citadel
  Date: 1 June, <u>2021 A.D.</u>
  Time: mid-day

"DRAPED IN CRIMSON, she slipped in crimson then twirled in crimson. Both were at her feet. 'Greatest success! You there! You! YOO-HOO! Remember?' With her toe, Clytemnestra nudged again at Stiffening Him. Howling with laughter, she pushed harder. 'Remember! Remember? You, the leader of more than a million men, have you forgotten your own advice? Remember your own back; Do not be blinded by what you see before you; Remember what's left behind!' Again she howled. Bending in hysteria, she stomped on Stiffening Him and grabbed the King's Cup from the crimson floor and drank to the dregs.

"Outside the windows, ravens cawed and hills reverberated, rumbling, thundering. 'Remembered.'

"Calmly, the queen slid over and washed her hands, turning the water in the gold lavabo to crimson. 'Wine!' she called. 'Our finest! Bring the finest from old, dead Atreus's reign.'

"The lover of five years, now the once-again-new King of one year, stepped over the crimson and slipped into her arms. 'Dead Old Atreus!' he whispered. Oh how he loved to slippery revelry that sexy crimson smell.

"She was remembering, in these also once-young arms, others, those of Stiffening Him down there, Agamemnon's once-younger arms: arms of a lover without comparison. But she stepped on that dead old lover and sighed and squirmed into these others, arms now, too, getting old. But he was Success. And alive. For now.

"Success. Aegisthos filled her with success, and he sighed and squirmed. He was young again in his mind. He was again new-King. Again his was the throne of Mycenae of Gold. Success.

"Outside the windows, lightning bolts split the sky, illuminating the splattered walls.

"'One revenge precedes another,' the Queen said. 'Let my next curse begin!' to her spirits Clytemnestra whispered so as not to wake this for-now alive New King."

~~~~

"The rumbling grew more ominous and, in the hills, it leapt from peak to peak, filling the valleys between with preparatory advent of sound. And then, in my dreaming state, as I, Selene, Merope's sister, leapt highest, the curls on the nape of my neck stood up as the claps of zigzagging, zinging light blazed past, blindingly, caused by our enforced warming of the air, by our leaping into electrostatic charges. Tiny ice particles forced by warm currents from across in Egypt collided, causing more charges and creating electric potentials within the long length of sky-rivers crossing the Great Sea, meeting the rise of under-clouds into where we were singing and jumping and causing the cap to move. And then, finally, our enforced, combined efforts sent lightning from that sky of red mammatus clouds, striking the ground in the barren sunburnt hills beyond, striking in the dry vineyard hills cracking without rainfall. And the flowering of the vines, ending too soon, was now totally ended by some spectacular resulting conflagrations. And we all began to realize what these omens meant down at the palace about the changing of the guard. Now the once-again New-King's heat would totally be on us, now to put out the fires our petitioning had caused. We would have to put out the fires or be set on fire. So our chanting and shaking and leaping intensified. The Votaress, lovely Cynthia, gave the signal. I stepped into position, all muscles primed, all eyes on me, all waiting for my call.

"The rumbling shook the ground under my about-to-soar feet. And then it happened. Wind shear spinning the updrafts almost tore me from the ground. And I woke to the reality of hundreds of eyes. All on me. Frightened eyes. Eyes wanting answers. And I knew they really had forsaken us: 'Queens, clouds, birds and winds.' Only barren wrong clouds were hearing us. And I knew only one real answer. My grandmother. My father's Mother. And there was only one way to get Grandmother Aliana's help.

"I grabbed a flask of water and downed it. I took another under my arm. Mother understood. I took the hand of my sister, Merope. And turned to the others.

"'Tell no one else other than your parents,' I said. 'I am off. I must get to Pylos before the downpours. The fires will not kill you if you protect yourselves in the caves up there away from the winds and smoke. Next, there are rains that are coming that will end everything. Rains from clouds meant not to revive but to drown. All. Harvests and vintages will be drowned, ended forever. Protect yourselves. I will get help. Now hurry. Get to those caves up there. The new king will believe we started this something that will not stop unless it and he are stopped by worse. Stay, all of you, there in these hills. Remember, only in those caves away from the winds. No matter what happens, I will be back with help for you. All.'

"'Selene! I'm coming, too!' That was my cousin Althea. Always willing."

"'No. It's your job, Althea, to keep them together. Share your lunches and waters.' I turned to my sister. 'Be frugal, Merope,' I said and returned her tight clutch. 'Merope, you're a brave girl and a good storyteller. This will take me some time. But I will be back. The more you amuse them with stories, the sooner I will be back.' Merope believed in me, though, unwillingly, she released me. Mother took her into her arms.

"Suddenly, little Merope was grasping me even tighter and whispered in my ear. I had to pry her unwilling fingers from me. She mouthed those whispered, fearful words again.

"I answered her whisper. 'You will, Merope-Moon Pour, definitely!' and gave her our secret sister sign. 'Moon Pour, I promise!' And I turned back to take the down path.

"She turned away in tears. 'No, I won't.'

"The early moon shone faintly but enough on the foot path and I was off in a flash. 'I will be back, Merope, within two days.'

"At my back, I heard her whisper: 'Bye.'"

Selene stood still and looked at me. "Hear and understand, please, Margaret. And heed: 'good queens, clouds, birds, wind.' Exactly as Merope told you."

~~~~

Margaret was no longer dreaming. Her hair was combed, her lips rouged. She was all dressed up for this surprise day and was seated among all her guests. But the enormity of the situation would not leave her. She was finally understanding that what was happening at the palace right there, only yards away from where she was sitting, surrounded by all these famous archaeologists, what was happening some thirty-two hundred and thirty-five years ago was not just a mythological story concocted by later dramatists or Mr. Homer. She was understanding that, indeed, murder had been committed and more murder was about to be committed all those millennia ago. And that such a murderess would, indeed, curse anyone in her way. And now Margaret was that anyone. She shivered in the knowledge of who she was against.

~~~~

"'I put a curse on you all! Rot in oblivion! FOREVER SILENT YOU WILL BE!'"

In her daydreaming, Maggie heard the voice of Clytemnestra and saw the red eyes turn to her. Instinctively, she closed her eyes and pretended to disappear.

"Oh, Maggie, hear and heed: We were just real girls until we began to sing. Then she cursed us. And that curse silenced and buried us. You must, please, find us. End it. Break it. Free us. Today the road will open! Beware for yourself. Do not let her perceive you. Close your eyes."

~~~~

"If only that Maggie could, just FOR A CHANGE, let someone else say something about them! This is BALONEY!"

She could not stop hearing the words she had heard all last night and all this early morning. But now, suddenly, there seemed to be an eruption from Andrew Stark's side of the room, and Margaret realized her neighbor had put a hand on her arm.

"I think, perhaps, you should stop the wine pourers," her neighbor, Agnes, kindly suggested. So, Maggie relinquished the warnings of Merope and Selene and looked up at those in her current world.

Indeed, it was becoming confrontational, as she had feared. And she could not just disappear. Or close her eyes.

"OH, MAGGIE, SHUT UP! Stop your posturing, pretending you know EVERYTHING about these FIGURINES! But, No! No!" Indeed, Andrew was now mimicking her and in falsetto. "Maggie knows all there is to know about the figurines. They were, of course, singing dolls for little girls! Dolls for little girls to play with. Didn't you know? This one" — he picked up his copy of her book and pointed to the cover girl, "this one is psychic, naturally. And psychic-psi 'Merope', she even told Maggie her name. And Psychic Merope told her about how they made their owners feel good! OH, BOSH! Just SHUT UP for a while and let the rest of us get some ideas in for a change! Let another idea in!" The voice rumbled through the room, its projection ending boisterous, happy talk. Like a clam, the talkative group shut down in startled silence.

"Oh, dear." Margaret put down her fork, raised her head and sniffed the temperature of the room. Again Agnes, her neighbor touched her wrist.

"Dreaming again?"

Maggie nodded. And though she did not say so, she was actually hearing again the voice of her cover girl. Yes, she was a little late understanding what, who, they really were. Well, a lot late. Figurines replicating those very real girls. Figurines, yes. But first, real girls. Real Khorus Girls who did important services for the community. Not just clay figurines in chic dresses with charming expressions. Had she said 'for little girls'? Of course, no one would have known about those real girls had not someone, somewhere, way back decided on this course of figurine representations of the most famous of these real, once-alive and singing girls. And no one now alive, except for her, Maggie, knew this extraordinary story and what had happened to those long-ago real girls. And even she was still greatly in the dark as to that. These real, these alive Khorus Girls had been cursed and had disappeared somewhere up there, and now she, Margaret, had been enlisted, entrusted, to actually save them from this curse, the murdering, obliterating curse of Queen Clytemnestra. Save them after thirty-two hundred and thirty-five years. Who would believe such a story?

Again, Agnes was questioning her. Maggie leaned over and whispered.

"Merope, this one," she pointed to the cover of the book that Agnes had next to her. "She has told me about a terrible curse on her, a curse on all the khorus girls by Clytemnestra. She told me so that I can immediately, after this business here, go save them somehow after all these millennia, and then correct and write the real, true story of who these girls had been and what they did to cause such a curse. I must start immediately after this," she murmured to the listening ear of her dear friend, Agnes Jones, Allison's teacher, who seemed startled by this revelation. "You know, Agnes, I've never wanted to be a renegade. I've always desired peace."

"Oh, Maggie," Agnes replied quietly with a chuckle, "you always find the most-interesting ways. Like, indeed, your Psychic Girl to tell you what to do. I think you love being the renegade."

Indeed. Well, Margaret now had to think this one through. But she did not have time.

"I'm also in danger," she said. "Grave danger. Not a grave joke. So much to accomplish once this event is over. It's that curse."

Again, Agnes touched her arm in sympathy and gave her a curious look.

Margaret had not been totally oblivious to the atmosphere in this room; she had just chosen to ignore it. While at her end there were "Congratulations" and "Happy to see you again" murmured over and over and many selfies taken, there had been more-overt and much less-happy boisterousness from Professor Stark's end of the room. But not too much as for her to signal, as Agnes suggested, no more wine to those serving. Indeed, until this moment, with, no doubt, help from that delicious wine from the Dassis vineyards, Margaret had been enjoying herself thoroughly, even forgetting for a moment the horrendous errors in that book she had just given to all these colleagues. And almost forgetting, as well, the great but unknown danger she was in. And it seemed that those gathered nearby, ignorant of both her distress over her huge mistakes and the somewhat psychic remonstrance by her colleague, were enjoying themselves as well.

She reached into her pocket for a tissue and found the folded page she had prepared. This she removed and slipped into Agnes's jacket pocket. Well, at the very least, she was sure that this would generate a message from Agnes in a few days. Now she smiled at Agnes, who was looking up at the cause of this controversy. Of course, as she herself surveyed the guests, Maggie was, in fact, surprised that Allison had invited so many really famous colleagues. And that they had come, many from far away. Like Agnes from Paris. And Allison had also organized for all the lovely townspeople, all of whom Maggie had known for ever so long, to also attend this delicious luncheon. Well, now town and gown were all here. And they would all, colleagues and friends and those less-friendly alike, take home a signed copy of a book that she now knew had umpteen totally wrong things, from beginning to end. Such a paper she would have to write and fast, denouncing and changing most of her book's statements. She wondered how charmingly her charming editor would react to this news. Now, suddenly, like a tummy ache, came the enmity with the dessert. A pin could have been heard dropping in the large room.

"Let someone else say something for a goddamn f#@&ing change about these figurines! Such rubbish. This book is rubbish!" Andrew's voice rumbled like the hills as he tossed his copy to the floor. "They were, as you should know, fashion models. As pictured in Paris or Milan magazines today. Models of what girls were wearing then. Fashionistas selling dresses. Not opera singers. Nor dolls. Certainly not psychic, talking dolls. Mannequins they were. A source of income. Not of religious frenzy. And I've never heard one note from any of them. Silent, unmoving, runway models. Useful for fashion-conscious ladies to choose their next year's wardrobe from."

The chair belonging to the occupant with the rumbly voice screeched as it was shoved back, outdoing the rumbling from the hills just outside.

Someone else scraped a chair, and that broke the ice as Donald Suskine from Canterbury Christ Church stood and pointed a long arm, like Zeus's bolt, and opened his mouth. Though all could see his mouth moving, the sound of his voice was obliterated by the suddenly fiercer rumbling from those hovering hills.

"Talk if you want to, Doctor Suskine," the originator of this crisis shouted, mocking, laughing.

Then all hell broke loose. A bolt flashed past the large windows. Then another. The words from the stately professor from Christ Church were again upstaged by more ominous rumbling. Then the lightning blasts struck, shaking the windows. Someone screamed. But the large man's voice was as Zeus-like as his arm's signal, and Donald Suskine's voice now took command to silence the room into some calm. Into hearing his repost.

"Professor from Philadelphia! Andrew Stark! You, too, have believed," his voice lowered, "sometimes, that the girls were ..." The speaker, tall and graceful, twirled about, waving. "Just statues of imaginary little girls. Kind of like dolls. Now you choose to tell us they were, instead" — his voice took on a falsetto — "statues called fashionistas. Mannequin dolls representing new fashions year after year. We've all heard and not complained about your belief. Beliefs. So why don't you make up your mind? And write your story? Or get some help from Dior."

"Fashionistas! Uh-oh! Takes one to know one, Andy!" Tones again in falsetto from the other direction came followed by a backflow of laughter.

Zeus walked thundering, shaking the hills.

Suskine strode closer to his opponent, speaking to the rhythmic jabs of his hand, orchestrated with thunder. "So, you've changed your mind? Again? Most of us do that. Quite regularly. And we let you believe what you choose. Let Dr. Margaret Benson believe and promote as her lights guide her. Today, Andrew, we are celebrating *her* twenty-five years of research and discovery through excavation here in Mycenae and at Pylos, in Kydonia, in Athens and at Elis. Your day may come if you work hard and long enough at whatever it is you believe. But for today, if I may, politely suggest, you shut up and let the rest of us, and her, enjoy."

The dignified man took a few deep breaths and got back his composure. Everyone listened when he spoke. It was not just his commanding presence but also his enormous academic stature. He had worked with all the greats: Blegen, Iakovides, Taylour, Dr. Elizabeth Wace French. His credentials were stellar and did reach the stars and call forth stars. He hated arguments. But archaeologists, like the stars they are, do have tempers, especially concerning their beliefs. And their loyalties.

And now, under and with Donald worked 'The Successor', William Kent, a young, brilliant man from California, the controversial finder of Agamemnon's throne. This young titan stood and began clapping.

"Bravo, bravo, Donald! Dr. Donald Suskine and Dr. Margaret Benson. Bravo to you both. Maggie, we all celebrate you! Bravo! We have all," he said as he put a finger to his lips, "quietly taken to the Mycenaean roads to surprise you, Margaret, and be with you here today.

To celebrate your work and discoveries. Let us celebrate the Khorus Girl figurines from Mycenae. And you, dear Dr. Margaret Benson."

She stood, bowed to him and made a little signal like, "Come over to chat." Did he understand? She had to get to him before he left. He had been named as a possible …

Everyone, almost, stood, clapped and shouted, "Margaret Benson! Bravo, Margaret!"

And then when that group from Berkeley, dressed in lightning-striped knit dresses in the Pucci style, fulfilled her dream and danced and sang about lightning in the hills, almost everyone was enthralled. Another standing ovation from almost all.

"The Khorus Girl dolls of 2021 A.D.!" almost all shouted.

Then, when the group all together presented and draped over her shoulders a lightning-striped, knitted shawl, well, that caused a big singing, shouting and dancing commotion over which anything she said would not be …

What could she then do to rectify this mess? She had to stand there and accept congratulations for what she now knew was almost totally wrong in the book. And then the knowledge there was a curse overriding this, upon which she would have to react as soon as they all left. Oh, if only she had more courage. And more information. If only she had more …

~~~~

… Now they had all gone. All the guests gone, even Allison and her assistant, Federica, taking with them the portfolios she had prepared for them. They had done a magnificent job of organizing and executing this wonderful and delicious surprise day. Finally, alone with the treasures of millennia past, Margaret stood in her Nikes in the darkened below-ground rooms of the museum at Mycenae, illuminated only by the lights in the various exhibition cases, waiting, key inserted in the lock, waiting to hear again from her girl, but up close. This was the announced moment for action. The eyes of all these little phi-, tau- and psi-shaped dolls seemed as always to be talking, telling, singing to her a story.

An ongoing story. One she had been trying to decipher for twenty-five years but only now was hearing correctly, the answer to her question: What were all of you really doing? Why were you made? A little late, she had learned the answer. No. Not quite. She had learned part of the answer. A little late, she had learned that this part of the answer required immediate search and recovery action. She was close to finding why they were made, but still the answer floated out there on a road yet to discover. The two roads were connected.

And so, tomorrow or the next, when at her new desk in Athens, having survived this impending catastrophe, she would stop all other work and put out a quick retracting paper stating her errors and her new conviction and admitting that she did not yet have all the answers. She would ask Donald to give the introduction. Well. It has been a long road, has it not? Since she had first taken the Bronze Age roads and come to Mycenae as a lowly assistant's assistant, these girls had captivated her. Those in cases over there were already here at the museum. And these, that one right there, front and center, and these she herself in her twenty-five years had unearthed from many locations here up at the citadel of the palace, and down below in many and various places as far away as Tiryns and Tegea; from between doors, and beneath floors from various levels of Mycenae's houses built over each other for over fifteen-hundred years, in so-called cult rooms here and as well as at Berbati and Midea, and even this one, another special one, buried here with a princess, elder daughter of Elektra, also clutched in her dying moments to her breast for comfort. And, of course, the star of them all, her Merope, for whom she was about to take off on a fantastic rescue voyage. They had not only captivated her imagination; they always gave her comfort. Now she felt adrift again, as though all these years had been wasted. But ...

"Forget all that! GET OUT FAST, NOW! GO! FIND US! RUN TO US! SAVE US!"

Suddenly, the dreaming ended. In front of her, they all were again jumping up and down, warning, "Curse on you, too!" They all waved their hands and shouted. Even those in Pucci dresses removed their hands and waved them and screamed, "FIND ME! ME! RESCUE US!

Good queens, clouds, birds, wind. GO! Rescue us from eternal silence. RUN! RESCUE ME! RESCUE US from obliteration!"

Fear ran like lightning through Margaret. With shaking hand, she turned the key and opened the glass case of her psychic Merope.

"Well," she sighed as she took her in her hands, "if those imaginative ideas in the book caused enmity, wait till I correct all my errors and then send out these theories." Her restatements would be the cause for further mockery.

"MAGGIE, STOP! That's all nothing. TURN NOW! GET OUT! RUN up those stairs! RUN! FAST! SAVE ME!" A little hand grabbed Maggie's finger.

Margaret had always been imaginative. Her mother called her "The Dreamer." She had tried to do as Mother often told her, tried to keep her imagination in check. But today's animosity, added with this now-definite directive and warning, encouraged her to follow her imaginative idea to run. Yet, on the other hand, Mycenae was known for the sounds of thunder in the double hills. It was a natural phenomenon, her friend who specialized in ancient weather patterns had told her. But again, there were those moments when nothing here felt natural. And today, even before Andrew Stark started his rampage, even before then, when all seemed light and gay, Maggie had felt that oppression. Ominous oppression. All the previous night, while she had dreamed ominous warnings, she had felt as though she was about to encounter a god. It was an out-of-her-head feeling. But then that feeling had flown in the rampage, and now she knew the rumbling was an ominous warning, and she smelled an oppressive mustiness. Maybe they just needed to open the windows in here once in a while and clear out the air-conditioning and let in real air. She clutched Merope with care and shut the case.

"Maggie, WAKE UP! GO! Wake up! NOW RUN! GET OUT!"

Maggie tried to do as her mother had told her, tried to keep her imagination in check.

"Just to be sure," she said, "One last time: Are you just part of my imagination?"

Her girl rolled her eyes and grabbed Maggie's finger tighter.

"Listen carefully," Merope said. "While you run out, I am going to tell you where to find us. And then you with me and Thanassis, that Menelaos guard, too, we are going there to the rescue. Remember? 'Good queens, clouds, birds and wind.'" She leaned over Margaret's hand and looked. "You've got your Nikes. Good, Maggie!"

"I remembered," Margaret said.

The lights flickered and went out. From Margaret's pocket, a light signaled that her phone was ringing. There was plenty of light still from the high clerestory windows for her to see. It was only four p.m. She took out her phone and answered it. It was Agamemnon Dassis. All the guests were now seated at all the various restaurants and cafes up and down Main Street in downtown Mycenae, including, of course, at his Belle Helene, enjoying more of his Uncle George's wines and pizzas from Spiros's Elektra Palace, and all were wondering, especially himself and his wife, when she would join them. He could fetch her.

Then Allison took the phone ... "He's gone. And his little tribe with him. The rest of us all want to spend more time with you. Let Agamemnon come to get you."

Maggie said something about no more dissing and assured Allison she would be there momentarily. Her car was down there in the parking lot, waiting. She just had to put some last papers in her briefcase.

"GO!" she heard from her hand. "Get Thanassis!"

"Is someone there with you?" Allison said. "Good. Come on over. Everyone's waiting for you. Even that funny woman Eva from down the road who says ..." The phone was snatched mid-word from Allison.

"And me, too, okay?" It was Agamemnon's voice.

"GO! RUN!" came from her hand. She felt little Merope grab her tighter.

"Okay. Okay, Agamemnon. — Oh, it's you now, Allison. Please tell Agamemnon thank you. I'll be there in fifteen minutes."

"GO!" Merope held on to Maggie's finger. "GO!"

After she returned the phone to her pocket, even in this gloom, thanks to the line of high windows, she could see to turn left toward her office. The comfortable room down here had been her office and storage area for valuable discoveries. As she hurried, the outside light from the last window up there flickered shockingly as lightning flashed past and the rumbling outside grew more ominous. She had get to that gathering soon. But first she had to do as Merope told her. As she reached for her briefcase, she was glad she had shoved all the current documents into the box she had packed for Allison. And, besides, without her at Agamemnon's street wine-and-pizza party, they could all say what they wanted. Actually, she was sorry Andrew had left. She had been hoping he would stay and get it all off his chest. She put away the keys and took her things.

"GO, MAGGIE! NOW!"

Merope clutched Maggie's fingers with her tiny hands.

"Maggie!" Maggie heard clearly. "RUN! It will make no difference unless you run out of here NOW. We were cursed and forced to sing. And that called wrong clouds. Which caused floods. And that caused us to be buried and forgotten. So let's go to where we are. Before it's too late. AGAIN, RUN! NOW! Drop the purse and case. RUN! Up into those hills you will find me."

Maggie almost dropped Merope, but she was holding tight.

"Where?" Maggie's feet were moving toward the exit. Again the phone rang. It sounded comforting. It was quite dark and totally silent down here except for the disquieting lightning strikes and thunder rumbling out there. She didn't recognize the phone number.

"Hello, Margaret Benson," she said. There was only static. She disconnected.

"Move, Maggie!" Merope said. "To the hills up there. I'll show you once we get to your car. With Thanassis. And Menelaos."

Maggie was scared. Where was Thanassis? Menelaos? "Okay, Merope." She turned and put Merope into her pocket and from her other pocket her phone rang again. Oh, the guardhouse. "Oh, Thanassis? Yes! Now! Come quick. I'll meet you. We have to leave fast. You and Menelaos must come with me. Us."

He wanted to know if she was alright. There was a blackout caused by the thunderstorms. He was on his way up with flashlights to get her to her car and come with her.

Then the light on her phone went out. There was a crash in the next room. Maggie screamed.

"GO!" came from her pocket, and Maggie did rush, retreating up the hall, feeling the walls for guidance. She went swiftly up the steps, holding the rail and began counting the fifteen steps. She could see the glass front door thanks to daylight from outside. Suddenly she was soaring up the last five steps, elevated as though she had been picked up. Close in back, she heard a breath. And a growl. A pant. "GO!"

Without turning, she shoved open the front door. Thank God she had not locked it. — "Oh, I can't take you, Merope!"

"RUN," Merope's voice begged. "FAST! Your car."

Maggie turned. Into a man. And screamed. Oh, gods! That statue of Alan B. Wace, dripping rain. She stumbled past the statue.

"RUN!"

Suddenly there was a dark oppressiveness, a sort of hedge of trees making it so. She hastened down the path.

"RUN, MAGGIE, RUN!" Merope was grasping her pocket, leaning into the storm. "RUN!"

The ground shook, and in back of her, the front door of the museum shattered. She screamed and ran, now protectively clutching the girl, stumbling down the hill. Then all heaven broke loose. Rain fell in torrents, so hard it knocked her to the ground. "Help!" But her words were knocked from her by a blow to her chest when she fell. Maggie now knew Mother had been wrong all along. And it might be too late. The flow of water sent her spiraling and tumbling head over heels. Suddenly she was picked up. "Thanassis! Thank the gods!"

He held her tight. "Let's go!" he said as he held her up. Down and down the hill they raced, the rain and wind at their backs actually helping. "Wow!" shouted Thanassis. "This is serious business. Hang on to me, Doctor."

"Call me Maggie!" she managed a laugh before water washed out her mouth.

"Say it!" shouted Merope from her pocket. "Say it!"

She spat and grabbed Thanassis's hand tighter. "GOOD QUEENS, CLOUDS, BIRDS," she shouted.

And he shouted, too.

And the voice from her pocket shouted, too. "GOOD QUEENS, CLOUDS, BIRDS! AND WIND!"

And when the wind blew them past the Lion Gate, Margaret was sure she saw a woman in a red dress up top down there shaking her fist at them. Was that ancient Greek she was shouting? Then the wind swept them higher into the air, their feet doing little of the racing, the wind doing it for them.

"Did you see her, Thanassis? Could you understand her?" She hoped her words were not lost in the gale. Suddenly, up over the cherry tree they flew. "I think we're going to Oz!" she shouted.

"Ozymandias! We need him now! And his best friend, the Great King, Agamemnon." Thanassis was trying to stay sane as, in a reverse action, in a sudden tornado of rain and wind, into obscuring clouds they were flung up and back over the citadel. And there, yes, through that cloudy veil, he could definitely see her, that woman in red standing beneath them on the wall of a great palace, shaking her bloodied fist up at them, shouting:

"Let them and YOU rot in hell of oblivion for the rest of existence."

"GOOD QUEENS, CLOUDS, BIRDS! AND WIND!" loudly countermanded from Maggie's pocket. "And close your eyes!"

Thanassis could also see that the suddenly arriving, obscuring clouds and gaggle of birds which were swarming, confused the angry, red woman. Suddenly, beneath her feet, with a great rumbling, the palace walls flew about and into the air, furniture catapulting into the vortex. And all crumbled down the hillside into the ravine.

Mother had definitely been wrong. This was not her imagination "Call!", shouted Margaret, closing her eyes. "GOOD QUEENS, CLOUDS, BIRDS!" And together, all three voices shouted in their version of Greek the mantra: "GOOD QUEENS, CLOUDS, BIRDS!"

"AND WIND!" shouted Merope.

"AND WIND!" the others joined her.

Behind them and under them, boulders and tons of dressed Cyclopean stones were equally uprooted like daisies by torrential flows that tumbled under them as easily as shells at the sea. The guardhouse went past, floating on a river of hillsides and monuments. Margaret did try to reach out for the door, but there was no longer any door. Nor was there any guard inside.

"Menelaos!" Thanassis shouted.

"Menelaos!" she called. But her eyes were flooded, and that empty guardhouse, filled with Mycenae soil, was the last thing she discerned before she was sent flying, still holding tight to Thanassis, spitting out debris, windborne, up over the whole of the Bronze Age site, past the sally port and up over the Chavros Gorge. But though she no longer felt much, she did feel another hand grab her other arm. And as she held Merope tightly in her pocket, she and Thanassis, with this new companion, were tossed higher into the air by a flood of raging water borne by winds. It almost seemed as if this new companion was picking them both up, and then, with Maggie's new lightning scarf wrapped around them, she and Thanassis were flying. She heard the sound of multiple wings. "Yippee!", she shouted.

"Yippee! Here we go!" Thanassis shouted, too.

They soared. And her lightning shawl unfurled like a parachute, sending them floating higher, something holding it open over them, she could not see what. Or who.

"Yippee!" came the smaller voice from her pocket.

"She really does talk," Thanassis shouted. "Yippee, Merope!"

~~~~

A mile downhill in the village of Mycenae, though those rumbles and lightning strikes continued like the backdrop in an ominous film, not a drop of rain fell nor did wind blow to mar the jolly gathering. The party continued with lots of table-hopping. Aromatic pizzas flowed endlessly from Spiros's wood-fired ovens to accompany the lovely wines from George Dassis's vineyards, complements of the Belle Helene.

Kati-Selene put down her glass and stood up.

"Where are you going, sweetheart?" Agamemnon was relaxed and enjoying this evening that they were offering to honor their dear, longtime friend Margaret Benson.

"I'm just going up there to hurry her." Kati-Selene gave him a kiss.

She got into her little car and turned uphill toward the citadel's parking lot. Before she reached the first tholos tomb of Atreus, she stopped and turned on her bright lights. Further up, toward the guardhouse, she could see a torrent like a moving mountain about to turn downhill. Horn blaring, she turned and retreated back, racing to the Belle Helene.

CHAPTER 13

FADE IN: *Who Is in Charge Tonight?*

SETTING:
Place: On the road to Pylos, Greece
Date: 1 to 2 June, 1214 B.C.
Broadcast to: Margaret Benson, unknown location, Mycenae
Date: 1 to 2 June, 2021 A.D.
Time: night into dawn

"SINCE THE TIME of the greatest king, King Atreus," Selene continued, "Mycenae was famous for its highways. And its routing signs. Because of my grandfather and father, I knew where I now had to go, what to look for. There with confidence I went at all my youthful speed and more-mature knowledge of who was counting on me, how many good people. So with a curse at my back urging me faster, hours before dawn, the village dust had flown from my shoes, and I was past skirted Tiryns, Argos far away to my side. They were now both in league with our new-again king, as was Sparta's returned-again King Tyndareus. Into my best stride, I could feel the positive wind of all the khorus of eyes on my back counting on me. I turned west and north, settling into this pace. I slowed. There was a freshwater pond around that bend with a roadside pavilion. My lightning-striped knitted dress was dragging at me.

So, after I refreshed with a drink and a shower, I tied it around my body. Though daylight was hours off, I had another eight hours-plus of running in front of me. Too many of my family and friends depended on me getting help. I looked back. The horrendous trembling under the earth was still competing with shocking displays of fireworks flashing down from the sky above Mycenae. Fantastical geological and meteorological phenomena, leaping up into a fiery cleaving within the pulsing mammatocumulos layer of clouds above those hills where the girls were, compelled and propelled me faster. Perhaps I would find a solar car at the next station.

"But I was gangly since birth like a colt and had always been a runner. My training for the Khorus was long-distance running to stretch my limbs, strengthen my diaphragm and give me a sense of freedom.

"I took to the roads by nature. And by birth. My father, Demetrios, and his father, Photos before, were our road engineers. My grandfather Photos had come from Krete in 1257 B.C. when a young man. And his engineering skills were soon brought to the attention of the Great King of Sparta, Tyndareus. Within a few years, Grandfather had been promoted to Chief Roads Engineer. Between King Tyndareus and the High King of Mycenae, Atreus, there was brotherly friendship forged to improve all their economies. So Grandfather Photos soon was traveling between Sparta and Mycenae weekly, drawing up plans and maps of where the highways should travel, where bridges should be built, securing, hiring and training local engineers, sourcing materials, and at the same time, hiring teams from both city-states. He was frequently at both palaces, that of Atreus and, naturally, that of Tyndareus.

"Suddenly, in 1255, King Atreus was murdered by his vengeful brother and his eleven-year-old son, Aegisthos.

"The young sons of murdered Atreus, Agamemnon and Menelaus fled and sought refuge with Sparta's King Tyndareus, where they were welcomed and treated like sons. Within three years, the two boys had grown into strong, warlike men, and with Tyndareus's support, they drove out the usurpers, the throne of Mycenae returning to Atreus's older son, Agamemnon, who by 1250, with my grandfather's engineering skills, built the signifying and defensive Lion Gate to announce who was in control.

"Then Tyndareus offered his daughter, Clytemnestra, in marriage to the now twenty-year-old Lion King Agamemnon, and thus the two city-states, Sparta and Mycenae, were even more firmly united.

"When younger Menelaus married Tyndareus's other daughter, Helen, the families' bond was cemented.

"From my family's more-immediate point of view, in 1250 B.C., Grandfather Photos's workload intensified as connecting roads were now built throughout the Peleponnesos to unify all points for economic and security purposes. Among the roads to the other Great Kings' cities, the first major ones were to King Nestor in Pylos in the west, near that sea of Io. From King Nestor's Citadel-Palace, locally-engineered roads already led to his natural harbors and seaport, connecting to the great arsenals with adjourning skyports that furnished Nestor the ships for sea and sky needed for his far-flung economies. But now these roads were put to ever more strenuous use, moving goods and troops and entrepreneurs between all the interconnected cities and the harbors. Towns sprung up along these broad freeways; entrances and exits and road markers had to be engineered and executed. For Grandfather Photos, there was constant upkeep and widening required to maintain his innovative improvements. One day while in Pylos, Grandfather, at a working lunch at Nestor's palace, met a young woman artist, Aliana, who was decorating with frescoes the palace walls. And as she said, they fell in love at first sight. After marriage, he moved in with his bride's family in Pylos, as was the custom in her Elian family, and together they travelled for the businesses they both loved: He to ally all the allies with a connective system of ever-greater improved freeways; Aliana to unite the allied palaces and princely households with evocative frescoes depicting the ancient heritages of the individual kings, including portraits of their uniting interconnected ancestors.

"As well, Aliana began to re-engineer an old idea to further unite the kingdom communities. Her mother, Thalia, had suggested a simple idea to further bond and unite, through passing on our ancient songs, not just of their three families (Thalia's husband's from Elis, Aliana's husband

Photos's from Krete, and now her own here in Pylos) but as well all the families within each kingdom. This was seconded by the Great King of Pylos, Nestor, who remembered the stories told of the powers of such a group in Krete. So Aliana began, during her travels, within each community what she called a khorus, a group of young khorai, or girls. Soon groups of khorus girls singing their families' songs evolved, at Nestor's further suggestion and seconded by his cousin, King of Elis, into groups to perform each year in a different city-state to further unify the Pelopid Kingdoms, first being cemented by roads and now by annual singing gatherings. Such gatherings that would 'Call upon all the gods from on high Olympus to hear,' Aliana said. 'A soaring singing to reach the highest peak,' King Nestor pronounced. Nestor's queen, Eurydice, said she would be on the steering committee and a participant as well. Tyndareus of Sparta, Grandfather Photos's first political allegiance, immediately gave his blessing and support. The Khorus Girls alliance had thus begun.

"Later, the expansion and success of the Khoruses put even more demands for widening and increasing of roads to carry in vans the large groups and their fancy dress throughout the kingdoms of the Peloponnesos. These gatherings caused the economy to boom in towns, all of which kept my engineering family very busy. Aliana and Photos's son, my father, Demetrios, keeping up the family engineering business and the now-established family protocol, he, when in his early twenties married a girl from Mycenae and moved in with his bride Cynthia's family. Later, in 1225, when The Great King, Agamemnon, flew off for the Peace Convocation in Troy, Father, in Mycenae, was elevated to Chief Engineer, keeping the roads transport-ready to all the ports north and south, east and west. And his bride, Cynthia, expanded the old idea of joining all the khoruses of the Peloponnesos with those of all the kingdoms in the economic and social Alliance. Soon, these girls and women were working and singing together and keeping their economies strong. My mother, Cynthia, in her travels to visit her new family in Pylos, noted how the songs of those khorus girls attracted the birds; then how the birds and the girls dancing and singing together attracted the clouds.

And Cynthia and Grandmother Aliana got other ideas of how to use this phenomenon.

"My thoughts were abruptly ended by a series of lightning bolts behind me, splitting the sky and searing the ground, shaking the earth like an earthquake. I paused my race and turned to a new, now fiery display and knew such horrors foretold a monumental disaster from where I had come. The evil of Clytemnestra throbbed in some dark places in my soul as did the words of my sister weigh on my shoulders and conscience. 'I will return, Merope,' I called aloud to the air from where I had come. 'I WILL!' Tears blinded me. Then, forth from a sudden opening in the red clouds, from the sky came the roar of a lion, that King of beasts, symbol of our great King, Agamemnon. And my heart truly broke, and I knelt and cried because heaven's announcement was surely of the death of our Lion King. 'Oh, Merope, I will return for you. I should never have left you.'"

"I had paused too long, burdened by grief. And after a drink, I took up my quest with renewed purpose. And with swifter steps I took the elevated roads. Memories of how it all began propelled me on this faster but more-even keel, keen to get to Grandmother's aid. And as I returned to my thoughts, I knew my choice of roads had been guided.

"Because of the confederation conference in Troy, and Spartan King Menelaus' prime involvement therein, Tyndareus had been forced to return to being Sparta's ruler and was, by now, in 1214, no doubt longing for the return of his adopted-son/his son-in-law, King Menelaus. I myself at this moment did not feel I would be welcomed in Sparta because surely word would have reached Tyndareus about this night's murder of the returned Trojan war hero, the Great Agamemnon, by his other daughter and the unwanted usurper, Aegisthos. No matter how much enmity he felt about the snake Aegisthos, Clytemnestra was his daughter. And my instincts told me that my trip would be seen as fleeing to King Nestor for aid against Tyndareus and his daughter. I would be detained and perhaps suffer a worse fate than if I had remained in Mycenae. So I stayed well above Sparta and continued the familiar roads toward Tegea, back roads my mother often drove when traffic out of or into Mycenae was backed up. Once when I was with her on such a jaunt, she raised her head and sang and sang to the skies and told me about times when she and her sister had been Bird-Swingers as well as Khorus Catchers. Today, the two of them were the Khorus Votaresses, 'as,' she had remarked, 'you and Merope will follow to also one day be.' Oh, if only.

"My father's grandmother, Grandfather Photo's mother, Myrtilis, from Krete, had been a handmaid to the little Queen, the Potnia Theron in Knossos. And from her came stories of how the two of them led the Bird Swinger Knossos Khorus. From that Kretan great-grandmother, the famous Myrtilis, it was said I had received a double shot of talent for the leaping and the singing.

"'Wrong,' my mother, Cynthia had interrupted one day at Grandfather's telling us this story. — (he and grandmother were visiting). 'Wrong. A quadruple shot'." Well, today, I sure needed it.

"My muscles were stretching more than ever and my stamina was being called upon as never before. But when I turned to look back, that streaming sea of red breasts of clouds, pulsing and flashing with lighting, let me know that soon torrents of rain would pummel the fire-devastated land of The Lion King and our families. My speed increased. And I prayed the girls were safe in those snug caves. Their supplies could last only another three days, at best. Their Votaress, the lovely Cynthia, was there to calm and bolster their spirits. And at home below in Mycenae city, home with a new baby, our longed-for baby brother, was his nurse and perhaps my father. I looked up and took another right turn up. And saw by the markers that I had still a way to go. I went down to another pavilion for water and a stretch, and then went faster.

"All these roads were my Pylian grandfather's and my Mycenaean father's roads: our wine roads, our perfume roads, our olive oil roads. Our great, wide freeways, enlarged and smoothed constantly for our departing caravan cars with goods to export and those with imports arriving, then for workers' cars and for our vans of diplomacy, and for our beautiful cars-of-state and our pleasure cars, in which Mycenae's ladies paraded their finery, visiting local friends and, naturally, shops, in Tiryns, Argos, Prosymna as well, gallivanting off to cousins and boutiques in Sparta and, certainly, to meet up with Queen Eurydice and her ladies in Pylos for an afternoon glass of her famous wines after purchasing her newest scents. Through my Mycenaean mother Cynthia's forays to and visits from her mother-in-law, Aliana from Pylos, my father heard of the long lines of vehicles of elegant ladies returning home, waiting on the road for convoys of commercial vehicles to clear. So father engineered raised roads over the commercial ones, exclusively for passenger vehicles.

"Thus, I got to know, since a baby, the imported spices and varied economic specialties of our joined kingdoms, all thanks to our dual system of roads. Since I was three of four, I began mapping out and running in back of Mother's and other ladies' parading cars on the raised roads and then took longer runs below behind father's engineers' solar carts, which were taking the workers to their repair jobs of the day. Then I began running in front of the carts. Soon, I was reading off the distance markers as I sped to wherever that day. One night at dinner, my father announced I would run some twenty-nine miles that day and added an extra portion of fried chicken to my plate, my all-time favorite dish from my Grandmother Aliana. That was the night Grandmother and Grandfather Photo were visiting. Grandfather looked up from his soup when my mother announced I had received a 'quadruple shot.'

"By then Grandfather Photos was unable to enjoy fried chicken, his wife's specialty, although, when no one was looking but me, he would spear the pieces she had shredded for his enjoyment. That night, he looked up from his soup and with a deep breath, pronounced: 'The girl is ready for the birds,' he puffed out after a large swallow of his wine.

"Everyone stopped, put down spoons, knives and glasses and listened in stunned silence. Grandfather had never pronounced, I later learned, on any aspect of the khoruses.

"'I've seen the best at Knossos and at Mallia,' he pronounced tonight. 'She's finer than my mother's sister, the famous bird swinger.' He looked at me and lowered his voice. 'Your great-great-aunt Sidonia.' He took another sip of his wine. My grandmother added more water to his glass. He continued to the rest of the room, 'Selene has a poise when leaping better than your Grandmother Aliana's mother, Thalia.' He looked at me and then at my grandmother, who now swallowed her astonishment to offer a large smile while patting his arm.

"'Grandfather, you descend from famous khorus girls,' my sister, Merope, solemnly spoke to him.

"'Yes, and you and your sister are and will be even more famous.'"

~~~~

"I ran faster. And as I remembered, I prayed and called to the Universe, up to the hills I was running among, 'Let it be!'"

"And as I prayed then my spirit seemed transported to you today, Margaret, to warn you of what you must join me in doing to save the Khorus Girls and to save yourself ..."

"Oh — let it be!"

~~~~

"Outside the palace, beyond the Lion Gate, the queen, still clad in dripping crimson, looked up and watched her other wish, her curse, begin. Clytemnestra smiled and, up where the cursed Khorus Girls were, the flaming mountain violently shook and rumbled and, at her gesture, the smoking hills rose and boulders and huge stones from the very top popped up and slid down one upon the other. And with another gesture, she brought forth rains from the pulsing scarlet and purple clouds. The downpour, *her downpour.* "At last!" And she conducted her rain to rain and rain and rain more. And with her downbeat, she knew for certain that no one would ever find them. No one would ever hear them again or learn who they were. But she, the great queen, would long be remembered. Forever remembered. As the real, the only, as the great Clytemnestra, as the great queen-votaress of the Khorus Girls. And she began to sing. And at her shrieks, the mountain answered and shook and rumbled and exploded and tumbled, and the rains fell and fell and the downpouring from above began to fulfill her curse.

"Then her inner eye spied a usurper, a something or other from another realm, flying high in the sky, calling, 'GOOD QUEENS,

CLOUDS, BIRDS, WINDS.' And with another shriek, Clytemnestra, flinging scarlet, destroyed that usurper while, with a wave of her arm, lightning flashed and crashed the usurper in two."

CHAPTER 14

FADE IN: *End of Day Two*

SETTING:
> Place: Mycenae Village
> Date: 2 June, <u>2021 A.D.</u>
> Time: early evening into night
>
> And ...
>
> Place: Western Hills of Vineyards above Mycenae Village
> Date: 2 June, <u>2021 A.D.</u>
> Time: early evening into night

THE WAXING MOON was rising. Allison, standing at the crossroads leading up to the devastation, gazed up at such delicate beauty in the sky and felt overwhelming dismay at what it shone down upon.

From dusk on the 1st of June, the village of Mycenae had been quickly and totally shut down, its populace removed swiftly to nearby houses of relatives and friends, though none of the flooding and landslides had actually reached the town. But all services, like electricity and gas, had been temporarily shut off as a precautionary measure. That mountain of water and cyclopean boulders had stopped as at an invisible barrier, right at the point opposite the tholos tomb called Treasury of Atreus, where Kati-Selene had stopped her car and retreated. Now, all the way up from there was a new mountain, a twenty-foot wall that angled forty degrees all the way up. The parking lot was no longer visible. The no parking lot. Somewhere, likewise, up east from there and under all that was the no fence, the no guardhouse, the no museum. No citadel.

"This must be as it was before any of us archaeologists arrived, as it was long before and until Schliemann," Allison said to herself as she stood there, looking at the barrier. And the tranquil moon rose higher. The Lions were no longer visible. It was as though that mountain in back had just swallowed it all. Somewhere under the new mountain were all those no longer visibles, the no longer tangibles: citadel palace, grave circle, cistern and posterns, Lion Gate. And lower down, the houses of Bronze Age Mycenae. And somewhere under it all were at least three guards. And Margaret Benson.

It was now almost twenty-four hours since the terror had begun, and Allison knew she had a mountain of work tomorrow, and tomorrow, and tomorrow, and far ahead of her.

It had been earlier this afternoon of this, the second day, as she was setting up the field office here at the crossroads from the village up to the site, when Kati-Selene and Agamemnon Dassis had walked over and invited her to go with and stay with them as a member of their family at his Uncle George's, as Margaret would have done if… no, when. But Allison had declined and was now standing here, wondering what to do next. She had to stay here at her post close to the site. Soon, early tomorrow, she knew, the rescue efforts would begin. She was needed here. Mycenae was now her responsibility.

She felt something wet and cold on her hand.

"Oh, Old Dog." She rubbed his ears. "Hungry, Old Dog? Of course, you are." So, with Old Dog at her heels, Allison walked back to the porch of the Hotel Belle Helene to find dinner for Old Dog.

Before they left in the late afternoon for his relatives in those westerly hills above, Agamemnon spoke confidently about how they would find Margaret, who was "so practical and resourceful. They will find her. In fact, she may have gotten out and will find us," he had added as he turned his face to brush away his tears. Then Agamemnon and

Kati-Selene gave Allison and Federica warm hugs, reluctant to leave them. Allison followed them back to the hotel and they showed her the keys and gave her instructions about rooms and cots and showed her the sheets for those who would be coming in for the rescue. In effect, the Dassis family offered the Belle Helene as a staging place for those who were needed to begin and carry out the rescue of Margaret and Bronze Age Mycenae.

~~~~

Up in those westerly hills, about the same time as Allison was dishing up Old Dog's dinner, Kati-Selene helped Agamemnon's aunt serve a most aromatic dinner. Having unexpected visitors seemed like a treat for Aunt Philia. Her avgolemono was soothing and truly delicious. And when Uncle George opened a bottle of his best Mavrofilero, Kati breathed in, took a sip and breathed out.

"Oh yes, the wine whose flowers smell like violets," she said. She took another sip.

"What did I tell you, Agamemnon?" Uncle George gave a rare smile as he poured more wine. "She is a natural! You've got to let her come to work with us here at the winery."

"With your lamb and okra, Aunt, Uncle, this wine is perfection." Agamemnon had a healthy appetite.

"You have had quite a fright. Both of you." Aunt Philia served Kati-Selene more of the spring lamb. "Especially, I am happy to have you here, my — our — new niece."

Though no doubt everyone enjoyed dinner, conversation had become stilted. Kati-Selene took another taste and savored the wine with the lamb. Yes, last night had been very frightening. She had stood out on the terrace all night, every moment expecting that wall of boulders and debris to swallow the town. But she couldn't say those thoughts. Was she becoming part of some conspiracy? Those terrifying rumbles had continued relentlessly. No one in the town, she was sure, had slept. No one got into beds. Except for Agamemnon. All the Belle Helene guests, except Dr. Allison and her chief assistant, had fled as fast as they could. For their part, Allison said, she and Federica had responsibilities; they had to remain to rescue. And as Kati-Selene had watched all night from the terrace, though Federica slept fitfully on a cot on the terrace in back of her, Allison had come to stand, take her hand and keep watch.

Now Kati-Selene sighed and took another taste of that violet-scented wine. "Yes," she thought, "Rescue. *Diasosi,*" she murmured.

Aunt Philia looked up.

"Tell me, Aunt." She liked her new aunt, uncle and grandfather, and felt they had welcomed her as warmly as their dear nephew Agamemnon. "Can you tell me, please, why everyone, including Aga here, pretends that those terrible rumbles that the mountains make, as they did all day yesterday, are nothing?"

Aga put down his fork. "I told you. Because they are nothing. End of that, Kati-Selene!"

"But Aga, that's not true. They were something. Something terrible. Why, Papa, does everyone in Mycenae pretend they signify nothing? Likely, our dear — your dear — Dr. Margaret and three of your own darling boys are lost, maybe even buried out there right now."

"Papa", Agamemnon's grandfather, had finished his dinner and sat before the fireplace, working with the vine cuttings, creating stakes for the new growth. He put down his glass, took out a pipe and did not seem as though he had heard her.

Her new aunt started clearing the dishes. Kati-Selene turned her attention to helping.

Later, when her aunt and uncle were also working on the staves for the vineyards and Agamemnon was reading the newspapers in the study, Kati-Selene went out into the garden. The vineyards surrounded the back of the house. Closest must be the *mavrofilero*. In the evening the aroma of violets was less powerful but more seductive as the new flowers closed. It was quiet and peaceful. In the sky, thanks to the waxing moon, she could see that one constellation so bright. The deluge had cleared heaven. Kati-Selene's special friends up there, the seven sisters she had always wanted, winked. The Pleaides sparkled like blue diamonds, west of Orion and his dog. She clicked off their names. She had imagined them as her sisters since she was little and had watched them, lying in the grass on warm nights in her family's garden.

"You, Sterope and Elektra, blinking like you're about to shower the earth with more stars for dreaming. And Maia. And you up there, Merope, you look about to run over the hill and jump down to join me here. Come on, little sister, come!" She was sure she could see eleven sisters, though she had been told there were seven. When she turned her gaze down valley, she could see down to Mycenae.

"I've been waiting to jump down to you, big sister Selene."

Clearly, she heard this reply from the sky. Kati-Selene stared back up at that one pulsing star in the Pleiades.

"Agamemnon tells you it is nothing ..."

She whipped around.

Papa was standing on the porch. He continued as he came down to join her ... "Because he is afraid to name it. We all are. We all have been afraid to mention it, I do believe, since Mycenae the Great was destroyed, all those hundreds of years ago. Thousands now." He sat on the bench in the starry night. "Look at it." He waved his match down toward the darkness of the ancient, ruined city, "When that day happened so long ago, it must have been terrifying. All those people in there. From here, yesterday, we could see it. And we could hear it. Even after it grew dark. Thank the gods Agamemnon answered his phone. We were terrified for you. We are all worried about our great-nephew, Thanassis. And now we fear, too, for his cousin, Menelaos-Stavros. My sister and her daughter over that way are inconsolable over the other possibility that Phaestos was with them as well. Three of the brightest boys ever. All the way up here, we, little Kati-Selene, could hear that terrible sound for the last two days. It still has not stopped. But thank the gods there are no longer other citizens in there. Just the horrors of the past."

"Not quite, Papa." Kati-Selene said as she sat next to him. He took her hand. "There was also, for sure, a good friend of your family in there. We do not know if she got out. Dr. Margaret Benson, I mean. I had been at her lunch just before with Agamemnon. And the noise from up there at the citadel was horrific. I could not believe all of those smart, educated people stayed and enjoyed themselves and no one said anything about it. Truly, I was relieved when we left."

"You were the one to give the warning? You were the one to see it?"

"Yes, Papa. A more-terrifying sight I hope never to see again. A mountain coming toward me. A moving mountain. Oh, Papa, where is Dr. Margaret? Where is cousin Thanassis?"

"Our other wonderful boys, too. Oh, little one," he sighed, "Thanassis's mother is not sure if he was at the citadel or if he was in school in Khora. She has not been able to reach him. Tomorrow she will go down and inquire. And the parents of Phaestos, they share not only our blood but our vineyards, too, you know. He had come to help with the vines and the Rogation. And Thanassis was taking his place. But suddenly, Phaestos announced he had to return to help at the guard house in case Thanassis had classes to attend despite the holidays. So, his parents are down in town now at your Belle Helene, staying, I think, with Dr. Margaret's assistant. But what can they do? They have no phone connection to him. And the schools are closed because of all this."

"They need to be close, Papa. It's their …"

"Come in, Kati-Selene. Time you get some sleep." Agamemnon still sounded gruff. He turned and went back inside.

"He's just frightened, that's all. And he does not know how to tell you that that sound we all pretend to ignore really frightens him, too." He smoked his pipe. "You know, I have worked a long time, all my life, almost, to cultivate this particular, aromatic clone of that *Mavrofilero* grape. It is a very old grape, very special and highly mutational. So, I must be on guard to keep it the way it is."

"The aroma of violets, Papa, is most entrancing." They both became quite still and inhaled the soft evening air. "Have there been vineyards here a long time?"

"*Enthousiasmos.* Yes. Strange you should ask. Only yesterday I was thinking how entrancing the aroma from those grapes is." He got up and walked toward the vineyards. She followed him. "You know, we Dassis have owned these vineyards for now ten generations. That's a long time. Some almost 400 years, I think." His smoke wreathed around, joining them. "I have felt, almost since I became in charge here, that sometimes when I walk these rows, I am walking with many others," the vines waved in the breeze of their passing, tendrils twining about them, "walking with those long-past grandfathers and ancestors. And even before the Dassis were here, I think, yes, yes, there were other vineyardists loving these fields, loving their vines. Just now when I spoke of that cataclysm that ended the Great Mycenae around 1200 B.C., I had a fleeting thought of the people who saw it from here, from right here, from their homes nestled in their vineyards. Way back then. The vine is long. The vine is Dionysos, and he is a very old god. And I do feel, as I put my feet into these vineyards, that far below us, there are vines from the past. And vineyardists walking the rows. What do you think? Do you think we could get some of those archaeologists from down at the citadel up here to excavate?"

"I think you have another good idea, Papa. Vineyards from ancient times from which were made the wines served at the Great Mycenae. Maybe Dr. Margaret and her assistants will find them. And you could resuscitate them."

"Yes, little Kat-Selene," he said, using Agamemnon's familiar name for her. He turned and led them back to the house. "I would be very happy to have a girl work with me in these vineyards, the next generation to pass our vines to. You, I hope. Well, we shall see." He knocked the ash from his pipe. "I mean it, Kati. You have a great instinct for the vines." He stood next to her, the light from the kitchen shining on her, turning her hair to gold. "One day when Agamemnon is in the right mood, I will bring it up again." He turned and went inside, leaving Kati-Selene as she had been, looking at the stars.

"Merope?" She looked up and saw her star she called Merope winking blue lights. "Merope, did you really say that? Are you coming? Come to help us, Merope?"

"I am coming again, little Kati-Selene. We are sisters. And we will be united when you least expect. I will come singing the cloud-calling songs to end the rumbling and open the doors to catch good dreams."

~~~~

At about the same time as Allison staggered and fell into her cot on the terrace of Hotel Belle Helene down in Mycenae, Kati-Selene fell into the welcoming arms of Agamemnon in the best guest room at Aunt and Uncle's home in the vineyards above.

CHAPTER 15

FADE IN: *Curses at My Back*

SETTING:
      Place: Solar Cars Speed Things
      Date: 2 June, <u>1214 B.C.</u>
Broadcast coming through to:
      Date: 2 June, <u>2021 A.D.</u>
      Time: noon to early night

"GRANDFATHER'S BRIGHT EYES receded from my memory," Selene looked up from her thoughts and slowed her pace. All these family stories, memories and plotting had carried her without a thought to how far she had run. But when she sighted the next sign post, she was already close to Tegea. "In Tegea, I found a carter who knew me. He had long worked the highways for my grandfather; his son now worked for my father. He was most willing to drive me in his old-fashioned vehicle the rest of the way. Together we could see the conflagrations and knew the situation for Mycenae and all nearby was grave.

"'Hurry, please,' I prayed aloud as I pointed back up at the pulsing, fiery red ceiling of bumper-to-bumper cloud breasts. 'Look! Those flaming clouds!'

"'Those are nothing bad,' the carter assured me as he settled me into a comfortable spot with a cushion. 'They will put out those fires. Nothing bad. Maybe nothing good. Maybe nothing at all. Nothing but rumbling. Nothing.'

"'Yes, something.' I could not take my eyes from seeing how they were more swiftly running in, crowding in from the southeast. 'Something very dangerous. The red flashing up there are rivers of clouds on fire in the sky, come on hot winds from Egypt. And those sky rivers will bring flooding torrents. We Khorus Girls were forced by the queen to call them. And they came. They came for the wrong reasons. For her evil reasons. And what they bring will destroy Mycenae and Tiryns, perhaps Argos, and who knows? Even here? We must please hurry to Pylos and then return to rescue them all.'

"'You Khorus Girls called? Well, giddyap! — You could be right.' His wife, daughter and granddaughter were in the khorus. 'I've only seen such once, when I was a child up north. And the torrents and earthquake migrated us here.' He pushed for faster speed. 'Ended the harvests; the vineyards never produced that year. But we had departed. My father knew better than to stay.'

"But now his granddaughter's family was over there near Argos. We crossed the bridge over a small stream, changed vehicles and, after skirting the triple mountains that announced Megalopoli, picked up a solar car from his cousin. The aura had changed and Pylos would not be much farther. Those vines surrounding the great palace city, these vines I could smell, were safe; they were in full flower with aromas of violets and of pears, and these fields were green. Vineyardists were at work in the fields and waved as we flashed by their several vineyards, all advertising wine tastings.

"Then we slipped between the university area and its numerous, high classroom and research buildings and libraries, and we drove down into Khora. All the while, our warning sirens wailed and the driver shouted, 'Out of the way! Khorus Girl from Mycenae!' Students dodged the madman as he raced us through town and out, using the lower, normally swifter Trade Road. But then our passage was halted as large vans filled with amphorae of wines going to the harbor for export moved slowly over to the side. Finally freed, waving thanks, he drove us down and toward the citadel palace of Nestor.

"Perhaps it is more through shared adversities, through shared understandings of personal losses and disasters than through great successes, that true friendships are forged, annealed and bonded lifelong and true. King Nestor told me once that it was only through the horrors and sufferings he witnessed at Troy that he began to really understand the importance of Woman, of his own dear Eurydice. Later, my daughter, Nepthaulia, would know this story even more intimately from Nestor's son, Peisistratos. But for now, all that was hidden by the veils of time in space.

"My mother, the beautiful and happy Cynthia, had told me the whole history of the Khorus Girls ever since I could remember, as told to her by her mother, Aglaia, and her grandmother, Echo, who had the gift of singing into the hills and hearing her voice repeated.

"'The khoruses form a perpetual chain from one generation into another,' she said, 'and so will continue to develop and exist as long as there are girls like you and Merope and, one day, your own girls. Your Grandfather Photo and I were both right and wrong: counting Aglaia and Echo, did you get a quadruple shot.' She always said those words as she finished the oft-repeated Khorus story. I would never see my mother or hear her tell that story again. But that was also mercifully hidden to me. 'The Khorus Girls really truly began here on the mainland under enlightened rulers, Kings Atreus, Nelius and his son, today's King Nestor, and Eleius of Elis,' she told me, 'and their four queens'. But in the long run, I would learn that the idea and long development of the khoruses did come from Krete, as my father's mother, Grandmother Aliana, always said. And the sustained belief that the graces given by the khoruses to aid ordinary citizens as well as knights and kings in times of need would return to end in Krete. That, too, was hidden from me and would only come much later at the end. Today, the lovely Cynthia was in those smoky hills with all the girls, safely, I prayed, in those caves.

"'Merope,' I sang inwardly. 'Merope, I am coming!'

"I held tight to the door, anxious as the carter pushed his vehicle, powered by the sun, even faster. The sun was getting closer to the western horizon.

"'Cloud Khorus Girl from Mycenae,' the driver continued to call, tooting his horn. It looked like everyone in the town was out on the roads. When the face of this carter, well-known in Pylos, raced down the hill from Khora, many were the runners following and shouting questions. On either side were makeshift tents and people bearing bundles of clothing and baskets of foods and drinks. This did not seem to be the normal celebration of the spring flowering of the vines. Besides, it was not yet time.

"'What?' I asked. But the noise of the populous shouting questions drowned my query to the carter.

"Thus, we arrived at the busy Pylos center just downhill from the palace citadel. There hundreds were unloading bundles from carts and cars were gathered there, too. Tents were set along both sides for receiving and packing goods, and streetside storefronts were also commandeered for receiving and packing. From among the crowd of curious soldiers and men and women jostling for a view, suddenly there was a parting, allowing one man to ford the stream. Arms that still bore the scars of his unfortunate years in Troy opened wide and enveloped me in warmth and the aroma of roses.

"'Welcome, little Selene, daughter of Cynthia, granddaughter of Aliana,' he said. 'We are glad you made it through. We've heard the news since last night. And could see from this high vantage to the northeast," he pointed into the sky, "the sky-high devastating fires that were most suddenly overshadowed by a humongous gathering of dark-red clouds spiked with sky god's bolts. Visible all this distance. Since dawn from them a strange deluge of fire and water has poured. Come here. Look.' And he held me up higher. And I could see the black curtain shot through with red, signifying strange, torrential rain. 'Better view from my balcony up there. Where …?'

"Mid-question, he stopped and turned around. A small hand had reached up to tap him on the shoulder. Behind the great king, I saw

Queen Eurydice. She stepped forward and gave me another warm, rose-scented embrace.

"'We will rescue them. Do not worry, child.' Then, in a breath of rose, she moved aside, giving place to that small hand's owner, a figure with big eyes and a bigger smile.

"'Oh, darling Selene. How you've grown.' Grandmother Aliana spoke softly in the same accent as my father. Soft her voice was, but it projected, as did the voices of all Khorus Girls.

"'Oh, Grandmother! Grandmother!' Tears ran down my face. I could not stop them. 'I've come all this way to get your help.' I knelt to look directly into her eyes. 'All the Khorus Girls in Mycenae are in great danger, hiding in the hills across from those where the fires began. Mother and Merope ...'

"'Your mother? No, she's at home with the baby.'

"'No, Grandmother. She came up to us in the hills at the command of the evil queen. She and Merope and cousin Althea are there now up in the caves with all the khorus girls and women, sharing little food. After the smoke from the fires, they will be overwhelmed by torrents of rain. Please, help me get help to rescue them. Please, Grandmother, please.'

"'Should I tell her about the terrible curse?' I wondered. The king had overheard. And understood. He took my hand.

"'Your father is on the way to locate your mother,' he interjected. 'He was working with his teams and heard you were headed this way. At word of further disasters in your wake, Queen Eurydice and I have sent and are putting together, as you see, these and more rescue operations from all our towns. All this day, many have left and must be close by now.'

"Then he waved forward my saving carter to meet with his chief men. Altogether with them the king consulted. And at his clap on the back, each one ran to join the rescue teams. The queen, front and center, was also moving in every direction, organizing, talking, calling and gathering and sending off a train of carts back from where I had come, along with faster cars and larger vans loaded with blankets and provisions already gathered and packed. With the king's escort they would travel the Kings's Highways and get there faster.

"To the queen I ran and explained how the Khorus Girls had been forced to sing in those fiery and rumbling back hills and about my mother being called and how the new baby was with the nurse in town.

"'Father will not find mother at home,' I said. 'Only baby with nurse. He'll be frantic. We must, I must, get word. I must go back. I promised Merope I would be back with help. And then there is that terrible …'

"My grandmother, with a soothing hug, interrupted me, and she stepped with me into the middle of the road.

"'Join me,' she said. She raised her face and began to sing to the skies, singing for clouds, birds and winds to lift the Khorus Girls, to save those they loved. 'May the rescuers arrive in time.' As my little grandmother sang, the queen herself and all the rest joined her and sang. The town of Pylos sang for the rescue of the Khorus Girls and the populous of Mycenae.

"The queen offered her hand and I clasped it tight as the verse ended. I looked into her beautiful eyes.

"'I'm going, dear queen," I said. "I must get word to Father, and I, only I, can lead the rescuers to where the Khorus Girls …to where I left them. I promised …'

"'No, no, Selene!' my grandmother said. "It's too dangerous. You've done the best part. Now, no more.'

"'Dangerous?' I knelt in the twilit road. 'Grandmother, I must. There is my sister, Merope, and I promised her. And our cousin, Althea, too. And, Grandmother, my mother and aunt. All of the Khorus Korai are there, hiding from the fires in those caves. I must go to show the rescuers the way to find them. Grannie, I promised Merope.'

"'No, no.'" My grandmother's tears were hard to resist.

"The queen took my grandmother and talked quietly to her. And I took this opportunity and ran to the leader of the search-and-rescue expedition.

"In the background, keeping a close watch, was a man whom everyone knew. He delivered amphorae of wine and of water and wool blankets and mingled with the townspeople, who obviously knew him. Often they thanked and conversed with him as someone well-known.

"From the palace road stepped a tall man about the same age. The two men hugged as best friends would, and the man with the amphorae of wine and water called out to his departing friend, the eldest son of King Nestor, 'Save me a place!'

"Just then I was pulled into one of the moving carts. My savior was none other than Queen Eurydice. And when I looked back, I saw that man was seated not far away from us.

"'My son's best friend,' the Queen smiled at me as she handed me a more comfortable cushion."

"And we set out under a rising moon colored purple from the smoke and fires."

CHAPTER 16

FADE IN: *Rescue?*

SETTING:
>Place: Mycenae Village and High Citadel, Mycenae, Greece
>Date: 3 June, <u>2021 A.D.</u>
>Time: before dawn to late night

WAKENED BEFORE two a.m. on the 3rd day of June by the urgent ringing of phones left in hidden locations, Allison and her assistant, Federica, had taken turns fielding calls from around the world, calls which paid no attention to other matters of urgency or time of day.

Yesterday, June 2, together they had set up a sort of field office at the crossroads of Main Street and Citadel Road. All that day across the desks the two had studied the maps and surveys, preparing for the rescue teams' arrivals.

These surveys and photos were of the very top level of the archaeological site, levels most recently excavated and now totally covered over and obscured by the new mountain staring at them. Vital were these pages. They meant that this excavating work *in extremis* could commence as soon as geology told them it was stable enough.

Allison, Federica and the others staying with them at the Hotel Belle Helene had been left plentiful amounts of food, water and wine by

Agamemnon and Kati-Selene, and pizza fixings by Stelios at Elektra Palace so that, with the pages from Margaret, they could all survive while they, with the arriving geologists, engineers and archaeologists, began the work of re-uncovering Mycenae.

Allison had been so tired at the end of yesterday, she had hardly tasted her pizza before falling into her cot on the terrace of the Belle Helene. But now, all that new mountain out there had downloaded into her unconscious and, at not yet 2 a.m., she was suddenly wide awake. Something licked her hand. Old Street Dog was keeping her company.

"Hungry, Old Street?" she whispered to him, reaching out a hand, which he licked. He lay right alongside her cot and stared at her. Among her snoring neighbors were a few vanguard-arrived engineers. From the parents of one missing guard, Phaestos, came more gentle snores. They had not believed they would sleep, but finally, the tensions left with the second glass of the Dassis's wine, and they were still asleep not far away on the terrace. But pressure was like that mountain on her. And Old Street Dog's large eyes were watching her. She was now his source for food and water. And comfort. Tomorrow, soon — her eyes began to close — soon she would be needed by the arriving teams of government search and rescue teams. Tomorrow. No. Her eyes opened. Tomorrow had become today: June 3. She looked at her phone and put it back down on the floor.

At 3 a.m. there was more than that mountain out there bothering Allison's rest.

Three nights ago, the evening of the thirty-first, after their jolly dinner with Agamemnon and Kati-Selene, after giving Allison the pages of photos and surveys and maps of the latest excavations, Maggie had mentioned that she still had to put into her briefcase some "last, even newer" papers, which copies she would give Allison after the surprise lunch the next day. Margaret had handed Allison that portfolio marked "BRONZE AGE MYCENAE STRUCTURE AND INFRASTRUCTURE, INCLUDING THE TOWN BELOW," explaining that she, Allison, now archaeologist in charge of Mycenae, would need this and should keep it at all times in a place she would be able to get to it, and never to leave without a copy when travelling.

Allison knew that as of today, Margaret's new office would be set up in the Athens' Archaeological Museum. Indeed, earlier two mornings ago, before Margaret's big surprise day, when Allison walked up from the parking lot on the road to the citadel, she had passed the van from the Athens Archaeological Museum at the guardhouse. The driver had bid her "Kalimera" as he and their guard on duty, Balthazar, loaded all those boxes packed by Margaret into the van. So, as she studied the Bronze Age Mycenae Structure portfolio, she felt pretty certain all those other boxes of records had been sent along to Athens.

Now mentally she closed that portfolio with gratitude to Margaret. It would be their guidebook to recovering. Later this morning, she would reach out to their guard, Balthazar, to make sure they had loaded all of Margaret's boxes. Balthazar had been on the night shift, which was ending just as Allison had arrived. So, she was fairly certain he was among the survivors. But that briefcase. Where was Margaret's briefcase?

Now at 3 a.m. from her cot on the balcony, as she looked into the eyes of Old Dog, Allison knew she was probably the only person who actually had the most-important records of the site, one of the few who had seen what had happened and could direct the efforts to save as much of Bronze Age Mycenae as possible. And she would insist that, beginning this morning, all of those in the first teams who came to help would continue to call this a rescue mission. It was not yet time for mourning. There was much to be found and rescued. Margaret. Thanassis. Menelaos-Stavros. Phaestos. The other guards. Her eyes felt heavy. She had to get some sleep. Oh. Where is Margaret's briefcase? Suddenly another image flashed across her inner eye, and she started to worry that somewhere in all that mess were also all those Khorus Girls figurines, including Margaret's little Merope. Could they be what Margaret meant by "the real girls"? Somehow, she knew they were very important in this rescue mission to find Margaret. She turned over, thumping the pillow.

Flickering in and out of her dreams, Allison kept hearing Margaret speaking to her while holding out that briefcase and clasping to her heart her Merope figurine. Maggie was talking about Merope "being a real girl" and how she, Margaret, had the key to finding her. Was that what she had been saying? The key? Had she also heard singing?

Finally, at around four in the morning, under the brightness of the waxing gibbous moon and the blue Pleiades, Allison gave up trying to get back to sleep and that dream sort of flew out on the notes of a song, floating out into the stars. And Allison got up, walked quietly from the porch, stood in the road, looked at the mountain staring her down, and worried. From down here at their new crossroads office up to the terrible mess she stared, feeling small and useless.

Something licked her hand. Old Street Dog was keeping watch, too.

And all too soon, June 3, Day Two of rescue, was upon them. Allison assigned the receiving and returning of calls, emails and texts to capable and willing Federica. And she, Allison, stayed at her rescue mission desk, right where she had stood early this morning, here at the infamous 4,000-year-old crossroads leading from town to that famous, now-buried citadel, fielding hundreds of questions, giving directions, as had many generals long before her. She insisted on keeping to the word "rescue," though she was not unperceptive to the situation, especially given the remarks she had overheard. Along with geologists, two teams of archaeologists arrived, all bearing their latest versions of geophysical survey equipment as well as dinosaur-sized cranes and plows to move the new mountain, and had checked into the hotel. By ten a.m. on this second morning after the catastrophe, given more and newly informed remarks, the reality of the situation seemed far more ... no, far less ... oh, well. She continued to hold out hope. Who knew where exactly the very inventive Margaret was? Allison could see as well as everyone else that where the museum building had been was now covered by that mountain. But she knew Margaret's office was below ground. So, maybe this was still a rescue operation. She stood at the bottom of all the terrible mess and, though a fleeting feeling of hopelessness passed through her, she could not, would not give up. She breathed out and opened Margaret's portfolio of the excavations. It was ...

"Pretty daunting, is it not?"

Allison turned to look into the sky-blue eyes of ...

"Director of operations for UNESCO, Oscar Hammerstein."

"Really? Oscar Hammerstein himself?" Allison had to smile. "Hum something for me, please. From *The Sound of Music*, key of F. That 'Hills' song would be good just now." She hummed, and took his outstretched hand.

"Great-great nephew or something. Yes, I'm theatrical. Look at the stage I've been assigned to produce on today." He gestured at the grand mess. "I would say we've got a lot of work to do until production, wouldn't you?" He released her hand. "You're the archaeologist with the details? The one who was here? One of the ones up there, too. Yes?"

"Allison Greer. And yes, Oscar, I do have the details. Here. The most-important ones. Well, remembering that there is, somewhere, in a briefcase that is missing, more possibly of what you may want to know. There are many unknowns still out there. So I was just now standing here among this — this," she repeated, waving at the destruction and all of the newly arrived trucks, filled with technology and people, "feeling totally lost. Thank you and all these men and women for coming."

Just before her tears would have come, he perceived and gave her a quick hug. "It's what we do," he said. "I would say you need to get some rest. But I think you would rather I propose another route? And some coffee?"

Before she could assess the possibilities or accept, a whirring, and wind whooshed from above as a helicopter put down only meters away, right in the middle of Main Street in front of Belle Helene. The door opened, and before the noise stopped, out jumped a man.

"Mr. Hammerstein?" he shouted as he ran, hand outstretched.

"Yes?"

"Neil Simon. Geological survey. Photogrammetry. Wave-Form Close Range with relative reflectance. Our 3-D data with our camera systems, integrated with your programs and laser-scanning historical records, can get pretty much down under this mess and find and map out exactly where your, ... Dr. Greer ..." He nodded, patted her on the back and shook Allison's hand, "Where your citadel and all the other structures are. Precisely. Our images are georeferenced. We can also detect where the least stability is so as to avoid it. And the reverse is true, too: for using the most-stable areas to set up high-resolution imagery and orthophotography equipment to digitally mark these unstable and stable features. Which we have done. And are doing now. High up there." He pointed at the newly exposed hills to their right. "So now, with you and the rescue teams, we will also find Dr. Benson and the guards."

Those words actually gave Allison a moment of real hope.

"You know," he said, pulling out grids and maps and flattening them on a tumbled boulder, "we measure range from light pulses. Any object we encounter will be thoroughly detected and detailed. But." He turned to them. "We are going to need both of you to work with us on this very difficult job. For your engineering teams' work, Mr. Hammerstein, we can provide you with information on those areas of least and most stability. And with you, Dr. Greer, for swiftness, we will work closely and you will provide direction to your sites' specific areas of most importance."

"Will you be able to find …?" She couldn't finish.

"Yes. We will find Dr. Benson if, indeed, she was on the site at the time."

Again, she felt a wave of relief. She grasped his sleeve. "How long?"

"If we start now, maybe three hours." He rolled up his papers and pointed to the top of the newly arranged mountain. "Our equipment's up there, ready to go, in two helicopters. There," he said, pointing again, "on the mountain's slope in those areas of stability, approved by Mr. Hammerstein's team. So if you will come with me, Dr. Allison." He led them into a still-whirring and waiting helicopter.

"Allison, please."

"Allison. And you, Mr. Hammerstein."

"Neil Simon?" Oscar and Allison exchanged a smiling glance. "Oscar, Neil. Yes, my engineering equipment is already up there. Ready?"

"Then we should have answers shortly. Oscar."

Allison sat between them. Neil, continued in full voice so as to be heard over the noise.

"We're from BGS," he said. "Also called in by UNESCO as part of the Environmental Research Council to determine the impact on this important world heritage stage. Anthropologists work with us as well."

Neil smiled broadly and gestured below as he hummed the opening bars of "The Hills are Alive" at them. "And since you, Allison, and the other archaeologists have, we hope, the newest and well-detailed records of where all the recovered citadel and town and early burial sites are located, as well as very good recording of the many unexcavated areas and their underlying contents, the geologists are more than happy to work as one team." He turned to them more somberly. "Everyone knows there are huge priorities and huge dangers. Each is armed with a signal tracking device in case of further mudslides. As you will be."

Allison handed him a copy of Margaret's portfolio.

He paused, reviewing it, when a gust whipped the helicopter suddenly up. They were preparing to land. Allison grabbed his arm.

What he did not say, as he took her hand in his, was that not one of the UNESCO or geological survey teams believed anyone could have survived. Though Dr. Benson was last known to be inside the museum building and the guards in the guardhouse, everyone who knew the site could see that the museum building's area was now covered by some ten-to-twenty or more feet of mud and boulders. If the museum building was still intact, Margaret Benson would have little oxygen. But the geophysical scan also showed that the building had mostly been crushed by huge boulders toppling from the mountains in back. No one had yet had the heart to tell Dr. Allison, who continued to believe.

Allison knew all this. But as she sat on a boulder high above a changed mountain slope, watching the rescue teams prepare to go to work, looking at the terrible mess below and comparing it with Margaret's more-recent maps and surveys — now hers — even though this part up here was totally changed, she continued to have hope. "Rescue," she breathed in.

The sun showed it was nearly noon. And someone stood in her light. She turned and looked up. Neil Simon offered her a hand up.

"Ready?" he said. "We've located somethings interesting. Something from Dr. Benson and the guard."

"Phaestos?"

"No, that's not his name."

She followed him into the helicopter and silently watched as they took the strange trip back in time down past the no citadel, the no Lion Gate, the no anything, swooping down over dense mud over the no gardens to the base of what was now considerably above the no parking lot. The ground had been stabilized by the geologists and the engineers. Landing pads had been set out. "A sort of helicopter parking lot," she thought as she got out to stand next to Neil.

Several workers were talking into devices, ordering about cranes and bulldozers. Down here, great hunks of mudslide (like huge spoons of chocolate pudding, she thought) were being removed. They walked to the edge of an excavated area and she saw Margaret's car down in there. The workers moved away and Neil, switching on a very dirty cell phone, showed her some numbers.

"Is this?" Allison said, staring at Margaret's car.

"No, Allison, she's not there. But look here." Again, he showed her the numbers displayed on his phone. She frowned, not sure what he wanted her to see. She reached to touch it, and just then, Neil pressed something and she heard a voice from inside his palm.

"Dr. Benson?" she heard.

"Hello? Thanassis?" she heard Margaret's voice replying. "Yes, it's time. Come quickly." Then another voice, a small voice: "RUN, MAGGIE!" ... Allison swirled and wondered and then looked up toward the stereophonic sound. She was hearing the same voices from two directions. One was in Neil's hand. The other came from the air. "Thanassis?" Allison stretched and reached but could not possibly get to the very familiar sound. There it was, though, high up there in branches peeking out of the mud above them to her right. That cell phone peeking out of the muddy, broken branch of the cherry tree, from which she also could hear that terrible rumbling in the recorded background, was either Margaret's or Thannasis's. A geologist ran up with a ladder, and in a second, he had plucked it from the branch. Heart thumping, Allison listened carefully. She listened as the voice of Thanassis was answered by Margaret's. And another small, unfamiliar voice. Neil took it and replayed the messages.

"I did not mean to frighten you, Doctor," Thanassis said. "But your phone disconnected. And without any power in there, we wanted to make sure you are alright. Are you ready to leave? I'm on my …" And as Allison received Thanassis's phone from Neil, she heard another phone in the background disconnect. Was that one Margaret's? Then again it rang, the other one in her hand, and they listened carefully to Margaret's voice. "Thanassis? Yes, it's time. Come quickly. We have to leave now." And then that other, that small voice repeated, "NOW! NOW! RUN!" Then Allison heard a crash and running, and then — she almost dropped the phone, but Neil's hand was there to steady hers—then there was the unmistakable sound of the roar of a lion. And then again, that small voice shouted, "RUN! MAGGIE, RUN! GO! FAST! YOUR CAR!" And Maggie shouted, "Oh, I cannot take you, Merope!" Within the sounds of downpouring rain and thunder, Allison heard Margaret say, "Did you see her, Thanassis? I think we are going to Oz!" Again the sounds of water and wind, and again Allison heard Thanassis: "Ozymandias! We need him now! And his best friend, the great King Agamemnon. Oh, gods, look! That woman in red!" And then a strange, new, very angry voice … from far below it seemed to come, and it came into range then went out as though the phone capturing it was moving fast past the shouter. "Them and YOU rot in hell of SILENT oblivion."

Allison murmured. "Could that be Bronze Age Greek? Something no one has ever heard. I'm only sure that she's very angry." Then she heard Margaret: "Together, Thanassis: GOOD QUEENS, CLOUDS, BIRDS!" And she heard them begin together this new mantra: "GOOD QUEENS!" "Yippee!" "Yippee! Here we go!" And the small voice called, "AND WINDS!" And after that, there was a huge noise that Allison did not want to hear, that of boulders tumbling and rain gushing. Neil took his phone from her shaking hand.

And from his other pocket Neil took something and handed it to Allison: Margaret's notebook.

"I transferred all their messages into my phone and linked them," he said. "Listen again, please." Again he touched a button on the phone and played back the last messages. "Who is there with Margaret besides Thanassis? Do you think that language is from the Bronze Age?"

Allison was staring at the small, muddy notebook. "The little voice," she blurted. "That's the voice of her Merope, I'm sure. I've never heard her, of course. Maggie said she spoke to her. That must be her voice." She wiped off the little booklet, opened it, read a little of the last pages then enfolded it with great care in another handkerchief that Neil offered. "Why would Margaret be taking her out of the museum?"

"To a place of greater safety?" he said. "You heard Margaret, too, wonder why." Neil put the notebook into her other pocket, along with Thanassis's phone.

As she looked up to thank him and he reached over to wipe her tears, she heard someone calling her name. That someone was waving them over. She touched the package in her pocket.

"As long as her phone is missing, with this I feel we are connected," Allison said. "Let's find them in time, Neil."

And Neil took her arm. "Are you alright?"

She stumbled across to the waving person. "Neil, I know you know that's a silly question." Her lips trembled. She shook. But she took a deep breath. What would Margaret say? What had she said that day they were excavating together? "Get it together. You're an archaeologist. They're all dead. Do your work. But dream, too. Archaeology is not a hard and known science. We work in the dark and must be creative and informed. And if this is the job for you, soon you will discover some of them are less dead than others. Those will speak to you." Maggie had noticed Allison's expression. "Their bones will. First it will be the artifacts that talk. You think that's strange?" Allison had knelt beside her as they brushed in the dirt. "Artifacts of a great, once very alive person are imbued with his or her sensibilities, loves. Artifacts, like this" — and she held up an encrusted but glistening golden chain — "may tell a story not heard in some thirty-four hundred years. We shall see." And carefully she had documented the location of the chain and, sitting back on her heels, continued.

"Schliemann listened to his informed instincts and look what he found. It's not rocket science. It's about human nature; about human differences and our human ideas of structure. Based on where we are up here," Margaret had said, tapping her head, "and here." She tapped her heart. "Look at that structure right out there," she had said, gesturing to the citadel of Mycenae, "and figure out what its form was based on at the very end, at the top level there, left for us to find first, when those defensive walls were doubled and the cisterns and granary were suddenly built. That queen who likely killed the king, was preparing for a siege. She was in charge."

Allison could hear Margaret's voice coming from inside her head, and at the same time, stereophonically, from those cell phones. She stopped listening and touched Neil's arm.

"Neil, you have found quite a lot: Thanassis's cell phone. And I suggest we use Margaret's last notes about the last queen killing the Lion King to put herself in charge up there as a point of reference." She gestured to where the great citadel and palace were again invisible under a mountain. "Those very areas where in 1214 B.C., Clytemnestra was getting ready for siege. We've both heard two strange voices in the messages, speaking, yes, I do think, Bronze Age Greek. And we heard the messages of Margaret and Thanassis. And still none of the teams out there have any sign of either of them. I think that gives me a reason to continue to hope. I also think some things very, very strange happened and that we actually heard them happening. My instincts tell me that the fourth voice we heard was that of Queen Clytemnestra. I want a copy of this sent to Dr. Theodoros Manasakis in Athens at the Acropolis Museum. He would know that language. That woman spoke in Greek so old, no one has ever heard it. Well, I know that puts me into a category called ..."

"Overstressed," Neil said as he took her arm and led her in another direction, where Oscar waited. "Well, it's not all good. Oscar's engineers found something more."

She trembled as they walked over. "Overstressed? I am definitely. But this whole situation is growing in overstressing strangeness." She reached out a hand to greet Oscar.

"I'm beginning to see that," Oscar agreed.

At the other end of the no parking lot, his team had found Phaestos. The burly guard's body was partially shoved under his recovered SUV. He had been crushed by boulders. And drowned. Those boulders she had heard crashing in the background over the phone. He was buried under meters of mud. His arm had alerted the searchers. He was reaching up to the door. To the handle.

"Another thing is more puzzling, Allison," said Oscar as he gestured to her, offering a hand. "Come over this way. It's steep and slippery, so hold on."

He pulled her up the steps cut into the mud on a steep incline. They were, she judged by looking about, somewhere atop where the museum entrance walk had been. Oscar brought them to a spot that was cordoned off and stabilized by heavy boarding. On the ground had been laid more boarding for walking. Over a small wall, they peered down and into the wide trench-hole that had been dug.

"Oh," she said. Instinctively, she turned away.

"Who is that? Do you recognize him?" Oscar queried gently.

"Yes. That's Fabrice. I'm almost sure. He's a close associate of Andrew Stark." She was sickened by what she saw and hesitated to look again. "What happened to him?" The man's face and body had been mauled and one arm had been pulled from its socket. It lay on top of the body, bloody with huge tears all over it. The sleeves of his clothing were in shreds. His remains lay on what had been the walkway to and from the museum.

"Looks to us like that wild animal we heard was really there and got him," Oscar said. "Now look at what else is there. This was in that hand." Oscar pointed to the top hand, from which fingers had been ripped. He reached down and received from an associate a very bloody cloth sack, which he offered to Allison. Two severed fingers clutching the top were attached.

She shivered. "Could you please? I do not think ..."

Carefully enfolding it in a large handkerchief, he opened the sack, and when she looked inside the sack, she drew back quickly and looked at the two men.

"What are they?" Oscar asked as gently as he could.

"Many of Maggie's special figurines. This morning I was worrying about them down in the museum there, tumbled around in all that mud. But why would Fabrice, who has no responsibilities here, be taking out a bag filled with them?" She reflected a moment, recalling again that little voice on the phones. "What was he doing in there?" She reached out. "I would very much like to study them. Make sure they are all accounted for. What was he doing? Why?"

Neil touched her pocket. "Perhaps this man, Fabrice, was taking them to that place of greater safety from the storm?"

"They were deadly enemies. He and his dear friend and associate, Andrew Stark, made a great joke of Margaret and her work. At the luncheon for her three days ago. Right in the museum. Just a short while before all this happened, they made mockery of Margaret at her own event, in public. And of what she had published about these very figurines. They hated Margaret. He must have been up to something to harm Margaret even more when he took them." She touched the sack. "I would like to study them, please." She was greatly disturbed by this, more than anything else so far. "Oh, dear, I am truly afraid now. What has happened here? That wild animal?" She looked at Oscar with growing shock. "There are no wild animals here. At least ..." She took a deep, shaky breath and, wiping her face, tried to do as Margaret had told her, to think with information but outside the box. "At least not four-footed ones and not since around 1200 B.C. Until then, this was an area," she said, pointing, "in those very hills and mountains, of lions. European lions. Then the last of the lions seem to have vanished, and suddenly, from here. Along with this civilization. It was different west at Pylos, where they remained another hundred-plus years. Climate change? Poachers? New regimes? All are likely suspects."

She pointed to the mountain slope to the west, slightly downhill from them, toward where the Lion Gate was now covered over.

"About fifty years before that, some of the last of the huge lions were replicated into their stone counterparts and placed over the grand entrance up there. — The Lion Gate, commissioned by the Great Lion King himself, Agamemnon. Those European lions were not as lions in Kenya are today. Different. Much larger."

An engineer from Oscar's team was carefully removing the remains of Fabrice. Oscar turned to the man, handing him the handkerchief with the severed fingers. "Ask forensics to test them against lion bites."

Then Neil turned to one of his geologists, "And could you ask Allison's assistant, Federica — she's down below in the street at the desk — to call Dr. Andrew Stark and request him to return to identify his colleague here?" He carefully wrapped the sack of figurines and gave them to Allison.

Allison followed Neil and Oscar back to the waiting helicopter. "Any signs of the other guards?" she asked.

"None so far. But as you can see," Neil said, looking to Oscar for confirmation, "we have a long way yet to go. With all the smart technology all these really smart people are using, we will have more answers by the end of the day; certainly tomorrow. As we are discovering, Margaret Benson and that guard, Thanassis, could be anywhere. And whoever else was with them. That small voice, the other 'Yippee!' voice?"

"Those three sounded as though they were flying," Allison murmured and pointed up. "Like they were flying in that direction, I would guess, from down there near the cherry tree, where it's likely those fierce winds ripped from his hand and carried Thanassis's phone. So, they were flying up." She turned to Neil and Oscar. "Is that idea also in the overstressed category?"

"Actually, no," Neil replied immediately. "In fact, I'm mulling over your comment about the fourth voice, that angry voice. The non-flyer, standing somewhere high up there and shouting in strange Greek as the others flew over and past. We have no candidates for who would have been up here in that torrent, who could have been shouting at Margaret and Thanassis. I want you to tell me more about these ideas. Later. But for now, we have much to continue on." He turned to Oscar, who was now also quite puzzled. "Sorry, Oscar, you're coming in on this a tad late. I'll play the messages for you to hear so you can give your opinion."

Therefore, and despite, Allison insisted to herself this was still a *rescue* mission. It was not yet to be considered a time for mourning. Along with Margaret and Thanassis, another two guards were still missing and presumed ... "Alive!" she whispered. "Alive."

Now she would tell Phaestos's family.

And amid hope for the others, that evening, quietly, a ceremony familiar to the village was held for Phaestos's family. The village ladies returned, each bearing a traditional dish. Tables and chairs were set up in the cleaned Main Street. And solemn music of ancient days was played on old instruments. Then, with the breaking of the flat breads and with the first toast to Phaestos consummated with the delicious wines of George Dassis, the solemnity gave way to happy stories of this well-loved, precious and talented son of a long-established family.

Yet it was still not appropriately a time for mourning. There were the families of the other two guards to think of, helping them hold on to hope. For the Dassis family to hope for both their children, Thanassis and Menelaos-Stavros. And hope for Margaret. But what needed to be done to begin healing for Phaestos's mother and father had been begun as it should.

In the night, in time for a bite and a shower, Donald Suskine, his successor and their team returned. Along with Maggie's friend and Allison's mentor, Dr. Agnes Jones.

And very late in the night, in Maggie's room in the Belle Helene, under a bright mobile phone light shining on a large cloth, Allison and Agnes carefully studied all the little figurines. Little Merope was missing. Allison took out Maggie's very soiled notebook. And Agnes pulled from her pocket a still-folded page. These they laid out in the light on the bed. While each studied the other's findings, Allison played the recording of the flight over Mycenae.

Agnes, too, was struck by the menacing female voice. "Bronze Age Greek, I would guess," she said. "How valuable this is. You did well to send it to Theodoros. He will know." She touched the phone and then, with Allison, thumbed through Maggie's notebook, where they found details of Maggie's fear of Clytemnestra. Agnes spread out the page Margaret had slipped into her pocket. "Well, take a look at this." And she read aloud, "'I'm going up to find caves high in the hills behind the citadel. Merope told me she and her whole khorus were cursed by Clytemnestra, sentenced to "silent oblivion." And that area high up back there seems like the likeliest place for "silent oblivion" and the most-likely place for caves. Though I've never yet seen caves up there.'" She handed the page to Allison. "Indeed, what caves? Where, more precisely, would they be?"

Allison held the paper closer to the light and studied it. "I've never seen or heard of caves up there. But to rescue thirty-two-hundred-year-old girls ..."

Agnes shook her head, took back the paper and pondered. "She was quite certain of this new evidence for correcting her book. We did not have time to talk much at the lunch. So many wanted a moment with her. And then Andrew's awful confrontation. Just after I got to a hotel in Nafplio and the news began coming in about how truly devastating this earthquake was, as I was hanging up my jacket, I found this paper in my pocket. Maggie obviously knew she had to tell someone where she was planning to go."

"Agnes, considering what Maggie says about Clytemnestra, and the voice we have recorded, what do you think is going on?"

CHAPTER 17

FADE IN: *Phantom Cry Over Mycenae, Resonating Through Time*

SETTING:
    Place: The Roads to Rescue from Nestor's Pylos to Hills above
        Mycenae
    Date: 3 June, <u>1214 B.C.</u>
    Time: before dawn to dark night
    Broadcast to Margaret Benson's Cell Phone
    Date: 3 June, <u>2021 A.D.</u>
    Time: before dawn to dark night

WHEN THE FIRST rescue cars passed Tiryns, Selene looked up at the clear, early-morning sky. They had driven all night, picking up more citizens and supplies at every township they had passed en route back to rescue Mycenae's khorus. Now they were near. Selene tilted her head and looked for familiar, early morning, winking stars. And, yes, there they were, her favorites, those that often accompanied her on her before school exercises, the Pleiades, clustering like her own sisters. Yes, there was the name-sake for her dearest little Merope, winking, showing the way.

"We are near the turn-off now, the turn-off up to the hills and the Khorus Girls," Selene called to the driver. "I could run ahead to show the way."

"There is no need, little Selene."

She felt Queen Eurydice's comforting arm pulling her into an embrace.

"But my lady, Queen Eurydice." Selene turned and pointed up at the stars. "They are leading me, calling me to come. And my legs are longing to stretch. Would you mind if I take a run? I'm longing to call up my reply to our Khorus Girls: 'We're here!' To tell my sister I am back for her. Let mother know all is now well. Soon she will be reunited with baby. To let all of them know they are safe. Then I will return to you to show the way."

"Then go. Stretch those lovely, long legs and alert those waiting girls."

Selene jumped down, and heart pounding, started off with anticipation, and urgent need. "I'm back, Merope! Mother, Mother, I am coming!" She knew she was too far off to be heard, but she was too anxious not to shout it out. "I am back!" she called to the still-darkened hills some distance in front of her, waving her arms. "I promised you. I'm back, Merope! MEROPE! MOTHER! CYNTHIA!" She listened, but the stillness did not reverberate echoes of her sister's name. "MEROPE!" No echo. Only a strange, burnt smell permeated the silent land.

For lack of light she could not quite see, but she sensed that in the opposite, still-distant hills, there were no longer any fires. The deluge had certainly put those out. But she sniffed again, and her nose picked up an odd, rancid, putrid smell. By now, her long legs felt they knew the way, and she relaxed into her pace, knowing she was getting closer, nearing the familiar big turn. She was headed toward the expected turn in the road to her right from which the caravan would turn up the long highway leading to the hills, and then there would be the path down which she had run. Suddenly, she slowed, insecure and confused. Disoriented.

These were not the hills she had expected. What had she done wrong? She knew the roads she had taken were the correct ones. She knew the hills to her left were the ones that had been on fire two nights ago. She could almost see the disfigured and blackened trees and the charred remnants of vineyards high up there, just catching some early light. Or was that her imagination? It was that time of darkest before dawn. She ran on. But as she looked again to her right, there were no small hills leading down from those caves. No path down which she could have run as she had confidently called back, "I will return." She put her head back and cupped her lips and called, "MEROPE! MEROPE! I HAVE RETURNED! MEROPE! MEROPE! MOTHER! CYNTHIA!" She felt she was crying, but she was not sure of anything. "MEROPE!" she called over and over. "Where are you?" The fires were out. Maybe the girls had all gone home. But this, too, put fear into her heart. With the erratic king and equally mad queen now in charge, Selene hoped mother had listened to her and resisted any such urge.

She ran and ran toward the faint streaks of dawn. Suddenly, as a bright spark from Helios hit the top of one of the larger mountains in the east, she looked with a growing frown and anxiousness. Again, she knew she was right, but again, she could see in front of her that she was wrong. Very. Had she, could she, have led them all — the rescuers in back of her — astray? She searched about for some familiar road signs or for that path up. But she saw none. Nothing familiar. Oh, she was ahead of herself, that was it. So, she slowed to allow the sun god to give her bearings. All was so very quiet. "Hmmm," she thought, "too quiet for a clear, dawning day. The birds should be up, busy at their gathering breakfasts of seeds and beetles." She stopped completely to make no competing noise. Not one bird's song. She almost stopped breathing to listen. And the sun's orange beams hit the undersides of dawn's pink clouds and shone upon the hills opposite. Clearly now she could see the charring from the fires she had run from two nights ago. She *was* in the right place. But she was not. Across from the burnt hills should be the hills of the caves where the Khorus Girls were waiting for her. But all was silent. And strange.

"MEROPE! I HAVE COME! MEROPE! CYNTHIA! MOTHER! OH, MOTHER!" Selene called as, again, at first anxiously, and then with growing confidence, she picked up her pace. And ran forward toward where — this must be the place — where the road curved and there would be that path to her right, that familiar back way to Mycenae. She had over-anticipated. This was the stretch where soon those caves would soon appear up there on her right. Soon. Again, she paused to call, "Merope! Merope! I kept my promise. I am back! Merope! Althea! We're here for you all! Oh, Mother."

But her voice did not resound as it should have. It sounded hollow. As she took the bend, preparing to call again, her feet slowed and, mid-step, she stopped. She was stopped. There was no more road. She was stopped by a huge boulder. Many huge boulders. Piles of them, higher than the Lion Gate. And trees ripped from their roots. All encapsulated within a wall of mud. A wall of a new mountain of mud. The whole once-highway was piled with mounds of massive boulders and broken trees and more boulders and more ... She shaded her eyes and looked up toward where she knew for certain was that path down which she had run two nights ago, leaving them to save them, calling behind her. She scaled a boulder, but the mud could not be traversed. She jumped down. "MEROPE!" She cupped her lips and called again. "MEROPE!" She backed up to see better and heard again those words her prescient little sister had muttered into her shoulder: "I'll never see you again." At that moment, as she looked at the devastation, she knew her mother, the lovely Cynthia, had been wrong all along about this one thing. Merope had not been too imaginative; she was psychic. And Selene should have believed her. And now it was too late. "Oh, Merope, I should have taken you with me. Oh, Merope." The tears fell down her face as she looked up at the destruction, at the new mountain formed from the bigger one in back. Everything familiar was gone, overwhelmed by mud.

A hand touched her shoulder and she turned quickly. "Merope!"

"No, my dear. I am here, Selene, here to hold you close. And to say we must not lose hope." Queen Eurydice's embrace felt like her mother's. "They are probably up there safe and waiting. We will send experienced men to search when day arrives. It is not a time for mourning. Come, come, let's have something to eat and drink. It's been a long, tiring night. Come. Rest. Then we will search and we will find."

"Please, madame, we must send round the other way, the southwest road into the town. We must send rescuers that route to find Father. He will be at the house and frantic about Mother."

"There is already a group taking that road. They will go first to him, trust me."

"Then he will show them the front way up to the hill caves. He will rescue Mother and my sister and ..." And then the tears fell full down her face as she remembered. "Oh, madame. She, she did it! She stood up there," Selene said, pointing to where they had all been only two days ago, "and cursed us all. Cursed us, vowing our oblivion, our silent oblivion forevermore. How can we overcome so evil a curse? How can we rescue them from that?"

"Who, Selene? Who?"

"The horrid, the evil queen."

"Clytemnestra?" Eurydice said the name and shivered.

Selene nodded.

And as Helios shone a beam upon her, the good queen of Pylos, Eurydice, raised her arms and faced toward where the caves were and called to the universe.

"Murderous queen! Your curse will reverberate upon you! I vow the Khorus Girls will be rescued and found. I promise Merope will become famous, known around the world one day. And I curse you, wretched queen, to the lowest realms of misery forevermore. You will be known and remembered for treachery and as an evil queen. Little Merope will be known for her exuberance, her singing, her leaping with the Khorus Girls, who sang for joy, who sang for the joy of their great King Agamemnon, the joy of their families, sang to save their harvests in times of need. Long will live the Khorus Girls of Mycenae."

The day came up full upon them and once again, birds sang.

~~~~

It was not yet the time for mourning. But there needed to be prayers to the gods for the souls of those feared lost and perhaps in need of mourning. If, indeed, they were lost in the devastation that was now visible to all the rescue groups, they were in no need of the dust of this earth to assure their salvation. They were, indeed, truly well-buried.

But it was still not yet the time for mourning. The ablest among the hundreds of would-be rescuers had found among the provisions, stout ropes, and, wearing their stoutest shoes, they had taken off, after a quick breakfast of well-watered wine and fruit, to climb into those burnt hills opposite the devastation sites. From there, they hoped to have a much better vantage point to determine the extent of the damage across the way and the possible routes to the caves. But even here as they began, they encountered obstacles, such as sliding earth. It was not obvious from the ground that up there, the fires had destroyed all the once-verdant vineyards on this side, and the rains, combined with the shaking, trembling earth, had created a subsurface that was highly unstable. While some of the men were able to get higher than others, using flattened boards tied to their shoes and carrying poles for grabbing hold of and pulling up upon, even they discovered there were treacheries unseen at every step. Two men had been buried. One had been freed unhurt. The other had broken bones from falling boulders. Another had fallen off an unstable cliff face and could not be reached. Not that it would have helped. It was clear he was no longer among the rescuers. But a few did make it high enough to see the side opposite, where Selene said there were caves in which the Khorus Girls took refuge. Not only were there no signs of caves, the hills themselves had disappeared. Instead, there was one enormous, continuous mountain. The even-larger mountain in back had simply appropriated the smaller one. And now there was one smooth-looking, treacherous mountain. The three remaining men then turned their attentions to west and south, down to where the palace and citadel of Mycenae was, where the monumental Lion Gate once welcomed all passing through. But they were not high enough to see far enough. If only they had available several hovering airships! Perhaps they would not come too late. And for the rescue of those feared to be high up in the caves, that would have to wait until this new mountain stabilized and unearthing could begin. That was their professional estimation. Special emergency equipment would be brought when needed.

One of these men was Elios, a prosperous vintner from Pylos, son of a cousin of King Nestor and best friend of Prince Thrasymedes. He had explained the danger to the queen. But Elios's eyes were fixed most upon the figure sitting alone on a boulder, quietly staring at the mountain in front. Elios went over to her to offer comfort. Putting a hand on her shoulder, he said, "It is not yet time for mourning. This is still a rescue mission. Have hope. We will search and discover more tomorrow."

At twilight a ceremony was held, led by Queen Eurydice, singing and praying to the gods for the recovery of those who were, perhaps, behind the huge wall of mountain in those caves and for all in the town of Mycenae.

"… Queen Eurydice came and held me, Maggie. And recounted a story from a group of palace workers fleeing Mycenae. They told that Agamemnon had returned that same evening into a home of treachery. I recalled the phantom cry of the lion. And so prayers were added for the king and, likewise, for the many worker-citizens presumed also at the citadel, the palace where the murdering usurpers were in charge. As well we prayed for those of our own who had given their lives to help save the Khorus Girls.

"After the ceremony, the queen moved among groups, offering comfort or sharing experiences. And a communal sharing of food baskets was enjoyed. Elios offered his wines. The queen with him, went to give comfort and nourishment to all of the rescuers."

Selene's thoughts were with her family, and she smiled acceptance and thanks for a small cup, but conversation was not something she could entertain. Though few were lighthearted, many were so tired laughter burst forth at odd moments. And from the heavy of heart among the hundreds whose hopes were dashed that evening as they prepared for another night under the stars, came stories about the Khorus Girls. And some began to sing their songs. On the morrow, the return to the southwest approach to Mycenae would commence. Tonight they sang Khorus Girl songs.

"… I distanced myself from the others and made my bed by the side of the road, looking up at the stars. The last thing I remembered was seeing Merope wink at me. And I heard clearly in my first dream, 'I love you, my dearest sister.' Would it ever be the time to mourn? Mother? My sister? Perhaps my little brother? Cousins? Aunts and Uncles? Perhaps when I am an old lady like my grandmother." ... Before the thought was finished, Selene was asleep.

CHAPTER 18

FADE IN: *The Hills are Alive*

SETTING:

Place: Int./Ext.: Mycenae Village and Hills low, middle and high
Date: 4 June, <u>2021 A.D.</u>
Time: from very early morning to mid-afternoon

IN HER COT on the Hotel Belle Helene's balcony, Allison dreamed of the tremendously huge possibilities. She saw people from the past and people from, she guessed, the future, and she saw Margaret. And she saw Margaret's Psychic Girl. Merope had grown and morphed into a real girl, just as Maggie had confided to her three nights ago, and was walking toward her.

"Merope is my name, Allison. Margaret has told you that. I am going to tell you my story and where to find me. Are you ready?" — And Allison opened her eyes. What had wakened her? — "Where to find me" — floated over her on a passing breeze that smelled intriguingly of violets. — "Find me ..."

She lay there a moment with images of all that had happened these last days flooding prismatically, re-forming kaleidoscopically over her, and she wished she could go back and somehow stop it all, could put up her Super Woman hand and send it all back into real time, to May 31st.

"But you cannot. So shall we discover what today holds?"

Clearly Allison heard these words. And recognized that voice. But how? Where had it come from? Quietly and quickly, she sat up on her cot. Day had not arrived. The street was very dark. Syncopated, small, snuffled snores came from her various guests. The Belle Helene's long and broad terrace had entertained quite a full house last night. And the grieving parents of Phaestos had been comforted by the warmth of these strangers and the familial gathering of all their friends and neighbors. Phaestos's mother had momentarily forgotten her loss when helping Allison stoke the pizza oven over at Elektra. Her husband had also seemed to feel the warmth, and he did enjoy opening, telling about, and tasting the wines of his neighbor, George Dassis. And when they finally camped for one more night on their neighboring cots, holding hands, they seemed to pass immediately into oblivion. And in that state, they remained, as far as Allison could discern in the gloom. The small moon and brilliant pre-dawn stars were shedding faint light. And as her eyes adjusted, she saw among her other guests many more archaeologists, including Donald Suskine, who had returned quite late, racing back from London with his successor, William Kent. There was also a larger number of geologists who had joined Neil and his team. And then, even later, quite a new contingent of anthropologists of all stripes had arrived. And Oscar's team of engineers had more than doubled. All seemed to be still enjoying a good sleep after a hugely exhausting and emotional roller coaster couple of days. None, she could discern, was the owner of the voice speaking to her.

As soon as Allison's legs touched the terrace floor, Old Street Dog suddenly and immediately was at her side, tongue out. "Hungry?" she whispered as she patted him.

"Naturally."

Allison turned around. "Who? Where are you?" she whispered, turning again. That voice was the voice she had recognized. But, whose? It was at the tip of her mind, tingling, tickling her thoughts. But she couldn't quite grasp it and bring it forward. She saw no one else awake. "Who said that?" she repeated very quietly.

"I. Merope."

Quickly, Allison followed Old Street's already inquisitive nosing under her cot, and, leaning down, pushed him aside and looked. She had forgotten she had stored for safety many of her things under the cot, including the handkerchief enfolding Thanassis's cell phone. Her hand was shaking, so she put the handkerchief down on the cot. And carefully unwrapped the device.

"Thank you for rescuing me, Allison. But my real rescue is yet to come."

"Who really is this? Where are you calling from?" She leaned forward to see better in the dark before dawn. The phone sent in a picture, and there she was: Margaret's 'Psychic Merope' was looking at her with large eyes.

"Yes. It's me. Maggie's Merope."

Allison looked about, worried the little voice would wake and startle a guest. So, tossing a sweater over her shoulders, she carefully went down the steps, into the street and over toward the field desk in the road while little Merope continued.

"You heard me telling Maggie to run and to take me. Once she got started and Thanassis arrived, things went quite swiftly. But in the catastrophic wind and turmoil, this device was dropped, and now through it you will follow my instructions and will rescue us. I will be Psychic Girl to you as well, Allison. Keep this safe and close. Through this I will guide you. Please listen."

~~~~

Late the night before, at the end of the town's communal dinner, Donald Suskine and his assistant, William Kent, and several of their team had returned. After a bite, a glass or two and a quick shower, they had happily bunked down onto cots on the terrace. From all around William soft snores were gently punctuating the beginnings of the day.

He had been deeply asleep, deep into dreams of strange places and odd people who all knew him. And that made him uneasy, and this unease is what must have woken him. He opened one then two eyes and oriented himself and then heard a small voice talking. A very small voice.

What was it saying? Was it Greek? English? He could not discern. So he lay still and listened and waited for understanding to arrive. He knew where he was. But who could be talking like that? And while he listened, he heard someone walking on the porch on which he was lying with many sleeping colleagues and families of Mycenae. Cautiously, he raised his head and turned to look. Someone was walking down toward the street. With care not to waken his neighbors, William stood and grabbed his sweater. It was a very chilly pre-dawn.

Quietly, he stepped around the sleepers and stood at the well-photographed balustrade that had welcomed many famous people since Schliemann. He could see long, blond hair shimmer in the moonlight. Likely that was Margaret Benson's replacement, who had welcomed them last night. What was she doing out there, hours before dawn? She certainly seemed to be talking to someone. Must be on her cellular as she was looking at her hand. She was even more lovely in this magical light, standing alone, attentive to the voice. And then, it seemed to him as he watched, she gathered all the elements together and they lay spangled at her feet, waiting for her command. — He shook himself from this fascination, stretched and went back to his cot, pulling the blanket over his body to keep away that morning chill.

Just as he was falling back into a deep sleep, he thought he heard her return.

~~~~

And now, before Allison could totally grasp all that was happening and all she had to do, her day was full on. All those important guests were here to do important work. "And I'm suddenly a big part of this new order. Not something to relish," she thought.

"Allison, Maggie's chief assistant," Donald Suskine determined, was in charge of this whole thing, though he was officially, for now, the new Director of Coordinating. After that announcement, he had taken off to find a spot inside the hotel where he could commandeer a desk, make calls and send out texts and emails. So, Allison had restarted her new job by first assigning some of Neil's geology teams to some anthropology teams, and then she linked up some of Oscar's engineers with archaeologists, who each had details of the areas they were to concentrate on. For now, she assigned herself the assessment and staking-out operations right here, downhill of the once-again buried Bronze Age town. The same enormous flooding that had swept down and covered it over around 1200 B.C. had returned to open areas all over the site, many not previously considered for excavating. And the same tumult had re-hidden all of the enormous excavation work of the last two centuries. There was so much to organize. And many precautions to be followed. Affixing her tracking device in case she fell into a crevasse, and, after lacing up field boots, Allison waded through mud and debris to her real assignment. And tried to look like the Chief.

She began not far away at the Bronze Age town areas with the assembled teams of assistant anthropologists, assistant-assistant archaeologists and some engineers Oscar had sent over with their students. She formed them into smaller teams, assigned duties by assessing priorities, following and coordinating the lists as best she could, lists handed her by the archaeological teams and by Oscar's engineering teams. And after she aligned others with the geological list from Neil, before sending them off to waiting helicopters or to more nearby geology, anthropology and archaeology search- and rescue-groups, she cautioned careful digging.

"This is still a rescue operation," she reminded them. Each worker was given a tracking device and taught how to use it. By ten a.m., she was focusing on the last of these teams. Some had arrived from Athens and places beyond only an hour ago and had just finished a breakfast of sorts. — And now that each was armed with cautions and a tracking device, she looked into faces eager and mostly ready to tackle this difficult and challenging day. Series of days. She gathered them close for a last talk and any questions. This group she had saved for last so as to be able to work with them herself. Some in this group were already practicing and others still students of forensic archaeology. And anthropology. Most were quite familiar with Mycenae and this spot, this as-yet-to-be-excavated town below the main citadel walls that had, with the devastation, again after 3,000 years been opened up in many areas.

"If you've no more questions, let's begin," she said to the team members after handing them their assignments.

"Dr. Greer?"

Allison was still not used to the doctor part. She turned with an outstretched hand. "Allison, please."

"William Kent, Allison, assistant to Donald Suskine. Sorry to interrupt you. But it sounds as though I am just in time." And, as he looked into her amazingly green eyes, he was not disappointed that he had allowed Donald to send him back to Mycenae when he had been looking forward to a few weeks of vacation. He took her hand. "Shamrock green. Is Greer Irish?"

"I beg your pardon?"

"Your eyes are so green, I was wondering if you are Irish."

"It is shamrocks in Ireland, Dr. Kent, not eyes, that are green. But Irish eyes smile. However today, I'm sorry to tell you, my, yes, Irish eyes find smiles more difficult to come by than shamrocks. So please tell me for what it is you are just in time." She rescued her hand.

"Oh." Though he had attended the Margaret Benson celebration she had organized, somehow he had failed to notice those amazing eyes. And the rest of her was pretty lovely, too, despite that golden hair being tucked up under a hard-hat. And he had heard she was doing most-impressive work here at Mycenae. So he sighed and turned her away from the very attentive group. "I'm in time to redirect you. If you'll allow." He took her arm.

Allison was taken off guard, and for a moment she could find no response other than to free her arm. "You found Agamemnon's throne, didn't you?"

"Yes. Well, there's some controversy. But I still think …"

"There's always controversy over something that shakes up the world we feel secure within. Remember back to Mr. Schliemann? Still causing controversy." She smiled.

He turned and pointed. "Up there in the Chavros Ravine." He returned the smile.

"You know it well?"

"Of course."

"Could you offer an idea, or ideas, as to where ..."

"That is, in a way, why I am here." He took her arm again, this time without resistance. "I want to try to reconstruct with you where she likely could have been when that earthquake and storm ... where all the others ..."

Allison could see in his eyes an understanding of her pain.

She interrupted. "You believe there was an earthquake? I do, too."

"Yes. I hear you have audio which might give location clues. Where she could have been is what we want to get to."

"And the guards. Do not forget. The newest guard, Thanassis, was definitely with Margaret. He, too, is on that audio. But there were, we think, still two other guards."

Her mobile rang, but his expression was so intriguing, she did not answer it.

William stood closer. "Are we speaking of the same 'she'? By 'she,' I was referring to that voice, the voice perhaps of Clytemnestra. Which I hear you have on that recording. And you? Oh, you are talking about the voice of Dr. Margaret. No matter. They are on the same recording. And, yes, I would like a copy. I think I might be able to help translate it. Then ... well, and as to the guards, probably they were gone by then."

"No. Only Thanassis was out of the guard-house. He had gone to help Margaret get out of her office. The others would not have left. Including Menelaos-Stavros. The reason we have the audio of Margaret's escape is because Thanassis had used Menelaos-Stavros's cell phone to call Margaret from the guard-house. Later we found Menelaos' phone buried near the guard-house and Thanassis' high in a near-by tree. So Menelaos-Stavros, and one other guard, should also be presumed to be missing.

"This recovery mission is very lucky to have you." William looked intently into her green eyes, "Meanwhile, having also worked with many of this team," he said, indicating the UNESCO-sent team members already at work in small groups, "I know that once you have assigned them their site and tasks, as you have, they will accomplish what you want. And will be waiting with results documented when you return. Most, as you know, are quite experienced."

"Return? From where? Mister, uh Dr. Kent, from which department have you come to redirect me?" She had to work hard to gather her wits about her with his intense focus on her.

"William." He smiled. "Well, this team which specializes in forensic archaeology and forensics, and another of some UNESCO engineers, like Oscar, both sent me for you. You may not know yet that late yesterday afternoon at twilight, engineers, returning the helicopters up there, passed over an area not seen before. And discovered some things that did not seem right. So different, in fact, that early this morning, they went back. They've just briefed me and taken me up there. We think you should come now to see. And then I really would like to re-hear that audio you have." He smiled. "And get a copy. But now, let's get up there to Oscar."

And she did not look away. "Do you think you might ..." Allison held out her phone. "understand ...?" Her sentence was left dangling as she searched for the message ...

"William!" The familiar voice came over his cell phone.

"Yes, Donald?" He turned to his boss's call.

"William! Where are you?"

Allison, oblivious, continued searching for the message ... "You would understand ... oh where is it?"

"Not far from you, I would guess," William replied to Donald. "I'm with Allison Greer. We're about to meet Oscar Hammerstein up above the Chavros Gorge to see ..."

Alison moved out of the sun, "... you both definitely would understand Bronze Age Greek. Oh. Here the message is." She handed her phone to William. "Here."

"That's fine," came from William's cell. "But Andrew Stark is here. And I think you both should first come to hear what he has to say about his pal Fabrice."

Smiling into the fierce, green eyes, William whispered, "I'll give it a go." He was mesmerized by those eyes.

"William!" Dr. Suskine's voice was filled with impatience. "William, to whom are you speaking? Come here now!"

"ALLISON!"

Before William and Allison could turn around and head back to base camp, her name, shouted, stopped Allison mid-step. Neil called it out again as he ran. "Allison! ALLISON! Quick, this way, come on." Neil reached her and grabbed her arm. "The guys in forensics called in a Forensic Odontologist. Anthropology is her background. Within an hour of arriving what she has already discovered will amaze and interest you greatly. Come on."

"Just a minute." William grabbed Allison's other arm again.

She resisted this tug-of-war. "A who? What?" 'Overwhelm' just kept coming at her, sending her off-kilter. "Odontologist?" Her brain fought to grasp the meaning of the word while she tried to retain her composure. Oscar. Donald. William. Now Neil with *forensic odontology.* She turned her back on William, and, facing Neil, she gnashed her teeth, "Oh, odontology." She showed her teeth and gave him a big smile.

"Right you are. This *forensics anthropologist odontologist,*" he laughed, "Dr. Litsa Polichroni, has identified and, with DNA, confirmed and linked with computer-generated comparisons, to form a most-likely scenario of what happened to Fabrice. You must come to hear what she has to say." With Allison in tow, Neil started off then turned back. "You too, Dr. Kent. Come on!"

Allison felt Neil's excitement and, toward the series of tents set up near the once parking lot, they ran in tandem.

But William followed slower, calling Donald back. "I'm not sure we can come over to you right now to see Andrew Stark. Perhaps you and Andrew Stark should come to see what engineering and geology and forensic anthropology has discovered about Andrew's partner's death. I'm just up the hill from the town and will wait on the road for you." He walked back down the road.

When William, with Donald and Andrew, entered the tent, the odontologist was deep into showing comparisons of archived bite marks and tooth impressions of the "European lion, now long extinct," with those bites on Fabrice to a very involved Allison and Neil. "Interesting how, almost delicately, the teeth removed this man's fingers from his hand, keeping them intact, while he was still holding the bag," the odontologist said.

"This lion was not enraged. She was doing a job. I've never seen such before."

"Can you repeat from the beginning, please," William asked. "We missed ..."

Carefully, Dr. Polichroni showed again the graphic photographs and her enlargements side-by-side along with a DNA panel.

"These confirm something amazing," she said. "Your colleague Fabrice was attacked by a lion. A not very old but a very large, female lion. Not an African lion but a European lion. The likes of which has not been seen here in, as Allison pointed out, over thirty-four hundred years. It looks like she was protecting her young. But after looking at the rest of the injuries, it is possible something else actually killed your colleague. Along with loss of blood, he also sustained huge blows to his torso and head. The body has been brought to the medical forensics team for more precise determination."

"That's all rubbish," Andrew Stark shouted. "GIMME THAT!"

Dr. Polichroni and her colleagues, as well as the archaeologists, geologists and engineers, turned quickly to see the cause of such an outburst and found themselves staring at a man who did not look quite sane. Andrew had the look more of a man who was still on a binge. His face was red and his clothes dirty and rumpled. His hair was in total disarray. He staggered over to the table.

Instinctively, the doctor covered her work protectively.

"Gimme that!" he shouted again as he shoved her arm. Donald Suskine and Neil pulled him away. "It was all a JOKE!" he shouted louder. "Listen. He says it himself." He took out his cell phone and pressed buttons, and a loud, laughing voice was heard. The speaker was almost in hysterics: "I've gotten them, almost all of them. Can you believe the bitch left the cage open. Whoops!" He laughed. "Case, I meant. Open. So I scooped them up and will bring them to you. She will have a stroke when she finds them all gone. WHAT A JOKE!" His laughter suddenly was choked off by a scream and a choking sound, followed by more screams and then the loud, proud roar of a lion. There was no mistaking that sound. It was almost a lonely sound, that roar.

"Lion," the anthropologist said quietly. "Protecting her young." They all stood in silent attention. Along with the horrific devastation all around, this described scene playing out vividly as their inner eyes compared the photos before them was so very strange.

Allison moved first. She reached for the cell phone. Andrew seemed as shocked at what had played on the phone and, in a daze, he let her have it.

"We will make a recording of this, Dr. Stark, and return the phone to you within the hour," Allison said. She turned to go out toward another tent but returned to the odontologist. "I'll have another copy made for you and your records, too." Allison ran out while the doctor put away her evidence.

"Has Fabrice's cell phone been found?" Donald Suskine asked.

"No. But Oscar's engineers will dig in that area again." Neil spotted the two engineers who had discovered Fabrice's body and quickly stepped into the bright sunshine and almost into returning Allison. He took her arm. "Allison, come with us now. Has William told you?"

Frowning in the light, she turned to Neil, her hand raised to shield her eyes. "Can you be more precise? This is getting so complicated. First, William and I were off to find Oscar when you came to get me." She turned again, and found Oscar arriving. "Oh, and here you are." She reached out a hand and gave Oscar a big smile.

Donald Suskine took William aside and said, "Keep me informed. I have to see about Andrew." He returned to the Odontologist's tent.

"Okay, everybody," Oscar took Allison's arm from Neil and walked her with him. "My A-team has discovered something else that we know you will all want to, and need to see."

"Indeed, this really is something more that Allison does need to see," William said. "What we were en route to an hour ago, Neil. Come on, man."

Together, the group walked toward the once-parking lot where the helicopters waited.

And Allison was swept into Oscar's fast pace, but then stopped. She lifted her arms, gesturing to the whole site.

"It's so amazing," she said, "what we are experiencing. Margaret was a magician. She directed all of this that we are experiencing. Everything we find here will continue to be amazing. Taking us off-guard, like Dr. Polichroni's lion's teeth marks and Andrew's phone's recording just did." They all stopped, quietly listening. "I know it is hard to believe your ears when you hear such strange words and things, unreal almost. Indeed unreal except for actually hearing them, as we did from Thanassis's phone. And now from Andrew Stark's. But Neil, Oscar, you two are just learning about the incredible woman we are searching for. I predict if we listen again closely with very open minds — unblindfolded, unprejudiced minds — perhaps we will understand what we are hearing much quicker. And maybe it all will form one amazing picture. One great, magical story."

"Well, maybe that's what we are about to do," Neil said, taking her arm and walking with her to his helicopter. "Blow open our blind, stodgy, twenty-first century minds."

Oscar rejoined his team at his helicopter and gave a call and a wave. "Up top! See you!"

In the lead plane, when they passed the again mud-covered Bronze Age site of Mycenae, William pointed. "Chavros Gorge. Right there, where that huge boulder is, is where I found the remains of Agamemnon's throne. The rest is still there, somewhere directly downhill from where the palace megaron would have been. It looks discouraging. All that down there. Everywhere. So much work. Mountains to be removed. But it can all be done by imagining what is below all that and thinking about blowing away all our stodginess, Allison. So let's see what Oscar is going to show us."

The pilot swooped up, preparing to land. Allison caught his arm. He put his hand over hers. "It's nothing." He set the plane down and turned off the engine.

"I know," she said. "I'm just not used to it, and all these new revelations are piling up. It's so strange. I am, we all are, very grateful to all of you for your time and expertise."

The pilot held the door open and offered a hand.

"This way," Neil guided them.

Seeing where they were, high above the site, up high in the hills, Allison took out Thanassis's cell phone and played again Maggie and Thanassis as they seemed to be flying stereophonically.

"Yippee! Yippee!" Maggie shouted.

"Yippee! Here we go!" Thanassis echoed. "GOOD QUEENS, CLOUDS, BIRDS!"

"YIPPEE!" from that small, feminine voice. "GOOD QUEENS, CLOUDS, BIRDS! AND WIND! it called.

And as they listened, the winds began to grow. And from between Allison's hands, the sounds of the winds continued and grew in intensity, with background shouting of "Yippee" from three voices flying in and out of vibrancy until, suddenly, the winds were much louder than before and at the same time were overtaken by the sounds of thousands of birds.

Then the sound of that small voice saying , "BIRDS! BIRDS! HERE COME THE BIRDS!" And the sounds of thousands of jubilant birds overwhelmed all other noise.

Allison almost dropped the device, she was so astonished to hear the thousands of birds. "That was not on the phone before, was it?"

Neil shook his head.

"I know the birds are not on the other guard's phone."

Also astonished, she could tell, was the normally unperturbable William. He took the phone and listened again. "I've never heard anything like this," he said, handing back the still- chirping phone. "It is possible we have already stepped into the realms of blowing open our stodgy A.D. minds?"

"Definitely none of what we have just heard could be considered normal by stodgy A.D. minds," Neil took the phone from William. "'Winds!' they called, and obviously, winds came. 'Birds!' they called, and quite definitely, birds came. Can we listen again? I want to hear it all, especially that small voice, the 'yippee' voice. And then there is the part where that ghastly sounding woman's voice cries out that curse which Allison translates as 'rot in eternal oblivion.'"

They formed a circle and played the whole thing all over, ending with the birds.

Neil handed back the phone. "I think it is time we really come up with what most would call crazy ideas. Like Allison's."

They stood still in their small circle, feeling a need for a protective closeness. William looked at Allison curiously. She seemed quite shaken. "Your idea," he said, "so, you first."

She took a deep breath. "As I told Neil, and as I hereby madly, wildly, reconfirm, I think the woman's voice recorded on these phones is that of Clytemnestra. But I'm certainly no expert in Bronze Age Greek. I can only loosely put together some of those sounds. I've sent a copy to Dr. Theodoros. He will know."

"Allison! You are Irish!" William laughed. He took the phone and replayed what they had heard. "So, whose is that one, this small, sweet-sounding voice?"

Neil put up his hands, gesturing. "Oh, please don't laugh. This is a time to stop being afraid of madness or we won't solve it, right? No one believed yesterday that it was possible that we had also heard the roar of a lion. And look at what we have found: pretty good proof of an extinct species of lion mauling a man thirty-four hundred years after such a noble beast was last seen here."

"Oh, while I may be smiling, I'm far from scoffing nor laughing at any wild ideas," William said. "I am Irish, do not forget, and we are quite mad." William shook Neil's arm in a collegiate manner.

"Sorry, old man. I'm over-protective perhaps of this wonderful person we have all just met and have each fallen in love with." Neil blushed as he took Allison's hand and gave it a kiss. "And," he coughed, "you, William, you are right on target here." Neil put an arm around both colleagues. "Time, don't we think, time we all get a little Irish, a lot fey, if you will, and listen to what we are hearing, as William says, with open ears and seeing with cleared eyes." He turned and walked up the hill toward some trees and pointed up toward where Oscar's helicopter was landing. "Oscar will need to hear this, too."

A minute later Oscar jumped out running and pointing up to those same trees. "Look! We've just spotted something more! There," Oscar said. "Up there. What is that?" And at the highest branches of the tallest tree, they saw something waving.

"Oh!" Allison's heart skipped a beat. "Is it? Can we get it down?" She called into the wind and at the same time gave her all into a jump. But she was far from achieving what she wished.

One of the teams Allison had assigned to this area was not far off. One excavator heard her and came running. "Let me!"

"Another one of us in love with her," William leaned over and whispered to Neil.

Nimble as a monkey, the excavator climbed the swaying tree. Then, as the top began to bend, he more-carefully shimmied up high and higher and carefully, branch by branch, removed a large piece of cloth and waved it in the breeze.

"Maggie's Lightning Girl scarf," Allison said, holding her breath and watching the rescue of the tangled scarf.

But before the finder was able to get down to present it, a bevy of birds *apparitioned* out of nowhere and broke into groups, each snatching a side of the cloth and, taking it out of his hands, unfurled it so it opened like a sail. The birds flew high and higher into the hills, waving this parachute-like cloth, swinging it between their groups.

"Bird groups working together! They are quite confident of what they are doing. And by looking at them, I would say they're up to something," Allison said. She pointed. "Look! They know how to open it and make it into a sail of some sort. Can birds be Irish, William?" She ran into the clearing and shouted toward where the birds were flying. "MAGGIE! FIND MAGGIE! DO YOU KNOW WHERE MAGGIE IS?" And then she called again, "MEROPE! MEROPE! WE ARE HERE!" And taking out Thanassis's phone she played the recording of the birds.

Suddenly, the recording was augmented once more, this time by the sounds of voices singing in Greek.

"Ancient Greek. Positively," William whispered, stepping close, leaning over her and listening carefully.

And on a dime, on the sounds of the singing, the birds from high up swooped back, sailing down toward them with the scarf billowing. And when they got over the group, all together the birds released it and departed as swiftly as they had arrived, the scarf settling much slower to the ground at the feet of the astonished, now quite silent Irish group.

Oscar picked it up, and with Neil's help, they billowed it out and put it around Allison's shoulders, letting the back portion fall to her ankles. And with that, Oscar Hammerstein stood back, lifted his head to the hills and began to sing, "The hills are alive with the sound of music!"

"Oscar's definitely Irish, too," Neil exclaimed before he walked over and joined in. Then did Allison. Finally, William joined the khorus. Then once again, Allison played the sounds of the voices singing in Greek. She put her head back and tried to sing along with them.

And again, as swiftly as they had departed, the birds, joined by hundreds more, arrived and swooped in formation over them, whistling and warbling and zooming around and above. And then "magically, Irishly," as William would later describe it, the birds grouped in and surrounded Allison, scattering the startled men. Allison looked back to see her Irishmen distanced from her by treasures of birds who were, she felt, somehow telegraphing to each other what they were intending. Fear again threatened to overwhelm her when, just as suddenly, the birds gathered into three teams, each taking a corner of the scarf and, in a synchronized act, wrapping it like a swing around Allison and sailed her into the air.

Holding on for life, Allison was not as surprised as she would have been had she not visualized from the recording what those birds and girls must have been doing while they chirped and sang. She held on as she sat in the scarf swing between the hundreds of birds, to be followed by a chorus of hundreds more.

Into the billowing clouds they swooped and sailed with Allison who, with their movements, was swinging back and forth high over the hills while she tried very hard to contain her fear. Earth seemed perilously far below, and she heard Oscar still singing down there, and from the cellular in her pocket, the voices continued louder, singing and singing. And then, as the clouds opened in front of her, she saw the birds' objective: a huge bankside in the hills even higher above. The birds continued up with her. And up. And into a billow of apparitioning silky clouds.

Allison knew she had now disappeared from view of the group below on the hillside. She became again quite uneasy and tried to remember what Margaret had said about thinking outside the box. She took deep breaths and said a prayer. Though she did all this, she was not quite capable of relaxing. In these clouds she could see nothing of what else she might be sailing into, nor could anyone out there see her. But then, suddenly, like the abracadabra unveiling in one of Margaret's magic tricks, Allison was sailed out of the whispery cloud prison. And what she saw made her feel pretty positively that she needed the whole team up here.

Swiftly and gently, she was lowered to an open hillside. It took her some moments to scramble to her feet and extract herself from the huge scarf. When she finally stood and looked about, she discovered that as swiftly as her escorts had arrived, they had departed.

Allison fumbled and turned on her cell phone. Merope's face appeared, "You are on the right track," she said.

"Oh, yes I am," Allison realized. She dialed.

Neil answered. He could not hear her clearly, the sound of winds being overwhelming. But then he did hear her.

"Can you track me through my device? I am seeing, well, things. Get Oscar and his geologists up here with you and your engineers. Quick, please, Neil. And Neil," her voice suddenly growing somber, "before you do that, it is imperative you call for medics."

Next, she texted William. "Get Donald. You two are the ancient cave experts. There is a series of caves up here. I have landed near them. And am hiking up. Caves recently opened, I presume, by this earthquake and deluge. Signs I see of habitation. Please, all you guys, all of you, come quickly. And, send medics."

Indeed, as she trekked up the hill, slipping and sliding in mud, the caves and their contents came into better focus, beginning to make spine-tingling sense. Suddenly, she heard someone. And she looked past a large boulder. And she knew it was not yet a time for mourning.

Below, William read her text aloud to the group. "Let's go!" He started toward the helicopters. "Come on!" But when he looked up, William saw that Oscar was ahead of him, running and talking on his cellular. "Oscar,"

William shouted, "you call medics. Get medics up where we're going. "Call for medics!"

Oscar's pilot was already on it, tracing Allison's tracking device. Oscar pointed. "He's got the location. Medics are on the way. — And look who has arrived ..."

Federica quickly organized the engineers in one helicopter and the geologists in another. "We brought a good supply of water, she told Oscar. Allison texted me. Okay. Are you gentlemen ready?"

"Where is Allison?"

"High up there on that southeast slope," Federica said, pointing. "Come on, let's get to her."

When William jumped aboard with the forensics team and Neil with his, Oscar, making sure all of the teams were accounted for and seated in the two helicopters, suddenly jumped from his copter and ran to join Neil and William. "Irish stick together," he strapped himself in with a smile at his two newest best friends.

Federica, finished her tally, strapped herself in, gave the signal and the three copters took off, the pilots chattering to each other. "Hey, everybody, another medic's copter is already following," Federica said into her microphone.

Inside the first two copters, all were glued to cell phones tracking Allison's device while scanning the terrain below. All except for William, who again was talking on his cellular.

"Caves very high up, sir. — No, sir. Higher. Much above even from where we are taking off." William Kent was talking to his boss. "Yes, Donald, I know you are the expert in this. And it was Allison who said I must call you to come ... Yes, sir, I know. But sir, Allison directed that I call you to come because these are caves none of us knew about ... No, sir, they cannot be seen from where you are. You are on the other side of that mountain. ... Yes, that's a first for us all. Suddenly exposed. ... Yes. Must have been the earthquake. ... Indeed, to the east. We followed Allison's signal. She had gotten herself up there. ... What, sir? ... Oh, that's another story. ... But, well, sir, she says the new-opened caves are filled with evidence of habitation. And she asks that we bring water. And medics, sir. We have water but, sir, please bring more. More medics, sir.

Donald, you, too, get here. Allison needs you. She said something about needing you. ... What? ... Likely closed since that last earthquake around 1200 B.C. Get another copter, sir. And, sir, get a camera crew. Come fast, sir. And get medics."

"Where? More exactly where?" Donald Suskine was making notes. This call had abruptly again switched him into another world from that he had been in after returning to his makeshift office at the hotel. Since learning of the lion-mauling episode, he had expanded his outreach to colleagues all over the world for additional help for this search and rescue. Now had come another whiplash confrontation. Perhaps he was returning to something he had not felt in decades: excitement. "How did Allison?" This announcement from William had startled him, to say the least. That lion business was strange enough. "Caves closed since the Bronze Age? Where exactly are they, William?" — Yes, excitement. — He was halfway to his waiting helicopter.

PART II

The Rest of the Story …
Keeping our Bargain

CHAPTER 1

FADE IN: *Payback Begins*

SETTING:

> Place: High Citadel Over Athens, Greece
> Date: 4 June, <u>1185 B.C.</u>
> Time: very early morning
> Simulcast with:
> Place: Hills high over Pylos, Greece
> Date: 4 June, <u>1205 B.C.</u>
> Time: very early morning
> Simulcast with:
> Place: Mountains high over Mycenae, Greece
> Date: 4 June, <u>2021 A.D.</u>
> Time: dream time (where time has no meaning)

"TODAY I, NEPTHAULIA, speak to you, Margaret, as a time-traveler. Not by using our space-time ship do I come to you, but through a special gift from Queen Eurydice. I promised you that if you saved the Khorus girls of Mycenae, I would help you solve the rest of your story. Now you will hear the story of how the real Khorus girls became figurines. So that now you can truly save yourself.

"Here, where I am, it is 1185 B.C., as you count such things. And I am in Athens, where you found my figurine.

"And Margaret, from here last night I, Nepthaulia, dreamed I was home again in Pylos. And the year there was 1205 B.C. And in Pylos on this same night in June, we became figurines. Here is that story of how that happened.

"The sound of my mother Selene's voice, Votaress of her name-sake, the moon goddess Selene, was unmistakable. And in my dream, mother's voice brought me back to Pylos, and I was standing on those high hills surrounding the citadel of the king. And I, Napthaulia, was eight years old. And the month was June. The 1205 season of the flowering of the vines was just over. It had stayed dry, giving a successful flowering, followed by a growing season with masses of grape clusters, young rosebuds and crops abundant, the fields abuzz with bees. But now, suddenly, there was a different situation. There was no rain. Daily the drought grew. And the bees became less as the grapes shriveled, as the rosebuds did not open and the olive flowers fell.

"The sound of my mother's voice in tones like sweetly falling silvery rain shimmered on my ears and my heart and came as a reminding phantom morphing, weaving, into that last night's dream. I was there with them all, home again on that most frightening night in 1205, when rain was now most-urgently needed, a night when all we khoruses joined on the hilltops of Pylos, feeling the drops that had halfheartedly, parsimoniously begun — eked out as if reluctantly persuaded, — hesitate and then dry up, making us beg fruitlessly in song and dance for the needed more. Then, at the sound of Mother's voice, the great moon goddess drove her team silently through the swift, passing, impotent clouds. Her glory startled the clouds so that at last they paused overhead. And paid attention. We hoped. We held our breath.

"We desperately needed those drops to return, to save what had started as a fine harvest but now was in desperate need of saving. For this we had been called. And my mother, Selene, had been saying to my Aunt Rhoda, my father Elios's sister, that whenever there was such a need, she heard the voice of her mother, Cynthia, the votaress of Mycenae, as she sang that old hymn to the goddess moon. Cynthia, my mother said, always began her petitioning of the clouds by calling for the goddess in that very old song taught to her by her mother-in-law, my great-grandmother, Aliana, who learned the songs from her mother-in-law, the votaress of the khorus from Krete.

"And as my mother began that old song, in my dream I saw again the hooves of the horses of the goddess's chariot. The goddess Selene's beams shone directly upon Mother's uplifted face, turning her long hair into gold. The goddess persisted in her efforts for her name-sake. When her votaress put her head back and continued that old, beguiling song, lightning flickered over the hillsides, the dry hillsides filled with now-shriveling, once-fat grapes, hillsides of orchards of all kinds, high valleys of olives and roses that were drooping in desperate need. But now, enchanted by the song of her votaress, the swift-passing, fleeing clouds stood at attention in awe of the goddess and enchanted by my mother's song. We watched as moon goddess's lunar light gilded the dark underbellies of swift-arriving and the now-stopping fat clouds. For hours they had not listened. They simply would not stop and offer their contents despite our best efforts. Their now-stationary appearance gave new energy to the khorus. Our team leaders sent out the Runners to reposition the Singers and the Dancers. With dawn still tiptoeing in the surrounding hills far away east of Tiryns, three groups of Cloud Tossers reconnoitered, regrouping, sending the more-experienced to the middle while the periphery unfastened their tight-woven mantles. These they tossed into the air, keeping hold of the ends to form a jumping net. And the Cloud Khorus Girls sang in rounds as they turned, entreating the darkening skies.

"Mother gestured to me and I readied myself. The various khoruses began The Chant.

"And so they sang. 'Come clouds, come,' I hear them call in my dream. 'Come water the vines, make plump the olives, sweetly give drink to thirsty roses.' The singing filled out as various groups of khorus girls joined. 'Come clouds, come!' The Grandmothers, the Clappers, clapped one to the other, donning hats of fantasy designed to capture the rain. The matrons, too, the Rain Wavers, wearing their polos hats, took up the khorus, now waving their rain scarves. And the khoruses altogether sang and sang and waved and clapped and shimmered and enticed down the clouds. Now the younger girls, the Jumpers, the Cloud Jumper Girls, came forth, and with sweet song, they joined hands, and when the Clappers fluffed and caught the silk woven into nets and passed them on to the Joiners, now began the khorus of the younger girls, the Jumpers and Flyers. Thus all the khoruses took shape and form. And at such pleading sounds, what cloud could resist? Clouds lowered and whispered each to each, forming magnificent shapes filled with magical, pulsating colors as they, too, joined into fluidity, filling the sky with glory.

"Down below, the various khoruses felt the cooperation. The Jumpers and Catchers gathered their equipment of tightly woven netting, lightning netting, cloud netting, rain netting. And in my dream, they massed into formation. All the while, the khoruses continued singing cloud-enchanting beckoning songs. Up above, the clouds formed a huge munificence of white and pink and purple. And the Catchers called the rain-calling songs to bring on the gray and black clouds. And the Catchers, in a larger circle, fluffed out the great net.

"'Come, clouds come,' the singers sang as they twirled in circles. Above, enchanted, the long line of incoming clouds continued to touch, bank and lower over the khoruses as enchanted.

"The Clappers clapped and syncopated. And the Whistlers began their irresistible warbling, and so came the crowds of birds, replying in like tones, flying in formations over the Bird Khorus Girls.

"The Gatherers' exuberance grew. In back, the Matrons clapped and sang and called and danced, shaking their bracelets and anklets, setting them chiming as they waved and stomped, tossing the silk netting from their shoulders into the air. The birds swarmed and caught the ends and swirled in their dance, opening the many cloud-colored nettings in back of the Jumpers, who grabbed hold. And each by each jumped into the large net to get tossed by the Khorus Tossers, who sang as they tossed high and higher. And the Jumpers harnessed the clouds, flying, singing in rhythm of winds, each singing to each cloud. And the clouds, seeing their destinies, loving their capturers, joined in the event and gave their all.

"Rain, rain, rain," the many khoruses called. And the clouds agreed and down fell the rain.

"Today, 4 June, 1185 B.C., I am in Athens. I talk to you from far away in time and space, in the king's home, high upon the Acropolis.

Last night here I dreamed of the sound of salvation, dreamed of the sound of my mother's song accompanied by rain. In my swirling dream, the oldest Matron Khorus Girl, Grannie, clicked her tongue and pulled the wool thread of purple. She was making a cloak for her Wanax, her king, named ... she could not remember which wanax was in charge now. She clicked her tongue again, fussing at the truant baby Khorus Girls who refused to join in. This behavior was unseemly. They paid her no attention; no attention to Grannie. She tossed her skirts at the truants, and her arms ordered them back to their dancing circles. Back from their games, back to their Tossers and back to their birds. As she stomped and ordered them back, she began to sing and hum, and then her hum became very loud and commanding. The babies stopped their foolish nonsense and looked up, startled and interested. After all, she was Grannie to them all. Everyone loved Grannie. And because they loved Grannie, they normally ignored her and did as they pleased. But this sound Grannie was suddenly sending at them was more interesting than their dolls. And they dropped the dolls, gathering around Grannie, who continued gathering all of them, singing this magnificent dreaming song. And it penetrated and grew in their brains, and their bodies reached and reached and reached. And it grew in my dream like salvation needed.

"And when the Cloud Khorus Girls called forth the Flying Babies, circling them, ready to toss them and catch them on their return, they ran flying into Catcher's hands to be tossed into the air, to begin their jumping and calling to their birds. And the birds flew over the Baby Cloud Catchers.

"'Come clouds, come,' the little Catchers sang enticingly. And their birds warbled in tune with their flying babies. Now they were being tossed by their sister Tossers and they were seeing sights caused by Grannie's song they had never dreamed of before, of clouds and light and colors. They joined hands and jumped, and their birds caught them, slinging the silk netting under little, plump bottoms, soaring them into the clouds, which by now were, too, enchanted.

"And Grannie walked and gestured and hummed as vigorously as she had done as a young Khorus Girl. And the song she heard in her head was not her song but that of her great-grandmother, and the memory of her singing and jumping inspired visions in Grannie of wind and rain and of silver drops, and suddenly, she was jumping, flying in air, buoyed on the 'Great-Grannie Song' she heard and hummed. And she flew and hung onto the cloud next to her best friend forever, Terpsikhore, and together they jumped and swirled on Grannie's hum, on Grannie's ribbon, and together the two enchanted the clouds to glow magenta, and then the red and gold and silver drops fell, and with the girls, they fell into the mantles of the Catchers, rising and falling. And all the girls and Baby Jumpers fell to safety like silver raindrops into the waving mantles. And when the last Khorus Girl was safely enfolded by her khorus, the rain fell in bronze drops and drowned out Grannie's humming.

"And the Catcher Girls caught the Jumper Girls who caught the Bird Girls, and they all took hands and jumped together, turning somersaults, helping each other to fly higher into the now brilliantly-colored clouds, signaling morning's arrival. Grannie's song became a solid thing on which they hung like a tightrope or a wide ribbon leading to the sky, a ribbon on which they could walk, it seemed. Grannie's song hung like a light in the sky, and the girls knew how to get to it. They jumped and called and laughed and dreamed of rain, rain, rain.

"And rain began to fall and fall. Big rain. Silver rain. Rain fell in torrents.

"In my dream, I, Nepthaulia, was back in Pylos, on that night when the rain began to fall and when the rest of it all began. It was again 1205 B.C. And I was eight years old when the rest of the story you need to know began.

"Today I am no longer eight. I am here in Athens on the high citadel, asleep with my husband, King Peisistratos, in the palace of his friend, our friend, the now king of Athens, the last king, Orestes. And it is 4 June, 1185 B.C. Many of those of whom I dreamed are no longer with us. Most took advantage and flew away. Some were less fortunate. The rest are with us. It is now almost the end.

"And somehow in the same dream, I see your eyes Margaret, you who found my figurine up here, and you are looking at me, asking again who I was. Who we were. Asking from your time, your day, on 4 June,

2021 A.D. So tonight in this story I have begun to keep my promise and tell the story of the figurines. But more, much more is yet to be told to you of us real girls becoming figurines.

"For now, this is the beginning of how it all came to be. Yet still, Margaret Benson, there is more for you to know to be rescued yourself. My great-aunt Merope is there with you, helping you. Please listen to the rest of our story and rescue, rescue, really rescue the cursed Khorus Girls. And yourself.

"It was the voice of my mother, Selene, that brought me back to the rest of our story.

"Listen to the rest. And rescue…"

CHAPTER 2

FADE IN: *Magical Rescue of the Real Khorus Girls of Mycenae*

SETTING:

Place: Mountains very high above Citadel of Mycenae, Greece
Date: 4 June, 2021 A.D.
Time: mid-afternoon to early evening

THE THREE HELICOPTERS followed each other up into the hills over the devastation, beamed up on the beeping from Allison's tracking device and now, as well, on a small signal coming from Margaret Benson's cellular. To Neil, Oscar and William, it was some sort of miracle that her phone could continue all this time. But there was no mistaking that it was Margaret's. They tried ringing it. There was no answer, but there was that small, persistent signal.

The faces of the men and women inside the helicopters were pressed against the windows, searching for places to land and looking for Allison. Her tracking device's signal was clear and they were on its beam. Now where to land? Though their faces looked tense, inside each of these men and women, geologists and archaeologists, engineers, medics and pilots too, was a feeling of excitement and anticipation. Allison had said the magic words: "Bring medics. Bring water!" It was a rescue mission they were on. And that in itself was exciting. But the archaeologists and the other "ologists" and "eers" were seeing other exciting possibilities, too.

The three pilots were talking to each other.

"There!" Suddenly Neil shouted, pointing. "There! That has to be. We see you, Allison! We see you!" He shouted as though she could hear him.

Oscar pushed him over to take a look. All faces on the right sides of the copters were pressed against the windows, looking.

And there she was. Allison. Pointing. Jumping.

The pilots took her directive and swooped down and around. And caves higher up, caves directly up and over in a cleft high in the eastern back of the now-reburied Bronze Age Mycenae, came into view. And pointing toward the largest, waving Maggie's scarf, was Allison. Jumping. And waving.

The copter pilots made another pass over, chattering to each other. There was a place for one copter near where Allison was indicating. Actually, on another pass, it became a space large enough for the second copter, too. Federica decided that had to be the medics' copter. As they continued around the mountain, there was spotted, not far around, a place for the landing of the third. The terrain looked traversable, so they readied for landings. The first one came in followed by the medics in the second.

"ALLISON, ALLISON, ALLISON!" Allison heard her rescuers, Neil, Oscar and William, call as each leapt down and started running toward her. The copters were on a narrow shelf. But these guys were expert climbers, and they raced up toward their colleague who was signaling, "Urgent!"

"We're here! ALLISON!"

"As you said, it's not yet a time ..." William, panting, said as he reached her first.

Allison interrupted. "Get the medics. Over there!" she pointed as she ran. "He's losing blood," she called.

Immediately, William texted the medics while running toward Allison. The rest of the Irish team was right on his heels.

When they reached her, Allison was bent down, leaning over something.

"Thanassis," she said gently. She gestured her team over. "This is Thanassis," she said, grabbing a bottle of water from Neil and kneeling to pour. She had a handkerchief beneath Thanassis's mouth. What he dribbled she used to wipe his face.

Oscar tore off his shirt and wrapped it, forming a tourniquet on Thanassis's leg. "Medic!" Oscar shouted.

Neil introduced himself then moved aside for the others, giving the name and field of expertise of each to the smiling guard. "Over here!" he ran out and gestured to the running medic.

"He's not in good shape," the medic said while addressing the deep wound in Thanassis's leg. Thanassis was covered in dirt, which made the medic's job more difficult. But Allison poured water, cleaning where the medic indicated. Then, when William — not to be outdone by Oscar — handed her his shirt, she wiped the blood and mess from Thanassis's face and arms, and more of his injuries became apparent.

Thanassis managed a smile, "Thank you." But even talking caused him to cough and the movement made him moan.

Allison touched his arm. "This arm looks broken."

"Yes." The chief medic, had finished the tourniquet and was now inspecting the injured man. "And this leg. Can you move it, Thanassis? No? That's far enough." He patted Thanassis on the shoulder, turned to his team members, who had arrived with a stretcher, and told them how to place Thanassis to fly him to the hospital in Nafplio. Then he made a series of calls to the hospital. "Definitely concerned about that," he said to someone on the other end. "He looks like he's been in a war. Lost a lot of blood." Pocketing his mobile, he turned back to the man now on a stretcher.

Thanassis was drinking more water.

"Not!" he croaked. "Not me. Maggie! Help doctor Maggie."

"But, Thanassis?" Allison hesitated. The hydration line was being put into his good arm. She tried again. "Oh, Thanassis, where, where is …?'

"There." His eyes told them where Maggie must be. "I fell trying to get water to her. She's been without water for a long while."

Neil took off in the direction indicated, jumping over stones and debris.

Allison was ahead of him. Over boulders and rocks and mud she clambered, calling, "Maggie! We're here! We're here!" Neil and William were just behind her. Above and to the left inside the cave, Oscar could be seen searching.

"Here!" Allison shouted as she clambered over piles of boulders to kneel beside an almost unrecognizable woman.

"Oh, Maggie," she whispered as she bent closer. Maggie was covered in mud and dirt and blood and looked more like a skeleton than alive. But somehow, those eyes opened and were brilliant with life. Maggie tried to reach, but had to let her hand fall onto Allison's arm. Allison slowly poured water for her. Maggie dribbled most of it, creating a pathway through the dirt on her face. Then she choked. And though gently the medic raised her to clear her throat, with the movement she screamed in pain. He wiped her lips and pressed a wet cloth to them.

"Suck," he instructed. At the same time, he gently moved aside her torn shirtsleeve and washed her arm before inserting a hydration line. "I hope this does not hurt," he murmured.

Maggie tried a smile. Her cracked lips looked more spectral than happy, yet she whispered, "So happy. Loo …" she croaked and tried to point. "Found mmm. Mmm."

Allison directed the flashlight of her cellular toward where Maggie had pointed. "What is it, Maggie?"

"Merpe," Maggie tried. And as she sucked more moisture and swallowed, they began to understand her clearer talk. Behind rocks right above where Maggie had fallen, Neil carefully inspected desiccated skeletal remains of what was obviously a long-ago young human, next to which Maggie had placed the figurine she had taken from the museum. The little figurine lay within reach of the hand of the skeleton.

Allison reached down and touched a shard that was folded in the skeletal finger bones upon which she shone her mobile's light.

"Merope," she said. "William, come, look. 'Merope.'"

"More," they heard Maggie croak and turned to see her eyes turned as far as she could into the cave. "More. More girls."

Neil shone his light further into the cave and gasped. "Allison! Here they are. Oh, all over! Come!" He played the light over a large surface, up and down in the cave. "Oscar! Go over that way," and he shone beams toward the left side. "Hey, William, go over there!" And his light flashed up to the right.

William and Oscar began taking photos and talking into their cellulars, up and down, left and right, carefully stepping over the remains, over boulders and jagged stones.

"So far, Maggie, I've found fifteen," Oscar called. "What about you, William?"

Oscar was bent over, photographing. William turned to come back, walking carefully over the surface, also kneeling here and there in areas he lit, bending closer, studying and photographing before returning to Maggie.

He stooped and gave her a kiss. Then, following her eyes and Allison's request, he bent over the remains of that nearby little hand and looked carefully.

"Yes. Yes." William read, "Yes. Definitely 'Merope.' It reads 'Merope,' and ..." He had to swallow to maintain composure. "And all the rest, all of them scratched their own names on shards of stone before the ... before the end." He looked up, bewildered and almost overcome. He wiped a tear. "Like all the rest, Merope, little Merope, scratched her own name." He turned and went back to Maggie. "You found her, Maggie." Then he carefully photographed the little shard with Bronze Age writing. And then took photos of Maggie with her Merope.

Oscar came running down to them, calling "Maggie! Maggie!" He knelt over Maggie and kissed her cheek. "You did it, Margaret Benson! You sure did. Maybe some scoffed, but, Doctor Margaret, you did it." He showed her the photos he had taken.

Allison broke in. "You rescued them, Maggie."

"Real girls! Real girls," Maggie whispered, reaching a shaky hand to touch Oscar's screen. "My girls!" And a tear fell, making a track down her face. "Your name?"

Oscar carefully wiped her face with a damp cloth. "Oscar Hammerstein, engineer. I am proud to meet you, Maggie. You've sent me, us, on quite an adventure. Meet my friends."

Neil and William were there, bending over to smile at her.

"Neil Simon, geologist," he said, backing away, wiping his tears.

"Hi, Maggie, remember me?" And William bent and gave her cheek a kiss. "We'll have that meeting you wanted very soon."

While the medic gave last instructions to his team about picking her up, Oscar poured her more water and gave her drops, which she avidly licked.

Allison returned from investigating. "Maggie, you sure did it!" Allison said. "Maggie, you, you …" She leaned down to Maggie. "You rescued them all; the real Khorus Girls of Mycenae of 1214 B.C." She gave Maggie's cheek a kiss, stood aside to let the medics work, then backing up and indicating the whole cave with a wide gesture, she shouted, "Maggie's girls: the Khorus Girls of 1214 B.C! Maggie, you are a magician!"

Margaret beamed as much as her parched lips allowed. "Magic," she whispered. "Merope," she murmured. "And Cynthia. And, and, and you take Merope, Allison." … She touched Oscar's arm. "Your name?"

He told her again.

"Oh, Oscar, oh, Allison," she said, touching Allison's arm. "Thank you for rescuing our Girls; for rescuing me. Take care of our Khorus Girls." Her eyes closed, and the medics had her on the stretcher and lifted it for her trip to Nafplio.

Just in time to wave to her, Maggie's biggest champion and supporter, Donald Suskine, jumped from his helicopter and ran over, blowing a kiss, sending Margaret on her way. And Federica ran over with a warm shawl for the medic to put over her. And the helicopter lifted her into the twilight sky over Mycenae and banked south toward Nafplio late on the afternoon of 4 June, 2021, A.D.

"Come this way, Donald," William said, taking his boss's arm. "You will really want to see …"

"To see what Dr. Benson has found, sir," Allison interrupted. "It's pretty incredible. They're all there. They are real. Her girls." Allison could contain herself no longer. She burst into tears. This was not a time for mourning. Oscar took her into his arms and let her cry.

"Lucky bastard," Neil whispered to William.

CHAPTER 3

FADE IN: *After the Fall; After the Rain, We Began to Become ...*

SETTING:
　　Place: Hills High Above Pylos, Greece
　　Date: 4 to 5 June, <u>1205 B.C.</u>
　　Time: 11 p.m. to 5 a.m.
Simulcast with:
　　Place: Nafplio Hospital, Nafplio, Greece
　　Date: 4 to 5 June, <u>2021 A.D.</u>
　　Time: 11 p.m. to 5 a.m.

"MARGARET! YOU SAVED US. And yourself. You listened, Margaret. And now we will continue to tell you how we became ... I, Nepthaulia, will reveal the rest ...

"Despite the curse and collapse at Mycenae, the real girls who were the Khorus Girls continued our evolution from harbingers of historic stories to community uniters, to community savers. Our songs enchanted the elements as much as the people. Everyone wanted to embrace the Cloud Khorus Girls. But that is not all our story. As you now know.

"So, today, Margaret, now that you know a large part of our story, I will tell you all the rest you were promised, how we real Khorus Girls came to be as you know us, figurines. And why these figurines became so loved.

"Tonight it is almost 5 June in 1205, and I am in Pylos, my hometown, Margaret. And tonight, 4 June, you are with me as all the townspeople are gathered below the top of the highest hillside, at the very top of which we are. Remember I have begun that story of how now, in 1205, all our harvests were in danger, needing rain? And how tonight, even King Nestor stood watching and listening at his spot, below where we, the Cloud Khorus Girls, were petitioning heaven to again work magic and save this year's harvests. King Nestor will play a large role in what comes next.

"Behind the king and around him were the town's notables, the Chief Winemakers, the Important Rose Perfumers, the leadership from the Olive Oil Consortium. They had pled with Nestor. And the king had gone to his queen. And Eurydice, as queen-votaress, had called upon Cloud Khorus head votaress, my mother, Selene. And thus, this special night of pleading to the clouds.

"As King Nestor later told me, while he stood that night, listening to the old, old songs to the clouds, he was returned to when he was a lad, a very young prince, remembering when he first heard the Cloud Khorus Girls. With the sounds of our songs, Nestor's eyes saw clearly those other clouds, and he heard the old, old songs, songs from 1287 B.C., those songs sung by the citizens of the Griffin Warrior, Nestor's great-great uncle, his great-great-grandmother's son. From Krete, the Griffin Warrior had come across the trade-sea and founded Pylos.

"The walls in Nestor's throne room have long portrayed that perfect description of the Griffin Warrior and his politics to all who came in homage and supplication, in diplomacy and in friendship. What Nestor's kingdom still represented has always surrounded and guided him as he proclaimed from his seat of guidance. Then as now, the fresco images announce to all who come: the griffin lying in peace and harmony with the lion.

"Tonight he waited and watched, as much as he could from the highest point to which all non-Khorus Girls could climb. And from under the billowing, teeming clouds, Nestor heard our singing above grow and reverberate, bringing, like rain, a sense of release. The older khorus voices sang and the younger Jumpers jumped, soaring over the clouds they sang to, and the king could see as they fell that they were soaked. With rain. And he could see that as the Jumpers soared up through those full clouds, they fell bringing the fat drops, and the Catchers, he visualized, were billowing their veils to catch the Jumpers. All together they sang and the songs came down to the king. Then Eurydice, the queen-votaress, left his side and walked higher to join her Cloud Khorus Girls. And as they all sang together, now King Nestor could hear the familiar voice of his wife, Eurydice. Suddenly, he saw them all sail into the sky, jumping and calling, his wife among the khorus. And as they soared up then down, lowered on parachutes of billowing mantles, the rain fell with them. Clearly, the king could see. Clearly, the king could feel. The rain fell in buckets.

"And the sound of that rain returned Nestor to those other falling drops, to those remembered songs, less-soaring, mournful sounds that fell upon his ears as he was returned to the sad songs sung by the khoruses so long ago, sung for the Griffin Warrior. That year was 1287 in our era. Up, in his memory, up from the old palace and then across the field, they came that evening, the mourners, singing of eternal life among the vines the Warrior loved, and up the last steep slope, still singing, they carried their Griffin Warrior to the place prepared, looking toward his vines and his rose gardens. The young warrior was their Wanax Lord and they loved him. In the twilight dappling through the surrounding olive trees, the faithful converged, singing. The grave was prepared as well as could be. He was too young to die. No one was ready for his fall. He, least of all.

"As King Nestor watched his khoruses on this now pre-dawn morning in 1205, watched the Jumpers soaring for the last jump through the pelting clouds, his real sight was still with that long-ago rain, so long ago, and those songs ... those long-ago songs and that day's rain had found him standing not far from this very spot with his mother and father and grandfathers and all his family, watching, participating in the solemn ceremony that long-ago early evening. As little Nestor was not much taller than the top of the grave, he was returned intimately to the sight of the care, the tenderness with which his great-great-uncle was being arranged on his right side, the side which would leave him facing the Gulf he loved to sail upon. All his grave treasures were displayed, attesting to his significance. Then, with deference, his final treasures, his personal treasures, were offered him. His small sword of lovely work was placed carefully, and then his favorite kylix wine cup was as well. Finally, his great-great-uncle's niece, Nestor's great-aunt, came forward. First, and, with shaking hands, she offered for the close family a viewing and then, bowing to the Griffin Warrior, lowered herself to place this last treasure. His fingers were pried open, and within them, his favorite treasure, his little Cloud Khorus Girl figurine with waving arms, which had come with him from faraway Krete when he was a young man, was enfolded in his hand, close to his heart, enfolded as well as his niece Thalassa could. Her uncle did not smell good, so she could not wait to confirm how well she had done her job, she later told her great-nephew.

"And as that sight faded from Nestor's memory, the new dawning day's cloud fall became intense. That day long ago had been a time for mourning. But today was not such a time. Instead, the hands of the Vintner, of the Olive Oil Producer, of the Rose Perfumer, the hands of all of Nestor's town leaders patted him, and, squinting in the shining rain-light, he looked up at today, this early-dawning morning, looked upon 5 June, 1205 B.C. All around him, his townsfolk, who had spent the night near him, watching and hoping, began cheering and shouting and clapping him on the back. His sight of the grave of the Griffin Warrior faded, and he looked again upon the triumph of his Cloud Khorus Girls of 1205 B.C. True, they were indeed also Dream Catchers. And his memories and the vision of the Griffin Warrior's special Khorus Girl gave him a new idea. Yes, indeed. He had another idea. And his step was youthful as he joined his community in praise of the Cloud Khorus Girls of 1205."

~~~~

"And this, Margaret Benson, Nestor told me, Nepthaulia, is the most-important of the three parts of this story about who we, your girls, were.

And this is why I, Nepthaulia, relate this part of the interconnected story of the Khorus Girls as told to me by King Nestor, who later became my father-in-law. But that is another story.

"There is still more for you to learn about us. More parts to be told."

Nepthaulia, the Khorus Girl she had found on the Athens Acropolis, bowed in Maggie's strange dreams and faded to blackness. "Remember this story, Maggie. Remember."

CHAPTER 4

FADE IN: *Khorus Girl Saviors*

SETTING:
      Place: High, High Hills Above Pylos, Greece
      Date: 5 June, <u>1205 B.C.</u>
      Time: early morning
Simulcast with:
      Place: Nafplio Hospital, Nafplio, Greece
      Date: 5 June, <u>2021 A.D.</u>
      Time: early morning

"OH, THAT HURT," she thought. Somewhere, wherever she was, lots hurt. Someone picked up each limb and examined it carefully. "Stop that!" There was a sharp sensation of pain that came through the clouds in her brain, and again Margaret gave a complaining sound.

"She's in considerable pain." A young man's voice accompanied that painful probing.

"Well, I could have told them that myself," Margaret dreamed.

"She's got lots wrong. But we will fix it all. Give her intravenous another small dose of the pain medication and I will get to work setting these bones."

While someone else's hands picked her up and moved her more gently, she did, indeed, feel less pain, and her mind returned to the familiar storytelling voice that began to speak to her again.

"I've heard all that before," Maggie whispered to the air. "Tell me more, Nepthaulia. Tell me the rest of your ... oh, ouch!"

With that "ouch," Margaret swam back from talking to Nepthaulia and tried to open her eyes. But what Nepthaulia was saying was too interesting.

With that "ouch," the doctor paused and looked at her. He had been listening with half an ear as he set Margaret's arm. She was talking to herself, which was not unusual in patients under light sedation. He continued his work.

And Nepthaulia continued her story. "My Aunt Merope guided you, and you rescued the Khorus of Mycenae from the evil queen's deadly curse, from which you now are recovering. And you also now know how I, Nepthaulia, with the Khoruses and my votaress mother, Selene, later saved the harvest in 1205 B.C. in Pylos. But there is more to this story which you need in order to connect all these stories of how all we Khorus Girls were turned into figurines: this is the rest of the story of how we real Khorus Girls became your figurines."

"Yes, yes, the figurines of my girls," Maggie whispered.

The doctor looked over at his patient, smiled and went back to work on her arm.

"I don't get much opportunity to hear archaeologists under sedation," he said and smiled at the pretty anesthesiologist.

Margaret tried to speak to Nepthaulia but could not. She moved her hand.

"It really did start with something Mother said. The sound of her voice," Nepthaulia continued. "Her tones, like gentle rain, fell like silver on my ears and on my heart and came as a reminding phantom, morphing into last night's dream. I was again in Pylos on the hilltop above Pylos on that most-special night and early morning when we needed the rain to fall. And, Margaret, it fell. Oh, how it fell at our petitioning! And that was the beginning of the transformation of real

Khorus Girls into figurines. That success began our change into clay figurines.

"Later, after the rain, when my mother, Selene, was answering my Aunt Rhoda, her sister-in-law, her reply truly began the rest of this mysterious story. This most-important story.

"Yezz, importanze …" Maggie slurred her words.

"You have heard how for hours the clouds had not listened. They simply would not come despite. The birds were anxious, as were the jumping babies. We desperately needed the rain. But no matter the enchantments called up to them by the Cloud Callers, no matter, no matter, the clouds did not move, stuck far away, from probably somewhere over Sparta in the east where, surely, those Khorus Girls were drenched with success.

"But then, after our mother stepped forward and sang the song to Selene, the moon goddess, who suddenly sailed in, the jealous clouds suddenly appeared, as though they wanted to steal the show from her. And the rest is, I guess, as my aunt did later say, Khorus history.

"This is what happened: 'Time?' My aunt called up to my mother. Aunt Rhoda was director of the Bird Girl khoruses. Mother, director of all the khoruses, nodded. 'Call!' mother replied. And Aunt held her hands to her mouth and called a warbling note.

"On that cue, the Bird Khorus Girls massed around behind the Cloud Tosser Khorus. In each hand, each Bird Girl held reins attached to a dozen birds. And uplifting their lovely faces to the first falling, silver rain, they called and whistled over their shoulders to their anxious birds. I could feel the whirring of wings in back of me, getting more excited with anticipation. I held the mantle firm and Khloris, my baby sister, scampered from over my shoulders into the net. The Baby Cloud Jumpers were in position. And the Rainbow Khorus, too. Amazing tiny tumblers, already their little, pumping legs were sending them soaring into the drizzling sky. Now the birds were released and each slid a sling under each plump bottom to bring their charges high into the sky. High and higher they flew, the babies who held tightly to the sling sides operated by their birds. And as the birds entered the clouds, they gathered the slings with babies into the fat and fatter clouds. And the babies began to swing in the clouds. And the birds sang to the babies with open slings full of clouds; The babies were swinging higher and higher into more clouds. And having gathered enough clouds, the Bird Khorus Girls reversed their sailing by parachuting back down to the Cloud Tossers and Singing Khoruses.

"'Ready, Tossers? Come, khorus! Come now,' I called, directing the rhythm, singing out the beat. And the two groups undulated the whole knitted net, sending the babies back high into the plump, dark clouds gathering faster and faster in the sky, coming lower and lower with each caress of the laughing babies. As the little ones landed in the netting, they landed and swiftly flipped back into the sky like little silver dolphins.

"'SING! SING, NEPTHAULIA! SING! ALL, SING!' Mother Selene called out over and over, now turning and gesturing to the groups of Hill Khorus Girls massed, dancing on the surrounding hills overlooking the city of Pylos and the sea of Io.

"'Sing, sing, sing, Nepthaulia,' was called to the hillsides, passed from hill to hill from khorus to khorus. All eyes were on Mother. At her upbeat, I, Nepthaulia, began the Song to the Clouds. I raised my arms and all the voices joined in, the sounds carried on the cloud wind and the sounds lifted into the skies. At that exact moment, the older Bird Girls began their ascent. Beneath them, the Tossers and Catchers circled with their cloths knitted to cushions and then return skyward the Bird Girl Soarers.

"Up and up their birds brought them, and, at the soaring third khorus, the girls flew into the clouds with their harnessing ropes, catching the clouds, springing into the clouds over and over until, enticed by the game, they relinquished, releasing this newest girth of water. Again it began to rain. And rain. Rain poured.

"As the girls the birds released sailed down into the Catchers' webs, others went soaring past, up into the clouds. 'Come rain, come! Come rain, come! Come rain! More rain! Come, beautiful rain. The harvest is waiting. The people are waiting. We thank you, clouds. We bless you, clouds. Come rain, come!'

"'Nepthaulia!' called the votaress. 'Nepthaulia,' echoed from all the khoruses.

"I relinquished my place at the net to an alternate Catcher and a Tosser and, with a somersaulting vault, flipped up into the center of the netting. Altogether, the Tossers undulated. And I gathered myself. And with one huge release of energy, buoyed by the net, I soared into the sky, into the clouds. The birds flew under me with nets and tossed me higher into the biggest, darkest cloud. And with my net unfurled, I caught the cloud and soared back, passing the other Jumpers.

"Over and over, the verses reached into the clouds, and the girls soared up into the clouds. The Catchers caught and the girls soared again and again.

"The rain continued falling heavily. The huge pithoi lining the hills, lining the roads, lining the city's streets, at each doorstep down there, all were being filled. The large cistern was being filled. The ponds and lakes were being filled. All that water sounded like laughter to my ears.

"Farmers and tillers, vintners and herdsmen and women had been waiting all night, listening and waiting. Now, in well-organized groups, they sent the water moving, flowing through trenches and swales, diverting the precious water into canals and cisterns and over and into irrigation ditches into fields.

"The large, upside-down-umbrella polos hats of the Khorus Girl Matrons on the hills were overflowing, too. And they bent as one losing the precious liquid into the fields and vines among which they stood singing. And still the rain fell. Again, the Girl Matrons unloaded their polos hats and kept singing.

"On and on we all sang. All the girls together sang, calling more and more clouds to us from over the eastern hills. We sang for our lives. We sang for our king. We sang for our parents and with our parents. And on and on the clouds pushed at one another for pride of place, demonstrating their prowess. And the rain fell and fell.

"Mother was our votaress. And when she sings out the 'Blessing To The Clouds' song, we know our work is almost done for the night. Now she began, and all the khoruses joined her in the Cloud- Blessing song.

"Still the rain fell and fell. And just when the last pitchers were overflowing, when all the ditches were perilously full, Mother gave the downbeat. We stopped singing. And instantly the rain stopped as abruptly as it had started. Such sudden silence made me shimmer within. Shimmer as I looked at the silvered fields, spangled vineyards, orchards of olives all drenched in silver, at the clouds of steam from the huddled whiteness in pastures full of sheep and goats.

"My aunt gave me her signal, meaning 'The Birds'. And I knew my work was far from done. First the Cloud Birds. Handing my little sister, wrapped in my lightning mantle, to my aunt, I made sure that the Bird Khorus Girls were feeding and drying and grooming and pampering their charges. These precious creatures, each carefully named, had taken several seasons to train for their positions and specific jobs. The younger Bird Girls were constantly training the next generations, testing and teaching.

"Now for my team, my special charges, the Khorus Cloud Jumpers. I went over to each and satisfied myself each was safe and sound. Except for Daphne. But Daphne had jumped down too soon, too far from my catching net to reach her. Our team of Catchers had been taken off-guard, and Daphne's ankle was now swollen. The Aesclepian priest in attendance wound a poultice around it and assured Daphne and me that nothing was broken. She was a good friend. I embraced the girl and got her assurances she would stay off the foot for two weeks as the physician had advised. After thanking the Aesclepian, and reclaiming Khloris, letting her snuggle into the pouch on my back, I turned to see about the rest, knowing Daphne would be well-rewarded for this hurt. She was our best Jumper-Soarer, and I knew that word was spreading like rain, first from the physician himself, then to her many followers lining the roads. By the time Daphne would reach home, her doorsteps would be saturated with bouquets and jars of honey and amphorae of wines; rounds of cheeses and pots of rose creams. I made sure that the queen's youngest daughter, Polycaste, my neighbor and best friend forever, who had been with the Tossers the whole night, had determined herself to be Daphne's chief nurse and would, with an arm around her for support, accompany her home to put rose oils on and bathe the swelling in cool waters.

"Thus, assured all were well, I gave nods to Aunt and to Mother.

"Their jobs, also done, other team leaders were at attention.

"Our votaress emptied her umbrella-polos hat as the signal that tonight's work was, indeed, done.

"All followed, emptying the last drops into the nearby water channels.

"The Votaress clapped. 'Khoruses! Singers! Lightning Dancers! Enchanters! Birds! Clouds Jumpers! Catchers!' As she called, each khorus stood in rank at attention. 'Littlest Flyers!'

"When all the khoruses were lined in rank, my aunt, the head of the Bird Khorus, called, 'Work successfully complete! At attention!'

"Each Khorus team struck the team pose: the lightning-gowned Phi, the rain-striped Psi, and the cloud-robed Tau.

"'Bravo!' called the Votaress. 'Home, khoruses! In formation. All together.'

"Dawn broke with a bruised mien on the horizon. The Head Votaress gave the marching beat. And, too excited to feel tired, the teams of Khorus Girls, arms around each other, began the downhill 'Song to the Clouds.' Suddenly, a brilliant bolt of lightning followed by a thunderous clap gave too-precipitous a notice from the sky god as herald of the efficacy of our night's work: a blinding downpouring. The rains fell and fell and fell. And we slipped and slid downhill, formations slipping as we clung to each other, still joyous, still singing, though we could not now hear our own voices.

"All the way down, the rains fell unrelenting and blinding. We felt more than heard or saw an added thunder, more rhythmic than the bass resounding from the hills. As we passed and the road narrowed, we gradually discerned them, appearing like phantoms, stomping and clapping together: the farmers, the vintners, the herdsmen and women, the spinners and corders, my schoolteacher. Even the town Mayor and all the leaders, beaming and smiling, shining wet. Still, the rain fell relentlessly as though from clouds ashamed of being so negligent to the loving importuning we had poured onto them. Our normally springy knit gowns were sopping, dragging. Their useful shapes depleted, they clung to us, making walking awkward. But we pulled them up and, flinging the lightning-bolt drapery over our arms, we continued downhill, still linked to one another. Through the downpour, dawn did arrive, allowing us to see better our surroundings and the crowds that continued to swell with welcome praise. But it did not dawn on me until much later what had truly happened that night, my joy was so immense.

"'Her grandmother will be very proud,' I heard my aunt say in back of me.

"And my mother stepped aside from her duties as votaress and in her own lovely, slivery toned voice answered 'Sister Rhoda, something must be done. Something will have to be done before it's all for ...' The sound of her voice conveyed what? Danger? Worry? Excitement?

"Rolling thunder rumbled following a bolt from sky god somewhere in the fields behind Khora and drowned out the rest of Mother's reply. We marched downhill as the pounding drops grew fatter. But as we rounded the last hillside, even the driving rain was outmatched by the rhythmic shouting that surrounded us, overwhelming any other sensation.

"Wreathed in shimmering drops, her long hair dripping them like coins, there was our Queen, open arms embracing us. She took my hand and, as the last of our group continued downhill, put it in an outstretched large one. I looked to see to whom Queen Eurydice had handed me, to see who owned the warm, brown hand clasping mine. He was beaming at me. Our king. The great creator and savior of our civilization, Nestor himself. He leaned down. I could smell the rose oil Queen Eurydice was famous for producing. I could see the oft remarked-upon blue eyes shining into mine. And before I knew what was going to happen, I was sent into the air again, this time not flung up but lifted and kept in a warm embrace of strong hands, wreathed with sounds of laughter.

"'You've done it again! She's done it again! Nepthaulia! By the gods, you have!' Nestor said. He kissed my cheeks, put me down. And plucked my little sister from the sagging pouch, pulling her over my shoulder to toss her almost as high as I had done to send her up to the clouds.

"My breath caught as I saw her get into position to soar. There was no net and no birds to take her. But she was savvy and knew this was not the real thing. She giggled and turned herself down, a born actor, flipping easily into Nestor's waiting hands.

"'Grandpa!' Her name for the king. She laughed with him and patted his face.

"And he kissed those damp, plump, dimpled cheeks. 'My little Khloris.' He put her back into her seat over my shoulder. He whispered again, 'Khloris'. It was the name of his mother. 'We will see you both soon.'

"And we were off. While I could hear the king continue clapping and prattling and praising, I began to wonder what my mother and my aunt were worried about and what plans they could be hatching. Together, they were great hatchers."

CHAPTER 5

FADE IN: *The Rest of the Story*

SETTING:
      Place: Pylos Village, Pylos, Greece
      Date: 5 June, <u>1205 B.C.</u>
      Time: morning
Simulcast with:
      Place: Nafplio Hospital, Nafplio, Greece
      Date: 5 June, <u>2021 A.D.</u>
      Time: morning

"WE LIVED IN a large house at the edge of Father's vineyards, which were also the palace vineyards of the king," Nepthaulia continued. "Father was a well-known winemaker, so well-respected that he had been appointed Chief Winemaker for King Nestor and for the palace and for Nestor's family.

"Later that morning, by the time I had bathed my little sister, combed her hair into braids, fastening them on the sides of her head, dressed her warmly and done the same for myself while she played with her Cloud Doll, we had begun to notice that, though normally up here in our rooms we heard nothing from downstairs, the noise of voices had been audible for some time and was growing louder. My father's laugh signaled he was enjoying the growing group below. Usually he was very quiet and let our mother and aunt do all the talking. A guffaw, loud enough to interrupt the story my little sister was telling her doll and me, made Khloris drop her doll. And she went running out through the rooms to look over the stair rail.

"She was already halfway down by the time I took her hand. Downstairs, among the voices of our parents, there were many, many unfamiliar voices. One in particular kept taking center stage. It was his voice that had so intrigued Khloris.

"Two strong hands reached up and took Khloris and carried her into the kitchen, where many of our neighbors and other friends and family were gathered. It looked like a party. But it was too early and we had to get to school. 'What's going on?' I whispered to Mother.

"'And here she is, our most famous Jumper, Singer, Tosser, Catcher. The famous Nepthaulia, Khorus Girl supreme,' my father called out, to my embarrassment, as he surfaced from his wine cave bearing several bottles.

"I could see the date on the Amphorae. '1216.' It was our most-famous vintage. We hardly ever opened one.

"The strong-handed guest put Khloris down so he could help Father. He took one and looked carefully at the label. 'Your finest, Elios,' said this man I had never seen before. He set the bottles on the countertop in the kitchen.

"Much smaller hands opened a way through the neighbors and townspeople, gathered as though magnetized around the front entrance, and I noticed it was Polycaste who had surfaced through that large and growing group. Then the Mayor stepped in behind her.

"Polycaste edged over to us and said, 'What's going on?'

"Khloris shrugged her shoulders. 'It has to be a party. But it's morning. I don't know. Who are all these people, Nepthaulia?' She tried to whisper, but I could see her words had reached some people nearby, who turned with large smiles.

"'Shush. They are guests. So let's grab something to eat and we'll let them do their thing,' I said. 'We've got to get to school.

"'How's Daphne?' I asked Polycaste as the three of us tried to sneak toward the dishes set in the middle of the dining table in the large room. There were boiled eggs, Khloris' favorite, and lentils, and Mother arrived with a dish of olives. Polycaste was addicted to Mother's sun-dried olives stored in their oil. Khloris grabbed a slice of warm bread and dipped it into the dish of olive oil. As I handed a plate for her to place her toast and breakfast, I listened to Polycaste say that Daphne should be back at school tomorrow.

"At the head of our family table was that man neither Khloris nor I had ever seen before. But perhaps I had noticed him among the townspeople watching from the hills this morning. I was not sure.

"He put down an empty amphora on the table as we came to take our places. 'Bravo!' he said. His voice was quiet and he had a smiling quality in his soft eyes. 'Sit, sit, girls,' he said. 'You need nourishment.' Aunt Rhoda put toast and olive oil in front of us. Father again left the room. Mother and the cook brought more eggs and lentils to the sideboard, and Father returned with another three bottles.

"'Again your finest, Elios?' Mother said. 'It's a little …'

"No, no!" Father picked one up and began to open it. 'It's a big day. Nepthaulia's big day! The Girls' big day!'"

Father chipped off the wax and, with his sharp blade, removed the cork seal. Immediately the aroma filled the room.

"Again that wine. 'The eleven-year-old wine! The wine with the aroma of violets.' It just popped out of my mouth.

"'How does she know?' My aunt was across from me. 'Is it, Elios?'

"'I've smelled its aroma since I was a baby, Aunt Rhoda. When I was three, Father opened a bottle. And when I was four, he let me taste as well as sniff it. That was when Khloris was born.'

"Aunt Rhoda picked up the amphora, looked at its tag and whistled. 'It sure is the eleven-year-old wine. The wine of 1216 B.C. The wine I helped make here.'

"'She has a great nose,' Father said, beaming at me.

"'And so did I help. In Mycenae. With our mother, Cynthia. All we girls that year…1216.'" Mother picked up one amphora. "'Yes, Rhoda,' she said. 'We all helped make this vintage. I with my mother there, and you with yours here. I with my baby sister, Merope, too.' — It seemed a special memory passed between them, and mother allowed my father to serve her some. 'Oh, yes. That aroma. It does bring me back. But how does she know?' Mother was talking about me. She wiped a tear from her cheek.

'"Did I help?' Khloris bit into her toast.

'"You? — You? No, sweet silly, I said. I jostled her in her seat. 'You were not yet. We were not yet …'

'"She does have a great nose,' Father said, passing the lentils to his guest. 'You see, Khloris, in 1216, the men were still off at Troy.' Father poured more wine for Aunt Rhoda, then he poured two drops into Khloris's kylix. 'Sniff,' he told her. She did. Pride was shining in his face. I could feel it passing through his hands. About to pour his own kylix, he stopped and brought the bottle near and poured precious drops into my water glass. All glasses were at lips. 'Ladies. Gentlemen,' he said as he looked at everyone. 'Aren't we forgetting something important?'

'"Elios!' Mother was quick. 'Elios, she's too …'

'"Too what?' Father said. 'Too famous not to taste with us and celebrate her heritage today of all days? In fact, if our guests will pardon me, I'll, after the libation to Dionysos, make the first toast to Nepthaulia. And to Khloris. And to Polycaste. And to you, ladies.'" He stood and poured drops into a glass of water and offered it to Polycaste before pouring another drop into Khloris's water. Then he poured his own. 'Now, first we offer the libation to Dionysos,' he said, and we lifted our glasses to the god before pouring the god's portion into the small trench that led under the table to the garden where was his shrine. Father again put water in our glasses, added precious wine to them and now poured wine for their guest, Aunt Rhoda, Mother and himself. The cook and her husband poured wine for all the guests. "To Nepthaulia! To Khloris! To Polycaste! And to all the Khorus Girls of Pylos!' He touched Polycaste's glass and smiled. 'Today, my darlings, you saved our kingdom. We will have, after all, a harvest.' And again he refilled all the kylixes and glasses with this, his most-prized vintage, the vintage of 1216 B.C. 'And to all you ladies who saved our kingdom while we were off at Troy in 1216.'

"'A great harvest,' this special guest intoned, then he and my father took their sips. 'And as we all know, those of us alive then, this extraordinary vintage of 1216 was made even more extraordinary because it was made,' he nodded at me, 'as your father said, by your mother and grandmothers and your Aunt Rhoda. You ladies, all school girls, helped make this wine. All the ladies of Pylos. And Mycenae.'

"'Here in Pylos with our queen, Eurydice, it was made,' my mother, Selene, spoke after taking her first taste. Immediately, her face took on a meditative look. She raised her glass and stood. 'And to the ladies of Mycenae.' Quickly she wiped something from her cheek. Then, after a small pause, she took her second taste, and her face brightened into a picture of loveliness. 'You are quite right, Dromo. It is an extraordinary wine.' She took another sip. 'It brings back good memories of Mycenae, of me next to my mother, Cynthia. And my little sister, Merope.' I watched her quickly brush another something. 'I wonder, don't you, Dromo, don't you, Elios, if this vintage in Mycenae would be as good today as this one made here by Rhoda and Queen Eurydice, if there was any spared by the devastation? Likely none was.'

"'Well, about that I cannot say. But perhaps with this late rain, after heat stressing those vines, this current vintage may even surpass the vintage of ...'

"'Bite your tongue, Dromo!' my mother almost shouted. 'Do not tempt Dionysos with assumptions on his grace.'

"Khloris picked up her kylix and sniffed. 'Violets?' she quietly said, looking at me for approval. I patted her on the head. Khloris looked at mother. 'May, may I?' She hesitated, spilling a few drops.

"Mother smiled and nodded and Khloris drank from her cup.

"'You see, Khloris, I was off at Troy,' my father said, continuing his story. 'It would be another two years before I would meet your mother. While all the men were off at war, the ladies in all these kingdoms made the wines. This particular vintage is the finest made in maybe a hundred years. What do you think, Dromo? Have you made anything to surpass it?'

"Our guest did not reply. He took two more appreciative tastes. Then he looked at me, Polycaste and Khloris, who was sitting next to him, spellbound. 'Would you like to know why I am here?'

"Without taking her gaze from him, Khloris reached for an egg, nodding agreement.

"'Let me help you.' The guest took the egg from the fingers of the mesmerized Khloris. And while he peeled her egg, he began. 'This morning, your mother sent for me. Such an offer made from the Khorus votaress! I came immediately. In fact, I was not yet home from watching the rainfall when your cook's son reached me. Shortly followed by your …'

"'Let me tell them, Dromo, why I sent for you.' Mother looked now at me and at Khloris. 'It's all because Aunt Rhoda reminded me today that while you are quite famous here, you, Polycaste, you really do not know your own famous history. You do not know about the fame of the khoruses of the past. We want your achievements to be recognized. And remembered. And with you, we also want the famous khorus past to be remembered. Dromo, here, is not only famous for his wines.'

"A figure darkened the doorway and the crowd parted. In silhouette, I could only see a very tall person, but his outline was familiar.

"'More famous than I,' Father interrupted Mother, and, before finishing his thought, he lifted his cup to his lips and was taking a big taste when, over the rim, he noticed his new guest.

"Khloris had already recognized our visitor. A large, brown hand patted Polycaste on the head, and before I could identify …

"'Grandpa!' Khloris laughed and jumped down from her chair, rushing to the figure, her arms upraised. 'Grandpa!'

"Father had put down his glass and was bowing. 'Welcome, King Nestor. Welcome.' He turned, looking for the serving lady, but her son was already there with a chair.

"The king, with Khloris in the crook of his arm, took the chair, sat between father and Dromo, picked up Father's wine cup and took a large taste. 'Oh, yes, oh, yes. Delicious. This, little Khloris, is one reason why I am here.' He put father's cup down and accepted the kylix of wine and water from Father. 'But it is only one of my two reasons. Go finish your breakfast.' He put Khloris down.

"Mother had risen and selected for the king from the buffet. She put the plate in front of him, and Cookie brought more eggs. Only then did she continue, 'You see, your Majesty, I was just about to explain to Nepthaulia and Khloris and Polycaste about Dromo .' She made sure the king had been well-served. 'About Dromo, which is, I believe, your second reason for being here. Listen to me, girls. Besides being famous for making great wines, Dromo is even more famous as a sculptor. I am sure you, Polycaste, know him well.' She smiled at Polycaste who, too, seemed dazed by this. 'His sculptures adorn your home, adorn your palace, sweetheart, the palace of your father, our great king, Nestor.' She took her kylix and raised it in toast to the king and smiled at him. 'Welcome, Majesty.' After Nestor poured a libation to the god and Father served him more wine and water, she continued. 'Dromo's sculptures also are front and center in Odysseus's palace. And his sculptures are in the great hall of Sparta and were, I remember, pride of place in Agamemnon's throne room before the ... before.' Hastily she took another sip. 'But Drumo also ...'

"Dromo interrupted. 'But I also began making some special things years ago, some small sculptures. I came here from Berbati. You may know it? Near Mycenae? There also is exceptionally pure and fine clay, and I began some long years ago when I was about your age'— he looked at me and Polycaste — 'making small sculptures of local people from that Berbati clay. Then one day, when it was needed most, when the Rogation songs of the high priests and even those by the great Agamemnon himself failed to get rain, the Khorus Girls of Mycenae and those khoruses of Tiryns gathered on all the hills, and after their importuning, the rains finally came and came as fiercely as those you called last night. And overnight, these girls became the go-to girls, the famous Khorus Girls of Mycenae of 1230 B.C., as they became known. Among them are ladies you know today. And I began making images of them, of their varied and different khoruses in their different gowns. And soon the people wanted copies of their favorite Khorus Girls.'

He put sea salt on Khloris's egg and olive oil on another slice of toast for her.

"'I have not done such again these twenty-plus years. But today, when your cook's son came to fetch me, followed shortly by Polycaste's brother, Prince Peisistratos, arriving at the request of his father,' — Dromo looked up and nodded at the king — 'at your request, Majesty, also to fetch me here, I knew why. After all, I had been at the rainfall last night with the whole town. I knew why.'

"The king put down his empty kylix, placed the stone of an olive on his plate and gestured to Dromo. 'And I,' said Nestor, quite happily interrupting, 'really originally decided to come here about ordering some of this greatest of vintages for my private stock in the palace, but then …' He thumped his kylix on the table again to show it was empty, making Father jump to grab the bottle and give a good pour, with cook's son adding water. 'Thank you, Elios. Thank you, son.'

"'And meanwhile, Majesty,' our mother said, continuing the interrupting game, 'I, seeing Dromo among the throng as we came back down the hill, reminded me of what I had to do. So, when I got back here, I sent for our friend.' Mother reached over and took Khloris's dish. She began mashing the egg the way she liked it. Khloris took back the fork. She wanted to do it herself this time. 'I asked him to come so we might talk of his making similar images of you, Nepthaulia, and Khloris and Polycaste and several of the others in the various khorus groups. You should all be memorialized for what you accomplished last night.'

"I was quite rocked back. Astonished. 'Memorialized?'

"Aunt Rhoda often reads my thoughts, so I was not too surprised to hear her words: 'You, perhaps, Nepthaulia, and you, Khloris, do not know that this fame, this talent, runs in our family.' She accepted the dish of lentils from my father, her brother. 'Your grandmothers and your great-grandmothers were, perhaps, the most-famous of the Cloud Khorus Girls. Ever. Your grandmother was …'

"'Head of the Leaper Khorus that year, that 1230 year.' Now it was Mother's turn to interrupt. Our heads swiveled from one to the other. 'And your, great-great-grandmother in 1270 as well. She lived in Elis then and came from a long line that extended back, she said to your mother and me one day, Rhoda, a line that extended here to Pylos as far back as 1400. That's quite a long generation of talented Khorus Girls. A quadruple shot at success my grandfather Photos predicted for me. So you have a pentuple shot at Khorus girl talent.' Nestor smiled, enjoying these interruptions. 'In 1270, King Nestor's father, King Nelius, had just died. And …'

"All this while, the king had continued enjoying his boiled egg, mashing it exactly as Khloris had hers, sipping his wine and taking the lentils offered and olives, too. He took another large sip, and with a larger thump, he set down his empty kylix, gave a discrete burp and interrupted what mother was saying.

"'And I,' said the king, prolonging his jolly interrupting game, 'have come here not only about this.' He again thumped his kylix on the table, and Father gave it another double dose of wine and water. 'I did send Peisistratos for Dromo and have come here not only about ordering this exceptional vintage of 1216 but also to commission figurines. To do exactly like your mother,' he gestured at me and Khloris, 'memorialize your talents and contributions to our society. Memorialize you in figurines of you, little Khloris, and of you, my dear daughter.' Polycaste blushed and took some olives on her plate. 'And especially of you, Nephaulia'. He waved his napkin at mother before wiping his lips, 'Also of you, Selene, you the quadruple shot Khorus Girl. So, Dromo, I would also like to commission, besides the figurines of all our Khorus Girls here of 1205 B.C., those of the Khorus Girls of 1214 B.C. Those from Mycenae. Those of that Khorus, like little Merope, sister to your mother.' He looked at Khloris. 'Sister to Selene and daughter of the votaress Cynthia, Selene's mother, your grandmother, Khloris, so they, too, are memorialized. They were well-loved by so many, so many who still remember. All who became Khorus Girls of Fire. All those also, Dromo, of the Khorus Girls like those your great-great-grandfather made on Krete. I want to make famous the figurine my wife, Eurydice, especially asked me for, that, of your grandmother, Nepthaulia and Khloris, the votaress in 1214 B.C., Cynthia. And her little Merope. Will you, Dromo, accept my commission?' He put down his glass and wiped a tear from his whiskers. 'Daily Eurydice remembers the rescue mission with you leading, Selene, and she wants to commemorate your family with you, Selene, to commemorate the cursed Khorus Girls of 1214 B.C. And you, the savior Khorus Girls of 1205 B.C. You girls.'

"There was silence in the room. The guests standing and sitting all around put down their kylix cups and plates and listened for the reply.

"Dromo put down his kylix and stood. 'So, sir, I will accept your commission and Selene's request as well and will make sculptures,' he said, looking at Nepthaulia, 'of you and of you, Khloris, and of Polycaste.' He was almost drowned out by cheers, but he put up his hands to continue. 'And of all the Khorus Girls as requested by you, our dear king. I would like to make as many as possible from the real, actual girls for exact likenesses in various poses for the jumps for which they are renown, in their varied dress signifying their khorus groups. As well as for those from the past for whom good likenesses remain, like the khorus votaress, Cynthia, the greatest singer of the anthem to the moon goddess and the cloud-blessing song. For that, you, Selene will direct me.'

"'And of my sister, Merope, and cousin Althea,' Mother added, again putting her napkin to her cheek.

"Everyone stood with glasses raised and cheered. And when the king gave Dromo a bear hug, they all rushed to do the same, all talking and telling him remembered Khorus stories. The king returned to his breakfast and his kylix.

"Khloris finished her egg. It was time for us to take off for school. But just then Dromo, released by our curious neighbors, turned to us. He took Khloris's hand. And looked at me. And Polycaste. 'You must come to my studio. You father will bring you. So I can make models. Do you agree?'

"I looked at Father. I looked at Mother. I touched Khloris's arm. She took a last swallow of her water and wine and nodded. I looked at Polycaste, who put down her toast and looked first at Khloris and then at me and nodded. I looked at sculptor Dromo and nodded, too.

"'Yes,' I said. 'Thank you, sir.'

"My father filled the king's kylix and Dromo's and his again. Then he lifted his. 'Again,' he said, 'I offer a toast to you, the Khorus Girls of

1205. You, Nepthaulia, and you Polycaste, raise your glasses and toast with us. Enjoy this celebratory wine with all of your family.'

"'I raise my glass, too,' came from Khloris, who was raising her glass and looking at the king. When he took a taste, she did so as well.

"Through stifled laughs, the assembly raised its glasses along with Khloris and our king and tasted the wine in honor of this successful negotiation to create the Khorus Girls figurines. This time Mother said nothing while we tasted with Khloris and the king and all our friends. The wine was even more delicious than I had remembered from tasting it three years ago, when Khloris was born. Mother seemed to be remembering that day, too, because she was both crying and smiling as she joined this universal acceptance of the Khorus Girls figurines plan. And Aunt Rhoda put out her glass for another pour.

"'To the Khorus Girls of 1205,' we heard the king intone. I wiped Khloris's mouth and took her hand. It was high time we got to school.

"As we left, along with my best friend forever, Polycaste, we heard him still: 'And Elios, as I said. I am also here about this famous vintage of 1216. I need to order several dozens of amphorae. All our eight vineyard townships are preparing for the annual Rogation Day and prayers to the sky in gratitude. When do you think they can be ...'

"And so it was done. The hatching of my mother and her sister-in-law would result in the creation of clay likenesses of all of us Khorus Girls, those of 1205 B.C. and those of the cursed Khorus of Mycenae from 1214 B.C., the girls doomed to become the Khorus of Fire.

"And we three were off to school in the drizzling morning."

~~~~

"And so now, Margaret Benson, you know the rest of the story, as promised."

CHAPTER 6

FADE IN: *A Vision from the Past*

SETTING:
Place: Hotel Belle Helene, Mycenae Village
Date: 10 June, 2021 A.D.
Time: morning

"WE GOT CAMERAS up in there this morning. ... Yes, yes. — Of course they were most careful, Maggie. All of them were trained by you. — Naturally. — Archaeologists and Anthropologists were in charge. All led by Allison and Federica ... Yes, dear friend, they filmed the whole area. I've seen some of what they found. ... Yes, yes, dear Maggie. — Indeed it is. It's all, most, extremely in fact, amazing. ... Mags, stop worrying. — We are, they are being very careful with your. ... Yes ... Yes, you were right on. — We have found all that, just as you said, dear. — And more. — We do not know how you managed to find all you did, injured as you were. ... Yes, yes. And Thanassis, too, yes. ... Of course I spoke with your doctor; just now in fact. ... Hum? ... Naturally it's a 'yes' to that. It's not a concern. — We most definitely will keep your time-table front and center in planning the release of your retraction. — Instead of you doing all that typing, which the doctor is frowning about, before he quashes the whole scheme, I have arranged for two of your favorite grad students to take it all down from you. ... Thank goodness. — So, well then. — All is in order? ... Yes. ... Well, to that I say, you let me know. But Maggie, before all is said and filmed and done, we will talk many times. ... What? ... Yes. I promise. Now you rest. Though you understand why I cannot get there to see you for several more days, we're sure to communicate tomorrow." And Donald Suskine put down the phone. He was standing in Maggie's former room in the Hotel Belle Helene in Mycenae. Now his office this last week.

Kati-Selene ran past, waving at him, followed by a group of men with cans of paint and ladders.

She returned and peeked in. "Will you join us for dinner, Dr. Suskine? On the balcony around seven?" And at his nod she rushed off.

There had been so much coming and going through this little, historic hotel, with all the teams from UNESCO and all his colleagues, it was a wonder Kati-Selene was still smiling, Dr. Suskine thought as he watched her hurry into the corridor. In fact, it was a wonder she had begun organizing the refurbishing of the hotel so soon. She and Agamemnon had only returned from his uncle's house in the hills three days ago, and here she was with workers racing after her, doing her bidding.

"She's quite a worker, your wife," Donald said, smiling at Agamemnon as he came by.

"She always finds something that needs doing, even if no one else would notice." He shrugged and went into the coffee area. "Would you like a coffee, doctor?" he called over his shoulder.

Before Donald had much time to give the question a thought, his host was back and handing him a small, white cup containing a steaming, aromatic brew.

"It's sweet." Agamemnon managed a smile. He, too, was busy getting things going again, but he was also grateful for all these paying archaeologists. UNESCO and all those universities were generous, so he would be generous with them, too. After all, their accommodations were spartan at best. Cots instead of beds. But the water in the baths was hot again, and the towels, and sheets and blankets were clean and sweet-smelling. And no one seemed upset about sleeping on the balcony in cots until the engineers determined the building to be totally safe. In fact, they all were most friendly. "There is more in the pantry," he said, glancing around Dr. Suskine's office, which really was Dr. Margaret's room. "Please help yourself." He turned to go see about the cleaning of the balcony but turned back. "Dr. Suskine, sir, excuse me."

Such a long string of words was so unusual for the normally taciturn Agamemnon that Donald stopped his work and looked up and gestured him in. "Yes, Agamemnon. What is it?"

"Dr. Suskine, sir." — Agamemnon seemed to have something holding down his tongue, something that prevented him from forming the sentiment into words. — He sipped his coffee and tried again. "Doctor, we are, my wife and I are, indeed we all in the village are most grateful to you and to you all for having found and rescued our friend, our long-time friend Dr. Margaret Benson. Indeed, sir, we are all in your debt. She has been a true friend for many years. Thank you." Agamemnon had to turn away swiftly. A tear was coursing down his cheek. "And, sir," — he could hardly say the words — "our cousin Thanassis."

Donald got up and followed the man out to the balcony, where he joined him in watching the passing traffic of the rescue efforts while they sipped coffee. Stelios and Anthula across the street waved and smiled and waved again.

"Come for pizza, Doctor," Stelios shouted. He kissed his finger tips and little Anthula called, "Zaaa," and stuck her fist in her mouth and laughed.

In back of Donald and Agamemnon, on the balcony, the housekeepers had moved all the cots to the sides and were sweeping and mopping. Donald's cup rested on the ledge next to Agamemnon's. Donald looked the equally tall Agamemnon in the eye. "We, naturally, are all saddened, Agamemnon, by the deaths of your nephew Menelaos-Stavros and cousin Phaestos. Good men. Faithful in their duties and talented. And, indeed, we mourn with their families." He patted the man on the shoulder. "And we, too, are so, most grateful that Maggie was found alive and rescued. Truly thanks to Thanassis. She still has a way to go, but her doctor assured me an hour ago that she is out of the woods."

Agamemnon frowned. "Was she in a woods?"

Donald had to control his automatic response. He pretended to sneeze into a handkerchief behind which he pulled down the corners of his smiling lips.

"Oh, forgive me, Agamemnon." He wiped the smile and put away the handkerchief. "That's an American expression. It means she will come out of this ordeal just fine. She will mend and be back to work pretty soon." He turned to go. "And Thanassis, too. He is young and will mend quickly. But, you know, with you, Agamemnon, we all are thankful that Allison and those men got there when they did. Another night up there and the outcome might not have been so positive. For both of them." He picked up his cup and took the last, sweet sip. "Thank you for the coffee. And the talk. We are all grateful to you and your wife and staff for the comfort and kindness with which we are treated here. It's long been a place for archaeologists. And if we have anything to do about it, it will remain so for many generations to come." He turned and went back to his temporary office.

Donald's cell rang, and as he walked, he talked to the team up top at the cave where the excavations of Maggie's discovery were ongoing. Now, assured they were photographing and videoing everything carefully, he stood looking out the back window of Maggie's room — his temporary office — looking up to the hills to the north-west. In the far distance, he could see the wealth of vineyards, the rows marching up and down those hills. His call had ended but still he stood, sort of mesmerized by the symmetry of the landscape.

"Those vineyards have been in Agamemnon's family for over ten generations," he heard in back of him and turned to see Kati-Selene standing in the door. She was holding a large bolt of material. "May I come in, Doctor?" She waved and unwound a bit of the cloth. The pattern was quite lovely and simple.

"Naturally," he said, smiling at her.

"If you do not mind, I would like the draper who is here to measure the windows. It will not take but a minute. We are having made new curtains that will match the new paint."

The draper did the quick measurement.

Kati-Selene stood at the window next to him and pointed to where he had been gazing. "Those vineyards are very old, planted in grapes that have existed in this area for so long, no one knows how long." — He looked up where she pointed. — "Doctor," she continued, "I have something I would like to ask you professionally. May I?"

"Naturally, Kati-Selene." She was so darling, like a living example of those Khorus Girls, almost, he was thinking. A very smart one, too. "What would you like to know?"

"I have a feeling, a large feeling, Doctor, about the vineyards of Agamemnon's uncle and grandfather up there. You know, that's where we stayed the last week after the earthquake and all."

He turned from gazing at the vineyards to look at her. She was intense with what she wanted to say.

"Often, Papa — that's Agamemnon's grandfather — and I stood up there at night looking down here, and he talked about what they saw that day and evening when the cataclysm happened. And he talked about what the inhabitants of those vineyards all those millennia ago, in 1214 B.C., when another such cataclysm happened, and worse, he said, what those inhabitants must have seen from that vantage then. And while he talked, I had a vision of those vineyards, those vineyards that provided the wines for King Agamemnon's tables. And I would like to ask if you could possibly consider coming up there with me one day to see if, perhaps, many feet below our vineyards, there might be the remains of Bronze Age vineyards."

Donald stood looking at her, at her intensity, and in him formed a vision from hers of those Bronze Age vintners among their vines looking down as the destruction of the palace and the citadel happened in 1214 B.C.

"Kati-Selene, that's something we have not even thought about before: the lives of the more-ordinary citizens who provided all the wherewithal for the palace society." He turned and looked again at the vines in the distance. — "I think that's a great idea. We definitely will do that once all this is sorted out. It may not be for some time, but depend on it. You and I will have time to talk about this, and I will go up there with you and we will make a plan." He turned to see a large smile on her lips and in her eyes. "With Dr. Margaret, of course."

She gave his arm a pat. "That's wonderful. I'm very excited." And on a dime, she spun about, preparing to take off to meet the workers. Then she stopped on another dime and turned back. "Doctor, Doctor, I hear that Dr. Margaret found wonderful things up there. What sort of wonderful things did she find? We are, naturally, all quite curious."

"She found —" he hesitated. There was so much, he wondered where to begin. And then there was the surprise element to be saved for Margaret's announcement. Then he looked and saw the excitement in Kati-Selene's eyes. "She found her 'Merope'," he replied.

Kati-Selene tried to open her mouth and found it hard to swallow. Then she blurted, "Merope? She found Merope? Is that what you said?" Kati-Selene had a look of astonishment on her face.

"Indeed. That's what she calls her special figurine Khorus Girl. Well, soon you will learn more. And so will I. That's about all I can say for now." He pulled out the desk chair to get to his computer. And she turned to join the draper, who was waiting for her in the hall. "Oh, and thank you again for making us comfortable," he called.

She beamed a great smile at him and waved, then turned back. "Oh, Doctor, if it's not a problem, tomorrow or the next day, after we have finished repainting the room next door, would you mind moving in there so we can get Dr. Margaret's room done, too?"

He smiled and nodded. And opened his computer.

And she ran after the draper.

~~~~

"Thank the gods it was not a time for mourning for Margaret Benson," all the inhabitants of the Belle Helene were thinking.

"Merope. Merope, Merope. You're here!'" Kati-Selene was also thinking. "Merope," she whispered aloud.

CHAPTER 7

FADE IN: *Fifteen Days Later: "Anticipation"*

SETTING:

Place: Hotel Belle Helene, Mycenae Village

Date: 25 June, <u>2021 A.D.</u>

Time: all morning

THE AFTERNOON BEFORE, after the Blessing of the Flowering of the Vines ceremony and after the celebration that followed, which lasted into the evening, Papa had decided it was wiser to stay the night than to drive home. So they had joined the troops and slept very well on cots on the terrace of the Belle Helene. It had been fun. But there was lots to do today. Papa yawned as he turned back from the car park, stepped up onto the bottom step, shooing the cat away, and waved to Agamemnon.

"Back soon!" he called before returning to the car.

"Back soon!" chorused Uncle George and Aunt Philia as they drove off.

Agamemnon put down his cup and looked at his watch. It was already 9 a.m. "I hope not," he murmured as he waved *antio*, then turned and shook the hands of the carpet layers. Their job was finished early and they were on their way to begin the day. And though it was early, Agamemnon offered them their choice of coffee or wine. They had not celebrated with the others but instead had been working all night and had done an excellent job with the new carpets, as well as making the rest of the installations possible.

"Back soon!" they, too called as they left. Again, Aga murmured that he hoped not. He had to get this place into shape after all the guests these past weeks and this refurbishment Kat had insisted upon. As they drove off, Agamemnon tossed into recycling the empty bottles of Papa Dassis's wine, poured himself a second cup of sweet coffee, looked up to see Kati-Selene and frowned even more. What was she doing all dressed like for a …? Oh. He walked back out onto the terrace.

"No, no, sweetheart," he called. "It's not until tomorrow."

"Aga," she said as she came up onto the terrace with a laugh. "Why are you dawdling? It's time you were dressed. We'll be late."

She had been bidding Father Kristophoros *antio*. Yesterday evening while he conducted the annual blessing of the flowering vines, Father Kristophoros had asked them all to join in singing an extraordinary song in praise of the great weather promoting such excellent, long, flowering. And he prayed a special prayer for continued divine aid for this growing season of vintage 2021. He was such a wonderful priest. Now, after making sure Father Kristophoros had followed her direction and turned his car uphill toward the once-citadel, Kati leaned over to pick up a stray cup left by a departing archaeologist, then turned to approve with her housekeepers that the last cots were being folded and packed away into the storage house in back. Walking toward her still coffee-sipping, daydreaming husband, she turned *en route* and stopped to kiss cousin Nikko.

"Back soon," Nikko, too, called as he ran down the steps. He had just finished delivering new beds to the guest rooms from his workshop in the hills near Papa Dassis's vineyards. He was rushing to return with another shipment of chests. His old truck complained as he backed out.

Agamemnon was in another world. He had to let go of the tension he felt over everyone's obviously friendly calls of "back soon."

"They feel at home here. That's all," he mused. "Relax." He flexed his fingers and breathed in. It had been such a hectic three weeks. He would now enjoy sipping his coffee while again watching as he leaned on his balcony, mesmerized (as if he was seeing an old film), by this passing scene of cars and more cars going up to where the excavated citadel had been only three weeks ago when all this began. Other signs of returning to normalcy: Old Street Dog was back sleeping in the street and watching all the passing cars.

"Yes," Agamemnon thought. "It is great to be back." This time, though their neighbors still sat fanning themselves, still pretending nothing was going on, this time Agamemnon waved his cup at the passing motorists, all of whom he now knew. They were back to work up there, uncovering the parking lot and replacing the guard's house, no doubt. Then it would be the Lions' turn to get unearthed. Soon he would have to go up there to check on the progress being made. He would take Stelios, who was right there across the street now, waving at the procession. But not today. Someone tooted and called something that sounded like, "See you soon." He waved and smiled and sipped the last drops. All of them in those cars had been his guests for the last three weeks, sleeping on those now-packed cots: archaeologists, anthropologists, engineers, UNESCO people. He had enjoyed getting to know them. Another car honked. He waved his cup. After all, soon all would be back in order. And they would all be back in real rooms at the refreshed Belle Helene. He sighed. Tonight, he would ask a few to describe what they were all doing up there. Certainly, the line of cars was endless today.

Kati-Selene could see he was in another world so, against his dreaming and the noise of the cars and Cousin's old truck, she talked louder.

"Why are you dawdling, Aga?" she said, slapping his coverall-clad bottom. "Cute!" she whispered in his ear. "But you should be dressed. Go change your clothes. We'll be late. Did you forget?" She turned to the honker and waved.

He smiled. "No, darling." He twisted a lock of her hair and held her for a moment before she was off. "*Anticipation,*" he hummed. He was thrilled to see that in her happiness about going to Athens tomorrow for the belated birthday celebration, she had mixed up the days. "*Anticipation.*" He followed her inside. "I have not, sweetheart. But you have." But the words had hardly come out before he quickly swiveled back at the odd sight of an ambulance sandwiched between the last cars. "Strange," he murmured, then he blotted out the sight and poured himself another cup of coffee. Adding sugar, he took Kati's hand and kissed it. "Sweetheart, it's not until …"

But Kati-Selene had already made herself air. She was chatting with the departing paperhangers. Then she grabbed a bag from someone leaving, calling to Sophia's husband, Phokis, for assistance.

Hearing another car honk, Agamemnon stepped outside and found Kati-Selene was there waving, calling at yet another departing car, "See you later." She ran back up on the porch and took his hand, walking them back inside. "Cousin Amalia," she explained. Cousin Amalia was a decorator and had come from Athens to help the refurbishment. "She's just off to get the last two chairs. She'll be back. Did you not hear me, darling? You'll …"

In the bright day out there, he could see Amalia's little car speeding away. Agamemnon picked up his steaming cup of coffee. "Kat-Selene. Sweetheart." He had to be gentle. "You're mixing up the days. It's tomorrow, sweetheart. Tomorrow we leave."

"No, Aga. Today. Now. Get dressed now. We will be late for Dr. Margaret's welcome back. We're supposed to be there in ten minutes. And that was five minutes ago."

Agamemnon swallowed the hot coffee too fast and sputtered, slamming down the cup and saucer, and turned from a confused man into an enlightened flash down the corridor toward their rooms. "Oh, my gods!" she could hear. And when she had caught up with him, he was already in a new, pressed shirt and was jumping into his Sunday trousers. Kati again swatted him on the bottom. "Tomorrow!" she promised him. "Now hurry."

She ran out toward the car. Then turned back to call up to Sophia - who was carrying in the freshly laundered sheets, to "make up all those new beds" and "leave the windows open, please, Sophia." Kati wanted the smell of paint out by the time the archaeologists, engineers, anthropologists and geologists returned and the new guests arrived that evening. "What a surprise is in store for them," she thought.

"At last, after almost three weeks on those cots, all sharing two bathrooms."

She was singing by the time Agamemnon jumped into the car. And as she turned the corner and passed over an invisible line where she had stopped that frightful night three weeks ago, she made the Sign of the Cross and said a quiet prayer of thanks that so many had survived. Turning up higher on the once-again road, there was, to her left, the new guardhouse, and the guards waved them up. Agamemnon waved back. And so she headed up a little further, parking where directed, not far from the still buried Lion Gate. She took Agamemnon's arm, and they walked up toward the bright, white tents.

CHAPTER 8

FADE IN: *The Return of the Magician of Mycenae*

SETTING:
    Place: Tent Museum, Mycenae Archaeological Site, Mycenae,
       Greece
    Date: 25 June, 2021 A.D.
    Time: late morning to early afternoon

THREE MINUTES LATER, Kati-Selene and Agamemnon found a now-familiar group of archaeologists and geologists and anthropologists and engineers all gathered and chatting and calling out to welcome them as part of this family, which they now had really become. Some were beginning to take seats in the first of a newly erected series of large tents attached to the few remaining recovered rooms of the Mycenae Museum. Others were still chatting in various sections, old and new.

    Donald Suskine escorted the Dassis couple to their seats in the front. Many of their hotel guests came over to chat. They felt very welcomed by this august group.

    "They're here!" Federica said, pointing, showing Allison.

    "Oh, goodie!" Allison turned and waved at the couple. Then she touched the microphone at the front. "Now that we are all here, it is time," she said. "Time we welcome back Dr. Margaret Benson to her home!"

The group stood and shouted, "Welcome home, Maggie!" Stragglers raced to their places. And three medics and a hobbling Thanassis carried in, in a sort of sedan chair, a bruised, bandaged, splinted and smiling Maggie. She waved and was then ensconced up center.

"Probably not since the Bronze Age have so many from all across the globe converged up here twice in one month," Margaret's voice did not carry as well as before, so she was using a small microphone that Allison had affixed on her jacket collar. She had to stop often and take breaths, but Allison, Federica and Thanassis were right there to help her and continue when she got too breathless.

Maggie pointed to the large screen at her right. With her gesture, the screen lit up with a display of many clay figurines of her girls. This time, though, they were not arranged as usual on various levels in glass cases. Instead, these figurines were shown all lying down in rows.

"Though I often call them my girls," Maggie explained, "these figurines of girls have been found by many archaeologists, by Lisa French principally. However, these figurines you now see here are exclusively of the Khorus Girls from Mycenae, clay replicas of real girls who perished here in 1214 B.C. Their clay sisters from other city-states are not represented with this group. How do we know? Because they are presented here in the order that we discovered their real, actual selves, high up there in the cave. Each figurine has been identified by comparing each to the recreated likeness of a real Khorus Girl by our anthropologists here, determined from skeletal remains."

Margaret paused to take a breath. "Now you will see what a remarkable, in fact, stunning job they have accomplished." Again she found it hard to talk, but she gestured for the next view. "Between the guidance from our guide, the real Merope, speaking to us through her figurine," (many murmurs) "which we have on cellular" (even more murmurs when Thanassis stood and held up his cellular) "and the name-shard found in the hand of every real Girl …" She paused to change the focus on-screen and felt the images generated a most-thoughtful, palpable, intake. "We have, after thirty-two-hundred and thirty-five years, joined each clay figurine with her real self. We have also been able to learn the name of each, thanks to these identifying shards each clasped.

Here you see the clay figurines joined to the recreated image of each real Khorus Girls, as each looked that day as a member of the 1214 B.C. Khorus Girls of Mycenae."

On the screen was a long, composite shot of the cave filled with skeletons. "And here you can see ... look here." A close-up of several skeletal hands came up. A gasp was heard from the audience. "Yes. Each is clasping something in her left hand. They are name-shards. And here we have a close-up of them." There was murmuring from some in the audience. "Yes," Maggie continued, "they are all in Linear B, all names, names of each girl, scratched by each girl herself, we must assume, as each is different. And here," she said as the next scene came into focus, "is a sort of Khorus lineup showing the reproduction of each girl done by our anthropologists to show you not only how many we rescued but how each looked on that day of their last performance, June 1, 1214 B.C., when they were sealed in the cave by the avalanche. Caused by Clytemnestra's curse."

This caused murmurs mixed with clapping. Many were the faces being wiped with tissues.

"The actual girls' remains will remain where they have been since that June day in 1214 B.C. The shards show they wanted to be remembered. Next photo, please, Allison."

A video began, starting with a broad overview of the large cave. Then the camera panned throughout the cave, showing, from right to left and back again and from the back to the front of the cave, each skeleton's remains. And each shard with a name scratched on it in individual handwritings was shown. Last, the focus was on four remains next to each other.

"Please, Allison, can you and Federica read these?" Margaret's voice was too full of tears to do it.

"Cynthia," began Allison. A close-up showed the shard in her hand. "The votaress, the mother of ..."

"One moment, please," Margaret changed the video focus to the next remains and into a close-up of that hand. "Thanassis, say this name, please. Thanassis?" Margaret gestured him forward. And though he was walking with a cane, Thanassis proudly stood on the other side of the screen.

"Merope!" He said it loudly. "Merope! We found Merope, guided by Merope!" He was so proud to say it to all of Maggie's friends. As one, the assembly stood, cheering and clapping and crying, too. At Allison's gesture, they returned to their seats while, again, the camera panned to a close-up of Merope's left hand and the shard scratched with Linear B.

"Merope." This time, Thanassis was joined by Maggie and the whole gathering. "And please," he went on, "look carefully at Merope's other hand." He pointed at the next close-up on the screen. On Merope's other hand was laid the little figurine that had held court from her case in this museum since she had been discovered. "Maggie asked me to put it there for this shot. This little figurine, I must repeat, guided us every step of the way, first to her real girl self, and then to all her khorus. She guided us to rescue all these real girls who had been cursed by Clytemnestra so long ago."

Federica took the microphone, "And this photo shows Merope with her mother, Cynthia, and her Aunt Thalia and cousin Althea, as reconstructed by our anthropologist."

"There is so much to tell," Maggie said as she set down a glass of water. "As you can see, Thanassis and I went on a great adventure with Merope as our guide. We were not sure we would make it back. But Merope had promised that if we did as she asked, we would not only rescue all of her khorus of real girls, we would be saved, too, from Clytemnestra's curse."

The last of the remains were shown and then another full screen shot of the whole cave of the Khorus Girls.

"Rescued, at last after thirty-two-hundred and thirty-five years. The Khorus Girls of Mycenae. The Cloud Callers, the Bird Callers, our Khorus Girls. And, as Merope and her niece Nepthaulia, also call them, the Fire Girls. All real girls. Many represented by the figurines many of us have speculated about for so very long. And," she said as she reached out a hand and Thanassis crossed over to take it in his, "as promised by Merope, for saving those real girls, we are here, too."

The audience stood up and applauded. "Merope!" Donald Suskine said most loudly. "Maggie's girl!" And the video close-up again clearly showed the scratched name 'Merope.'"

"Now," Allison spoke up, "here is one last shot to show all the names of the Khorus that Maggie and Thanassis rescued. Close-up, please, on that large boulder." And in close-up on the screen was a large boulder on which were scratched names. "Merope's mother, votaress Cynthia, has here inscribed all the names of her khorus. And here, as you see, she wrote out the story of what happened to them. The curse of Clytemnestra. And how her other daughter, Selene, went for help in Pylos but did not return in time before the fires made them flee into the caves where the earthquake buried them. They did survive two days with some little water and food. But soon, all air was expended in the cave, whose entrance was blocked by boulders and mudslides. They sang these songs to the end. And here she inscribed the words of the 'Cloud Calling Song.'" Maggie read each word. "This song will have music composed for it by some of you, using the songs from Merope recorded on our cellulars. And I hope at our next meeting, we can try to learn and sing in praise of these, our Mycenae Khorus Girls of 1214 B.C. It is true this all sounds like fantasy and not archaeological factual. But there it is for you to judge."

Then Margaret continued.

"After our last meeting, I was finally beginning to put together all that Merope and Nepthaulia were telling me, beginning to understand the enormity of my mistakes, those I had just printed, about who these little figurines had really been. And I had decided to immediately write a retraction and create a sort of compendium to the original book, calling it *Errors of an Archaeologist.* Now, as Merope promised me, I have a far better book to attach to the first one. With photographs and quotations from our cellular recordings, some of which I will now play with the help of Thanassis, who was there with me, saving me the whole time. I would not be here were it not for Thanassis, for his strength to get us to survive where we were dropped far above here and his enthusiasm for all these real girls and women, especially the one he has fallen in love with, little Merope. I want us all to show Thanassis how much what he accomplished means to what the world will learn about Mycenae. And the real Khorus Girls of Mycenae of 1214 B.C."

Thanassis took the microphone. Quieting the applause, he described the three days and nights they were up there, not knowing if anyone would ever find them before another storm might come and cover them up, too, along with the remains from the Bronze Age Khorus Girls. He then showed the video taken by Allison, William, Oscar and Neil when they had spotted them.

The Irish Team then took turns reading aloud each name of each girl. As each name, held in a skeletal hand, appeared on the screen, the audience, too, began calling them.

Donald Suskine took the stage with Thanassis and Allison. The tall, distinguished professor was beaming. "Margaret Benson, twenty-five days ago, you were scheduled to leave this site and head to your new office in Athens to begin reconstructing the end of the Bronze Age throughout the Peleponnesos. Since then, as we all know and witnessed, the mountains, and a Bronze Age curse, almost decided otherwise. But today, we're here with a large contingent of your rescuers from all our disciplines and joined by many colleagues who were here twenty-five days ago to congratulate you on your new book and new appointment. Now I make an announcement. One to which Margaret herself is not yet privy. As of today, and until the Lions are visible and roaring again from atop their gate, Margaret Benson, your office will remain here."

The audience erupted with shouts, but putting his hand up, Donald finished what he had to say.

"Margaret, you can begin your new work from right here while, with the able co-leadership of Allison and Federica, you will also now direct the re-uncovering of Mycenae." The audience rose and shouted "Bravo!" "Yes!" "Congratulations!"

And under the watch of so pleased an audience, and with Thanassis's help, Margaret got up and hugged Donald and then, leaning on Thanassis, walked toward a central arch. It was covered with a banner. Margaret gestured to Thanasis. He took the cord and pulled it to reveal:

"THE MYCENAE DREAM CATCHER CLOUD KHORUS GIRLS OF 1214 B.C.: THE MEROPE WING."

"The Mycenae Dream Catcher Cloud Khorus Girls of 1214 B.C.: The Merope Wing!" Everyone called back. "Yes!" "Merope!"

Margaret took back the microphone. "When completed, this room will be solely dedicated to what Thanassis and I discovered with Merope as our guide, and what is still to be discovered about the Khorus Girls and their last days up where we found them," Maggie said. "Now begins the next step in this discovery of the real Khorus Girls, again with the help of their figurines. I will continue my search to find out how Merope's figurine, made in Pylos, came back here to be discovered where she belonged, in Mycenae." Maggie held up the figurine of Merope. And from a pocket, she took the little figurine of Nepthaulia. "Merope's niece, Nepthaulia. She holds the secrets to the next step in uncovering the mysteries of Pylos, of how and why this clay figurine of Nepthaulia, also made in Pylos, ended up in Athens where I found her. Donald?"

"Maggie, anything you wish to do with the figurines, we all agree you should," Donald turned to the guests. "Yes?" The audience just kept on clapping. "And after all, you are still director in charge here. And they are all your girls." The audience called, "Maggie's girls!" She kissed both figurines and returned them to a special case Thanassis had made.

~~~~

As Kati-Selene and Agamemnon walked to their car, they were stopped a hundred times by pats on the back and hugs. "See you soon," most called.

Agamemnon got into the car with a puzzled expression. "I know they are staying with us, but I've never heard them express how happy they are to be returning. And soon," he murmured to Kat-Selene as she started the car.

CHAPTER 9

FADE IN: *Homecoming*

SETTING:

Place: Hotel Belle Helene, Mycenae Village
Date: 25 June, <u>2021 A.D.</u>
Time: early afternoon to early evening

WHEN KATI-SELENE drove up, the painters, speckled with their work, were putting their things into their battered truck.

"Back soon!" Georgios called before he jumped in with the others.

The paperhangers were on the terrace, handing glasses to Sophia. They came down the steps and waved at Kati-Selene and Agamemnon. "All done. See you soon."

And when Papa drove up with Uncle and Aunt and waved at the couple, Agamemnon could stand it no longer. He jumped from the car and called out to departing Georgios, "I thought you finished this morning!"

All he got in reply was a nod, a wave and a "See you soon."

Agamemnon raced up the steps toward Kati, who was helping his aunt spread the family's best tablecloth on a large table set on the terrace. "What's happening, Kati-Selene?" he fairly shouted. "Why are they all calling, 'Back soon'? Back soon? They left this morning. What are they doing coming back this afternoon? What's going on?"

Papa came out with Uncle and they began opening bottles on a separate table Sophia's husband had brought out. And before Agamemnon could hear Kati-Selene's reply, he heard cars and more cars arriving and stopping. And then he saw people laughing and talking and calling to each other, getting out of those cars and coming up onto the terrace, all smiling at him.

"Thank you for inviting us," they each said in one fashion or the other before going to kiss Kati-Selene and accepting a glass of wine. Stelios, accompanied by his wife, who was carrying Anthula, came from across the street with two large pizzas. After his wife gave little Anthula to Kati-Selene to hold for a moment, she ran back to get more pizza, followed by Stelios.

"More over there!" Spiros called back to Agamemnon.

When the two men returned with four more pies, the whole town including all the neighbors who usually never leave their own balconies, were gathered, talking and laughing and enjoying. Not to mention the throng from Dr. Margaret's ceremony. The cars lined both sides of Main Street from the interstate turnoff and around the corner up toward the citadel. All the archaeologists and all their guests ran up, clapping Agamemnon on the back and happily accepting wine from Kati-S. At some point, when he turned from offering pizza and meze to accepting hands, he saw that Dr. Margaret had joined them and was sitting on a lounge chair, cat in her lap. She patted his hand before accepting a slice.

"At last you join us! Welcome home!" he whispered in her ear.

Then Father Kristoforos drove up and his altar boy got out, following. They had two large boxes with them. And when they reappeared from behind a curtain hanging over the entrance that Agamemnon had not noticed before, Father Kristoforos was robed in his finest ecclesiastical garb, carrying a silver hyssop. He dipped this into the chalice of holy water that the altar boy carried at his side, and Father began sprinkling that new curtain over the entrance. Everyone joined in the responses to his prayers for happiness in this house and God's blessings on all who will come to stay and enjoy.

As Father's basso voice boomed out the song of the special Blessing to all of the guests of the hotel, Kati-Selene brought Papa over to one side of that new curtain that was hiding the entrance. Agamemnon was brought to the other.

"What is this, Kat-Selene?" Agamemnon said, feeling strange with all this commotion.

"When I signal, pull the cord," she whispered and put the cord in his hand.

She stepped back, and Father tossed sprinkles of holy water all over the curtain, soaking Agamemnon. He could hardly see when Kati-Selene gave the signal. She had to call, "Pull, Aga!" And he pulled. Everyone was clapping and shouting, and Father boomed, "I christen you the Hotel of Dream Catcher Khorus Girl Merope!" And everyone shouted back, "Hotel of Dream Catcher Khorus Girl Merope!"

"What?" Agamemnon was struggling to see what they were all shouting about and looking at. But everyone kept getting in his way, hugging him and kissing him. When he finally stepped aside and wiped his face, he stared up at the newly painted words over the door: Hotel of Dream Catcher Khorus Girl Merope. He was stunned. He turned to Kati-Selene, who was beaming at him with Papa beside her.

"Isn't it wonderful, Aga?" She kissed him so warmly that he suddenly changed his mind.

"Yes, darling, it is the most-wonderful ever." And when she let him come up for air, he looked at the image of Merope looking back at him. Did she wink or was his imagination running wild?

"I told you we would meet soon, my dear sister Kati-Selene," Kati heard as clear as clear despite all the hubbub.

"Yes, you did, little Merope, little sister," Kati-Selene whispered. "And I look forward to our being together a very long time."

Allison brought a glass of wine to Maggie, and Thanassis pulled over a chair. Their conversation was soon interrupted by three admirers bringing over plates of food and more wine. Donald Suskine joined the group.

"Congratulations to us all," he called out after clinking his glass for silence. "Congratulations to us are in order. Margaret Benson has agreed that she will share the directorship of the excavations here at Mycenae with Allison and Federica. So we are not losing but keeping the great, wonderful Margaret; and welcoming into new positions these lovely archaeologists, Allison, and Federica, both of whom have shown intelligence and bravery and brawn during these last weeks. Congratulations to us all. We anticipate the new, uncovered Mycenae and Maggie's, Allison's and Federica's discoveries."

"Are you forgetting us? The Irish Team!" And three rowdy men, perhaps somewhat intoxicated, staggered forward. Donald announced them. "In order of appearance here on this stage: Oscar, Neil and William." They took bows and went back to surrounding Allison.

Old Street Dog took up his post in the middle of the road. It was a lazy afternoon in Mycenae.

EPILOGUE

FADE IN: *Falling Stars Meet Clouds of Fire Over Western Aegean Sea*

SETTING:
Place: King's Palace, Athens Acropolis, Athens, Greece
Date: 26 June, <u>1185 B.C</u>
Time: 4 a.m.
Simulcast with:
Place: Hotel Merope, Mycenae Village, Mycenae, Greece
Date: 26 June, <u>2021 A.D.</u>
Time: 4 a.m

"AGAIN, LAST NIGHT the stars were falling far to the west over our once-land of Pylos," Nepthaulia continued.

"From far away we could see: they fell blindingly in numbers so vast, we knew the end was near.

"Again last night I dreamed I was home in Pylos, in the old days of Nestor.

"Was it the sound of the rain on the tiles of the king's palace in Athens that brought me home?

"Or the beat of my heart?

"Or the variable elasticity of space in dreaming time?

"It was all that and my longing for home; for Nestor's Pylos and all it stood for.

"Tonight, we Khorus Girls will sing one last time from decks of the ships offered us by King Orestes.

"Selene, our votaress, and Khloris, my sister, and I, with Queen Eurydice and the Khorus Girls of Pylos who made it through with us, all of us will sing from the ships. Clouds and birds will guide our people to a new land.

"But while we sing for a new land, we are singing of the old.

"We were the Khorus Girls.

"Once upon a time, we danced in vibrant hills of great kingdoms.

"Once upon a time, we twirled as we sang, vaulting high in the surrounding hills.

"Vaulting as the great goddess taught us, sailing into the clouds we called.

"We sang our kingdoms into being; and sang, keeping our kingdoms.

"Once upon a time, we were an alliance for our kingdoms and for our people.

"With lions and turtles, we sang and soared to our songs in the hills.

"Once upon a time, we danced in those hills. Vaulted with birds, clapping and soaring, catching our sounds in echoes, calling for universal harmony. "Harmony," called the birds, called the clouds, and saved our harvests, singing and singing until our songs called clouds of fire.

"Now our kingdom is fallen into the sea. Our great kings are gone with the winds. Gone with the fires. Gone under the sea. Gone to the gods.

"And today we begin again, with the blessing of the new goddess, Wisdom. We begin again, flying off to seek new lands where again we can sing and save. And live.

"Oh, Margaret, remember us, remember our stories, remember to tell all who come to visit our old lands; tell them about the Khorus Girls who sang our lands and our incredible, fabulous civilization into being."

~~~~

The new bed was so comfortable. Too comfortable. The day had been so happy, so tiring, so exhilarating. Her healing bones ached, and Margaret turned and thumped the pillows and dropped again into dreams so vivid, she was really there with Nepthaulia.

"Tell me all about the end, Nepthaulia," she mumbled into her soft pillow.

~~~~

"And the sea rose, and the earth, up to meet the stars. The land shook and shook and exploded until the mountains fell and the great universities and hospitals and observatories and arsenals and even the space-time machine all fell into the seas. And the people. Then came fires of heaven. The clouds of fire.

"Nestor did not see the end. The falling stars were not his end. His heart was broken."

Margaret sighed at this and reached out to take Nepthaulia's hand as she fell back into a deep sleep. And there again was Nepthaulia, standing on a high hill with a temple behind her. Surrounding her, Margaret could see, were many, many people, all watching her.

"I promised to tell you the rest of our story, Margaret. — In Pylos, the stars continued to fall. The scientists were prepared to counterattack with the most violence possible, if necessary. The rumors of the Sea People and their destructions continued to arrive daily by emissaries sent from every nation in the confederation. We were never sure whether or not these Sea People or Sky People actually existed or actually used their weapons of mass destruction. Or if, indeed, the conflagration was planet-made. Did volcanoes outside of all imagining spew simultaneously from all mountains to join concurrently with rising seas, with stars falling, to converge with Sky People using weapons of the same atomic energy? All together in one catastrophic dance of death, mountains fell and seas rose, and altogether everything was destroyed in our golden land, our Pylos. Certainly, the king forbade use of our violent weapons. He was not there to see this destruction.

"Nestor did not die in the final conflagration; not in that last star-fall. In 1189, not long after Nestor's meetings with the most-trusted people in his scientific community, his oldest son, King Thrasymedes, playing polo, fell from his horse and died of a blow to the head.

"Thrasymedes also loved sailing and swimming in the spectacular omega-shaped bay he called the Bay of Everything. Indeed, it became his Omega, his last home from where he could survey all that he loved most. Everything. His land, his sea, his universe. Pylos and the Sea.

"His father, almost prostrate with grief, commissioned a magnificent tholos tomb on the hills overlooking Thrasymedes's Bay of Everything. And there at twilight, in the spring of 1188, on a fiery night when the stars fell continually into the sea beyond, Nestor, with Thrasymedes's mother, Eurydice, with all the family and all our town-ships of Pylos, all of us, including Thrasymedes's sister, my best friend, Polycaste, now queen of Ithaka, with her husband, Telemachos, came to visit with King Thrasymedes and taste one last time the great vintage of 1216, before the tholos's entrance was sealed.

"Afterward, upon entering the palace, now the palace run by the new king, Peisistratos, my husband, the old king, staggered against the guard, grabbed for him and called out, 'Eurydice! Eurydice!' He fell into her arms.

And overhead, the stars fell in greater and greater numbers.

"It was best he was not with us to witness the destruction of all he had created and loved. Eurydice, as always, was our leader in moving us out of harm. As many as possible left with us before the mountains erupted and the sea rose and the stars fell and the heavens burst into flames and the earth tumbled into the Arsenals filled with waiting ships, into warehouses filled with enterprise waiting all the ships, over the vineyards and into homes, demolishing whole villages, sending Pylos sliding into the sea. All who had not fled with the queen were utterly destroyed.

"Few were the possessions we could grab as we fled. — Children. — One man grabbed one vine by the roots and tossed it behind his wife and children in his car. — My father, Elios, did take one amphorae of his precious vintage, but somewhere along the route, it must have fallen.

We were fleeing. King Peisistratos, my husband, tried to keep the people together and keep spirits up. But we were fleeing for our lives and many succumbed along the way. The roads, my grandfather's and father's roads, no matter how well engineered, could not stand the tension and load and upheavals, and those elevated highways collapsed onto the low freeways, and such destruction made them impassible. But many carts and cars and trains managed to continue. Many had to be abandoned. And the passengers had to walk if neighbors had no room.

"Among the things I took along with our two babies, the queen and I grabbed the little Khorus Girl statues the king had commissioned. Our dear friend Orestes, along with us, cared for them all along the route to Mycenae. We had decided to stop at Mycenae before continuing in order to see Orestes's son Tisamenos, King of Mycenae.

"Tisamenos received us as well as possible given that they, while not in as disastrous a situation as in the far west in Pylos, were also inundated with upheavals, earthquakes and shortages. And falling stars. And though we begged him to join us, he stayed to be with his people for as long as possible. So, with Tisamenos, Eurydice and I left the tiny statues my mother, Selene, and Eurydice had commissioned of those Khorus Girls of Fire who gave their lives in the curse of Clytemnestra: Merope and Cynthia and Great Aunt Thalia and so many others, cherished friends of my mother. These precious mementoes of the heroic work of our Khorus Girls, who gave all for the citizens of Mycenae, were accepted with humility and pride by Tisamenos. He positioned the statue of Merope on his own desk. She had bonded with him immediately. Her spirit was palpable through the clay, he said.

"Before we left, before hugging his son one last time, Orestes picked up clay Merope and gave her a kiss. Then we were off to Athens and whatever the gods had in store for us.

"The people of Athens, desperate in these desperate times, welcomed us as saviors
and crowned Orestes king of Athens. He was installed in the once-magnificent palace of Erechtheos at the top of the Acropolis, next to the temple to Wisdom.

"There, this morning, 26 June, 1185 B.C., as the sun rose, Orestes and I and Peisistratos, with Queen Eurydice, went again to supplicate the goddess of wisdom. Today, to her, I brought my own little Khorus Girl statue and asked Wisdom to protect us, to watch over us from her vantage and keep us safe on our travels across the skies and seas. I left my figurine as suppliant at her feet.

"And at twilight we sailed, flying into skies full of stars and seas of dolphins: Peisistratos and I and Queen Eurydice and as many of our people as were still with us. Orestes and the Athenians sent us off in the best ships left to them. We were bound west for a new land to recreate our Pylos once more. Would we? Would we reclaim the dream? The dream of the Griffin Warrior? The dream of King Nestor?

"As we sailed through skies of falling stars, I thought of the stories King Nestor had told me of the stars falling. Of the stories of The Griffin Warrior and his voyage guided by the sense of smell to a new home. Though to our north-east again we could see the stars falling and missiles streaking across and tumbling down, and though we could see, near the Isthmus, the earth rising up and tumbling into the sea, and though the seas below us often rose terrifyingly high, we were on a new mission for home. I looked back and knew Wisdom was protecting us. And on we sailed ever west into the darkening night across the seas. Dolphins of the stars and of the seas came alongside and guided us to a new land.

"Later, we learned from enterprising merchants, who had salvaged what they could of our warehouses, that all of the western Peloponnesos had been destroyed by fire and storms, and earthquakes and missiles falling from the stars. The destruction was so complete, nothing could be recognized, according to those who braved and attempted to discover. Swiftly, our old paradise had become a land of darkness, cold and barren. Perpetual night shrouded and froze our once-fertile and verdant land. And people, those who survived, lived, we learned, in caves.

"Now, Margaret, I leave it to you to discover all you can about us. And tell the world about the famous Khorus Girls who saved their once-great societies, saved the harvests, saved the kingdoms: the Cloud Girls, the Bird Girls, the Girls of Wind and the Girls of Song. The Khorus Girls.

Tell about the fabled, learned, humanitarian society our singing brought into and kept in existence: the civilization of King Nestor.

"It was the sound of rain that brought Mother's voice back to me. She was singing the song to the moon and to the clouds. And all around her were gathered the Khorus Girls, waiting for her upbeat to begin."

FADE OUT ...

AUTHOR'S NOTES

FADE IN: *Author's Letter on The What and Who Made This Story Possible*

CENTER STAGE: The Girls.

Found by Carl Blegen at Nestor's Palace.
Photo by the author.

These little statues may be viewed and visited in the museums attached to the sites where they were discovered by archaeologists.

Madeleine in Mycenae
Museum with The Girls.
Photo taken by her pal,
Anthula Gross.

At Mycenae, at the astonishing site of the Bronze Age Palace of Agamemnon, down-hill from the Lion Gate (where the lions are still roaring after 3,271 years!), you will find The Girls in places of honor in the modern museum.

At the western end of the Peloponnesos, not far from today's modern town of Pylos, a few kilometers up the road from the Bronze Age Palace of Nestor, in the old and charming village of Khora, in the Carl Blegen Museum, the oldest figurines of The Girls are also in places of honor. And archaeologists, Sharon Stocker and Jack Davis, are kept over-busy reconfiguring that building for the recently discovered art and artifacts from the Tomb of the Griffin Warrior. A visit to this museum is well-rewarded. And all contributions at the museum are greatly appreciated.

In Athens, in both the National Archaeological Museum and the New Acropolis Museum, you will find little statues of The Girls, still waving.

The Girls in Archaeological Museum at
Archaeology Site of Delphi, Greece. Photo
taken by the author.

If you cross the Mediterranean, as the founders of the Peloponnesos
did, and arrive back in Krete, from whence they came, in Heraklion's
Archaeological Museum you will see The Girls. They are different in
dress and attitude: these are the Khorus Girls of Krete.

In these and in several other museums, The Girls are waiting for
your visit. You will feel their presence even before you spot them; they
are waving and wearing their special dress, designating their various roles
in the khoruses. And while they, like the Lions over Mycenae's Gate, are
very, very old, they do not look too much older than the day they were
created. You can feel they are gearing up, ready to soar, singing, into the
clouds. Likely, you will hear them.

Beyond these Bronze Age girls' figurines found in museums
throughout Greece, especially in Mycenae, Pylos, Athens, and on Krete,
you will find reproductions for sale in boutique shops. Though the
reasons The Girls have always been loved have been forgotten, the
collective-unconscious obviously maintains a fondness and respect for
them. If you have the opportunity to visit in the home of Greek friends,
there is a good chance you will find in places of honor reproductions of

the Khorus Girls. Somehow, in the subconscious, the knowledge that these girls are saviors is still alive.

Madeleine at The Lion Gate, Mycenae, taken by her pal, Anthula Gross. Anthula forgot the Lions.

The Lion Gate taken by Dr. Elizabeth Wace French, sent to me by Elizabeth Wace French with permission for me to use.

NEW SCENE: IN APPRECIATION

FADE IN: *The People and Places*

Though this is a work of historical fiction, Dr. Elizabeth Wace French is a very real archaeologist, daughter of Alan B. Wace. It was a question I had for Lisa in 1986 about a short story, a magical mystery story, that her archaeologist father had written, that first connected us. Since then Lisa has guided me and championed me. I am most grateful for her decades of friendship, for all the knowledge she shared, for stories about excavations at Mycenae, and permissions to use many personal photographs she took there. She not only sent me reams of information to keep me on the path — really on the path, with an actual map of the paths and old back roads in and out of and around Mycenae — (because of which I was able drive and plot the running route "Selene" took from Mycenae to Pylos in 1214 B.C.), but sent me to other magicians of the past for more. Her word opened modern and Bronze Age doors for me. When she asked, Dr. Sharon (Shari) Stocker and her partner-husband, archaeologist Jack Davis, opened arms and doors for me to visit their site in Pylos, and, with their guidance, learn about the Griffin Warrior and his society at Pylos. Without such this story could not have been written. Her name alone was enough for Dr. Martin Schaefer to open the doors of Athens' Archaeology Society Library, where he provided tomes of more magical findings of the past. I have come to realize that it was Lisa herself who was the greatest magician of them all. She moved mountains for me, and I did not even feel rumbling. She was ever a smiling and eager adventurer.

Sadly, I use the past tense. As I was finishing this manuscript I received word from her daughter, Ann, that darling, brilliant, wonderful Elizabeth Wace French died in June, 2021, A.D.

Lisa Wace near The Lion Gate, Mycenae, 8 years old, with local friends. Photo sent to author by Ann French, Elizabeth Wace French's daughter, with permission to use.

Dr. Sharon (Shari) Stocker and her husband, Dr. Jack Davis, are very real and extremely busy practicing archaeology, excavating at the Palace of King Nestor in ancient Pylos. In the last five years alone, together and with their teams, they have uncovered the Tomb of the Griffin Warrior, and more recently, two Bronze Age Tholos tombs which, likely, were lined in gold. I am privileged to have met Shari and to have spent time at the site with her and am most grateful to her and Jack for their generosity in sharing information.

Archaeologist Sharon (Shari)
Stocker, at Pylos, Greece. Shari
and her husband, Archaeologist
Jack Davis, uncovered the Tomb
of the Griffin Warrior and two
Bronze Age Tholos Tombs all at
the site of King Nestor's Palace at
Pylos, Greece.

Photo taken after dinner at Hotel
Philip in modern town of Pylos by
the author.

And Dr. Martin Schaefer, head librarian at Athens' Archaeological Society: To Martin I owe many thanks for his prescience in finding for me and having ready on a table in the reading room at his library, books that really sealed the deal: Elizabeth French's book on those Bronze Age roads in back and around the site of Mycenae, and the anthology of Pylos and Iklaina by Jack Davis and Sharon Stocker about many aspects of life at Pylos including the sea creatures and colorations used in frescoes. In what Martin chose I found enabling information.

Both the archaeological sites of Mycenae and Nestor's Palace at Pylos are open to visitors. A trip to visit these truly out-of-this-world sites is well worth the effort.

For visitors to Mycenae, the trip from Athens is not long by car. Also, one may find that for visiting Mycenae the sea-coast town of

Nafplio is convenient and most pleasant with lovely hotels, restaurants, and great vistas.

Equally for visiting King Nestor's Palace, while the trip by car from Athens is longer, there are most delightful hotels, like Hotel Philip, and restaurants there and in town along the bay front, as well as many other places of interest, even excellent golf courses.

The actual site of Nestor's Palace is about a fifteen minutes-drive from the modern town of Pylos on the dazzling Ionian coast. And about another fifteen minutes up from the Palace, in the ancient town of Khora, is the Carl Blegen Archaeology Museum.

Taken of the front porch of the Carl Blegen
Museum in Khora, Greece by author.

The Hotel Belle Helene in my story is a fictional hotel, modeled loosely on the real and historic hotel of that name. The Agamemnon Dassis in my story is a fictional character, bearing only the same name as today's manager of the historic Hotel-Restaurant La Belle Helene.

In the village of Mycenae, on the way up to the site of the Bronze Age Palace of Mycenae, visitors will pass right by the real and historic hotel, still as always named La Belle Helene. In the 1870s when Heinrich Schliemann began excavating at Mycenae's Bronze Age site, he rented rooms in the home of the Dassis family. By the 1890s, the Dassis family had turned their home into La Belle Helene Hotel. Today, it is owned and operated by George Achilleus Dassis and his 50-year-old grandson, Agamemnon. A stay there makes for the perfect jumping-off point for visiting the site of Mycenae. It also has a fine restaurant. Perhaps, it you stop at the hotel, you will have the good fortune to meet George Achilleus Dassis and his grandson, Agamemnon, current day manager.

ABOUT THE AUTHOR

Past and Future Works

Author photo by Anthula Gross

Her first novel, *Julius Caesar Invented Champagne*, in a zany, *Yellow Submarine*-ish travelogue, traces the history of wine from the mountains of northwestern China in 10000 B.C. forward to 51 B.C. to recount how Julius Caesar used his decommissioned troops after the Gallic Wars to create the greatest vineyards this planet knows, beginning with "la Romanee", co-planted with tribesmen of the Aedui, which land today is called Burgundy.

Madeleine's second book. *JULIA CHILD*, *a memoire of friendship*, has not one recipe in it. Instead, it is a personal story, an off-camera look at the wonderfully delightful, speedy, long-legged, Julia Child — America's French Chef.

Currently Madeleine is finishing a nonfiction book:

Three Wine Tastings That Changed The Then World.

Visit the author website:
http://www.madeleinedeJean.com

Or read the Madeleine's blog:
http://champagnetoujours.blogspot.com

Facebook:
https://www.facebook.com/MadeleinedeJeanBooks